"They're going to kill us!"

Jack leaned around the corner to see three rioters pulling a half-conscious policeman from the cab. Jack recognized him as the same cop who had said he'd try to call CTU. His face was covered in blood from a cut on his forehead, and his eyes weren't focused. He was as limp as a rag doll and no threat to anyone. But he was wearing a police uniform, and in the rioters' maddened state that's all it took. One of them stomped on his head.

Jack snatched the wire cutters from his rescuer's hand and shoved him out of the way. He reached the injured cop, and as another rioter raised his foot to stomp down, Jack kicked his base leg. The rioter screamed and toppled over. The other two looked at him in surprise. Jack punched one of them in the stomach with the hand holding the wire cutters. The beak of the cutters jabbed into the man's stomach and he crumpled to the floor. The third one grabbed Jack by the shirt, so Jack head-butted him in the nose and shoved him backward.

.

24 DECLASSIFIED Books
From HarperEntertainment

CAT'S CLAW
TROJAN HORSE
VETO POWER
OPERATION HELL GATE

Coming Soon

VANISHING POINT

DECLASSIFIED

CAT'S CLAW

JOHN WHITMAN

Based on the hit FOX series by Joel Surnow & Robert Cochran

HarperEntertainment
An Imprint of HarperCollins*Publishers*

This is a work of fiction. Names, characters, places, and incidents are products of the author's imagination or are used fictitiously and are not to be construed as real. Any resemblance to actual events, locales, organizations, or persons, living or dead, is entirely coincidental.

HARPERENTERTAINMENT
An Imprint of HarperCollins*Publishers*
10 East 53rd Street
New York, New York 10022-5299

ISBN: 978-0-06-084227-7
ISBN-10: 0-06-084227-X

HarperCollins®, 📖®, and HarperEntertainment™ are trademarks of HarperCollins Publishers.

First HarperEntertainment paperback printing: January 2007

Printed in the United States of America

Visit HarperEntertainment on the World Wide Web at
www.harpercollins.com.

10 9 8 7 6 5 4 3 2 1

After the 1993 World Trade Center attack, a division of the Central Intelligence Agency established a domestic unit tasked with protecting America from the threat of terrorism. Headquartered in Washington, D.C., the Counter Terrorist Unit established field offices in several American cities. From its inception, CTU faced hostility and skepticism from other Federal law enforcement agencies. Despite bureaucratic resistance, within a few years CTU had become a major force. After the war against terror began, a number of CTU missions were declassified. The following is one of them . . .

PROLOGUE

1 Month Ago

Detective Mercy Bennet eased her Audi A4 up to the curb of the big ranch-style house on Roscomare Road. It was only five o'clock, but the Bel Air hills blocked the sun and the street was mostly in shadow. Thick ivy covered the ground from the curb all the way up to the rose bushes leaning against the front side of the house. Mercy walked up the middle of the driveway, keeping well clear of the ivy. Her father had been a pest controller and had always told her that rats loved ivy. Mercy worked pest control, too. Just a different kind.

She gathered information as she walked through the front door. The doorjamb was smooth and the chain was intact, but the Karastan rug in the marble entryway was rumpled, and a single thick, crystal candlestick on the hallway table had been tipped on its side. The frameless beveled mirror on the wall behind her was askew. To the right of the hallway, a set of stairs climbed up to the second story, while straight ahead the corridor opened up into a high-ceilinged living room. The living room was decorated with the same sense of class as the hallway—ecru walls trimmed in white crown molding surrounded two brushed suede couches and a wrought-iron coffee table. There was a marble chess set sitting atop a small round table where two chairs squared off against each other, and an Alexandra Nikita print hung over the fireplace, with a tall fake ficus tree in a wicker basket nearby. Except for the fake tree, the room looked like a picture from a Restoration Hardware catalog.

Two uniformed policemen were already there, as were two paramedics with a gurney, and the crime scene technician. The forensics tech was crouched over the dead body in the middle of the living room. The body was lying facedown on the carpet with the head, or what was left of it, soaking in a pool of blood. This had been Gordon Gleed, a forty-three-year-old divorced businessman living alone. Habitually Mercy started collecting scenarios in the back of her head based on the facts she knew. These scenarios would fade away as the facts became more specific. Right now, given the fact that he was divorced, lived the bachelor life in a stylish Bel Air pad, and was obviously successful in business, Mercy thought *home invasion, angry ex-wife, angry gay lover, angry business associate.* They were clichés, but she noted them anyway. Ever since she'd read Malcolm Gladwell's *Blink*, she'd been keeping track of her first impressions at crime scenes. So far she was fifty-fifty on the hunches she formed.

Mercy didn't know either of the uniforms, but she had known Sam Kinsett, the forensics tech, since she was in uniform herself. His red hair had thinned as her waist had thickened, but both of them still looked pretty good ten years into their careers.

"Blunt trauma to the head," Sam said by way of hello.

"They taught you well. That the weapon?" She pointed to a crystal candlestick lying on the ground nearby, the mate of the one in the hall.

"All signs point to yes," Sam replied.

One of the uniforms joined in. "Neighbors called in because the door was open and said they heard sounds of a struggle. We showed up to find him like this."

"How's the rest of the house?" she asked.

"Tossed," the other uniform replied. "Really tossed. The whole place is a mess."

The rest of the forensics team arrived for pictures and prints while Mercy walked the house. The bedroom was a shambles, with clothes dumped from drawers and pictures taken off the walls. Gordon Gleed kept a home office, which had now been turned upside down, with most of the contents of his mahogany desk dumped across the top. The blue box of a Linksys wireless router sat in a corner, its lights still on, but the wireless laptop, if it existed, was now gone. The kitchen had been ransacked, plates broken and dish drawers left open. Even the refrigerator had been searched.

By the time Mercy returned to the living room, Sam and his team were packing up. "We're ready to move the body. You got anything else you want?"

Mercy didn't answer at first. Something about the house bothered her, but she couldn't put her finger on it. "How's his wallet?"

"Empty," said one of the uniformed cops. "No cash, I mean."

"The DVD player's gone from the den," said the other cop. "TV's still there. They only took light stuff."

"Any other reports of home invasions in this neighborhood?"

"Nada," said the first cop.

"Light stuff," Mercy repeated. She looked around the living room again. She was sure she'd seen those couches in a catalog. The coffee table, too. Catalogs, but expensive ones. She walked over to the plastic tree and touched its leaves. They looked real enough, but they felt waxy and stiff. She plucked one and it popped out. The leaves were held in place with a clever little ball-and-socket arrangement. It was well made, but it still didn't fit with the rest of the decor. She crouched down and looked at the big wicker basket that held the fake plant. Grabbing the basket with both hands, she pushed it aside.

"Look what I found," she muttered.

The plastic tree hid a small, round floor safe set beneath the carpet. She bent down, careful not to touch, and examined the combination lock and the hinges. Both were covered with dust. If the killer was looking for the valuables, he hadn't looked very hard. But he *had* tried hard to make it *look* as if he had tried hard.

This wasn't adding up, she thought. No one commits a home invasion robbery in this neighborhood to steal a few dollars in cash and a DVD player.

The next two hours passed quickly. The uniformed officers knocked on neighboring doors and asked questions. Mercy found recent copies of *Penthouse* under the piles of clothes strewn around his bedroom, which put a crimp in the gay lover theory. The ex-wife had been "ex" for seven years, had her own money and a new husband. That left Mercy with only one hunch left.

"Let's get to know Mr. Gleed's business contacts."

Five Days Ago

Jack Bauer stood at the bow of the *Catalina Express,* a huge hydrofoil boat that carried passengers from the mainland to Santa Catalina Island, twenty-six miles across the sea.

His wife, Teri, was standing next to him, holding her sweater close to her throat and pressing in against his body to ward off the breeze as the boat eased into its Long Beach dock. It had been a long time since she'd done that. It had been a long time since he'd missed it.

"It was a good trip," she said. "Thanks."

He nodded and let his cheek rest against her head. He didn't deserve the thanks—the trip hadn't really been his idea. Well, the specifics had been, maybe, but not the concept. Their marriage had been on shaky ground for a year, but Teri, not he, had had the courage to suggest they do something about it. A weekend away had seemed easy enough, so he'd rented a condo at Hamilton Cove on Catalina Island.

Her hair smelled like watermelon, and he breathed her in. He agreed. It was a good trip. When she pulled herself out of mommy mode and he stopped obsessing over his Counter Terrorist Unit caseload, they made a good pair.

"You think we can keep this up?" he wondered aloud.

He felt her shrug. "It's easy to be a holy man on top of a mountain."

Jack didn't enjoy philosophy. "Meaning?"

"Meaning the last two days have been great, but it wasn't the real world. That's the real world." She pointed to the dock ahead. The *Catalina Express* was just easing into its huge slip. On the walkway beyond, huge crowds of people walking past. Beyond lay the *Express*'s office building, and beyond that the buildings of Long Beach, and Los Angeles, and the mountains far off in the distance.

The ship docked, and Jack and Teri Bauer followed the passengers on their slow, small-stepped progress down the gangplank and onto shore. Crewmen carted all the bags onto the promenade. The Bauers picked theirs out. Jack shouldered his and Teri's, and they turned toward the crowd milling past.

"There must be a lot of people coming back from Catalina this weekend," Teri said.

One of the crewmen, overhearing, grunted, "Naw, you never get this many people from the island. These are all from Mexico or somewhere. A whole big fleet came in. Bunch of protestors."

"Protesting what?" Jack asked.

The crewman shrugged.

Hitching the two bags higher on his shoulders, Jack plunged into the crowd. The group was a mixture of South Americans—mostly short men and women dressed in poor clothing—and a species of political activist quite common to North America: twenty-something Caucasians in dreadlocks or stubbornly unwashed hair, wearing carefully selected secondhand clothes. Jack hadn't had any direct experience with the type, but he'd read enough profiles and attended enough briefings to guess what they were protesting—a G8 summit was scheduled to start in Los Angeles in a few days. Like the meetings of the World Trade Organization, the G8 sessions usually triggered waves of protests from anti-globalization and pro-environmental groups.

Distracted, Jack didn't see the other man until they collided. Without thinking, Jack pushed back, his right hand sliding under his jacket out of habit. The other man stumbled back a step and cursed under his breath, though Jack couldn't hear exactly what he said. He threw Jack an angry glare—just long enough for Jack to catch a dark face and bright, burning eyes. Then he hurried through the crowd. Jack watched him go.

"Don't start anything," Teri said, only half joking. "You pushed him."

"Yeah," Jack said distractedly. He took a few steps, then said, "That guy just looked familiar."

"Work familiar or old friend familiar?"

He didn't need to look at her to know that a resigned frown had settled across her face. They'd come down off the mountain already.

"Doesn't matter," he said. But Jack's eyes didn't leave the man until he was out of sight.

1 2 3 4 5 6 7 8 9
10 11 12 13 14 15 16 17
18 19 20 21 22 23 24

....

....

7:00 A.M. PST
Federal Building, West Los Angeles

It was just seven o'clock in the morning, and already the mob had gathered in front of the Federal Building. LAPD had blocked off Wilshire Boulevard, one of the city's main thoroughfares, for two miles in either direction. It was a concession to the size and force of the crowd. The original battle plan had called for the police to keep protestors at least five blocks away from the Federal Building, but no one in his right mind believed the protestors would obey that rule—just as no one in his right mind wanted images of L.A.'s finest beating and tear gassing hordes of protestors. So, at a permit meeting that felt more like a peace summit, the police had promised not to use excessive force if the protestors kept their feet on the wide green lawn surrounding the perimeter of the building and off the concrete plaza at its center. The protestors, in turn, had agreed to remain peaceful and keep their troops within the permit area.

Neither side expected the other to keep its word.

Jack Bauer moved through the crowd, following in his daughter Kim Bauer's wake. He worked to make his footsteps heavy and his eyes dull. He did this partly for the benefit of any protestors on the lookout for undercover cops, but also for the benefit of his daughter. He didn't want her to think he was on the job.

"These are my guys," Kim Bauer said, turning a quick smile on her father. She skipped forward until she bumped up against a group of other teens who'd formed their own island in the sea of protestors. Most of them wore blue T-shirts with the words "Teen Green" scrawled across the front and back. As Kim giggled with them, a short, wiry man with glasses, a bald head, and a weary smile navigated his way through them and stuck his hand out to Jack.

"Marshall Cooper. You the parent chaperone?" He enunciated quickly and crisply, and had a pale, vegetarian sort of look about him.

"Jack Bauer. No, sorry, I just—"

"I'm here, I'm here," said a harried and very loud female voice. A large woman with bright blond hair and a faux leopard-skin purse appeared beside them, grabbing Cooper's still-hovering hand. "Andi Parks. You must be Mr. Cooper, right? I knew it, Cindi said you were a granola type; no offense, of course, I mean we're all here for the same granola causes, right? That's what Teen Green is, right?"

And that was just her hello. Marshall Cooper tried to speak—Jack thought he was saying something about being Teen Green's student advisor—but he didn't stand much of a chance against Andi Parks's barrage of words. She went on talking to the little man even though she'd turned to look at the Teen Green girls already. Cooper glanced at Jack Bauer with a look that pleaded, *Are you sure you don't want to be the parent chaperone?* Jack shrugged sympathetically.

"Kim. Kim!" Jack called over the noise. She tore her gaze away from a boy with straight hair that hung down to his eyebrows. "I'm getting some coffee. I'll be back to check on things in a while." He was sure she hadn't heard a word, but she smiled and nodded anyway before turning her attention back to the boy.

Jack surveyed the sea of protestors around his daughter. What he saw was a collection of teens and twenty-somethings mingling with older, grizzled protestors from a faded generation. It might have been a grandparents and kids gathering, if not for the twenty-story Federal Building looming over them and the atmosphere electrified by tension. The protestors tended to gather into groups, but then those groups blended into larger factions. Often these factions shared a common purpose. More often, though, the only thing they shared was a common enemy—in this case, the G8.

The G8, or "Group of Eight" was composed of the world's leading industrialized nations, namely the United States, Britain, France, Germany, Italy, Japan, Canada, and Russia. This was, of course, an old boys' network of "leading" nations, since a number of countries rightly pointed out that Italy wasn't exactly a manufacturing powerhouse compared to the exporting power of many Asian nations, many of whom were currently lobbying for a place at the table. In fact, one of the main issues on the agenda for this particular G8 summit was the possible inclusion of China, whose exploding economy was being watched anxiously by every other market on the planet.

The entire Los Angeles headquarters of the Counter

Terrorist Unit had been subjected to several briefings on the G8 summit, of course. The briefings thus far hadn't amounted to much. In the aftermath of 9/11, the newspapers and local law enforcement agencies used phrases like "high-value target" in connection with an event like the G8, but the truth was, attacking the summit wouldn't be al-Qaeda's style. Terrorists connected to Islamic fundamentalism had thus far chosen two specific types of targets: military assets located in Arab countries and purely civilian targets that caused maximum fear and confusion. Al-Qaeda and its loose collection of affiliates would assume that the G8 summit was shielded by a nearly impenetrable security screen and, Jack knew, that assumption would be correct. And, more importantly, both sides knew that attacks, even successful ones, against political targets would generate more outrage than terror. If and when al-Qaeda ever struck inside the borders of the United States again, Jack was sure they would attack a train or a shopping mall, a soft target that promised gruesome results.

Even so, there were plenty of other terrorist organizations with far more specific political agendas, and for them, the G8 represented the most logical target. Jack had attended no fewer than five high-level security briefings in the past two weeks; at each of them, the various layers of security had been reviewed with agonizing thoroughness. Aside from the uniformed security in and around the Federal Building, response teams had been positioned all around the perimeter of the protest group, and plainclothes agents mixed freely with the protestors. In addition to those plainclothes officers, undercover agents had infiltrated several of the more belligerent activist groups. With all that security on hand, the presence of one additional CTU agent meant very little.

Which was exactly the point made to Jack by the chief of his department, Christopher Henderson.

"There's no need for you to be there," Henderson had said a day earlier, rejecting his request.

"There's no harm in it," Jack protested. "I'm telling you I saw him."

Henderson had tried unsuccessfully to hide his skepticism. He knew from past experience that Jack Bauer didn't make idle suggestions. Bauer had bucked the chain of command, ignored the opinions of his colleagues, and risked making a fool of himself and everyone around him. If Jack Bauer stomped into his office claiming to have uncovered a plot to assassinate the entire line of succession in the U.S. government, Henderson would probably believe him. But this . . .

"So you were just walking along the docks in Long Beach," Chris had said, "and you just happened to bump into Ayman al-Libbi."

"That's right," Jack avowed, stating his claim for the tenth time that day.

"Ayman al-Libbi, Jack! He's the jack of diamonds in our current deck of cards, one of the ten most wanted terrorists in the world."

Jack shook his head. "He's a bench player lately. The Libyans haven't used him since Kaddafi got religion, the Palestinians can't afford him anymore. He's a hired gun. He's ripe to be used by someone taking a potshot at the G8. He'd do it, too, just to put himself back in the spotlight."

Chris had put his feet up and made a determined effort to rein in the conversation. Jack worked at a furious pace, and it was easy to get dragged along in his wake. After a long pause, Henderson had said, "So let's say you're right and al-Libbi's in the country, even in the city. What are you going to do, walk around the Federal Building until you spot him?"

Moving through the crowd of protestors, Jack grinned in spite of himself. Goddamned Henderson. For a guy who'd been riding a desk for several years now, he was still quick on his feet. Here he was, meandering through throngs of thousands, every one of them shouting down the United States or its allies, protesting globalization, environmental degradation, human rights abuse, or whatever pet cause they'd adopted. The chances of spotting one man who was probably too smart to present himself in person anyway were less than zero.

Of course, Jack wasn't using only his own eyes and feet.

"Unit two?" he muttered into his sleeve, pretending to scratch his nose as he spoke into the microphone clipped under his cuff.

"Two here, over," said a sleepy voice into his ear piece. That was fellow field agent Tony Almeida.

"Did I wake you?" Jack asked.

"No, I'm still sleeping."

"Hilarious. Is the FRS up and running?"

7:10 A.M. PST
Federal Building Command Center,
West Los Angeles

Tony Almeida was straddling a molded plastic chair he'd spun backward so that the backrest touched his chest. He folded his arms across the top edge of the rest and settled his chin down on his forearms. He spoke in soft, narcotic tones that, along with his puppy dog eyes, convinced others that he was slow. This was an often serious, and sometimes fatal, mistake.

Tony had lodged himself in the basement security room of the Federal Building, a bunkerlike chamber that had been designated as the central command post for the various agencies involved in security during the G8 demonstrations.

Because the building was Federal property, the FBI had overall jurisdiction, but with the demonstration population expected to grow beyond ten thousand, they had grudgingly asked for help from the Los Angeles Police Department, Beverly Hills PD, and the L.A. Sheriff Department. Since the FBI expected to do all the brain work and just needed bodies, they hadn't invited CTU. For this reason, Tony hadn't exactly received a warm welcome when he'd walked into the command center asking to watch the security monitors. The two FBI agents working the visual equipment—pallid techies who'd spent their entire investigative careers, Tony was sure, sitting in little rooms just like this one—reluctantly shifted a little to make room. But no one offered to get him a more comfortable chair.

He was staring at a bank of twenty video monitors that showed images relayed from cameras all on and around the Federal Building and the plaza. From that small room, the surveillance team could monitor every part of the growing mob of demonstrators from several angles.

But Tony wasn't interested in those monitors. He was staring at five smaller screens stacked to the right of the main console. Those screens displayed snapshots of individual protestors, taken at random, that were fed into a highly sophisticated facial recognition system, or FRS, that compared those images to the government's growing database of known or suspected terrorists.

"Yeah, it's running," Tony replied finally, talking into a headset. "They're just pulling random images for now."

Jack Bauer's voice crackled over the radio link, its usual grit turned to even more of a growl as he spoke softly. "Get them to focus on short, dark hair—"

Tony laughed. "Jack, we had about five thousand people come up from Central America the other day to protest deforestation in the Amazon. Two-thirds of the crowd has short, dark hair. It's WASP-y types like you that stand out like a sore thumb."

"If you wanted an easy job, you should have become a postman."

"I'd rather read people's mail than deliver it."

7:13 A.M. PST
Federal Plaza, West Los Angeles

Jack allowed himself a half smile as he signed off. He and Tony Almeida weren't the best of friends and probably never would be, but some recent cases had brought them closer together, and each had earned the other's respect. Their working relationship, cold in past months, had thawed enough to allow for the occasional friendly insult. Almeida stayed inside the lines too often for Jack's taste, but he got the job done, so Jack couldn't complain.

Jack's mobile phone rang. He leaned up against a lamppost on Wilshire Boulevard so that he was out of the flow of foot traffic. "Bauer."

"Jack, it's Mercy."

Jack felt a stitch in his chest, that tightness he felt back in boot camp when the drill sergeant stormed in for barracks inspection, or even farther back, when a police car cruised by on the road. It was an irrational, automatic feeling of guilt despite having done nothing wrong.

"Mercy," he said hesitantly, "what's . . . ?"

"Relax, Jack, this is business."

"Oh." The stitch loosened.

"I'm working a case I want to talk to you about. I think it might involve you guys."

"Okay," he said, feeling his tongue loosening as she spoke. "You want to meet tomorrow?"

"No, I want to meet now. I can come to you. Where are you?"

"The Federal Building."

"Right, the G8. Where can I meet you?"

Jack looked around. He was in the middle of an ocean of bobbing heads and milling bodies that stretched for a block in either direction. The sun had risen high enough above the surrounding buildings to shine light over Federal Plaza and warm the demonstrators. Like seals responding to the sun, the demonstrators had begun to agitate more with each passing moment. "I'm not exactly in a great spot for a case review."

"There's a bus shelter on the corner of Wilshire and Federal, right next to the building," Mercy said.

"Right," Jack said, spotting the shelter. "I think it's currently the protest headquarters for the Latin American Coffee Growers."

"See you there at eight A.M."

"The crowd is huge. You'll never get here in twenty minutes.

"Jack, this is L.A. You can get anywhere in twenty minutes."

7:35 A.M. PST
West Los Angeles, California

He did not think of himself as a man of action. He was a man whose circumstances had imposed the need for action upon him. He had committed acts of violence, and planned to commit more such acts very soon, but he did not adore violence as did some others with whom he had worked. Unfortunately he could not denounce violence, either. Violence was a tool, and at times a very useful tool indeed, and he had long ago sworn to use any and all tools necessary to satisfy his ambitions.

He was lying across the bed of his room, studying the lines in the ceiling created by uneven plastering. The lines reminded him of aerial maps of the Fertile Crescent. The beige plaster served as desert, the rough patches were arid mountain ranges, and the long cracks wound their way across the landscape like overtaxed rivers.

His room was sparse. He didn't care—he spent very little time there. He had roomed in the best hotels in the world, and also spent nights in tents under desert skies or in jungles, and they were the same to him; strategic locations from which to plan his assaults on the powers aligned against him.

When he had begun his crusade, he had fought in the name of "his" people. They were his adopted people, of course, and he acknowledged that. But it made them no less his own, and he had poured all his energies into protecting them from occupiers and colonialists. The fight, back then, had been personal. As the years passed, the fight had grown, until now he saw himself as a crusader fighting for worldwide justice.

He smiled in spite of himself. He was self-aware enough to know that the image of the crusader existed only to satisfy his ego. Still, that did not make it untrue.

His mobile phone vibrated. He recognized the number. It belonged to someone sympathetic to his cause, someone well placed and therefore useful. He picked it up. "Yes," he said calmly.

"The Feds are getting involved."

He felt nervousness tighten his stomach, but he forced himself to relax. "Well, they intended to be here all along. After all, you are a 'Fed,' too."

"Part of a standard security team. These guys are looking for someone specific." The man on the phone recited a description.

"That could be anyone," the man in the hotel said.

"Which means it could be you. You make the call, I'm just passing on the information."

"These 'guys' to whom you referred. You know them?"

"Only by reputation. The point man is Jack Bauer. He's the one looking for you."

"And how close do you suppose he is to finding me?"

"Not very. But they have some kind of lead."

"I see," said the man in the hotel room. "Well, let's learn a little more about Mr. Bauer. We may have to pay him a visit."

7:45 A.M. PST
Federal Plaza, West Los Angeles

Jack had cruised by the Teen Green assembly and waved to Kim when his ear bud chirped.

"Jack, Tony. You're not going to believe this."

"Tell me anyway."

"I think we got something."

"Al-Libbi?"

"No, but a lead. How fast can you get to the southwest corner of the building?"

"They say you can get anywhere in L.A. in twenty minutes."

"Well, make it faster. There's something you'll want to see."

Jack turned on his heel. He had almost reached the northeast corner of Federal Plaza, putting him as far as possible from his destination. The fastest way to reach the far side would be to cut diagonally through the plaza itself. But looking over the heads of the still-growing mobs of protestors, he saw a line of uniformed riot police assembled along the perimeter of the building itself. So far the protestors had stuck to the script and stayed fifty yards away from the police line.

Jack decided that rushing toward that line of grim officers would cause a riot long before he had a chance to flash his badge.

He headed west on the Wilshire sidewalk, blading his way through the crowd. This was no easy task, as the number of protestors was swelling by the minute. The G8 summit was scheduled for opening statements and photo ops at eight-thirty, and the protestors were mustering for action. Placards were sprouting like angry weeds all over the place, and some of the crowds, relatively normal in their dress before, had now changed into costumes. Jack elbowed past a Grim Reaper wearing a sign that said GLOBALIZATION KILLS.

He neared the northwest corner and cut across the grass as close to the forbidden concrete plaza as he dared, then headed south. His phone rang again, but this time the screen read Home.

"Hey," he said, not slowing his pace.

"Hi, how's everything there?" his wife, Teri, asked.

"Crowded," Jack grunted. "You wouldn't believe the line to get coffee."

"Are you sure she's going to be okay?" Teri said worriedly. She had asked that question, in that same tone of voice, ten times since last night.

"She'll be fine." Jack wedged his elbow between two pale-faced grad students with uncallused hands whose matching T-shirts bore pictures of Che Guevera. "The student advisor is keeping them away from the front of the pack. If things get out of hand, they'll be far enough away."

"Plus she's got you with her."

Jack suspected that a mother's definition of "with" didn't include being separated by ten thousand political activists and platoons of anxious policemen. "I promise she'll be fine," was all he could say.

He heard soft static on the telephone. "Jack, are you okay?"

"Me? Of course."

"You've just got your work voice on."

"It's just the crowd," he replied. "It puts me on edge a little."

Teri's voice lightened. "Relax a little. You're not saving the world today, just taking care of your daughter."

"Saving the world is easier," he said. "I'll talk to you later."

7:55 A.M. PST
Southwest Corner of the Federal Building,
West Los Angeles

Jack hadn't been off the phone for more than sixty seconds when his ear bud chirped again. "Tony, I'm here," he said. "What am I looking for?"

"I see you," Almeida said from inside the command center. "Turn to your four o'clock and move to the street. Look south on Veteran Avenue. Hurry!"

Jack made a quarter turn to his right and slid through the crowd to the curb. Veteran Avenue, one of the streets bordering the Federal Building, had been closed off for security reasons and a barricade had been set up half a block down. A line of protestors had formed at the barricade, where police were doing cursory searches to ensure that no weapons got through, and most people, once they passed the police line, hurried toward the building. Jack looked just in time to see one man moving in the opposite direction. "Blue T-shirt, long sleeves, dark hair," Jack described.

"You've got him."

Jack sped up to a jog. "Who am I chasing?"

"The FRS thinks it looks an awful lot like Muhammad Abbas."

Jack broke into a run. "Can you get sound?"

"We're angling the shotgun mikes."

Muhammad Abbas, Palestinian refugee turned Lebanese parliament lap dog for the PLO, turned arms-dealing middleman. Abbas had been a functionary working in the shadows of real power brokers in the Middle East for twenty years. He had, in fact, served as the factotum for one particular terrorist: Ayman al-Libbi.

"I'm at the police barricade," Jack said, his breath coming shorter. He couldn't see beyond the barricade and the crowd waiting for approval to move past it. He looked around urgently, spotting a cement trash can. He jumped on top of it and looked over the crowd, spotting the blue T-shirt near a red Toyota Camry with the door open. There was another man standing there, but Jack couldn't get a clear view of them.

"I'll never get to them in time," Jack said. "How about those mikes?"

"We've got them, but—"

"But what?" Jack snapped. "Feed it through so I can hear it."

"Jack, they're not on Federal property anymore. We don't have a warrant to eavesdrop—"

"Screw it," Jack said. "If that's Muhammad Abbas, we have all the probable cause we need. Patch it through."

Over the radio, Tony made a short, disgruntled sound, but a minute later there was a burst of static, then Jack was hearing the voices of the two men talking half a block down the street.

". . . we thought, there's no way of doing it here." Based on their body language, Jack guessed that was the man in the blue T-shirt.

". . . meet in an hour or two. I will contact you to plan for tonight."

"Are you sure of success?"

Jack heard laughter, cold and flat in the microphone. "If it were easy, you would not need us. But we won't fail. They'll be—"

A truck rumbled by the two men, disrupting the signal.

"—dead."

Jack swore. "Did you guys get that?"

"Negative," Tony said. "Goddamned traffic."

1 2 3 4 5 6 7 8 9
10 11 12 13 14 15 16 17
18 19 20 21 22 23 24

• •

THE FOLLOWING TAKES PLACE
BETWEEN THE HOURS OF
8 A.M. AND 9 A.M.
PACIFIC STANDARD TIME

• •

8:00 A.M. PST
Southwest Corner of the Federal Building,
West Los Angeles

"Get off there!"

Jack felt someone grab his ankle. Without thinking, he raised his other leg and stomped down on the offender's wrist. Only then did he see the uniformed cop standing below him, his angry glare transformed instantly into shock and pain. The cop released Jack's ankle, but used his good hand to draw a collapsible baton from his belt. With a smooth snap of his wrist, he extended the baton and swung it. The hard aluminum connected with his shins. Jack's vision went suddenly white and he toppled, landing on top of the officer, who collapsed beneath his weight.

"Officer down!" someone yelled. A second later Jack felt more blows across his back, then hands dragged him off the cop and onto his stomach. Someone put a knee across the back of his neck. Pebbles from the street asphalt dug into his cheek.

"Get the hell off me!" he snarled. "I'm a Federal—"

"Shut up!" someone barked into his ear. "You have the right to—"

"I'm a Federal agent!" Jack said.

"Believe it or not, he is."

Jack heard Mercy's voice resound loudly but calmly over the turmoil.

There was some muttering that Jack couldn't hear—the knee across his neck had shifted and was crushing his ear—and then a moment later all the pressure was lifted from his back. He sat up and saw Detective Mercy Bennet staring down at him, smiling and holding out one hand. She was flanked by four uniformed police officers, one of whom was rubbing his wrist painfully.

Jack took her offered hand and let her pull him to his feet. "Sorry about that," he said to the uniform.

"I think you broke it," the cop grumbled. "You should ID yourself before pulling a stunt like that. This is a potential riot area."

"You've got to forgive him, he doesn't always work well with others," Mercy said. To Jack: "Walk with me?"

Jack looked back over his shoulder. The two men were gone, probably driven off by the disturbance he and the cop had created. Damn. He spoke into his mike. "Did you see where they went?"

"Negative," Almeida replied, sounding disgusted. "Down the street, but we couldn't get more than that. The cameras are blocked by the tree line. Those guys are gone."

Jack threw the uniformed cop an angry glare, but didn't

feel the drive to push it further. It wasn't the cop's fault.

"Hello, Jack?" Mercy said, waving her hand in front of his face. "Remember me?"

"Mercy," Jack said, "I know you wanted to meet, but I've got something going here."

"Me, too," the detective said. "I think this might be your area."

"Jack?" Tony Almeida's voice muttered in his ear.

"Stand by," Jack said. He refocused on Mercy. She looked as good now as the day they'd agreed not to speak ever again. She was a fascinating combination of shapes—a sharp nose on a round face framed by straight dark hair. It all came together in a way he found attractive, especially when coupled with her no-BS attitude. You'd have called her feisty except that she'd kick you in the groin for using that word. She was wearing a dark blue pant suit with a white blouse that offered just the slightest hint of her nearly perfect breasts.

Mercy Bennet had spent six months as LAPD's liaison to the Counter Terrorist Unit, a thankless task that required diplomacy, patience, and tact.

Mercy had not been good at the job.

The first time Jack met her, she walked into the conference room at CTU to accuse Ryan Chappelle of withholding information and holding LAPD suspects in custody without notifying local authorities. At least that was what she'd written in her report. The words she'd actually used to his face were more along the lines of "sandbagging son of a bitch" and "pencil-necked twit."

Jack liked her right away.

"All right," Jack said after a moment. "What have you got?"

8:10 A.M. PST
West Los Angeles

". . . just kill him," the man on the phone was saying.

"No, Nick," said the man from his room. "We're not going to kill anyone we don't have to kill. Besides, killing him will raise even more questions."

"Getting soft?"

The man grimaced, not so much at the challenge to his authority as to the tedium involved in defending himself. Nick was his inside man, one of the faithful—but he was a man of action, and like most men of action, he required constant affirmation of himself and his leaders.

"I am economical," he said. "You should know that by now."

"Well, you may have to spend a little something on this guy," Nick said. "From what I've heard, Bauer isn't the kind of guy to stop once he's on the scent."

"He's hardly 'on the scent.' "

"He just met with the detective on the Gordon Gleed case."

The man in the hotel room hesitated. He was rarely surprised, and rarely unsure of himself. But this information was surprising, and was surely cause for concern. He had not expected the Gleed case to move from the local to the federal level so quickly.

"In twenty-three hours it won't matter," he said. "We will have to convince Mr. Bauer to slow down his investigation."

8:16 A.M. PST
Southwest Corner of Federal Plaza,
West Los Angeles

Jack Bauer stood by the grill of Mercy's slick-top white Crown Victoria, where she had led him. "So what's the story?"

Mercy had just related to him the theory she'd been developing since the day Gordon Gleed was bludgeoned in his own home. From those first moments, she'd been convinced that Gleed had not been the victim of a robbery. The tossed house and stolen items were a feint. Gleed had been killed for political reasons.

"Gordon Gleed was president of the Free Enterprise Alliance. That's a business group that supports rural resource developers."

"Rural resource—?"

"A fancy name for loggers, real estate developers, like that. They file lawsuits to repeal environmental protection and fight against the Clean Water Act. The Free Enterprise Alliance is one of those groups that eats endangered spotted owls for dinner and takes baths in baby seal blood."

"How does that involve us?" Jack had asked.

"I did some research. The Free Enterprise Alliance had several clashes with some splinter groups from Earth First!, a radical environmental group. These splinter groups, like the Earth Liberation Front and some others, are on CTU's terrorist watch list."

Jack didn't even try to hide his shock. "A bunch of tree-huggers are on the terrorist watch list?"

"You should check into these guys, Jack. They aren't just a bunch of granola heads. They're eco-terrorists—organized, sophisticated. They've killed people, sabotaged companies. They're as radical as anyone else out there."

"No planes into buildings, though," Jack pointed out.

"No, but I wouldn't put it past some of them. There's a splinter group that left Earth First! because it felt that Earth First! was too soft. They sent a half-dozen death threats to Gordon Gleed in the last year or so."

"Even if this guy was murdered by eco-terrorists, it's not something I can focus on now." He spread his arms as if to embrace the entire Federal Building. "I've got the G8 to worry about, and a known political terrorist to track down."

"That's why I tracked *you* down. From what I could dig up, Gordon Gleed had taken matters into his own hands. No one at the Federal level did much for him, so he started digging up his own dirt on this splinter group. I think he found out they were planning something at the G8, and that's why they killed him."

"Planning what?"

"Jesus, Jack, if I knew I would have *started* this conversation there," she said, her temperature rising.

"Well, come on, Mercy!" Jack snapped back. "What do you expect me to do with this? You want me to drop a potential lead against a man who's responsible for about a hundred terrorist acts over the last ten years and look into a local murder because of some Greenpeace guys who are really, really upset?"

Mercy's neck reddened. She fought the urge to bite back, and kept her sentences short and factual. "Gleed was smart. He reported everything he learned to the FBI, even though they weren't really interested. He also did his own investigating. He heard this splinter group was planning something for the G8. Something big."

Jack held his hands up in appeasement. "Okay. That's not much, but it's something. This splinter group, does it have a name? A leader?"

Mercy fidgeted. "They call themselves the Monkey Wrench Gang."

"The Monkey Wrench Gang!" Jack said incredulously. "You can't be serious."

"I laughed it off, too," Mercy said defensively. "But it has meaning. *The Monkey Wrench Gang* was a book written by a guy named Edward Abbey. That was the book that inspired the founders of Earth First! In some ways it was the inspiration for the whole eco-terrorist movement."

"Who's the leader, Magilla Gorilla?"

Mercy bore the brunt of his jokes bravely. "According to Gleed's notes, he's known as Seldom Seen Smith." When Jack rolled his eyes, she added, "Another reference to the book."

"Right. Monkeywrench Gang. Seldom Seen Smith. Mercy, I hear what you're saying, but even if you're right, I don't have much to go on—"

"I have Gleed's notes. Run through them with me. We could dig up something—"

"—and I have a possible sighting of Ayman al-Libbi and a positive sighting of one of his lieutenants here already. I've got to stay on that. Why don't you take it to someone else?"

Now it was Mercy's turn for sarcasm. "After what we've been through, do you think I'd go to you first?"

Her statement hit Jack like a slap in the face. She hadn't wanted to see him. She had actively avoided it. And now she'd come to him only as a last resort. "Mercy . . ."

"The FBI had the same reaction you did. I'm telling you, these guys fly under the radar because no one puts eco-terrorism high on the list, and because the names are so ridiculous. But that's only going to last until they do something big. For God's sake, the Muslim Brotherhood sounds like it belongs in a comic book, but you take those guys seriously."

"Forget that for a minute," Jack said. "I want to"—he glanced around but none of the uniforms was paying any attention to them—"let's talk about you and me."

She didn't move a muscle, but to Jack it seemed as if she had stepped back. There was suddenly more distance between them. "There's nothing to talk about," she said flatly.

"You don't believe that any more than I do," Jack insisted. "Just because we stopped doesn't mean there's nothing there."

Mercy had been three months on the job as liaison when her weekly updates with CTU turned into one-on-one meetings with Jack Bauer, and those meetings became coffee, and then dates at the firing range for a little friendly competition, and then lunch . . .

Mercy smiled at him, the corners of her eyes wrinkling ever so slightly, and ever so sadly. "I didn't say there was nothing there. I said there's nothing to talk about." She stepped closer, so that even on the warming asphalt of a Los Angeles street Jack could smell her perfume. "Jack, I want you. We fit together. And I'm not going to pretend that you have to leave your wife first. But I don't want to sleep with you just because you need a little something extra. If there's a thing here, I'm all for it. But if it's just you feeling itchy, you need to set your sights on a different target."

Jack smiled awkwardly. He hated her for saying that, and loved her, too. She was blunt, factual, efficient; a bullet in the brain. She stated her case without equivocation. He had nothing but respect for that.

"Okay," he said. "I'll look at this when I can. But only for you. I . . ." He gathered himself. "I just want you to know that, no matter what happens, where we are, or whatever your situation . . . you'll always have someone who's on your side. Always."

Mercy smiled again, her eyes shining. "Thanks." She opened her car door and pulled out a stack of files. "Here," she said. "Read through those. If you finish and still don't think there's something here, forget it. Blow me off. But if this interests you, you know where to find me."

She handed him the file. As he took it, she brushed her finger along his hand. "Talk to you soon," she said, then slid into her car, started the engine, and drove away.

8:30 A.M. PST
Northeast Corner of Federal Plaza,
West Los Angeles

Kim Bauer was still talking to the boy with straight hair that hung down to his eyebrows. His name was Brad Gilmore. He was the current cutest boy in school, and half the reason Kim had joined Teen Green.

"So what does this meeting really have to do with the environment?" she asked Brad as they put the finishing touches on their posters. She knew the answer already, but she also knew boys. They liked to show off, and smart girls gave them every chance.

Brad pushed his hair behind his ears. "The G8 is made up of the biggest countries in the world. I mean, not the biggest exactly, but some of the biggest polluters. And they're also talking about letting China join up, and China is totally a big polluter, too. I went to Beijing one summer with my mom and you could taste the air."

"And demonstrations like this are going to help, right?"

Kim meant for her voice to sound cute and coy, but she was still Jack Bauer's daughter, and a hint of skepticism crept in.

Brad squirmed a little. Clearly he didn't want to get into a political debate with Kim. "I don't know," he said. "I mean, this is our planet, too, right? Maybe it's more ours than theirs, since we're going to be around longer. Besides, it's pretty cool to be here, isn't it?"

"That's the quote of the day!"

Both Kim and Brad turned to see who was talking to them. The man standing behind them was short and round, his belly pushing against the buttons of a blue button-down shirt. He smiled a puffy, big-cheeked smile from behind a pair of round black glasses. He was wearing a badge on a red ribbon around his neck, which he lifted and waved in front of their faces. "How're you doing? I'm Martin Olivera with the *L.A. Weekly*. You two have time for a quick interview?"

Kim looked from the short round man to Brad to Marshall Cooper, the club advisor. Mr. Cooper glanced at the press badge and then smiled and nodded.

"Sure," she said.

Martin Olivera plucked a pen out of his shirt pocket and lifted a small black notepad. "So what brings a group of teenagers down to a huge political demonstration like this?"

"Well," Kim said, winking at Brad, "I mean, this is our planet, too, isn't it? And like we're going to be around here longer, aren't we?"

Olivera scratched at his notebook. "That's good, that's really good. Can I have your name for the article?"

"Kim Bauer," she said. "And he's Brad Gilmore."

"Great, thanks. Have a good day."

He turned away, and Kim turned back to Brad. "Oh, hey, one more thing," the reporter said. He reached back and tapped Kim with the pen. The pen poked her on the wrist like a bee sting.

"Ow!"

"Oh, jeez, I'm sorry!" Olivera said. "I just wanted to make sure it's B-a-u-e-r."

"That hurt. Be careful with that thing," Kim said, bringing her wrist to her mouth and sucking at the spot where the pen had stabbed her. "Yeah, that's how you spell it."

"Thanks again," Olivera said with a smile. "Goodbye."

8:45 A.M. PST
Federal Building Command Center,
West Los Angeles

Tony Almeida watched Jack through the camera as he talked with the female detective. He'd seen her around CTU—some sort of liaison—but he'd forgotten her name. Jack had turned off his microphone, so he couldn't hear what they were saying.

"She's a hottie," said one of the two pallid FBI techs. The other one had gone on a break. This one grinned at Tony. He had a hard, Slavic look about the face, but his body was thin. "We could always use the shotgun mike on him."

Tony glared at him under his heavy eyelids. "How do you guys get off when you're not snooping?"

"Oh, we're always snooping," he said with a grin.

Tony shrugged. "You guys told me your names before. McKey and Dyson, right? Which one are you?"

The tech laughed. "We're interchangeable."

"Built out of spare parts at Quantico, that it?"

"Something like that. I'm Nick Dyson." He shook Tony's hand quickly. "So anyway, how about that shotgun mike?"

Tony shook his head. "If Bauer wanted us listening in, he'd have left his mike on."

"Suit yourself," the tech said. He stared at the bank of monitors and sighed. "This is going to be boring, I can tell already."

Almeida watched the human ocean roiling and crashing against the barricades. "Let's hope you're right," he prayed.

8:55 A.M. PST
Federal Plaza, West Los Angeles

One of the best parts of being a Federal agent was the parking. When Jack had brought Kim down to the rally, he'd parked in the Federal Building's main lot, which was now reserved only for personnel who worked in the building and, of course, Federal agents.

Jack climbed into his black SUV as his cell phone rang.

"Hey, Jack," Teri said. "How's it going out there?"

"Hey," he replied. "It's going fine. Listen, can you call Kim on her cell and tell her I'll be right back? I have to run over to the office for a minute."

The wireless connection went suddenly cold. "Jack, you're supposed to be with her."

He defended himself. "She's with the chaperone. And this is a quick trip. I just have to check on something. Do you mind calling her?"

"Fine," she said in a tone that indicated it was anything but. "I'll talk to you later." The call ended.

He would pay for that later, he could tell. But there was nothing to be done at the moment. Jack fired the engine, then rolled out of the lot and turned south on Federal Avenue. It would have been easier to turn north and take Wilshire Boulevard toward downtown, which would have led him closer to CTU headquarters, but Wilshire was, of course, blocked, so the only way to get away from the building was to follow a maze of detours through the narrow streets lined with tiny, well-kept Spanish bungalows that had sprung up just off the main thoroughfares. It was really just Los Angeles, but they called it Holmby Hills, or Rancho Park, or something else that sounded exclusive and desirable, so that the residents all felt good about their inflated property values.

He should have been focused on Ayman al-Libbi, or even Mercy's take on the eco-terrorist theory. But instead he was focused on Mercy Bennet herself, although his mind alternately, almost guiltily, went from Mercy to Teri Bauer and back, like a bad news reporter giving equal time even when the topics did not merit equal weight.

Mercy was right to hold him at arm's length. He knew that, and not because he subscribed to some outmoded sense of decency. Half the men he knew admitted cheating on their wives, and the other half were liars. Mercy didn't demand that he do the right thing—she just wanted assurance that she was making more than just a guest appearance in Jack's own personal drama.

And the truth was, he couldn't give her that assurance. He liked her. He knew that. But he loved Teri, even when she drove him crazy. Even in the depth of his discontent he had never thought of leaving her for another woman, until Mercy appeared. She was a new temptation, different from the others that Jack had resisted, a temptation that was more than distraction, a lure that seemed to be not just temporary relief but . . . an alternative.

And the truth was, Jack knew that in the end he was using her.

"You know what's really screwing you up," Jack growled to himself. "The fact that you're thinking of this at all. You need to focus on your job."

He had just finished speaking those words out loud when the pickup truck slammed into the passenger side of his car.

....

THE FOLLOWING TAKES PLACE
BETWEEN THE HOURS OF
9 A.M. AND 10 A.M.
PACIFIC STANDARD TIME

....

9:00 A.M.
Four Seasons Hotel, Beverly Hills

Kasim Turkel walked into the hotel lobby with the same sense of stupefied wonder he'd felt upon entering every building since his arrival in the United States. The evidence of abundance was overwhelming. The double doors were fashioned of wrought iron and glass. The tiles in the lobby were wide and smooth, with heavy stone tables supporting enormous porcelain vases filled with flower arrangements that towered over him. Beyond the tables stood a small wooden lectern, behind which stood a tall young man in a blue jacket who smiled at him professionally.

Instinctively Kasim hesitated until he felt Nurmamet Tuman's hand touch his arm reassuringly.

"Relax," Nurmamet said softly in Uygur. "We are just visiting the bar. It is done here all the time."

To the man in the blue coat, Nurmamet spoke in gently accented English. "Good morning. Where is the bar please?"

The young man pointed over Nurmamet's shoulder. "It's that way, sir. But I'm sorry, they're not serving."

"That's all right," Nurmamet replied, "we are just looking for a quiet place to sit for a few minutes."

Kasim nodded and summoned a smile as he passed the man in the blue coat, following Nurmamet's lead, and turned right. In this direction lay another set of double doors, this time of hand-carved wood, that opened on an opulent bar of gleaming wood flanked by deep-cushioned stools. Across from the bar, squads of tables guarded by leather chairs formed a small army. As the hotel employee had said, the bar was not open and the room was empty except for a man sitting at one of the tables, one leg crossed lazily over the other, a newspaper laid out before him and half lifted in his hands. He seemed not to have noticed the two men enter.

Undaunted, Nurmamet walked over to him and sat down, indicating that Kasim should do likewise. The man in the chair did not look up from his newspaper. He wore a blue silk suit with pinstripes so thin Kasim had not seem them from a distance. His tie was light green and knotted into a perfect triangle. In that opulent hotel, sitting across from the man in the expensive suit, Kasim felt uncomfortably underdressed, but Nurmamet had assured him that in Los Angeles it was sometimes fashionable to dress poorly. Attitude, he said, counted almost as much as appearance.

Kasim watched Nurmamet, who for the first time seemed the slightest bit nervous as he recited awkwardly: "Is this your first time at the Four Seasons?"

The well-dressed man let the newspaper fall flat and

looked up at the two newcomers. His eyes bulged slightly, his lids were heavy, and there were small bags of skin beneath each one that gave him the look of someone who had recently been crying. "Enough of the code words," he said dryly. "It's not necessary."

Nurmamet looked flustered. "But Mr. al-Libbi made it clear that we needed to identify ourselves."

"You are not the FBI," the man said with a smile. "I know this because you have not arrested me."

"We could be agents," Kasim blurted. "We could be trying to get to your employer through you."

The well-dressed man turned his sad eyes toward Kasim. "Are you?"

Kasim fidgeted and the man laughed again. "I did not think so. If you were the FBI, I would already be somewhere very unpleasant being asked questions in a very unpleasant way." He held out his hand lazily and when, after a moment, Nurmamet and Kasim each shook it, he said casually, "I am Muhammad Abbas. If you have the rest of the money, then I can take you to Mr. al-Libbi."

Kasim was baffled. This wasn't right. He looked at Nurmamet, who appeared equally confused. "This is not right. I understood that we were to meet Mr. al-Libbi here, not his assistant."

"Yes, but you are amateurs. Ayman al-Libbi does not take chances with amateurs."

"We are not—!"

"Don't deny it," Abbas said calmly. "You are rank amateurs. You tell me that you might be agents. What about me? I could be an agent trying to trick you."

Kasim stared at him, willing his heart to stop pounding. "Are you?" he said, his voice almost steady.

This amused Abbas. "Not bad! This one is good, Nurmamet. He is a leader where you come from, eh?" Nurmamet nodded. "Well," he said to Kasim, "don't be insulted. Mr. al-Libbi had urgent business to attend to, something that will make all this go more smoothly."

9:16 A.M.
Culver City, California

Jack woke, feeling as though he had overslept and urgently needed to be somewhere. A moment later he remembered a glimpse of a red pickup truck hurtling toward him, the spine-shivering sound of metal contorting metal, followed instantaneously by the pop of his air bag and then white blindness.

He opened his eyes, or thought he did. He was in complete darkness. He was lying down on a hard, cool surface, rough with pebbles and coarse dirt—a concrete floor. He sat up, carefully reaching his hands outward, upward, backward into the blackness. Wherever the ceiling was, it seemed high enough, so he stood. His knees wobbled a little beneath him. Jack used his hands to give himself a cursory search—he didn't seem to be bleeding, although his face felt tender, probably from the air bag. His left shoulder and his abdomen ached, most likely having been pressed into the seat belt during the crash. He felt another pain, this time on his left arm, but this was different. It was extremely localized and sharp, like a dime-sized bruise at the crook of his elbow.

Okay, Jack thought. *A car crash. Now I'm here, and "here" definitely does not feel like a good place*. He reached for his handgun but found that the SigSauer 9 mm was gone from his shoulder holster.

"Your weapon will be returned to you before we are done, Agent Bauer," said a firm but polite voice.

Who are you? Where am I? These were the questions that

popped instinctively into Jack's mind. He didn't ask them. The person who had put him in a dark hole would not be inclined to answer either question. Jack chose one that would get an answer. "What do you want?"

He heard a short grunt—somewhere above him—a sound of approval. "Right to the point. I like that. The truth is, Agent Bauer, I want nothing. I mean that literally, I want nothing. To be more specific, I want *you* to do nothing . . . for, let's say, the next twenty-four hours."

I've been kidnapped, Jack realized. *Stuck in a hole somewhere. Shit.*

"So I guess I'm staying here for a while?" Jack stared up, although he could see nothing. He was trying to gauge the height from which the voice originated.

"No," his captor replied. "No, although I confess I considered it. It was tempting, but not really workable. I suspect that if you go missing, people will come looking for you. So I'm going to have to release you in the next few minutes."

"Good," Jack said.

Who was this guy? Unconsciously Jack recorded information gathered from the man's speech: he was educated, confident, forward-thinking; his English was perfect, but there was a slight cadence to it, as though he was accustomed to speaking a different language.

Holding his hands outstretched, Jack took a step forward, trying to stay light on his feet. The room did not echo, which meant it wasn't very large. If he could find a wall, then he could find a way out.

"Before I release you, though, I'm going need a guarantee that you do absolutely nothing for the next day."

"Okay. I promise."

The man laughed. "In a better world, that would mean something, wouldn't it? But I'm afraid we live in this one, so I'm going to need some more assurance. Your reputation with the Counter Terrorism Unit is that you are tenacious. And I suspect you are not the kind of man who can be intentionally assaulted and kidnapped, and then simply forgive and forget."

Jack allowed himself to laugh. "It does put a crimp in our relationship," he quipped. His captor was urbane and seemed to appreciate dry wit. Jack would have preferred to put a bullet in his brain, but that could come later. He took another step, then another. His shoes crunched lightly on the dirt-sprinkled concrete.

"We are not destined to be friends," his captor agreed. "To explain how I am going to extract a guarantee from you, I need to tell you about a virus."

Jack froze. At the word *virus,* his focus changed. Escape was now secondary. Information was a priority.

"This virus comes in several strains. One of them, when injected into the bloodstream, begins to replicate within twelve to twenty-four hours but doesn't show any symptoms until then. After that, it is infectious and all but incurable and it is decidedly fatal."

Jack became conscious of the small, unique bruise on his left arm. "You injected me with the virus," he growled.

The man, wherever he was, laughed. "No. From what I understand, you are not the kind of man to be blackmailed by a threat to your person. I injected your daughter."

9:30 A.M.
CTU Headquarters, Los Angeles

Chris Henderson sat at the end of the conference table, staring down the row of faces on either side. He'd gotten to know most of the team members well during his stint as Director of Field Operations. They were a good team. He'd watched them perform well under severe strain in the months since he'd come on board, and he'd read case files on some of their activities before his assignment. They were an impressive bunch.

"Tony," he said to the speaker box squatting on the center of the table like a miniature spaceship. "Can you brief us on current activities at the Federal Building?"

Tony Almeida's voice resonated from the box. "We're approximately one hour into the demonstration, and so far so good as far as riots go. LAPD estimates the crowd at over ten thousand, but they figure on twice that before noon. It's going to start getting hotter then, too, so we may see tempers flare."

Tony Almeida was a sharp one, Chris thought. Even though the higher-ups in CTU continued to pressure him for budget cuts, he couldn't imagine letting Almeida go. The guy had Agent in Charge written all over him.

"How about your lead on Muhammad Abbas?" Chris asked. "Has Jack finished beating up cops?"

Almeida laughed. "We lost Abbas. Jack is on his way into the office to do follow-up."

Nina Myers, another first-class agent, spoke up. "If that was Abbas, and if he is still doing gruntwork for al-Libbi, then Jack's right and al-Libbi is in town. His target has to be the G8, right?"

"Or part of it," Almeida said. "Does it make sense for him to attack the whole summit? Al-Libbi's last client was Iran, which has been trading arms from France, so why would they allow France to get bombed?"

Nina Myers said, "We have to figure out who al-Libbi is working for."

Chris nodded. "What's al-Libbi's alignment these days?"

"Money," Nina said. "The CIA says he lost religion years ago, and now he just works for the highest bidder. Last known base of operations was Iraq, but he was booted out in early 2001 for taking a job with the Iranians. He's pretty much a hired gun, now."

"Which means he could be working for anyone," Almeida piped in. "We're a target, of course, but with Russia here, too, I wouldn't put it past the Chechens to go after the summit. They could easily have contacted al-Libbi."

"Don't forget China," Nina said. "Half the protestors out there are upset that the G8 is considering letting China into the club."

"Where's our short list of active anti-China groups?" Chris said.

Nina reached for the remote that controlled the conference room's display screen. She tapped a few buttons and a list popped onto the screen. "There's Free Taiwan and the religious group Falun Gong. According to the Chinese, there are also about forty groups in Xinjiang Uygur Autonomous Region, or what the locals like to call East Turkistan. They vary in size, and some are more violent than others, but all of them are pretty localized."

Chris nodded. All this had been covered in the advance work done several weeks prior to the summit. Most of the agencies involved—the FBI, Homeland Security, the CIA, and CTU—believed that China's presence would cause a huge political firestorm, but not a terrorist attack. Organizations with enough muscle and sophistication to launch an attack on U.S. soil, such as al-Qaeda, would go after the United States itself or Russia. Still, it had bothered Henderson during the advance meeting when no one seemed to know anything about these eastern Chinese groups.

"Have we gotten any more intelligence on them?" he asked.

Jessi Bandison, one of the analysts, spoke up, but she didn't look at Chris. "Not really. The Chinese government plays an interesting game. They work very hard to report on the horrible things that these separatist groups do, but they refuse to give out any real information about them."

"Do we know if any of them operate in the U.S. at all?" Chris asked.

"Only one," Nina said. "ETIM, or Eastern Turkistan Independence Movement. But they're small-scale, never done anything big even in their own region, and the CIA says they have no funding. Their cause isn't close enough to al-Libbi's heart to get him to work for free, and there's no way they can pay his salary."

Chris sighed. "Well, let's put someone on it anyway. Where's Jack?"

9:39 A.M. PST
Culver City

Blood pounded in Jack's ears. He felt his fingers flex involuntarily as he imagined squeezing the life out of this man, whoever he was.

"She'll be perfectly all right, Agent Bauer," said his captor. "I have an antidote."

"Let her go. Let me see her," Jack demanded.

"I don't have her. You're missing the point. I know how these stories go. There's a murder, or someone goes missing, and all of a sudden the cat is out of the bag. No one is going to go missing, Agent Bauer. Your daughter is going to go about her day. She doesn't know she has been exposed to the virus. She won't even become contagious for twenty-four hours. I am going to release you now, and you're going to go about your day. You are going back to your office, and you are going to sit there for the rest of the day. But you are going to stop your line of investigation. Tomorrow you will receive a small package with the antidote. Give it to your daughter by seven o'clock tomorrow morning, and all will be well. Do I make myself clear?"

"I understand," Jack growled.

"Good. I would like to tell you one more thing, and then our business will be concluded. I will be watching you, Agent Bauer. And I will be watching your daughter. I will know where you go, and where she goes. So what I expect you to do is go back to your office and sit there all day. If you leave it, I will know. If you try to get your daughter to a hospital, I will know. You will never hear from me again, and your daughter will die. Goodbye."

Jack heard a faint scuffle—clothing sliding along wood. A few seconds later there was a heavy thud, the sound of a circuit breaker being thrown. Then bright lights came on. Jack, after sitting in the dark, was blinded. He blinked, waiting for his pupils to contract. When he could see again, he found himself in a small, bare basement with a concrete floor. Dust covered the floor, and cobwebs hung in the corners. The stairs, or what was left of them, were broken and rotted, but a brand-new aluminum ladder climbed from the dusty floor to the next level.

Jack ran for the ladder and climbed it quickly. A short hallway led away from the basement, then opened up into a larger room, an abandoned warehouse of some kind. There were windows on all sides of the warehouse, but they'd been papered over. Morning light leaked through and around them. Jack ran for the door, stopping only to pick up a few items that had been left in plain sight: his gun, his wallet, and his mobile phone.

Jack opened the door and walked out onto an asphalt parking lot. There was a faded sign on the warehouse, which was in a row of warehouses packed between two retail districts. According to the street signs he was at the corner of Barrington and Ocean Park. Four or five cars drove by on each street. Any one of them could have held the man who had just poisoned his daughter.

9:44 A.M.
CTU Headquarters, Los Angeles

Henderson's phone rang. "Henderson here."

"Chris, it's Jack Bauer."

"Jack, I thought you'd be here by—"

"I need someone to come pick me up. I'm in Culver City. Tell them to meet me at the corner of Barrington and Ocean Park. Now."

Chris heard the urgency in Jack's voice. "Stand by." He opened another line. "Nina—"

"I'm working on—"

"I need you to get Jack Bauer at Barrington and Ocean Park. Something's going down."

"On my way."

Chris returned to his other line. "Nina's en route. What can you tell me?"

"Nothing over the phone." Jack thought fast. He needed people he could trust. "Can I meet with you, Almeida, and Nina when I get back?"

"I can make it happen."

"Thanks." He touched the bruise on his left arm. "I'm going to need a medical team and a scanning team at headquarters. I think I've got some kind of tracking bug in me somewhere."

"It's done."

"Good." Jack hung up without further ceremony. He dialed another number. "Kimmy?" he said as soon as the connection was made.

"Hey, Dad! That must be some line for coffee!"

Bauer forced his voice to sound calm. "Sorry. I thought Mom would call you—"

"She did, I'm just guilting you a little. Are you coming back, or should I get a ride?"

"I'll try to get back. Listen . . ." He hesitated. "How's it going there? Any trouble?"

Kim lowered her voice conspiratorially. "Actually, this is totally boring. We're just standing around. Mr. Cooper says it's important just to stand up and be counted, but this reeks. All Brad Gilmore wants to do is talk about greenhouse gas."

"Did you—have you met anyone else? Had trouble with any other groups?"

"Dad, stop asking about trouble. Everything is totally cool. I even got interviewed by a reporter. He's going to put my name in the paper, which is cool. He was kind of a dweeb, though. He was trying to talk to me and he nearly stabbed me to death with his pen."

Jack's heart sank. "His pen—?"

"Well, he didn't really stab me, but like he poked it at me. I have a red mark and everything."

Jack had held out the faint hope that his mysterious captor was bluffing. That hope now withered away. "But you're feeling okay?"

"Dad, yes! You're totally channeling Mom."

He couldn't tell her. There was no reason. There was nothing he could do from here. Not yet. "Okay. I'll see you soon."

9:53 A.M. PST
Four Seasons Hotel, Beverly Hills

Kasim had spent the last thirty minutes listening to Muhammad Abbas describe the plan to him. His head was swimming.

This was a whole different world for him—not just the physical world of expensive American hotels and silk suits, but
also the world of intrigue. He had plotted and schemed back
home, of course, but the plots had been straightforward and
the schemes had led almost immediately to action. And always the action had been at his own hands. In his heart, he
believed this hiring of a mercenary was distasteful and was
frowned upon by Allah. But, by the same token, it was Allah
who had led them to Nurmamet, who made all this possible,
so maybe it was just Kasim himself who frowned upon it.

"As I said," Abbas pontificated, "it is important for your
group to continue with its normal activities. If your people
would normally be at the protests, you must be there. Your
absence will make the FBI and others suspicious."

"It will also give us alibis," Nurmamet agreed.

"Which you will need," Abbas assured them. "After tonight, every law enforcement agency from every country in
the G8 will swarm over this city like flies on a carcass."

1 2 3 4 5 6 7 8 9.
10 11 12 13 14 15 16 17
18 19 20 21 22 23 24

· ·

THE FOLLOWING TAKES PLACE
BETWEEN THE HOURS OF
10 A.M. AND 11 A.M.
PACIFIC STANDARD TIME

· ·

10:00 A.M. PST
CTU Headquarters, Los Angeles

Nina was slowing the CTU car to a stop, but Jack had already jumped out and hit the ground, running through CTU's doors with a flash of his badge. Henderson was waiting for him in the main room.

"Medical team?" Jack said.

"Conference room," Henderson said, equally short.

Henderson, and Nina farther off but gaining, followed in Jack's wake as he burst into the conference room, where three techs with an array of electronic devices were waiting. Jack was already pulling off his shirt and pointing at the bruise on the inner side of his left elbow. It looked as though someone had drawn his blood.

"I'll explain everything in a minute," he said to the other agents. To the techs, he said, "Here's the deal. I think someone bugged me with a tracking device. I've got this bruise on this arm, so I'm putting two and two together and figuring that he inserted it there. Find it."

He sat on the edge of the conference table as they went to work. Over their shoulders and bobbing heads, he addressed Henderson and Nina, delivering a machine-gun summary of the events of the last hour.

"It's got to be al-Libbi," Jack said. "The grab was professional. I was in and out in less than an hour, clean and simple."

Henderson checked some notes he'd gathered while waiting for Jack. "There were no witnesses to the accident, but several residents called in reports on your car and the red pickup, which were left on the side of a residential street. LAPD is doing forensics on them, but I want to send our people down."

"I guess we have to, but be careful," Jack said. "This guy has someone on the inside."

Nina raised an eyebrow. "Not inside CTU?"

"I don't think inside CTU. He referred to us as 'Counter Terrorism Unit' instead of 'Counter Terrorist Unit.' That tells me he's not too familiar. But he knew we were on to him, and he knew I was the agent investigating pretty damned quick after that, and knew enough about me to know I had a daughter and that she was there. That's a hell of a lot of information to get in just a few minutes. It's got to be someone inside G8 security."

Chris pressed the intercom button on the conference room phone. "Jamey?"

"Here," Jamey Farrell, senior programmer, replied over the speakerphone.

"I need a list of everyone with every agency who is assigned to security on the summit, and who works as a liaison with CTU."

"Every agency?" Her voice sounded incredulous. "You realize we are talking about the G8, right? That means we're talking about all the local agencies, plus State, CIA, DOD intelligence—"

"Everyone, please."

Jack jumped in. "Start with everyone Tony's come in contact with."

"Go, Jamey. Thanks." Chris terminated the line.

Jack had been ignoring the poking and prodding of the techs, but one of them now stepped into his line of sight. "Excuse me."

"Did you get it out?" Jack asked.

"No. I mean, there's nothing there," said the tech.

Jack was surprised. "Really? This guy was positive about tracking me."

Nina shrugged. "He was bluffing. Maybe he's bluffing about Kim, too. We should bring her in and have her tested anyway."

The tech prepped a small syringe. "All I can tell you is that there's no transmitter embedded in your arm. Nothing on your clothes, either. It looks like they either drew blood from you or injected something into you. We're taking a blood sample just to make sure there's nothing nasty in your bloodstream."

Nina laughed. "Jack's got plenty of venom of his own."

10:12 A.M. PST
West Bureau, Los Angeles Police Department

Mercy Bennet had just reached her desk at LAPD's West Bureau. Her desk was bare except for file folders and paperwork from a stack of new cases. She hadn't had time yet to put up her picture of Tank, her chocolate Labrador, or her favorite quote. It said, "Nothing is ever as bad as it seems or as good as it sounds." She'd written it herself soon after making detective. In the middle of her first case—the murder of a small-time dealer in Venice that she'd hoped would break open a whole drug ring—when the trail was getting cold, she'd scribbled it on a yellow sticky note. The maxim applied to every area of her life, so she'd had the little sticky note laminated and taped to her computer screen. Her eyes went to it every time she heard news, whether pleasant or unpleasant.

But it wasn't there at the moment. She hadn't bothered unpacking yet. West Bureau had been her first assignment as a detective, six years earlier. She'd managed to scratch and claw her way up the ladder, fighting past other up-and-comers reaching for the next rung and pushing against the weight of mid-career sloths who wouldn't move aside for her, until she made it to the department's prestigious Robbery Homicide Division. She'd spent two years there, working the meaty cases requiring the biggest budgets, until she'd attracted the attention of a deputy chief looking for sharp minds and go-getters in the post-9/11 era. The minute Homeland Security was established and the department needed a liaison to work with the Feds and the Counter Terrorist Unit, Mercy volunteered. She assumed the move would be an ascension, a step up from tracking cop killers and high-profile celebrity murders to hunting terrorists alongside secret agents.

But as with many departmental changes related to Homeland Security, this job had evolved—or, rather, devolved—into administrative and bureaucratic nonsense. Instead of participating in midnight raids on al-Qaeda safe houses, Mercy served as nursemaid to LAPD officials whining about jurisdiction while playing coy with Federal officials whose egos were bloated by their budgets. She didn't like it, but for the first few months she did what any sane person does when confronted with intolerable government work: she gritted her teeth and bore it, knowing that eight more months of work would give her the Get Out of Jail Free card she needed to transfer to another department.

Unfortunately, all that had changed when she found herself on the receiving end of Ryan Chappelle's very unpleasant personality. Chappelle was the Regional Director of CTU and a complete twit. Some of the other leaders there had oversized egos, too—George Mason and Chris Henderson among them—but at least they were competent. Chappelle was just a rule book dressed up in a suit, as far as she could tell, and she let him know it whenever his rules got in her way.

The only saving grace—although maybe it was a curse—to her time as CTU liaison was Jack Bauer. She had known from the first day she met him that they were kindred spirits. She also knew he was married, and so when they first started talking to each other, she studiously avoided anything flirtatious. That was her first clue, really: they both tried not to flirt and in doing so they got to know each other well. Jack was a straight line cutting through the maze of life. Though he was always on the move, Mercy's image of him was that of a rock holding steady in the middle of a rushing stream. He had a sense of duty that belonged to another time and place, but he made it live and breathe here and now. She found herself spending more and more of her duty time with him.

Unfortunately, her own no-nonsense attitude had gotten her booted out of the job. This would have been okay with her, but Chappelle, toad fungus that he was, sensed that removal from his presence was more reward than punishment, and went after her career. Mercy found herself ejected from Robbery

Homicide altogether; she landed back down to West Bureau, where her caseload had consisted of a ring of residential burglaries (high school kids, she was sure) and a missing persons report (a runaway wife, as far as she could tell).

To her surprise, Jack Bauer kept calling. They had coffee. They had dinner. They had . . . they had come close. But Mercy was smart enough to sense that Jack was keeping something to himself, and though he was inscrutable, she guessed that this "something" was his wife. Not his wife as the woman to whom he was married—that fact didn't stop any man that she knew—but his wife as someone he actually loved. That stopped Mercy in her tracks. Jack had kindled in her the hope that she might actually meet someone who could match her spirit. She was willing to cross the line with him, to commit adultery, but only if he really loved her, really wanted *her*. If he still loved his wife, then Mercy would have none of it.

Those thoughts had consumed her for the past few weeks, far more than the purse snatchers and DVD thefts.

All that had changed when Mr. Gordon Gleed got himself murdered. As fate would have it, Bel Air fell under West Bureau's jurisdiction, and thanks to a minor miracle, Mercy had been atop the rotation when the call came in. Even so, she wouldn't have given the case much thought if the murderer hadn't worked so hard to toss the house. The fake robbery theory had led her to investigate Gleed's background, which was squeaky clean—well, at least as far as the law was concerned. Gleed's ethics, on the other hand, were more than questionable. Seventeen interviewees, four bios written for four separate corporate boards of directors, and two articles in *Business Week* and *Fortune* magazine all indicated that Gleed was a ruthless businessman who, if he had ever had an empathetic bone in his body, had obviously pawned it for growth capital. Gleed had spent the last four years running an association of "rural natural resource providers"—which meant logging companies, oil companies, and ranchers—battling environmental regulations. A press release copublished by several environmental groups called Gleed's Free Enterprise Alliance "the Gestapo of the U.S. industrial complex" and described Gleed himself as "a cowardly Faust, who has sold OUR souls to the devil instead of his own."

Environmental groups, Mercy decided, were made up mostly of liberal arts majors who had taken too many writing workshops in college.

Mercy knew her basic premise was sound: radical environmentalists had ratcheted up both their rhetoric and their violence in the last few years. It was only a matter of time before they graduated to full-fledged terrorism, and Gleed would certainly be at the top of any tree-hugger's list. The picture became clearer for the detective when she discovered that Gleed had launched a corollary campaign of his own. His Free Enterprise Alliance had funded several private investigations of the well-known environmental group Earth First! and its offspring. If the Sierra Club was Dr. Jekyll, Earth First! was Mr. Hyde. While other environmental groups chained themselves to trees to stop logging, Earth Firsters had (it was alleged) spiked trees to stop loggers. Tree spikes, apparently, chewed up the chainsaws the loggers used, and could conceivably cause serious damage.

Mercy had acquired a warrant to review the files created by the private investigators. The files indicated that Earth First! was too amorphous to pursue. Earth First! claimed to be a leaderless "nonorganization" with no official membership. In addition, this organization that didn't exist had published several statements over the years. The first statement claimed that Earth First! neither condemned nor condoned tree spiking or other violent acts. The second encouraged Earth Firsters to not spike trees since other methods had proved more useful.

Apparently, the Gleed files suggested, this hadn't sat well with some more radical environmentalists, who thought that Earth First! had lost its cojones. Earth First!'s new stance caused several spinoff organizations such as the Earth Liberation Front, the Rain Forest Network, and the ridiculously named Monkey Wrench Gang. Mercy wasn't involved enough to know if these groups were just fronts for Earth First!'s activities or if they were legitimate entities unto themselves, but she did know that Gleed had gone after them with a passion. The Monkey Wrench Gang had claimed responsibility for at least three acts of arson not only in the United States, but in the Amazonian rain forest as well, firebombing trucks and trailers owned by logging companies that paid dues to Gleed's Free Enterprise Alliance. Gleed had used political pressure to instigate arson investigations against a number of individuals in these loose organizations.

This, obviously, was where Mercy's radar started to beep. It didn't take a Robbery Homicide detective to establish a motive: pro-business advocate investigates violent environmental activists, who murder him in retaliation.

Her biggest obstacle wasn't the linkage: it was the attitudes of other investigators. The word *eco-terrorist* sounded like a Doonesbury joke or a Rush Limbaugh tag. Every investigator with every agency, from the FBI to the LAPD, considered environmental activists to be vegetable-eating tree-huggers, which in their minds meant they were pacifists. The only group that seemed to understand clearly what these groups were capable of was the Free Enterprise Alliance. But Mercy's problem was that the FEA was hardly impartial—they had plenty of reason to make the eco-terrorists look as evil as possible. Mercy had lucked out when Gleed's investigators turned her on to an environmental activist who actually *was* a tree-hugging pacifist. He went by the name of Willow.

And that's who Mercy decided to call.

"Hey," Willow said in a casual, familiar voice.

"How'd you know who was calling?" Mercy asked. Her cell phone was ID restricted.

"I didn't. I just always answer the phone that way."

The first time Mercy had spoken with Willow, she thought she'd have to run him in on a narcotics charge. But she soon realized that he wasn't doped up—he always talked and acted like he was stoned.

"Willow, I struck out again."

"That sucks," he said casually. "Those guys are a bunch of tight asses, aren't they?"

"You have no idea." The truth was, Mercy was pretty tight-assed herself, but for some reason Willow had taken a liking to her, so she played to his expectations as much as possible. "I can't get anyone to believe that an eco-terrorist would plan something big for the G8 summit."

Silence. Willow apparently didn't understand that this was his cue to contribute to the conversation.

"What do you think they might be planning, Will? I need something to go on."

"Man, I don't know," said the informant. "I told you I never liked their vibe. I stopped hanging with them a long time ago. I just heard from a friend that they were getting all postal and working themselves up, and that they were talking like the G8 was going to be jacked up."

This was about as far as Mercy had gotten last time with Willow. If he'd been her sole indicator, she wouldn't have given him a second thought. But since Gordon Gleed had been murdered for hearing the same information (at least that was her theory), she had to assume there was some truth behind it, if she could ever find the specifics behind Willow's vaguery.

Mercy decided it was time to stop playing softball with him. "Willow, I need to know who told you, and I need to know now."

"I told you, that's not cool with me. I've taken a vow against violence but I've also taken a vow against ratting out my friends."

"Well, your two vows are officially in conflict. If you don't put me in touch with someone who knows what's going on, then you'll as good as help cause whatever violence happens. So tell me—"

"Man, you are starting to sound like—"

Mercy pulled a piece of paper out of her files, checking his address. "Tell you what, you'll tell me in person instead. I'm going to be at your house in ten minutes." She cut the connection. Mercy grabbed her purse and stood up, then, at the last minute, picked up her desk phone and rang the dispatcher. "Roll a unit to 16150 West Washington," she said. "Occupant is a male Caucasian, twenty-six years old, five feet six, brown hair, approximately one hundred sixty pounds. He's not to go anywhere until I arrive."

10:17 A.M. PST
CTU Headquarters, Los Angeles

Jack buttoned his shirt back on as the techs left with a vial full of his blood.

"If he's trying to tail me, I'll lose him," he said to Chris. "Better yet, I'll catch the tail and get information."

Jamey Farrell appeared in the doorway, pushing her dark hair back from her face.

"That was fast," Chris Henderson said, impressed.

"Oh, we're not nearly done," Jamey said in a voice mixed with pride and annoyance. "But I wanted to update you. We did a first run on anyone we considered primary, including all of our liaisons to other agencies, the FBI surveillance teams at the Federal Building, and all of us."

"Us?" Nina barked, sounding offended. "You ran checks on us?"

Jamey shrugged. "SOP," she said, which was shorthand for "standard operating procedure." "You're clear, by the way," she said with a smile. "And so is everyone else. Not even a hint of anything that might suggest contact with al-Libbi. You'd expect clear records, of course, but there's not even a remote possibility. No one worked on anything that would put them close. No overseas assignments, no connections with intra-departmental groups that worked in Iraq, Afghanistan, or Israel."

"How far back?" Chris asked.

"Three years," Jamey said. "No sense in going farther, since most agents on the list were on other assignments prior. The G8 is a big deal, but we're talking about local surveillance here. Everyone being used on this is domestic, or at least pulled from areas that are not terrorist-related. *We* wouldn't even be involved if it weren't for—" She looked at Jack.

"Yeah, I get it," he said. "If it weren't for me. But so far it looks like I was right. How about vacations?"

Jamey raised her hands in an expression that said, *Everyone takes a vacation except you.* "Sure, vacations. The Bahamas, Costa Rica, the Amazon rain forest. But no one vacationed in Iran."

"We need to check on everyone's contacts for the last year. See if there's a link to their vacations with any movements of al-Libbi."

Jamey Farrell rolled her eyes. "Jack, you're asking for—"

"This asshole threatened my daughter!" Jack yelled. He felt pressure swell up inside him, like an angry sea rolling up under an unsteady boat. He realized that he'd been bottling up his anger at being assaulted and violated; he had focused on solving the problem. But now, at a pause in the crisis, he found his anger overwhelming him. "I don't care what I'm asking for. Just do it!"

"Jack." Chris Henderson's voice was calm. He had the sort of presence that calmed passionate men like Jack, because they knew Henderson had faced the same darkness they had faced. "We haven't been able to track al-Libbi's movements that accurately, or we'd have picked him up."

"Is there any chance there is no informant?" Nina asked. "This guy was bluffing about tracking you, maybe he was bluffing about everything."

Jack waved the suggestion off. "He knew who I was. He knew I was tracking him. He didn't read that in the *L.A. Times*."

Chris Henderson appeared lost in thought for a moment. Then he said, "Jack, go get your daughter. Get her away from the demonstrations, make sure she's okay. We've got eyes and ears all over the Federal Building. If they try anything, we're as ready as we can be with or without you there. You'll feel better once you know your daughter's okay."

Jack nodded reluctantly. Henderson was speaking reasonably, but Jack was in no mood to be reasonable. The violence inside him had not dissipated. He bit his lip, letting the pain focus his attention. He could hold his violence in check. He'd done it before. He would let it loose at the right time. When he found al-Libbi.

10:22 A.M. PST
Culver City

Mercy slid up to the red curb in front of 16150, ignoring the fire hydrant. Two uniformed police officers were on the front lawn of a yellow three-story apartment building, wrestling with a twenty-something man in jeans and an orange T-shirt.

By the time Mercy had exited the car and crossed the lawn, the uniforms had him on his stomach and were hooking him up.

"Hey, Willow," she said with a smile.

The young man craned his neck to look up at her, his indignant look clearly proving that he laid the blame for his predicament squarely on her.

"Stand him up, please," Mercy said.

The uniforms took hold of one shoulder each and pulled Willow to his feet. His hair was close-cropped and his chin was covered in a permanent fuzz.

"Man, Detective, you are turning into the man—"

She smiled. "Truth is, I was the man before we met." They were roughly the same height, and she forced him to meet her eyes. "I need to know who your friend is. You're going to tell me right now."

"No, I'm not!" he protested childishly.

"Yep," she said as though he'd agreed with her. "Because you're a pacifist and you hate to see people get hurt, and if you don't tell me, it's very possible people will die. Is that what you want?"

"Well, I don't friggin' want this," Willow said. "I don't want to turn my friends over to fascists, either."

Mercy realized she'd brandished the stick but had never offered the carrot. "Willow, you have my word. I have no interest in arresting your friends. I don't care right now if they've done something illegal. I just want to know what they know so that innocent people aren't killed."

Now it was Willow's turn to stare at Mercy. She allowed him to study her eyes. She wasn't sure what he was looking for, but she let him look. She liked Willow. He had all the makings of a flake, but in truth he had found his set of beliefs and preserved them against all comers, whether assaulted by the LAPD or by friends who pursued a more violent agenda than his own.

Either Willow found what he was looking for, or he gave in to his fear of law enforcement. Mercy found herself hoping it was the former. "Her name is Frankie Michaelmas. She's with the Earth Liberation Front. She said she heard some dudes talking about doing some serious damage at the G8."

"Great. Where can I find Frankie?"

"She's at the protest. Hundred percent, she's there."

"You have her number?"

Willow nodded.

"Great. Let's give Frankie a call."

10:28 A.M. PST
Four Seasons Hotel, Beverly Hills

Nurmamet and Kasim had departed. Muhammad Abbas sipped a small coffee and read the *New York Times* as Ayman al-Libbi walked into the deserted bar. Al-Libbi was clean-shaven, with short black hair. He wore a dark blue three-button suit over a light blue dress shirt with no tie, looking like no more than a second- or third-generation son of Middle Eastern or Latino immigrants. He spoke English with a California accent and walked with the casual confidence of a man who belonged wherever he was. These traits, along with scrupulously forged documents, had allowed him to cross the borders of dozens of countries over the years.

"How did it go?" Ayman asked as he sat down.

Muhammad folded the *Times*. "The money is in a briefcase beneath the table. I assume your project went well?"

"We'll see," Ayman said lazily. Muhammad had noticed this tone in his leader's voice in recent months. Ayman began projects with the same ruthless efficiency of years past, but once the gears were set, he seemed to lose his personal drive. In Bali, Muhammad had feared for Ayman's life, but these days he feared for himself. The Americans could be fooled, but once on the trail they were relentless. Muhammad had no desire to end up in Guantanamo Bay.

"Will your man do what he is told?" he asked with real concern.

"I have him under control. You counted the money?"

"They would not cheat us, Ayman. Yes!" he added hastily, fidgeting under the other's sour glare. "Yes, I'll count it." A question floated through his thoughts, a question he had considered voicing before. He stared down at the folded newspaper on the table as if the answers might be there. Finally he said, "Is it only the money now, Ayman?"

Ayman al-Libbi threw his arm over the back of the chair. "Muhammad," he said with a smile, "it was always the money."

Ayman's phone rang and he plucked it out of his breast pocket. "Hey . . . *al salaam a'alaykum.*" He listened for a moment. "Okay. I'll take care of it." He snapped his phone shut. "Apparently my new friend is becoming a bit of a problem."

10:39 A.M. PST
CTU Headquarters, Los Angeles

Jack hadn't driven more than five blocks when his phone rang. "Bauer."

"Agent Bauer, you are not obeying the rules."

The connection was crystal clear and the voice perfectly recognizable. "Go to hell," Jack said to the man who had threatened his daughter.

"It isn't my afterlife you should worry about. I told you not to continue your investigation. Yet you seem to be going somewhere."

"What are you talking about?" Jack growled.

"I am talking about the fact that you are heading west on Santa Monica Boulevard."

Jack jerked the wheel and pulled to a stop slantwise, the tail end of his SUV half blocking the right lane.

"Ah," the caller said. "That's better."

Jack slammed his fist down onto the dashboard. Was it a tail? He hadn't picked up any cars, and unless someone had CTU under surveillance, there was no way this mystery man—Jack could only assume it was al-Libbi—could know what he was doing. There had to be a bug of some kind. Jack instinctively ran his hands over his arms and touched the bruise at his elbow. He looked around his car for a moment, then opened the door and jumped out. He started walking west.

"Uh-oh, you're moving again, "the caller said. "I want to make this clear to you, Agent Bauer. Your daughter has been infected with a virus. There is a cure, but I guarantee you that the only person who has it is me. If I see you leave your office, you will never hear from me again and your daughter will die."

Jack stopped walking. The techs had screwed up somehow. There was a bug on him or in him somewhere. The caller was tracking him as he walked down the street. On a whim, he raised his hand and flipped a bird to the buildings around him. No reaction.

He returned to his car, ignoring the drivers honking at him, and climbed back in. Angry, he backed into traffic and whipped around in the middle of the street, heading back to the office.

Twenty minutes after putting the screws to Willow, Mercy was back at the Federal Building where she'd met Jack Bauer. The crowds had swelled in the last two hours. She'd heard on the police band that there were in excess of ten thousand people. Protestors were now pressed right up to the edge of the permit zone like kids with their toes just outside the door of their big brother's room. The outer edge of the crowd had pushed back nearly three full blocks in all directions, a swelling sea that undulated and splashed up against the island that was the Federal Building.

Mercy inched her car up Federal Avenue, which had shrunk down to a narrow aisle in the center of the street with police cars, paramedic trucks, and ambulances parked and double-parked all the way up to Wilshire Boulevard. She spotted an open space and double-parked next to another slick-topped car with the government "E" on the license plate. She got out and wove her way through small crowds of police officers taking breaks from their time on the line.

Willow's laid-back style of speech had been to Mercy's advantage. When he had called his friend Frankie Michaelmas, there had been no hint of nervousness in his voice, and in a few moments Mercy knew what Frankie looked like and where she was. She and a few of her friends had gathered in Sepulveda Park on the south side of Federal Plaza and across the street. Sepulveda Park was so crowded that the grass had disappeared. Finding a single person would be like looking for a needle in a stack of needles, but Willow had kindly arranged to meet Frankie at the drinking fountain next to the soccer field.

Across the street and half a block up, right in front of the Federal Building, protestors were chanting protest slogans.

Mercy couldn't make out the words but the sound suggested that it was something like "One-two-three-four, there's no G8 anymore!" She wondered why protesters always resorted to childlike rhythms. Were they as naïve as children? Or were they smart enough to know that the best messages were simple messages?

Over here in the park no one was chanting. This felt more like a sit-in, or even a picnic, than a protest. Twenty- and thirty-something Caucasians mingled with short, dark-haired men and women with Latin and Incan looks. Mercy thought wryly that the whole scene appeared as if someone had laid a J. Crew ad over the top of a Benetton ad. She passed through clouds of clove and marijuana and smiled at the image of a couple of uniforms barging through ten thousand people to arrest someone for possession of a baggy with two grams of pot. No one person, she thought, made the laws, but the *people* definitely did, and these ten or twenty thousand people had decided that a little ganja was okay.

Mercy reached the drinking fountain. There was a young woman standing there, her eyes scanning left and right, looking right past Mercy. She was short and broad but fit, like a gymnast, and wore her curly hair long and (Mercy suspected) artificially blond. She wore a ruby-red stud in her left nostril. These details matched Willow's description, so Mercy said, "Frankie Michaelmas?" and held out her badge.

Frankie's searching eyes focused in sharply. Mercy exercised Gladwell's *Blink* theory on Frankie as the other woman reacted to her: *thinks on her feet, dislikes authority, violent.* These were the instant impressions she felt when she saw Frankie's reaction, the last especially noticeable because of the flash in her eyes that Frankie hid so quickly Mercy nearly thought she'd imagined it. But if Mercy was going to stick to her theory, then she had to admit it was there—a moment of spite begging for a physical outlet.

Frankie didn't say anything.

"Detective Mercy Bennet, Los Angeles Police Department. You and I need to have a word." Mercy had learned long ago not to ask permission. Asking permission gave the subject the feeling she could object, and Mercy was beginning to suspect that she had very little time left for objections.

"I'll give you a few words. How about fu—"

"That's cute," Mercy interrupted, her voice intentionally thick with sarcasm. "I've never heard that before. I want to talk to you about the Earth Liberation Front."

A few of the people standing around them were now staring at Mercy, but none of them looked hostile. Mercy guessed that none of them were Frankie's friends. In fact, based on her tough grrrl appearance, Mercy suspected that she didn't want any of her friends to meet Willow, and therefore had brought no one to this meeting spot.

"Willow sold me out," she said with a shrug. "I should have figured. But you're barking up the wrong tree, you know?"

Mercy took a step closer. She wasn't used to being taller than her subjects. It was a good feeling. "I know that you told Willow something big and violent was going to happen here. I want to know what it is."

Frankie pushed her bleached blond hair back on her head. "Well, if you find out, will you tell me?"

"I figure your friends in the Earth Liberation Front already did."

Frankie smiled. "I'm not a member of the Earth Libera—"

"—not a member of the Earth Liberation Front," Mercy mocked. Supporting information was filling out her first impression of Frankie Michaelmas. The "fuck you" attitude wasn't exactly a false facade, but it wasn't the foundation of her personality, either. Mercy decided that Frankie floated on a wide but shallow sense of self-esteem.

"I didn't think you were dull enough to try that crap with me," she said disdainfully. "The ELF doesn't keep a membership, so technically no one is a member. But I'll tell you this." Mercy leaned even closer, until her chin nearly touched Frankie's forehead and she had to look down to see her. "You can all talk about how you're not members of the same club when you're serving time together. Because I'm taking you into custody, and the minute something bad happens, you're an accessory."

Frankie's eyes dimmed just a bit, but she straightened her back and said, "Like you're going to arrest me here, in the middle of all this? I don't think so."

She spun and pushed her way through the crowd.

Mercy smiled and followed.

10:58 A.M. PST
CTU Headquarters, Los Angeles

Jack stormed back into CTU Headquarters feeling enraged and humiliated. Chris Henderson saw him from his loftlike office overlooking the analysts' bullpen and was halfway down the stairs as Jack approached him.

"The techs messed up!" Jack snarled. He held up his cell phone as if it said everything. "The son of a bitch called me on my cell phone! Even when I got out of my car he knew I was walking!"

Chris's shoulders sagged. "All right, we'll have them test again—"

"We don't have to, sir."

The tech who'd helped Jack before reappeared. His face was screwed up, as though he was having trouble expressing surprise, admiration, and fear all at once. "We just finished a blood test on Agent Bauer."

"You better have found the damned transmitter. I don't care how small it is," Jack said.

The tech nodded. "We did, sort of. But it's not just small. It's . . ."

"I don't care what it is," Jack barked. "Get it out!"

"We don't know how," the tech admitted. "It's not a device somewhere in your body. The transmitter is laced throughout your entire body. It's in your blood."

1 2 3 4 **5** 6 7 8 9
10 11 12 13 14 15 16 17
18 19 20 21 22 23 24

• •

THE FOLLOWING TAKES PLACE
BETWEEN THE HOURS OF
11 A.M. AND 12 P.M.
PACIFIC STANDARD TIME

• •

11:00 A.M. PST
Federal Plaza, West Los Angeles

It wasn't easy, following a pint-sized twenty-something girl through a crowd of protestors at Federal Plaza. The blond hair helped, but Frankie was so short that several times Mercy lost her bobbing yellow head in the crowd. The good news was that the sea of people made it hard for Frankie to spot a tail. She did glance back once or twice, but Mercy had shifted off to one side, moving parallel to Frankie instead of behind her, and so the girl hadn't noticed her.

Eleven o'clock, and the sun had already turned the protestors into twenty thousand sweating bodies. Mercy's nose told her that more than a few of the people she passed kept personal hygiene fairly low on their lists of priorities. She rubbed up against one man with curly brown hair, his arm slick with sweat, and his stink clung to her like a plastic wrapper clinging to her fingers.

The first thing Frankie had done, after bolting away, was make a cell phone call. Mercy silently cursed Jack Bauer's stiff neck. If she'd had CTU's resources behind her, she could be listening in on that call right now and tracing it back to its source instead of elbowing her way through the masses. Now the girl was reaching the edge of the crowd at Veteran's Park. Wherever she was going, Mercy was determined to stay with her.

11:04 A.M. PST
Federal Building Command Center,
West Los Angeles

Tony Almeida came back from the bathroom, yawning and stretching, reluctant to plant himself back in his plastic chair in front of the video monitors. He had been on dozens of stakeouts—electronic and otherwise—and he was used to the boredom, but this drab cinder-block room seemed specially designed to suck the life out of the most determined officer.

"Anything?" he asked.

One of the two FBI agents was gone. The other one, the thin, Slavic-looking agent, shook his head. "Not much. I spotted that detective your guy was talking to. Looks like she was meeting with an informant in the crowd. There she is."

He jabbed a finger at one of the dozen screens. This was a very wide shot of the swelling crowd, probably from a camera positioned high up on the building. The agent pressed a toggle switch on his control board and the camera zoomed in. Tony saw the dark-haired LAPD officer moving through the crowd. He recognized the detective from her short stint as a CTU liaison. He hadn't known her well, but her first name was distinctive: Mercy.

"Stay on her," he said. "Not sure what's going on, but Jack doesn't waste time, so let's assume she's important."

"Trying," the agent said, leaning across to the other side of the control panel to flip some switches.

"Your friend's gone a lot," Tony observed.

"Tiny bladder," said the Slavic agent. "Plus he drinks that swill." He pointed to a paper cup on the counter with coffee dregs at the bottom.

"And you don't?" Tony said. He'd never met an FBI agent who didn't swig caffeine during surveillance.

"Oh, I drink coffee," the agent said with the air of a connoisseur. "But that's not coffee. You want to try real coffee, try fresh Costa Rican coffee beans."

"I just go to my coffee place and point," Tony said, sitting down.

The agent grunted. "You and everyone else. But Costa Rica, or Brazil, that's where the good stuff is. You know, there's a little coffee farm northeast of Rio de Janeiro in the province of Minas Gerais, the beans they grow there are amazing. It's like coffee and chocolate grown together."

Tony glanced at the screens. "I've never been."

"Oh, you've gotta go. I've been all over. The jungle is—" The agent smiled at himself. "Forget it, I could go on about this stuff forever. I'm kind of a rain forest addict."

"I took a canopy tour once," Tony said distractedly. "You know, sliding on those ropes in the treetops. It was amazing, except that I almost got bit by a monkey." He eyed the screen. "It looks like that detective is tailing someone."

They both watched. The detective was moving parallel to and slightly behind a short girl with artificially blond hair.

Even in that mass of bodies, Tony saw easily that the woman deliberately matched her pace to the girl's.

"You're right," Nick said. "Well, my turn to piss." He stood up. "I've been on those tours. I hope everybody goes on them, actually. Helps people know about the rain forests so maybe we stop destroying them."

"I guess it can help," Tony replied, turning his attention fully to the monitors.

"It better," Nick said. "They say a few more years and most of the forests will be gone."

"Well, at least we won't have to worry about the monkeys."

11:08 A.M. PST
CTU Headquarters, Los Angeles

It was a radio dye marker, also called a chemical emitter. The marker was a chemical compound that, when found in large enough quantities, emitted a low-frequency signal that could be tracked by satellite. The medical techs hadn't ever heard of it, but Jack had. The military had initiated the project a few years earlier to help with intelligence gathering, but the system had proved inefficient. The dye markers were no more accurate than more conventional transmitters, which could be miniaturized to the point of being nonexistent.

"Okay, it's in my blood," Jack said. "So get it the hell out."

The tech shook his head. "We've got a call in to Department of Defense," he said. "But I don't think anyone knows how to get this stuff out. It's not harmful, so I think they just figured it would eventually get processed out of the body someday."

Jack sneered. "Well, someday is today. I need this stuff out of my body right now!"

The tech stepped back. Chris Henderson rested a hand on Jack's arm like a tamer calming a lion. "We can leave you here, Jack. I'll put everyone else on the case."

"That's my daughter!" Jack jerked his arm away. "There's got to be some way to filter this dye out of my blood."

Jamey Farrell buzzed into the room over the intercom. "Chris, I've got someone on the line for you. They say it's about Jack."

"Is it Department of Defense?"

"No, Interior."

Chris raised an eyebrow. Why would someone from the Department of the Interior call CTU? "Okay."

There was a click, and a tentative male voice crackled over the conference room speakers. "H-hello?"

"This is Chris Henderson, Special Agent in Charge of Field Operations," Chris said crisply.

"Hi. What—what can I do for you?" the voice asked nervously.

Chris frowned. "I don't know. You called me."

"Oh, oh, well yes, but they told me to. I mean, I got a call from the Secretary herself. I've never gotten a call from—"

"Who are you?" Chris demanded.

The voice squeaked. "Dr.—I'm Martin Shue. Dr. Shue. What can I do—I mean, no one explained to me exactly why I was calling."

Chris's neck turned pink and he bit his lip, but his voice was calm. "What exactly do you do over there, Doctor?"

"Environmental work," the doctor said. By the sound of his voice, he was clearly relieved to be asked a question to which he knew the answer. "I was with the EPA for ten years, now here. I'm a zoologist."

"And Interior told you to call us?"

"That's—that's right. They said it was an emergency."

Chris shrugged. "By any chance do you know anything about radio dye markers or chemical emitters?"

"Oh, oh yes. Of course I do!" The zoologist's voice perked up even more. "Are you trying to track an animal of some kind?"

Chris smiled. Nina Myers laughed out loud. Jack just glowered. Chris said, "Not exactly. We want to get this emitter out of someone. Do you know how to do that?"

"Out of some*one*?" Dr. Shue mused. "I didn't realize anyone was still trying chemical emitters on people. The technology has sort of fallen into disuse, except for people in my field. We use them to track animals that are too small or delicate to be tagged with transmitter bands—"

"How do you get the stuff out!" Jack yelled.

The doctor squeaked again. "I'm—I'm not sure. That was never a priority, of course. But the chemicals aren't harmful. They break down in the body after a year or two anyway."

"We need it out right away," Chris said. "It is an emergency. Do you have any ideas?"

"Well, no, no, I don't, except, yes, maybe," Dr. Shue hemmed and hawed. Jack couldn't help thinking that he was the perfect scientist to work for the government.

"Is it yes or no?"

"Well, we never developed a process for removing the marker," Dr. Shue said. "It just wasn't necessary. But all you really need to do is filter the blood. You could probably use a regular dialysis machine."

"Dialysis," Henderson said. "You mean like for kidney patients?"

"Exactly. I couldn't guarantee it, but it would probably—"

"Thanks," Henderson said, hanging up.

Jack ran his fingers through his hair. "Dialysis. That takes hours, doesn't it?"

Chris nodded. "We'll put people out in the field for you—"

"Excuse me," the tech tried to interrupt.

"—I'll have Nina pick up your daughter, take her home or somewhere safe—"

"I think I can—" the tech tried.

"—we'll see if Tony can pick up any more leads on al-Libbi—"

"Hey!" the tech yelled.

The CTU agents, not accustomed to being interrupted by others, glared at the technician, who turned bright red. "I have an idea," he said meekly.

"Okay," Chris Henderson acknowledged.

"There's a dialysis machine at UCLA. It only takes thirty minutes."

11:14 A.M. PST
West Los Angeles

The cell phone rang again, and the man Jack Bauer wanted more than anything to meet face-to-face answered. He had left his hotel and was driving toward his next task. He had a big night planned, and many things to accomplish before night fell. "Yes?" he said calmly.

"One of your little errand monkeys picked up a tail," his informant said. "The blond girl, built like a fire plug."

"Frankie," the man said. "Thank you. Make sure no one on your end causes any more trouble."

He hung up and checked his watch, calculating where Frankie would be and what she would be doing at the moment. He frowned. Interference from the law would be extremely inconvenient at the moment. It would have to be dealt with. He dialed another number.

Tony Almeida camera hopped, his eyes switching from one screen to another as the female detective followed the blond girl across Veteran's Park. The crowd had thinned to a few stragglers, and Mercy had fallen back out of her quarry's line of sight. She was good, Tony thought approvingly.

The blond girl was walking away from the last camera that could track her. Tony zoomed in, but she was still fairly small in the screen. Tony thought he saw her reach into her pocket and pull out a phone, hold it to her ear for a minute, then put it away. Seconds later she swerved straight toward Sepulveda Boulevard, making her away across the wide parking lot that separated a YMCA building from the street.

Mercy changed direction to follow.

Frankie reached the sidewalk and turned south, heading against traffic. Mercy dropped back even farther.

"Hey." The coffee connoisseur returned. "You stare at the monitors like that and you'll go blind."

"She's almost out of camera shot," Tony said, his eyes glued to the screen.

Cars zoomed by on Sepulveda Boulevard. A big blue van slowed down, and for a moment Tony thought the blond girl would climb inside. But she walked right past it without paying much attention. Mercy, too, passed the van without paying attention. As she did, the van door slid open. Hands reached out and grabbed Mercy, dropping a hood over her head and dragging her into the vehicle. The door slammed shut.

"Holy shit!" Tony yelled. He reached for the radio.

He saw the movement behind him, but didn't perceive it as a danger until something heavy struck hard against the base of his neck, and by then it was too late.

11:19 A.M.
Sepulveda Boulevard, West Los Angeles

Mercy gasped for breath and felt the cloth from the hood suck into her mouth. She blew it out and kicked. She couldn't see a damned thing, but she felt her heel smash into something firm, like a face, and she was rewarded with a yelp of pain. Her arms were pinned, but she shook her right free and reached to her left. She felt hands on her biceps and wrist. She chose the wrist, digging her nails deep into the flesh.

"Goddamn!" someone yelled.

Pain like fire exploded on her face, and Mercy knew she'd been hit. She didn't let go of the hand, but tore a chunk of flesh out. Another painful sunburst erupted behind her eyes, and she lost consciousness.

11:21 A.M.
Federal Building Command Center,
West Los Angeles

Tony Almeida was lying with his face on the floor. His rattled brain tried to make sense of that fact; he believed for a moment that Nick Dyson had told him to lie flat as he slid along the rope during a canopy tour, while monkeys chattered all around him. But a second later he realized that was the concussion talking. He was lying down because he'd been flattened by a blow, and the chattering was actually the shouting of two men locked in some kind of struggle over him.

He propped himself up on his elbows, and a wave of nausea made him heave dryly. He turned on his right side and looked up. FBI Agent Nick Dyson had the other agent, McKey, in a bear hug with one arm pinned. McKey's free hand was pressed against Dyson's face, digging into his cheek.

". . . get off me, get the hell off me!"

". . . kill you!"

Tony's head was swimming. He didn't know who was yelling what, or why they were fighting. One of them had clubbed him over the head, but he wasn't sure which one. He saw Dyson land a knee to McKey's groin. McKey doubled over. Dyson grabbed his partner by the hair and slammed his face into the video console. McKey turned into a rag doll and slumped to the floor.

Tony managed to climb to his feet, but he was doubled over with his hands on his knees. There was a roaring sound inside his head. The room swayed back and forth like the deck of a ship and he had trouble maintaining his balance. Dyson, however, had no trouble. He covered the distance between them in two short steps and grabbed Tony by the hair just as he'd grabbed McKey. Tony didn't try to avoid the blow. Instead he slammed his left forearm down on Dyson's leg, jamming it before he could bend the knee. At the same time, he swung his right arm up, slapping the FBI agent hard in the groin. Dyson grunted, leaning over the top of the CTU agent. Tony bolted upright, the back of his skull slamming into the bottom of Dyson's jaw, and the FBI man staggered back a step. Tony lifted his right knee and stomped Dyson hard in the chest, and Dyson flew backward into the wall of the surveillance room. He dropped to the floor, leaving a small wet stain on the cinder blocks behind his head.

Tony doubled over and threw up.

11:24 A.M. PST
CTU Headquarters, Los Angeles

It took a determined man to travel from UCLA Medical Center to CTU Los Angeles in ten minutes. It took an even more determined man to make someone else do it. But eleven minutes after Jack made the call, an ambulance rolled up to the building, sirens wailing, and a team of doctors poured out, running like their own lives depended on speed. Jack and Nina Myers held the doors open for them, waving them through security.

"Hurry up!" he yelled.

"Dr. Viatour!" said the lead physician, his white coat swirling up behind him and his face scrunched into a look of serious displeasure. "It would have been faster if you'd come to us!"

"Can't. I'll explain while you work."

Three technicians rolling a stack of awkwardly piled equipment followed.

"What we're gong to do is called CAPD. Instead of regular hemodialysis, this system actually uses the peritoneal wall in the abdomen to help filter—"

"Great." Jack nodded. "And it only takes a half an hour?"

Dr. Viatour recoiled at his brusqueness. "Yes. Give us a few minutes to set you up, then we'll time the filtering for thirty minutes. Is there some sort of—?"

"Just make it thirty minutes," Nina said. "That'll be the longest Jack's ever sat still anyway."

Jack hustled the medical team into the conference room

like a muleskinner driving a team. "Go, go!" he yelled.

Dr. Viatour glared at him. "Sir, we're a dialysis unit, not an ER team."

"Right now you're an ER team," Jack said flatly. "Lives depend on this. Go!"

Dr. Viatour scampered back to his equipment.

"Jack, what do we do about your daughter?" Chris Henderson asked as they waited. "If she's really been infected with something . . ."

Jack shook his head. "I'm going to get her."

"What?" Chris said, shocked at Jack's response. "If that's what you want, we can bring her in."

"I'll do it," Jack said. "Whatever al-Libbi's got planned, he's done his job well." He picked me up with no problem, and he shot Kim full of something without her even knowing it. This tracking thing is pretty sophisticated, too. He says he's watching her, and I believe him. He may have injected her with the same thing he gave me. And she doesn't know she's involved. I want to take care of it."

"What kind of infection can it be?" Nina asked. "Maybe CDC will have a cure for it—"

Chris sat down in a chair and leaned his elbows onto his knees. "I've been thinking about that. It doesn't fit his MO. Ayman al-Libbi is a bomb maker. He blows people up. He drops grenades into crowds of women and children. He doesn't stab people with delayed reaction infections or whatever, and shoot up Federal agents with space age tracking devices. None of it fits."

Dr. Viatour reappeared. "Okay, look, the actual process takes thirty minutes, but we normally do a lot more prep work on our patients."

"Just do it," Jack growled.

Viatour shrugged. He held up a long thin tube. "Okay. We're going to insert this catheter into your abdomen and pump you full of a dilute salt solution. As your blood passes through the peritoneal membrane in your abdomen, the salt solution will filter out impurities. Lie down on the table."

Jack lay down on the table, filled his lungs with air, and let out a huge breath. *Thirty minutes*, he said to himself. *Think of all the times thirty minutes was too short. Let this not be one of those times.*

11:29 A.M. PST
Century Plaza Hotel, West Los Angeles

The real meetings didn't even take place at the Federal Building. The eight world leaders would have a perfunctory meeting at the Federal Building later in the day, but the real work would take place in secluded rooms far from the noise of contention. The protestors had chosen the Federal Building as a symbol of governmental abuse, and because the Century Plaza Hotel was private property and so the owners could deny them access without cause.

So while thousands gathered on all sides of the Federal Building, half a mile away at the Century Plaza Hotel, in a conference room guarded by multiple rings of security, eight men who controlled massive areas of the globe sat in discussion about the future of the world.

Well, thought President Barnes, not really *eight*. After all, the G8 still included France and Italy, for Christ's sake, and neither one of those "powers" was going to shake the world any time soon. But there was German Chancellor Gerhardt Schlessinger sitting across the table from him, and Russian President Novartov to his right, and those were men to be reckoned with. Japanese Prime Minister Kokushi Matsumoto, always a strong ally, was stationed to Barnes's left, and the Prime Minister of Great Britain, Christopher Straw, sat at the far end of the table. Straw, of course, might as well have been in Barnes's pocket.

French President Jacques Martin was, as usual, talking. ". . . I want the language on the environment revised by our staff," he intoned in his heavily accented baritone. "If it is not, we will issue our own statement. I want it clear that France considers these environmental concerns to be important."

Russian President Novartov smiled. He had the hungry look of a predator. His smile came across as a threat. "Wasn't it France that blew up a Greenpeace vessel?"

"Years ago." Martin brushed the comment aside. "The environmental constituency grows. I want them to know we are acting."

Barnes raised a finger. "You want them to *think* we are acting," he corrected. "We all know that the only real issue on the table at this summit is China."

China. The word hung in the air like an impolite comment the group could neither ignore nor accept. China was the loutish neighbor down the street that no one wanted to invite to the party, but everyone wanted to be friends with.

"Look," Christopher Straw said obsequiously, "let's take this down to brass tacks, shall we? We're not really letting them in without addressing the human rights issues, are we? I can't imagine voting for it."

"I find myself agreeing with the Prime Minister," Novartov said, as though the fact surprised him. "China still has much change to do in its human rights record before sitting at the table."

Schlessinger of Germany shifted in his seat. "This is a waste of time. We will all have our finance ministers, our trade representatives, and others, debate the real issues of the day. You know as well as I that China will not be denied."

"I do not know it," Novartov replied curtly. But he softened his tone almost immediately. "But, in the end, I will listen to our collective wisdom, of course."

"The world turns, Mr. President," Martin rumbled. "It will not be stopped."

Barnes sat back in his chair. He wasn't comfortable with philosophical talk; he especially disliked Martin's pompous French pseudo-intellectualism. But he also knew the Frenchman was right. China was coming at them all like a tidal wave, and if it wasn't invited into the G8 it would eventually make the G8 obsolete.

Of course, there were other truths floating around, unspoken truths. Like the fact that Russia couldn't care less about China's human rights record. Russia wanted to exclude China because the two countries' rivalry went back decades, and Novartov had no interest in allowing his hated opponent to the southeast to grow any stronger if he could help it. The Russian President's gut reaction—snapping at Schlessinger—interested Barnes more than his soft-sell follow-up. He wondered what Novartov had in mind for his next move. The human rights issue was a convenient cover for all of them to use—it allowed them to bully China (if China could be bullied at all) into making trade concessions.

"But again, the environment," Martin began when no one else spoke up. "You must be aware that five thousand people came up from South America, mostly from Brazil. *Cinq milles!* It is unheard of, is it not? Brazil will be the next to force a seat at our table. We must control the environmental issue now."

Novartov laughed. "I will pay attention to the issue when the trees can vote."

"If they haven't all been cut down by then," Barnes said darkly.

Jack stared at the tubes sticking into his abdomen. A diluted saline solution was still flowing into his body, creating pressure around his stomach. He imagined the solution mixing with his blood, filtering out the chemical transmitter. It tingled, but that was only in his head. He'd received a local anesthetic so there was no pain, but his mind still created the ghost of a feeling. The brain simply could not acknowledge the fact of foreign objects injected into the membrane lining his organs without attaching some sensation to it.

Six minutes on the machine. Twenty-four minutes to go.

The conference room phone beeped. Before it rang a second time, Henderson was in the room. "You'll want to hear this."

He slapped the speaker box and said, "Go ahead, Tony. I have Jack."

"Hey, Bauer," Tony said fuzzily.

"Tony, you sound like hell."

"Thanks. Damn, my nose is bleeding again, hold on." There was a pause. They heard Tony shuffling around. Then he came back on. "I'm back. Jack, I found the mole."

Jack's eyes lit up. "Hold on to him for twenty-three more minutes."

"Oh, he's not going anywhere. That's the problem. I noticed something going on the video monitors down here. He clubbed me. I'd be dead if it weren't for the other surveillance guy here, McKey. He fought Dyson—that's the subject—until I came to. I put Dyson down, but he's not regaining consciousness. He might be in a coma."

Jack bit his lip. This was the lead he needed. More work had gone into this one clue than anyone around him knew. He wished Tony had had the foresight to put on kid gloves, but he couldn't blame Almeida for fighting to survive. "Don't worry about it," he said with difficulty. "What do we have to go on? Are we digging into his background?"

"I have Jessi Bandison on it," Chris said. "So far, no connections to al-Libbi. But something will turn up."

"What triggered the attack?" Jack asked. "You've been with those guys all morning, right? There must have been something specific."

"I was about to sound the alarm . . . oh, shit!" Tony yelled, as though he'd just remembered something. "My brain must still be fractured. I was reaching for the phone to call because I saw that detective, what's her name, Bennet? She was grabbed." In his still-quavering voice, Almeida described Mercy Bennet's kidnapping.

Jack tried to will the frustration out of his body. "This never would have happened if she hadn't come to meet with me. I should have done a better job of dodging her."

Tony said, "I've already been in contact with LAPD. They're on the lookout for the blue van, but the angle was too bad for us to get a license plate. They gave me the information Bennet was focused on." Tony told Jack that Theodore Ozersky, a.k.a. Willow, had been taken into custody, and he passed along the name of Frankie Michaelmas.

"Okay," Jack said. "We need to deal with Ozersky eventually. Is he cooling his heels for now?"

"He's okay, there's no hurry there," Tony said. "I'm taking Agent Dyson to the hospital. I might have myself checked out, too."

"Good," Henderson said. "Keep us informed if he comes around."

"We should add in Gordon Gleed," Jack said. "He's deceased. That's the murder that started her investigation. There's bound to be some connection."

Chris Henderson scowled. "Well, then, we'd better get our

asses in gear. There's a terrorist plot happening tonight, and we don't have a clue yet what it is."

Jack looked at the tubes in his stomach and growled like a caged animal.

Twenty minutes left.

11:40 A.M. PST
West Los Angeles

He sat back in his chair. He slipped a maracuja leaf into his mouth and chewed it slowly. The Spanish had called the maracuja "passionflower" because the broad white flowers somehow reminded the conquistadores of the Passions of Christ. The native population was much more practical, of course, and had long understood the maracuja's natural properties. When taken in large doses, it acted as a sedative. In smaller quantities, such as he now absorbed, the maracuja had a pleasant, tranquilizing effect.

There was a small GPS tracker on the table next to him. The tiny blue dot was stationary at a location corresponding to CTU headquarters. He recalibrated the device, and a tiny red dot appeared at the Federal Building. Both Jack Bauer and his daughter were being well behaved.

He had just received a call from some of his operatives. Detective Mercy Bennet was in hand, and currently being transported to one of his two remaining safe houses in Los Angeles—the first having been used up during his temporary imprisonment of Jack Bauer. The involvement of CTU and the investigation by the LAPD both caused him anxiety, but now he felt the maracuja's chemicals easing through his body like ice water flowing into his veins, and he relaxed. He wondered if he should have killed Jack Bauer. He was not squeamish; he had killed people before, but only when necessary, and he had not perceived it as necessary to kill the CTU agent. It was almost beyond the realm of possibility that CTU or any other government agency could discover his purpose. Few of his own people knew his real name or his whereabouts, and they were true believers. None would betray him willingly. By tomorrow, of course, everyone would know him, but by then he would be safely out of the country. He only needed to delay CTU for a few more hours.

No, it wasn't Jack Bauer who disturbed him most. It was the LAPD detective who had thrown a monkey wrench into his own plans. He had her under wraps now, but how long would that last? Her absence would soon be noticed.

The man shrugged. Maybe it was the effects of the maracuja, but he found himself adopting a very Zen quality. The day would play out as fate would have it.

He picked up a vial that lay on the table next to the GPS. Its contents were clear liquid, basically water, but this was water no one should drink. In that liquid swam one of the most aggressive viruses nature had ever manufactured, a hemorrhagic fever so violent that it would kill a human being within hours. He had learned to weaken its strain ever so slightly. The smaller, weaker strains killed within a day, and they could be destroyed inside the body if the antidote were delivered on time. It was this smaller, weaker cousin that he had introduced into Kim Bauer's body. She might feel ill, but she was in no real danger for another day.

11:45 A.M. PST
Federal Plaza, West Los Angeles

As far as Kim Bauer was concerned, the demonstration was a bust. The weather had grown much warmer than anyone expected, she was surrounded by hot and sweaty people (none of whom, as far as she could tell, had bathed), and Brad Gilmore had turned out to be a major league dork. And to top it all off, she felt like she was coming down with something.

"I'm burning up," she said to Janet York, one of her best friends, who looked as bored with Teen Green as she felt.

"I'm so sticky it's disgusting," Janet said, tugging at her shirt to air herself out. "How much longer?"

Kim checked her watch. "We're supposed to stay during school hours if we want credit on the political science project."

Janet rolled her eyes. "As if." She glanced at their chaperone, Marshall Cooper, who was busy separating Brad Gilmore and another boy who had begun to wrestle for no apparent reason. "You want to skip out? We can hit the mall or whatever."

Kim touched her forehead and felt beads of sweat. *That is so attractive,* she thought sarcastically. "Maybe skip out, but I don't think I want to go shopping or anything. Let's just get out of here."

11:51 A.M. PST
CTU Headquarters, Los Angeles

Jack's cell phone rang. "Bauer."

"Agent Bauer."

It was the voice of his former captor. "What?" he demanded. He waved to Henderson and motioned for him to track the call. Henderson nodded and ran silently out of the room, hailing Jamey Farrell as he did so.

"I want to express my appreciation that you're being a good boy. I trust you haven't told anyone about our little arrangement."

Jack glanced at all the people working around him. "Not a soul," he lied.

"Unfortunately, it seems your daughter isn't behaving quite so well. I trust she's not being taken to a hospital?"

Jack frowned. "I don't know what you're talking about."

"What I'm talking about is the fact that your daughter has now left the Federal Building and is heading west on Wilshire Boulevard. I want to remind you, Agent Bauer, that I am not bluffing. No doctor you find in Los Angeles will have a cure for the fever she's about to contract. Once her symptoms start, she'll be dead before they can even diagnose it."

"I haven't talked to Kim in over an hour," Jack replied. "Maybe she's just going to get lunch."

"We'll see. If she travels more than one mile from the Federal Building, you'll never hear from me again."

The phone clicked off. Henderson came back in, and Jack knew by the look on his face that they hadn't had time to trace the call.

He slammed his fist onto the table. Three more minutes.

11:55 A.M. PST
Federal Plaza

Kim hadn't walked far when her phone rang. "Hey, Dad," she said.

"Kim, listen, I had to run to the office for a minute, but I'm coming back soon. You're still there, right?"

"Where else would I be?" Kim said.

Bauer grinned wryly. He couldn't fault his daughter for being a good liar. He was pretty accomplished himself. "Great," he lied back. "I just want to check up on you. I'll see you in a bit."

Kim snapped her phone shut and sighed at Janet. "Guess I'm sticking around."

11:56 A.M. PST
Minas Gerais, Brazil

Rickson Aruna waddled up to the house of Constantine Noguera. It wasn't quite noon yet and already his hip was hurting him. He was getting too old to be the constable of the village, but of course no one else would do the job. They all said it was because he, Rickson, had performed so ably over the years, but in truth it was because no one else wanted to bother. The town was dirty, the pay was low, and most people considered him more of a gossip than a policeman. And, of course, when he did need to act as a policeman, the cause was far too serious for most of these peasants: there were disturbances caused by the drunken antics of the timber cutters, and now and then the protests and sabotage of the environmentalists.

Usually with the environmentalists and the timber cutters it was political, and the federal police became involved. At these times Rickson was eager to step aside. He was a caretaker of the town, not a defender of the forest. He did not like the timber people—he had grown up in a town farther up the river, but now that whole area was clear cut, and erosion had washed half the land into the water. But he was only one man, and he was not inclined to fight the powerful companies from the north.

But the silence from Constantine Noguera's house, *that* was something he could deal with. Rickson rapped his knuckles on the rough-boarded door of Noguera's house. "Constantine!" he called. "How drunk can you be?"

There was no answer, not even a groan from inside.

Rickson pounded on the door again. "Constantine, get up! No one has seen you all day. Come out. The sun will do your hangover some good!"

Again there was no answer. Once more Rickson pounded on the door. This was too much for the old door. The lock broke and the door creaked open. Rickson Aruna found himself staring into Noguera's little shack, with its front room that served as a kitchen and living room and its one back room for sleeping. The stench of decaying flesh assaulted Rickson's nostrils and he staggered back. Rickson braced himself and entered, pushing through the stink until he reached the bedroom. When he got there he gagged, choking back bile. His nose had already told him Noguera was dead, but he was not prepared for what he saw: Noguera's body lay on his bed. The flesh looked as if it had turned to slag on the bones, and huge pustules had erupted all over the body.

Terrified, Rickson tried to hold his breath. He had seen these marks once before, when he was a child and the disease had swept through his village. This was in a time long before modern doctors and medicines. He did not know if the doctors had a name for this disease, or if they had even heard of it. But the old women of his childhood knew it. They called it *uña de gato*.

....

THE FOLLOWING TAKES PLACE
BETWEEN THE HOURS OF
12 P.M. AND 1 P.M.
PACIFIC STANDARD TIME

....

12:00 P.M. PST
CTU Headquarters, Los Angeles

Jack Bauer practically pulled the tubes out of his body himself.

"Hey, let that finish draining!" Dr. Viatour yelled. Thirty minutes after injecting the dialysis solution into his body, the doctors had drained it away, filling a clear plastic tube with a disgusting-looking, bile-colored liquid.

Dr. Viatour said, "This is the solution post-filtering. In theory, it's filtered impurities out of your blood, including this chemical marker, whatever it is."

"What do you mean, in theory?" Jack asked.

Viatour shrugged. "Well, peritoneal dialysis works. It's performed all the time. But usually it's done three or four times a day for patients with kidney dysfunction. I don't know anything about this chemical marker, so I can't tell you if one treatment has done the trick."

"We're going to find out," Jack demanded. "Stitch me up."

He lay back and let the doctors finish. The truth was, he felt nauseated. They'd filled his abdominal cavity with some kind of saline solution. As his blood passed through it, it had mixed with this solution and, in theory, had filtered impurities out of his body. With luck, that had included the chemical tracer that Ayman al-Libbi had inserted there. He had sat helpless and impatient during the procedure, but now that it was done, he felt spent. His stomach felt distended and awkward, and the large puncture wound in his stomach hurt like hell.

"Chris," Jack said to Chris Henderson, "soon as I'm on my feet, I'll leave CTU and see if they contact me again."

"Suppose he doesn't give you another warning, just packs up and leaves you and Kim?" Henderson pointed out.

Jack answered decisively. "Either way, I'm moving forward. If they've gotten hold of a virus, then it's going to be part of the plan. He's going to use it on the G8. I'm going to get Kim and make sure she's safe. I'll also get her blood so we can check it."

"And if al-Libbi is watching like you think he is?"

"I've got a plan."

12:05 P.M. PST
UCLA Medical Center

Tony Almeida sat in a private room with an ice pack on the back of his neck. Across from him in the bed lay Agent Dyson, motionless and comatose. Two uniformed policemen were stationed outside, and FBI agents had been in and out

of the room all day. They had all asked Tony the same questions and he'd given the same answers. They were at a loss
to explain Dyson's actions or to uncover his motivations.
This was no great shock to Almeida—over the years the FBI
had played host to any number of moles at various levels.

Unlike the FBI agents, who left when they learned Dyson
was comatose, Almeida waited. This was partly because his
head still felt like it had been split open with an axe, but also
because he didn't take kindly to having his head split
open . . . and he planned on being there when Dyson opened
his eyes.

Tony leaned his head back onto the ice pack. There was
time still to rest. Eventually Dyson would snap out of it.
Tony would ask him a few questions, and then put him into a
whole different kind of coma.

12:07 P.M. PST
West Los Angeles

Mercy Bennet had drifted in and out of consciousness for
God knew how long. Every time she drifted toward wakeful-
ness, she felt her face throb and her skin stretched tight over
what must be scabs on her face. Darkness was all around
her. A hood had been thrown over her head. She would sink
back down into forgetfulness.

Eventually, though, her conscious mind would not be denied, and she came to. She was lying on her side, hooded,
with her hands bound behind her back. Her ankles were tied
as well. She was lying on a hard floor. Voices from another
room drifted toward her.

". . . ill her. Jesus, we're in it this far. What difference does
it make," someone was saying.

"A great deal of difference," said another voice, a very

calm voice. "There is a distinction between killing for the cause and outright murder. You know that."

"I know that makes you comfortable to say it," replied the first speaker. "All I know is that I'm going to jail if they catch me, and so I don't want to be caught."

Mercy shifted her arms a little, trying to get some blood back into them. As she did, she felt something jab into her hand. It was a nail of some kind, sticking up from the floor-board. She rubbed her wrist on it and felt the cords catch. She listened again—the voices came through a wall. There was no other sound. If someone was in the room with her, he was quiet as a ghost. She rubbed the cord against the nail again . . .

12:10 A.M. PST
Federal Plaza, West Los Angeles

Driving a borrowed SUV with a siren, Jack made good time from CTU to Federal Plaza. No call came during the drive, which meant that either the dialysis had worked or the terror-ist wasn't bothering to issue another warning. Jack didn't care either way. He'd spent enough time lying down and leav-ing his daughter out in the cold. He was going to bring her in.

This whole day had turned to hell. He had planned it per-fectly, but like all plans it had gone awry, starting with Mercy Bennet's appearance at the Federal Building. Jack hadn't counted on that. Their meeting had triggered a series of events that had spun the whole day out of control, and drawn his daughter into danger she did not deserve. But he was determined to take care of that.

As he drove, Jack sorted his list of worries. He had to get Kim out of harm's way. He had to find al-Libbi and this virus. And he had to make sure al-Libbi's plot against the G8 was neutralized.

And then there was Mercy. She'd been taken by the terrorists. She might be dead, she might be under torture. And he was doing nothing about it. He recalled his own words to her: *you'll always have someone who's on your side.* Those words sounded empty to him now. Jack had broken promises before. He'd lied and misled before. But only to complete the mission. Only to corner the enemy. That was part of his job. But Mercy was an ally and he'd made her a promise. He kept promises to his friends.

Jack turned onto Westwood Boulevard, which marked the eastern edge of the protest perimeter, and drove south past Wilshire Boulevard until he reached Olympic Boulevard, then swung west until he came to Veteran. He turned right back up Veteran until he reached the same parking area Mercy had discovered. Jack parked and looked around for the nearest set of available uniformed cops.

"Hey, gentlemen, can you help me?" he asked, showing them his badge as he approached.

One of the cops turned toward him, and Jack recognized the face and the bandaged wrist at the same time. "Oh, it's you," the cop said. "You back for the other one?"

Jack hesitated for a fraction of a second. Then he thought of basic infantry training: in an ambush, attack the attack. "Special Agent Jack Bauer, Counter Terrorist Unit," he said in his command voice. "I need help from a few of you guys. Come with me, please."

12:20 P.M. PST
Brentwood, California

Ayman al-Libbi parked a dark blue Toyota Sentra close to the curb on a residential street in Brentwood, California. Brentwood was the next enclave over from Westwood, separated by the wide 405 Freeway. Not quite as large or wealthy as Beverly Hills, it was still drenched in money. The neighborhood was wealthy enough that his cheap auto would eventually draw attention, but for the rest of the day it would be mistaken for a car driven by a maid. By nightfall, it would no longer matter.

He checked the address. The house he was looking for was several doors down, a two-story house with a wide grass lawn, red-tiled roof, and a wall that hid a patio before the door. It reminded Ayman of the architecture of Spain. A green pickup truck was parked in front of the house, and he could hear the high-pitched whine of a leaf blower.

A leaf blower, he thought. The sound of the leaf blower made him angry in an irrational way. It seemed to represent everything he despised about the West—countries full of people too lazy to rake their own leaves, who used gasoline imported from the Middle East to power machines to move the leaves around for them. And then, of course, they would bomb those Middle Eastern countries to keep the price of gasoline low. It was the height of decadence.

By the time Ayman reached the Spanish house, the leaf blower had stopped. A pot-bellied Mexican man in green pants and a green shirt walked down to the sidewalk and put the leaf blower in the back of the white truck. He removed some kind of small shovel and then turned back toward the house. As Ayman approached, the gardener knelt down along a stone walkway that led up to the wall. Long-leafed agapanthus plants lined the walkway, resting in freshly dug soil.

"Those look good," Ayman said pleasantly.

The gardener turned, his round face covered in a sheen of sweat. "Eh? Oh, thank you," he said, saluting with his little shovel. He had a gentle Mexican accent. Ayman, who spoke four languages, understood how hard it could be to rid the tongue of the rhythms of home.

"Is this a good time to plant agapanthus?" Ayman asked.

The gardener had already turned back to his planting. Now he turned fully toward Ayman and smiled. "No. But . . ." He pointed the shovel toward the house and rolled his eyes.

Ayman nodded. "Well, we all work for someone."

The gardener stood up and wiped his brow. "That's the truth. Even though I like to think that I work for myself." He walked past Ayman toward his truck, which had the words "Sanchez Landscaping" on the side.

Ayman followed him to the truck. "If we are lucky, we serve our own ends. But we work for others. Have you owned your own business for long?"

The gardener, Sanchez, opened the passenger door of his truck and reached inside for a card. "Nine or ten years, I think. Here."

He turned to give Ayman the card and was surprised to find him standing so close. Ayman pushed the gardener almost gently back onto the passenger seat. As Sanchez lost balance, Ayman lifted a silenced .22-caliber semi-automatic handgun and shot him in the head.

12:34 P.M. PST
CTU Headquarters, Los Angeles

Jessi Bandison was potshot-ing. At least that was her word for it. Chris and Jamey had assigned her to track down any connections between the terrorist Ayman al-Libbi and any groups that might want to cause trouble at the G8. The problem, of course, was that there were a thousand groups that *might* want to cause trouble at the G8. Almost none of them had the resources to try. So Jessi had spent her first few hours analyzing those that did have resources: al-Qaeda, Falun Gong in China, Jemaah Islamiya (although they operated only in Southeast Asia), and a few others. But connecting al-Libbi and Falun Gong was like fitting a square peg in a round hole, and as far as al-Qaeda was concerned, al-Libbi didn't practice their kind of radical Islamism.

After that, Jessi had transferred from a resource-oriented search to a motive-oriented. Falun Gong came up again and was discarded. The East Turkistan Independence Movement, or ETIM, was the most likely candidate simply because they had an office in Los Angeles, which proved they were politically savvy and had some resources. But the "office" turned out to be a Mongolian barbecue restaurant in a strip mall, and every source Jessi dug up on ETIM in eastern China was roadblocked. Beijing was very tight-lipped about political activism, especially when it involved violence. As far as the Communist Party was concerned, ETIM didn't even exist because there was no East Turkistan at all.

"Any luck?" Chris Henderson asked.

"Nada," she said, stiffening a bit. Henderson had never been anything but cordial to her, but somehow he gave her the creeps.

Bits of data shining out of the computer screen reflected on her light chocolate-colored skin and round cheeks. "We don't have much data on activity inside China. I'm just potshot-ing now."

Chris read the screen, conscious of how close his hand was to her shoulder. "You're back on ETIM. I thought that was a dead end."

"Oh, I'm not, really," she said. "It's all the shotgun approach at this point. I've got the computers doing a random match on any names that appear to be of eastern Chinese origin with any other unusual activity, such as plane flights, fund transfers, that stuff. I think I'm using half the RAM in the entire network. I'm surprised Jamey hasn't—"

The screen flickered. Jessi stared at the screen as an enormous list of transactions appeared. "See, I knew there'd be too many to make the list usable—" She stopped speaking again. Her logarithm had ranked the listing in order of probability. The one at the top caught her attention: it had been ranked in the ninety-ninth percentile. She drilled down into the line and read the following:

TRSP $US2,000,000.00
FROM 343934425 TO 904900201* CAYMAN ISLDS
*ACCOUNT NO. ACTIVITY MATCH: EASTERN TURKISTAN INDE-
PENDENCE MOVEMENT

"Hmm," Jessi said, astounded.

Henderson patted her on the shoulder. "I'm taking you to Vegas."

"Yeah," she agreed. If the computer match was correct, it appeared that someone had transferred two million dollars to an account in the Cayman Islands—an account that had been connected to ETIM. So much for ETIM not having resources. "Let's find out who," Jessi said.

Henderson watched her work. He'd liked her from the moment he took over as Director of Field Operations. She was certainly a wizard on the computer, but every analyst at CTU could make that claim. Bandison had a level head and a detective's mind. One of his predecessors, Kelly Sharpton, had written her glowing reports.

"There," she said. He tore his eyes away from her to study the computer.

"Marcus Lee," he read. "Chinese American, living in Los Angeles. Now why would Mr. Lee want to give two million dollars to ETIM?"

Kim stomped her foot impatiently. "I don't care what my dad says, I need to get out of here."

Her face was flushed, and she was starting to perspire so much, she was sure her makeup would run.

"We should just go," Janet said, lifting her hair up from her shoulders to cool her neck. "There's like nothing happening here anyway."

Even as she said that, Brad Gilmore and another guy from Teen Green shoved into them, hitting Janet on the back and nearly knocking Kim off her feet.

"Hey, cut it out!" Kim yelled.

"It wasn't us!" Brad complained. "It's them!"

On the other side of Brad, two or three people Kim didn't know had started to push and shove each other—a middle-aged granola with shoulder-length gray hair, and a cute guy who looked like he was in college. They were yelling over each other, and Kim could barely understand the words. The college guy shoved the granola, who shoved back. The people around them simultaneously whooped encouragement and yelled at them to stop causing trouble.

In moments, four or five policemen were on the scene, pushing past the spectators and grabbing hold of the two men.

"Excuse me, miss."

Kim Bauer turned away from her conversation with Janet to find three policemen standing around her. They had serious looks on their faces.

"Yeah?" she replied.

"You'll have to come with us, please."

Kim looked around as if trying to discover something she'd done wrong. The fight was already breaking up, and she hadn't even been involved. "What do you mean?"

"Is there a problem, officer?" Marshall Cooper, the advisor, pushed past several gawking members of Teen Green. "Is something wrong here?"

One of the policemen with a bandage around his wrist said, "Step back, sir. We're going to have to take this girl inside for some questions."

Kim didn't like the sound of that. "What'd I do?" she asked fearfully.

The cop paused. "Disorderly conduct."

"That's ridiculous!" said a high-pitched voice. Andi Parks practically rolled over Cooper as she set herself between Kim and the policemen. "That's completely and totally ridiculous, I've been here the whole time and that girl hasn't done a thing, in fact she's not feeling very well, are you, Kimmy?"

Her onslaught was enough to make all three cops step back, but they recovered quickly. The injured cop puffed his chest out again. "Back off, ma'am. We're just doing our job. Now come along, miss." He took Kim by the arm gently but firmly.

Kim looked from Janet to Andi Parks to Mr. Cooper, who looked confused, outraged, and helpless, respectively.

12:45 P.M. PST
Federal Plaza, West Los Angeles

Jack watched from the crowd, a safe distance away. He was wearing a borrowed blue Dodgers cap that hid his blond hair, and he kept his chin tucked, hiding half his face in the collar of his shirt. If anyone was keeping an eye on Kim, he was sure they wouldn't recognize him in that throng of people.

The police officers had surrounded Kim and were leading

her toward the entrance to the Federal Building. Jack trailed them. He was vaguely aware that the shouting and arguments continued behind him.

12:50 *P.M. PST*
West Los Angeles

There is a single-mindedness that settles over a person about to die. For Mercy Bennet, that single-mindedness refined itself into the single, repetitive motion of her bound wrists along the edge of an exposed nail. Elbows bent, elbows straightened, elbows bent, elbows straightened. It was not monotonous. It was not tedious. It was, in fact, the single most thrilling and interesting event of her entire life, because her entire life depended on it.

They had argued twice more about killing her. "They" comprised at least five distinct individuals, though by the sound of footsteps there might be others coming in and out. She had no faces to match the voices, but she had begun to learn more about them. They used names with one another that had to be codes: Jack Mormon, Rudolf the Red . . . and at last, when one of them spoke to the man she thought of as the leader, she heard the name Smith. She guessed who it was: Seldom Seen Smith, the leader of the Monkey Wrench Gang. At one point during her captivity, Smith apparently left the room, and two others spoke of him in voices mixed with reverence and contempt.

"What's gotten in to him?" one male voice asked.

"Easy, Rudolf," a female voice said. "Smith's the man."

"He's turning in to some kind of Hayduke, though," said Rudolf.

Mercy was surprised to find that she understood the term, and she thanked her research on the Edward Abbey book from which the terrorists took their name. Hayduke was one of the most revered characters in the environmentalist book—he was famous in part for the fact that he studiously avoided causing harm to other people.

"That's not such a bad thing, is it?" the female voice asked.

Rudolf spoke stubbornly. "It is if it gets in the way of the goal. Hell, if we're going to talk and not do anything, we might as well join the Sierra Club."

"Quiet." This came from a new female voice. Mercy thought she recognized it as Frankie Michaelmas. "I was with him in Brazil. I saw what he did to those surveyors that time. Trust me, when the time comes, he'll kill her."

Conversations like that were very motivating. Mercy had managed to roll so that her body lay almost over her arms, which she moved ever so slightly to fray the ropes. Under her hood, she had no idea if anyone was watching her, so she had to make her movements imperceptible. Twice she heard footsteps approach, and felt heavy steps on the floorboards beneath her, and she froze. Only when the footsteps turned and walked away did she resume her cutting.

After what seemed like hours, she felt the ropes part. She stifled a gasp. Her hands were free, but her feet were still bound. If she sat up and someone discovered her now, she'd be nearly helpless. She listened carefully, reaching out with all her senses to gather information about the room. There was neither sound nor movement. She had to risk it.

In one fluid motion, Mercy sat up and pulled the hood from her head. She was sitting in a bare room with scratched wood floors and faded yellow walls. The single window had been covered in heavy drapes. The door was half closed. There was no furniture.

Quickly Mercy pulled at the ropes tying her ankles. They

were tied tightly, and at first her fingers fumbled over the knots. Although her heart was pounding, Mercy forced herself to stop. Focus, she told herself. Slow and steady wins the race.

She found the bit of rope that would loosen more easily, and tugged.

12:53 P.M. PST
Federal Building Command Center,
West Los Angeles

Kim Bauer's heart was pounding as she passed through the metal detectors and into the Federal Building itself. The doors closed behind her, and the sound and energy of the protest outside was sealed away as neatly as if it were a scene on television. She could still see the protestors fifty yards away from the glass walls of the lobby, but they seemed a world away from the quiet, air-conditioned interior.

The three policemen still surrounded her, and one was still holding her arm. "I really didn't do anything," she said to them, her voice rising a little in panic. "It was those guys next to us. They started the fight."

"Maybe so," said the cop with the bad wrist.

At their direction, Kim walked into an elevator and rode it down to a basement level. She was led along a beige corridor with fluorescent lighting past several rooms occupied by men and women in business attire, but wearing guns in shoulder harnesses like the one her dad wore sometimes.

The officers stopped at one door, which opened just as they arrived. Out walked two men: the cute college guy and the gray-haired hippie. Kim's eyes went wide. "That's them!" she said. "Those are the two guys who caused the trouble."

The gray-haired man smiled at her and looked back over his shoulder. "I guess you gotta be good at something," he said. He moved out of the way, and Kim saw the person to whom he'd addressed his comment.

"Dad!" she yelled.

Her father pulled her into his arms and held her as though his hug could squeeze the infection from her body. "Are you all right?"

"I'm okay, but these guys are arresting me and I didn't do anything—"

"I know, it's okay," he said. "You're not being arrested." He had already decided not to tell her about al-Libbi's threats, or the virus. The news would terrify her, and he could offer no comfort. For all he knew, the terrorist *was* lying about the virus. So he lied, too. "I had to get you out of there because, because we got information that a riot was about to start. I wanted to make sure you were okay."

Kim looked back out the door. "But what about Janet and Brad and everyone?"

"They're okay. They're being sent home." More lies. "I just needed to make sure you were okay. By the way, *are* you okay? Your face is red."

Kim felt her blond hair clinging to her forehead and pushed it back. "It's so hot out there. I think I've got a fever."

Jack saw his opening. He'd been wondering how he was going to get a sample of Kim's blood without telling her why. This was his chance.

"Okay, there's a doctor on call down here. I'm going to have her look at you. She's a pretty thorough lady. She may want to give you a complete checkup, is that okay?"

12:58 P.M. PST
West Los Angeles

Mercy dug her fingernail under a stubborn loop. She felt her fingernail tear away, but the loop came loose and she pulled hard. The ropes around her ankles fell away. She jumped to her feet but immediately stumbled as a thousand hot pins and needles stabbed at her legs.

A young man wearing a Lynyrd Skynyrd T-shirt walked into the room. His jaw dropped. "What the—?"

Mercy lunged toward him as fast as her numb legs would carry her. He had just enough sense to raise his hands as she punched him, and her knuckles smashed into the back of his hand, which in turn smashed into his forehead. Ignoring the pain in her legs, she kicked him in the groin.

He had no skill, but he was stubborn. As he doubled over, he lunged forward and wrapped his arms around her still-burning legs. She nearly lost her balance, but bent her knees forward, resting her shins on his shoulders and using her hands to push his face down into the floor. He grunted and loosened his grip. Mercy jerked her legs free and stomped on the back of his leg, then launched herself over him and out the door.

She was in a living room as bare as the room she'd left, except for a stack of five or six wooden crates filled with glass vials. Three people walked into the room from a hallway and gave Mercy the same surprised look that the first man had—except this time one of them moved more aggressively. He was another young man in his twenties, wiry and bald, with a hard look in his eyes as he threw himself at Mercy. She had no time to move. He wasn't much taller than she was, but he was stronger, and he grabbed her in a bear hug so hard, she thought her back would break.

Mercy had been in fights before. Coming up from the uniform ranks, working as a female cop in Los Angeles, of course she had. She dug her thumbs into his eyes and pushed up and back. He screamed and lifted his chin, flinching away from the pain. Mercy headbutted him on the nose and felt it crush beneath her. Lifting her own head away, she let go of his face with her right hand and punched him in the throat. He made a wet gurgling sound and threw her away from him. Mercy smashed into the stack of glass vials. Glass cut her skin and warm wetness spread across her back.

"You idiot!" yelled one of the other two. Mercy saw a tall man in his forties, slightly balding, with a fierce, hawkish face. The voice told her this was Seldom Seen Smith. "Do you realize what you've—"

He didn't bother to finish; his look of anger turned to horror and he started to back away. "Both strains," he said fearfully. Beside him, a girl spewed a stream of obscenities. Only then did Mercy realize that it was Frankie Michaelmas. She glared at Mercy but she, too, had begun to step back. Mercy scrambled up and away from the broken glass beneath her. She didn't know why they looked so suddenly upset, but her command instincts took over and she stepped forward as though she'd just drawn her gun. "Both of you, get down on your knees!"

Smith took one more look at the mess Mercy had made, turned, and ran.

12:59 P.M. PST
Federal Building, West Los Angeles

Jack Bauer walked out into the lobby of the Federal Building. He knew Kim was safe now, and there wasn't much he could do while the doctor examined her. He was afraid that

if he stayed, he'd give away his concern. So he'd come upstairs for some air. He knew something was wrong immediately, since the cops who manned the metal detectors and
X-ray machines were pacing back and forth along the tall
windows, and two of them now stood before the shut doors.

He looked beyond the glass and saw why.

Around the Federal Building, the sea of people had turned
into a storm. Protestors surged over the grass field and onto
the concrete plaza. Police wearing helmets and carrying
shields appeared out of nowhere, forming a hasty line before
the building doors. A plume of tear gas rose up from somewhere. The protest had turned into a full-scale riot.

•••

THE FOLLOWING TAKES PLACE
BETWEEN THE HOURS OF
1 P.M. AND 2 P.M.
PACIFIC STANDARD TIME

•••

1:00 P.M. PST
Federal Building, West Los Angeles

The elevator doors opened behind Jack and half a squad of uniformed policemen hustled out, hastily strapping on their riot helmets, their thick plastic riot shields bumping against one another as they hurried toward the doors.

LAPD had managed to form a perimeter ten yards out from the building itself, and the sight of their wall of shields had slowed the crowd. They formed their own line a few yards from the police, shouting epithets and chants, raising their fists and their voices in anger. They were two armies drawn up in battle, waiting for the moment to strike.

But ten thousand people, once roused, needed some outlet for their frustration. Over the heads of the vast crowd,

Jack saw smoke rising on the street, and he guessed that a car was burning. Jack's lip curled into a sneer. From his training with the L.A. Sheriff Department years ago to his time in Delta Force to CTU, Jack had seen more than his share of chaos. He understood that a mob generated its own energy, and that this energy had to be transferred somewhere, somehow. But understanding it did not mean he respected it. The soldier in him felt nothing but disdain for misdirected violence. As far as he was concerned, a crowd of people engaged in protest were exercising their rights in a democracy. He risked his life to defend that right, whether he agreed with them or not. But a mob that destroyed property and caused violence was just a bunch of low-level terrorists.

Jack's cell phone rang and he flipped it open. It was someone at CTU. "Bauer."

"Jack, it's Chris. I've got the surveillance team at the Federal Building on the line."

Jack looked down at the floor, as though he could see through several layers of concrete to the command center below. "I'm at the Federal Building."

"I know, but with Almeida at the hospital, they didn't know how to reach you. I'm patching them through."

There was a click, and Jack said again, "Bauer."

"Agent Bauer, this is Cynthia Rosen, FBI. Are you still on the premises?"

"Upstairs, watching the shit hit the fan."

"Listen, bear with me if I'm not sure about this, but my team just took over surveillance after whatever happened this morning, so I'm not totally up to speed. But your unit had requested FRS on a couple of people, didn't it?"

"That's right." Jack watched a glass bottle arc up and out of the mass of protestors and bounce off a policeman's riot shield.

"Well, we got something. Facial recognition on a guy you had videoed this morning."

Jack straightened. "Muhammad Abbas?"

"No. Based on the video you guys took, it was the subject he was talking to. We don't have his name, just a match with the previous video we captured."

"Better than nothing," Bauer said. "You have him now?"

"Affirmative. North side of the building."

"Roger." Jack slapped his phone shut and ran.

1:03 P.M. PST
West Los Angeles

Mercy had no gun, no badge, and no radio, so she had pursued her two subjects on foot. Frankie and Seldom Seen Smith had bolted out the front door and onto a residential street. The small Spanish-style houses and low-hanging power lines told Mercy she was somewhere in West Los Angeles, but she couldn't see any street signs.

Frankie and Smith ran together for several blocks, but then got smart and split up at a residential street, Frankie swerving west and Smith continuing north. Mercy stayed on Smith. Her feet started to ache almost immediately; having gone from near-zero circulation to a sudden sprint was too much for them. She'd have given anything for a radio, but she refused to quit. She wanted this bastard, if only to prove to Jack Bauer that she was right.

Fortunately, Smith was no athlete himself. She wasn't gaining on him, but she wasn't giving ground, either. And so far Smith hadn't opted for the one thing Mercy feared most—that he'd swerve up a driveway, over a fence, and turn the chase into an obstacle course. Thank god for middle-aged terrorists.

She stayed focused on Smith, but she became vaguely aware of the scene ahead of him. They were running toward a tall building, and there seemed to be some kind of loud noise and movement ahead. They crossed another residential street, and the Spanish bungalows gave way to small apartment buildings and duplexes. Mercy saw a cloud of white smoke in the distance and wondered if there was a fire of some kind. Then she picked up the faint acrid smell of chlorobenzylidene and knew that it wasn't smoke; it was tear gas. She lifted her eyes up from Smith's back and got her first clear view of the structure ahead of her.

It was the Federal Building.

Looking beyond Smith, she saw that the disturbance was a mass of people, frothing and surging like waves battering a sea rock. Another plume of tear gas rose up, and she heard wailing sirens mix with the roar of ten thousand people chanting.

Mercy realized what Smith was trying to do and she gave him her grudging respect. If Smith plunged into the midst of that chaos, he would be almost impossible to find.

Even as she thought this, he reached the edge of the crowd.

1:12 P.M. PST
CTU Headquarters, Los Angeles

Jessi Bandison hated puzzles. She hated puzzles in the same way she hated tangles in her curls—they were things that ought not to be, and she felt obliged to work them until they were out of her hair.

"Marcus Lee" was the current tangle she was trying to smooth away. A quick search had pulled up a file full of information on him, but none of it was of any consequence.

According to his file, Lee was a Chinese American who in 1998 had immigrated to the United States, where he already had several family members in residence. The FBI had a file on him, but it consisted of no more than a cursory background check that came up clean.

Jessi had contacted the CIA, hoping they might have done a workup on a former Chinese national. Through their database she managed to obtain a glimpse of the Chinese government's own files on Lee. The prospect excited her until she'd mined the data and found Lee to be about as interesting as a stucco wall. The man had just enough background to be real but not enough to be interesting: born in Shenzhen, educated at UCLA, then returned to China to work in computers, but never achieved any strong connections in the Communist Party. Eventually he earned a visa and immigrated to the United States, where he'd turned his IT savvy into a thriving software business. He lived in Brentwood, paid his taxes, committed the occasional parking violation, but that was it.

Jessi didn't like it. The story the data told her seemed believable, but the tangle was still in her hair, and now it was starting to bother her.

"I've got two choices," she said to herself, staring at her computer screen in CTU's bullpen full of computer terminals. "I can assume that my connection's wrong, that this bank account has nothing to do with Marcus Lee, and that Marcus Lee is a solid naturalized citizen."

But that didn't smooth the tangle, it just ignored it.

"Or I can assume that the account connection is right, and there's more to Marcus Lee than he wants me to know about."

It was the bank account that was the key. How was Lee connected to the bank account? Instead of running down Lee, Jessi turned her attention to the Cayman Islands and began to research account number 343934425. Like accounts in Swiss banks, the Cayman Islands accounts were kept confidential, but unlike the Swiss, the Cayman Islanders had neither the tradition nor the backbone to maintain that privacy under pressure. As she dug deeper, Jessi expected to find history on some FBI or CIA investigation that had linked the name Marcus Lee to account 343934425.

She was right that a prior investigation had matched Lee to the account. But to her surprise she found that the investigation itself was Russian. Jessi stared at the screen for a moment, baffled by the notation. But there was no mistake: Russian intelligence had fed the CIA the data. This wasn't completely unheard of, but to Jessi it was a gaping hole in the road.

Fortunately, she knew someone who might be able to help. She dialed a number she hated to admit she knew by heart.

"Hey," said the voice on the other end of the line.

"Hi Kelly," Jessi said. "How are you?"

"Well, better now," said Kelly Sharpton. "I've been hoping you'd call."

"It's business," Jessi said.

"Oh."

Kelly Sharpton had been her boss for a short time at CTU. He'd been brought in on temporary assignment during Jack Bauer's fall from grace. There'd been a spark between them, but Sharpton had left the unit some time ago, "seduced by the lure of filthy lucre," as he put it, and the spark had never started a fire. At least that was how Jessi thought of it. But they spoke every now and again when Kelly was in town, and Kelly had been growing more and more obvious with his hints.

"You have some contacts with the Russians, don't you?"

"Did," he corrected. "It's been a while."

"I'm following a trail that leads from a CIA file to Russian intelligence. Can you put the word out for me?"

"Do I get a dinner out of it?" Kelly laughed.

Jessi felt her heart flutter. She shouldn't be flirting with him. *He's older, he's traveling, his work might put us in conflict . . .* But she heard herself say, "Depends on how good you are."

"Deal," he said. "Expect a call."

1:20 P.M. PST
North Side of the Federal Building,
West Los Angeles

Jack slipped out of the double doors and ran behind the line of officers near the entrance of the Federal Building.

The scene was rapidly spiraling out of control. A bottle shattered on the ground a few feet behind him. Dark smoke mixed with the plumes of tear gas, and Jack knew that protestors had set fire to something, probably a car. He also knew that over at the Veteran Center, half a mile away, LAPD had mustered the horse-mounted squad. If the violence continued, they'd be charging down Wilshire Boulevard, backed up by rubber bullets.

Jack reached the north end of the Federal Building. "I'm here," he said into his mobile phone. "Talk to me."

He was still in touch with Cynthia Rosen downstairs in the command center. She talked back to him now. "He's still there. Getting tough to stay on him, though. Bodies are starting to fly around there."

"I'm there."

The north side of the Federal Building was the narrowest plot of land—an arcade no more than ten yards wide, with a grass lawn another twenty yards, and then the street.

LAPD's original plan had blocked traffic from the street, allowing the protestors to occupy the boulevard and leaving a healthy perimeter between them and the building. The riot had changed all that, and as Jack rounded the corner, the crowd was pushing its way onto the concrete. There was a police line there as well, and in Jack's view they were exercising admirable discipline. Protestors were pushing at their phalanx of riot shields, but they had yet to bring their batons to bear.

"He's at your nine o'clock," Rosen said. "Blue shirt."

Jack looked to his left. It was nearly impossible to get a clean look at anyone beyond the riot shields and in the swarming crowd. But a flash of blue caught his attention and he focused on it. The man wearing the shirt did not stand in the front ranks, but close enough to be noticed, raising his fist and yelling at the police line.

Jack hesitated before moving on. Something about this man's presence at the protest didn't make sense. Why would a terrorist working for Ayman al-Libbi bother with the political protest? It didn't make sense even to risk a showing. There was no upside, and al-Libbi could not be completely confident that Federal investigators hadn't identified at least some of his help. So this man was either so far down the food chain that al-Libbi considered him unimportant, or he had some other reason for keeping him at the protest. Jack tucked that thought away as he made his move.

He did not want the subject or anyone nearby to see him come from the Federal Building, so he turned back around the corner, then passed through the police line.

"Where do you think you're—?" one of the officers asked.

"Federal agent," Jack said, flashing his badge. He held it tight in his left hand, figuring he might need it again soon.

Crossing the line between the police phalanx and the

rioters, Jack felt like a sailor leaping from the ship and into a choppy sea.

"Who the hell are you?" a young man challenged, grabbing Jack as he pushed his way into the crowd.

Jack kneed him in the groin. "No one to mess with."

He stepped over the man and into the space created where he fell. A few more people yelled at him or clutched at him, but Jack ignored them, and a few steps later he was among people who hadn't seen him and didn't pay attention to him except for the second during which he pushed past them. They were all chanting in the same rhythm, but he had the impression the words changed from group to group, as though the rioters were made up of distinct groups with distinct messages who'd all fallen under the same spell. As he made his way through the crowd, rounding the corner of the building, a young Latino pushed him aside and threw a bottle. Jack watched it spin through the air toward a police officer, who ducked behind his shield as the bottle bounced away. The young man smiled at Jack and said something in Spanish that he didn't quite catch. Jack resisted the urge to punch him in the face and moved on.

He waded through the crowd and reached the north side. Using the building as perspective, he made his way back to the point where he'd seen the blue shirt. There was an ebb and flow to the mob as it pushed close to the police barricade and then gave way, and the blue-shirted man was no closer to his original position than a man overboard at sea. But Jack spotted him at last, a few yards away. He shoved his way past four or five short Latino men dressed in primitive costumes, with signs that read "DEJAR LA AMAZONA TRANQUILA!", elbowed through two men holding a banner that said, SAY NO TO CHINA! REMEMBER TIANANMEN! Finally, he forced an open space next to the man in the blue shirt.

Jack had expected him to look Middle Eastern, but if looks were any indicator, the man's background was farther east and north. He looked Chinese, or Slavic, or both. Jack had traveled in the "-stans" that were the former satellites of the old Soviet Union—Uzbekistan, Turkistan, Kyrgyzstan, and the like. The blue-shirted man reminded Jack of men from that region. This thought reminded Jack of something he'd heard in a briefing several weeks earlier, but he couldn't recall it at the moment.

Jack pulled out his cell phone and activated the camera feature. He knew the blue-shirted man wasn't paying much attention to him, but he pretended to enter a number and hold the phone to his ear. "What!" he yelled, just for show. "What?" He pulled the phone away from his ear the way people did who'd lost a connection, as though moving the phone a few inches away would improve the reception. In that moment the blue-shirted man's face appeared on the screen. Jack snapped the picture. A second later he forwarded it to CTU.

1:35 P.M. PST
UCLA Medical Center

Tony Almeida woke with a start when his chin fell forward into his chest. His headache had eased over the last hour, but he was still having that strange post-concussion sensation of layered awareness. Every ten minutes or so he felt as if now, finally, his mind was completely lucid . . . only to discover ten minutes later that his mind really hadn't been clear, but *now* it was . . . only to make the same discovery again in a few minutes, and so on.

He checked the big round clock on the hospital room wall. He'd been asleep only for a few seconds. Dyson was still in the bed, motionless, the monitors beeping along calmly. Dyson's skull had been fractured by his impact with the cinder-block wall.

Tony stood up and was glad when the room didn't spin. He walked over and stood next to the bed, looking down at Dyson. An oxygen tube hung under his nose and draped over his face.

Who are you working for? Tony asked silently. *Why did you try to kill me?*

The FBI had vetted Dyson's record and found nothing. Not trusting them, CTU had done its own research, and even Jamey Farrell, who was a tenacious analyst, had drawn a blank. As far as any of them could tell, Dyson had absolutely no connection to Ayman al-Libbi or any groups that might want to hire him.

Tony opened his cell phone and called CTU.

"Jamey Farrell."

"It's Tony. Have we had any luck tracking any of the people in the van that took Detective Bennet?"

She sounded mildly annoyed. "Not yet. There's nothing on the van at all. We ran a check on Frankie Michaelmas. No one knows where she's at. What makes you think she has anything to do with Ayman al-Libbi?"

"Jack's hunch," Tony said. "Why do you ask like that?"

"Ozersky's a granola. Goes by the name Willow, if that tells you anything. The girl is pretty much the same. She's an environmental freak, not a political activist. Do you know something I don't?"

"Just that Jack's hunches are often right."

Tony hung up. Jamey had no idea how far out on a limb he'd gone to pursue one of Jack's hunches. In fact, very few people in CTU knew how far he'd gone. To make it all turn out right, they needed a break—a big one.

"And so far, you're the only lead I've got," Tony said to Dyson.

As he looked down, he was sure he saw Dyson's finger twitch.

Mercy closed in on Seldom Seen Smith.

Smith's strategy had nearly worked. Mercy had lost him when he plunged into the crowd at the south end of the Federal Building. She'd plunged in after him, past jagged lines of people who seemed hesitant and uncertain. The protest chants had ceased, replaced by a loud, fearful buzz caused by the police activity a block or two to the north. She slid between people and stood on her toes, which did her no good.

She'd grabbed a cell phone out of someone's hand. "Hey!" the young girl complained. Mercy ignored her and dialed 911, but the circuits were busy. She'd dialed the direct line for her office, but the line rang until a recording came on saying, "Thank you for calling the Los Angeles Police Department's West Bureau. If this is an emergency, please hang up and dial 911 . . ."

Mercy closed the connection and tossed the phone back to the girl. If she needed another one, there'd be plenty around. She pushed forward, not knowing what else to do, knowing that Smith would do everything he could to lose himself in the huge crowd. As she moved forward, she made mental notes about his appearance: Caucasian male, over six feet, balding with brown hair, eye color probably brown, thin, probably under two hundred pounds . . .

And then she saw him. He had done the right thing, changing his pace, moving slowly to avoid attention. She would have missed him entirely if luck hadn't turned her in exactly his direction. Their eyes locked for a moment, his opening wide and hers narrowing sharply. He moved away from her and she moved forward.

She had tracked him that way through the crowd until now, at the far northeast edge of the crowd, almost two blocks away from the Federal Building, he was coming to the edge. Mercy saw open street beyond. More importantly, she saw two uniformed police officers stationed at the corner. Pinning her eyes to Smith's back, she moved toward the cops. "I'm a cop," she said. "Detective Bennet, West Bureau. I lost my badge during a pursuit. I need help with an arrest. Can you call for backup?"

"Who'd we call?" one of the uniforms said sarcastically. "Everyone's here."

"Then it's you two," she said.

"How do we know?"

"You don't," she admitted. "But who else is going to walk up to you and say they are a female detective from West Bureau?"

The uniformed cops nodded; not quite convinced, but willing to play this out. They followed her into the crowd. Smith had seen them. As they moved forward, he moved back into the crowd itself. *What's he doing?* Mercy wondered. She wasn't going to lose him, and the crowd meant that he moved more slowly.

Much more slowly, in fact. The two uniforms fanned out and easily flanked Smith. Mercy moved forward. Smith had slowed almost to a stop. Was he giving up?

The uniform on Smith's left moved in. Smith raised his hand and yelled, "I give up! I give up! Stop hurting me!" in a voice full of panic.

The cop stopped, taken aback by the fear in Smith's voice, since the cop hadn't touched him at all.

"Stop! Help!" Smith screamed in a high-pitched voice. He lunged forward at the cop, who held up his hands defensively. Smith clutched at the officer but yelled, "Let go of me! Help!"

"Hey, man, he's not fighting you," someone standing nearby said.

"Get off him, you freakin' fascist," said a blond kid in a Von Dutch T-shirt.

"Get him off me, get him off!" Smith yelled.

The second uniform rushed forward, seeing his partner in a struggle, and pulled Smith away and to the ground.

"Goddamned pig!" the blond kid yelled, angry now.

Mercy saw it happen, but couldn't stop it. Smith clutched at the officer, preventing him from standing up, but yelled, "Help! Help! He's breaking my arm!"

Two protestors yelled and grabbed the officer from behind, pulling him away. The officer swung wildly and hit the blond kid in the face. He jumped on the officer's back, and the first cop, who'd regained his feet, waded in to help. Before anyone could stop it, a huge fight had broken out, and the two uniforms disappeared under a pile of bodies.

Smith slipped away.

1:47 P.M. PST
CTU Headquarters, Los Angeles

At that moment, Jamey Farrell hated camera phones. Worse than useless, they gave the impression of being useful without delivering much on the promise.

She'd received the photo sent over by Jack Bauer—a grainy close-up of a dark-haired man in blue. It might as well have been an Impressionist painting. But Jamey knew her job and she did it well. Within minutes of receiving the file, Jamey fed the data over into CTU's image-enhancing software. A quick phone call to Jack confirmed that the man was of Slavic/Asian descent, which helped her nudge the program. The computers had spent the last few minutes reconstructing the subject's face. Every ten seconds or so her computer screen rolled like a wave, and a slightly sharper version of the man's face appeared. The image had just reached the point where Jamey felt it was worth running through CTU's facial recognition software.

She used the inter-office line and called over to Donovan Exley, a young analyst with graphics expertise. "Van, I'm going to feed you an image. Can you run FRS on it right away."

"No prob," he replied.

Jamey sent the file and nodded in satisfaction. The wonders of science would turn Jack Bauer's Impressionist painting into the complete biography of a terrorist suspect.

1:50 P.M. PST
North Side of the Federal Building,
West Los Angeles

Jack waited impatiently for Jamey Farrell to get off her ass and get him information. He knew that wasn't fair—Jamey was one of the most capable analysts he'd met. But standing in the midst of ten thousand screaming protestors with clouds of tear gas wafting through the mob did not increase his empathy.

He looked to the east, where the tear gas had been fired. There was dark smoke there, too, probably a car fire, but he hadn't seen people running from that direction. He guessed that the incident had been isolated. Tear gas had probably scattered the vandals, and so LAPD had backed off.

The blue-shirted man was still close by. Jack had spent the intervening minutes studying the people around him—they were a mix of Slavs and Asians, and they were definitely with the anti-China contingent. With nothing else to do except try to blend in, Jack joined in a chant (something about "China's record doesn't rate—keep them out of the G8") while he formed theories about his subject. He decided that there was only one way the subject could and would be seen at the protest: he was expected to be there. There was no other explanation for why a man with terrorist connections had been seen twice. He wanted to be seen—at least, he'd wanted to be seen the second time. The first time, when the security cameras had caught him in the middle of his meeting with Muhammad Abbas, had been luck—Abbas had stayed away from Federal property like a vampire avoiding a church. But now the blue-shirted man was doing everything he could to get noticed.

He's a member of an anti-China political group, Jack told himself. *Someone who'd be expected to be here. Whatever's going down at the summit, they know we'll go after everyone when it's over, and he doesn't want to do anything out of the ordinary.*

Jack smiled grimly at his own detective work. Who needed computers?

A moment later, he felt the change before he saw it. A wave of anxiety swept through the mob, moving like a murmur through a crowd, only stronger, more visceral. Row by row, lines of people turned their heads away from the Federal Building and toward the west. In the distance, someone screamed.

Jack stood as tall as he could, but saw nothing. At the edge of the plaza, near the sidewalk, was a row of short cement pylons. They were designed to look decorative, but their real purpose was to prevent car bombers from driving into the building. Jack pushed his way past murmuring, confused protestors until he found one of these pylons and stood up on it, raising himself a good two feet above the crowd. The screaming increased; the protest chants had turned to cries of fear and terror.

From his vantage point, Jack could see the far west edge

of the crowd folding back in on itself like a riptide. And he could see why they were running.

A line of mounted policemen was charging down Wilshire Boulevard to scatter the crowd. It was archaic, but no less terrifying for that fact: a line of horsemen twenty strong, the horses charging at a steady lope, their eyes rolling in their heads, the riders holding riot clubs, herding the crowd of people like so much cattle.

At that moment, Jack's phone rang. "Jack, it's Chris," Henderson said quickly. "Are you still in the crowd?"

"Oh yeah."

"Get out," Henderson commanded. "Some protestors just beat two cops nearly to death. LAPD is calling in the cavalry. They're using rubber bullets."

Jack hung up and looked for some escape route, but he already knew it was too late.

· ·

THE FOLLOWING TAKES PLACE
BETWEEN THE HOURS OF
2 P.M. AND 3 P.M.
PACIFIC STANDARD TIME

· ·

2:00 P.M. PST
CTU Headquarters, Los Angeles

Jessi Bandison's line buzzed. "Yes?"

It was CTU's call center. "You've got a call from the Russian Embassy."

"I'll take it," Jessi said.

"Jessi Bandison," she said as the connection was made.

"Miss Bandison," said a female voice in smooth English, with only a hint of accent around the edges. "I am Anastasia Odolova. Anna, if you like."

"Jessi, then. What can I do for you?"

"A mutual friend suggested I call you. I might be able to help you with what you're looking for."

Jessi found herself wondering what Odolova looked like.

Her accent was almost cartoonish, and Jessi couldn't help imagining a lean vamp in a slinky black dress. She herself was round and chocolate-skinned, the opposite of a Russian seductress. "Okay, thank you. I was hoping—"

"You wish to know about Marcus Lee."

"Right," Jessi said. She rolled her eyes. Maybe it was the smooth, almost studied lilt of the Russian accent, but Jessi felt ridiculously like a 1950s espionage agent. She ought to be wearing a trench coat. "I'm running down information on him and I noted that there's been an information exchange between us and the SVR," she explained, referring to Russia's foreign intelligence service. "I'm curious to know if you have any additional information I can use to corroborate my own." That was standard operating procedure when talking with foreign entities: never admit how little you know. But Jessi wasn't well versed in deception, and the words felt large and clumsy as she spoke them.

A smile spread itself across Odolova's words, as though she understood exactly what Jessi was not saying. "I am happy to help you," the Russian said with a slightly aspirated "H" in each word. "In fact, I believe I have what you need. We have a more extensive dossier on Marcus Lee, including"— Odolova paused for dramatic effect—"including his real name."

Jessi's heart skipped a bit. There were no aliases in her file, and no aliases according to the Chinese dossier she'd seen. To an analyst like her, a name was like the single thread that, when pulled, could undo the knot. "Yes?"

"I suggest you pursue the name Nurmamet Tuman. You will find that he is not from Shenzhen, but in fact he was born in Xinjiang Uygur Autonomous Region."

Jessi furrowed her brow. "Xinjiang Uygur Autonomous . . . ?"

"I believe the separatists refer to it as East Turkistan."

2:04 P.M. PST
Federal Building, West Los Angeles

Wilshire Boulevard had turned into a river of people, and
Kasim Turkel was being carried east by the current. The
mob surged en masse away from the charging horses. For a
split second, Kasim considered resisting, but he nearly lost
his footing. To fall meant being trampled to death by stomp-
ing feet and, afterward, galloping hooves. So he ran with the
crowd, swimming his way toward its edge like a man struggling toward the banks of a river. But each person he tried to
push past panicked and clawed at him. The protestors and
their chants were gone, replaced by mid-brained primates
fleeing a pack of predators. Screams and shouts of anger and
fear filled Kasim's ears, punctuated by the sharp report of
gunfire.

   Kasim had been in that place of terror before—in the streets
of Urumchi when the Chinese soldiers charged the pro-inde-
pendence demonstrators. Kasim had been a teenager then;
that afternoon had become a jumbled memory of arms and
legs and screams, smoke, and tear gas. In his panic, Kasim
saw once more rifle butts raised up and brought down violently
on the heads of wailing Uygur women, children screaming
for their parents, and men being dragged into waiting trucks.
Though the images had blurred into one long scene of terror,
the emotions of that night were as sharply defined today as
they were ten years ago. That was the night of Kasim's meta-
morphosis. That was the night the independence-minded boy
was transformed into a freedom fighter.

   Kasim had no idea where he was going. He knew the policemen on horses were behind him, but ahead he saw black
smoke, like the smoke of burning tires, mixed with the
white smoke of tear gas. Tear gas meant the police were
close by, and he feared the American police were boxing

them in to kill them all. Somewhere in his skull, a tiny piece of his mind told him that the Americans did not operate this way, but that tiny fragment was overwhelmed by the seething reptile of his mid-brain that understood only fear and anger. Terror had gripped him as it had gripped all those around him.

In the midst of all that confusion, Kasim looked around for an escape route, and his eyes fell on the face of an American man. The man had blond hair and wore a green shirt, but it was his eyes that caught Kasim's attention. Those eyes were locked on Kasim with fierce intent. And in that moment, the same reptilian brain that drove Kasim along with the terrorized crowd told him that this man was a predator, and he was the prey.

Forgetting the crowd, risking the loss of his footing, Kasim turned at an angle to the human current and swam toward the far side of the street, scratching and clawing his way through anyone and everyone in his path. Someone shrieked at him and scratched at his face, but he pushed him down, stepped over him, and surged forward. He reached the sidewalk. The crowd was thinner here. He was facing a wall and knew that on the other side was a wide open space—a graveyard of soldiers, the Veteran's Memorial. Kasim slithered along the wall, buffeted by people running past him. He reached the corner, the Federal Building still looming on the south side of the street; here on the north side, he was standing before a huge engraving built into the wall of the memorial. There were three figures carved in alabaster, three men with soldier's uniforms from different time periods. Beside the memorial was a side street, far less crowded. Kasim started to run.

Instantly he felt something hard and heavy slam into his back. He flew forward and hit the ground hard, cutting open his chin and shoving all the air out of his body in one agonizing punch. He gasped for breath. Before he could regain his senses he felt strong hands grab his shoulder and spin him over. Kasim blinked up into the blue sky and sunlight. He was looking up into the face of the blond-haired predator.

"Don't move," the man snarled in a voice that sounded like smashing gravel. "Federal—"

But his words were cut off. In the same instant that he had spoken, dark shadows appeared behind him, blotting out the sun. More hands grabbed the blond man and pulled him off Kasim, slamming him to the ground. Kasim started to rise, but someone's knee planted itself firmly on his chest. "LAPD, stay down!" someone ordered, and Kasim had no strength left to argue.

At the edge of his vision he saw the struggle as uniformed policemen restrained the blond man, who was yelling something. One of the policemen jabbed a small canister into the blond man's face. There was a hissing sound, and the blond man gagged and coughed.

2:08 P.M. PST
Federal Building, West Los Angeles

Chaos and hell.

Those two words kept repeating in Mercy's head like a violent mantra. The general vicinity of the Federal Building had exploded into a full-scale riot. Packs of protestors ran this way or that, some of them fleeing the scene. Others seemed to have produced bandanas and masks from nowhere. She saw a Latino man in a "Save the Rain Forest" T-shirt light a Molotov cocktail and throw it at a police car. A man and a woman staggered past her, supporting each other as they walked. Both were bleeding from the head.

It had taken Mercy twenty minutes to travel the three blocks from the street she'd been on—somewhere east of the Federal Building—to Veteran, following the furtive movements of Smith. They were both moving against the current, which several times threatened to carry Mercy backward.

"Don't go that way!" a well-meaning protestor said, wrapping one arm around Mercy's shoulder. "They've got horses! They're clubbing people!"

Mercy shoved him off. "I'm a cop!"

"Then fuck you!" he yelled, and was carried off by the stream of bodies.

Her twenty minutes of working against the crowd had paid off. She was exhausted, but as she reached the western edge of the riot she saw Smith again. He was cagey, sometimes sprinting ahead, sometimes slowing down to the pace of the crowd, often changing directions. But though he was sneaky, Mercy was tenacious. She had him in her sights, and she simply refused to lose him.

Mercy's eyes stung from the tear gas. Though she hadn't been in proximity to any shells, there was enough of the stuff in the air now that everyone was feeling some effects— runny noses, teary eyes, labored breathing. She wished that was all that was slowing her down. She'd done more running in the last hour than she had in the last year. She swore that if she got through this case, she'd get back on the treadmill.

Though she couldn't see well, she knew she was near the veterans' cemetery because she could see the alabaster statue. Smith had just passed it. Mercy hurried that way as well, when she saw several uniforms hauling protestors into a paddy wagon.

2:10 P.M. PST
Federal Building, West Los Angeles

Jack Bauer sputtered and coughed, spitting mucus out of his mouth, trying to gather enough air in his lungs to speak. The goddamned cops had blasted him with enough oleoresin capsicum, or OC spray, to drop an entire cell block. He was blind and he could feel snot running down his nose. His mouth frothed. His hands were secured with flex cuffs behind his back, and angry hands were hauling him to his feet.

"I'm a . . ." He coughed. "I'm a Fed—"

"Shut up and move!" a cop yelled, softening him with a punch to the stomach.

2:11 P.M. PST
Federal Building, West Los Angeles

Mercy saw two cops half dragging one protestor toward the black police wagon. One of the officers punched the protestor in the stomach and he doubled over, his wispy blond hair quivering atop his head.

That's Jack! Mercy thought.

She took one step toward the officers, but hesitated. She would lose Smith. She would lose him, and the Monkey Wrench Gang would fade away, and she had no idea if she had disrupted their plans or not. Jack would have to take care of himself. Eventually the cops would figure out that he was a Federal agent and release him. She had lives to save and a terrorist to capture.

2:12 P.M. PST
Federal Building, West Los Angeles

Smith looked back to see if he was still being followed. His eyes, too, had been attracted to the cops on the corner. He saw the police officer punch his captive, and his eyes flew wide.

Agent Bauer! The man was indeed resourceful. Smith's last GPS reading had shown Bauer still sitting inside CTU headquarters, doing nothing. How had he evaded the chemical markers?

In that moment Smith felt all the energy sucked out of his plans like the sap draining from a tree. Mercy Bennet had broken open the vials of his virus. Jack Bauer had evaded his tracking device. This was more than he had bargained for. He'd gone up against the full forces of the Federal government for the first time and found himself lacking. But he still had his anonymity. The riot had given him the cover he needed, and Mercy Bennet had not yet been able to call in support. If he could get away from her with his anonymity intact, he would have time to regroup and leave the country. He could go back to the Amazon, where he felt most at home, and fade into the forest for as long as the forest still stood.

He ran.

2:15 P.M. PST
CTU Headquarters, Los Angeles

Jessi presented her findings to a room full of people that included Chris Henderson, Nina Myers, Jamey Farrell, District Director George Mason, and even Regional Division Director Ryan Chappelle. Both had been called in from other appointments as the protests at the Federal Building heated up.

"The entire investigation began with a lead from Jack Bauer," Jessi began. Immediately Ryan Chappelle shifted in his seat. The Regional Division Director had no patience for a man he considered a troublemaker. "Agent Bauer was certain he spotted the known terrorist Ayman al-Libbi slipping past border security aboard a flotilla of ships sailing up from Central America to protest the G8 summit.

"These suspicions were strengthened when Bauer was kidnapped briefly, then released, by subjects unknown but assumed to be al-Libbi. We began to search for connections between al-Libbi and the G8."

"Al-Libbi's a gun for hire these days," Chappelle said in a high voice that, along with his narrow face, contributed to his reputation as a weasel. He did, however, do his homework.

"Yes, sir," Jessi said. "Since China is at the top of the G8 agenda, we searched for groups with motivations in that area. A random search for anomalies uncovered a transfer of two million dollars to an account associated with the East Turkistan Independence Movement, or ETIM. Two million dollars is a huge sum of money for a movement that small. The money was then immediately withdrawn from that account, destination unknown. We traced backwards. The transfer came from a Cayman Islands account associated with one Marcus Lee, a Chinese national."

"Would a Chinese-born person want to help a separatist group?" Mason asked.

"We almost hit a dead end there," Jessi continued. "But I discovered that our information on Marcus Lee and the Cayman Islands account had actually come from a data exchange with the Russian SVR. I had a contact there, and through them I learned that Marcus Lee has an alias that the

Chinese withheld from us. In fact, Marcus Lee is pretty much an invented person. Marcus Lee's real name is Nurmamet Tuman. He was born in Urumchi, in what the Chinese refer to as the Xinjiang Uygur Autonomous Region."

"East Turkistan," Chappelle murmured. "So the money trail leads from this Nurmamet whatever to ETIM and then possibly to al-Libbi. To do what? Do we have ID on al-Libbi except for Bauer seeing someone who looks like him in a crowd?"

Henderson hid a grimace. That was Chappelle summed up in two sentences: a mind sharp enough to put the details together in a snap, and a tongue sharp enough to insult everyone who'd done the work before him.

"Nurmamet *Tuman*"—Jessi emphasized the name—"is one of our leads. Under the alias Marcus Lee he lives in Los Angeles."

"I plan to bring him in," Chris said. He looked to George Mason for approval, and Mason nodded.

"You said one of our leads," Chappelle noted. "What's the other?"

Jessi continued. "Earlier in the day surveillance spotted someone who looked very much like Muhammad Abbas, al-Libbi's aide-de-camp, meeting with an unknown subject. A short time ago, Bauer, who is still at the Federal Building, spotted the same man."

Jessi looked to Jamey Farrell, who took over the narrative. "Bauer sent us a photo of the man, which we ran through computer enhancement and facial recognition. We have a nearly one hundred percent match for a man named Kasim Turkel, another Chinese national. His record was a little more transparent than Tuman's. No criminal record we could find, but he's from Urumchi as well."

Henderson summed things up. "Turkel meets Abbas. Abbas means al-Libbi is around somewhere. Money goes from Nurmamet Tuman to ETIM, and then disappears. We're guessing it went to al-Libbi as payment for whatever he's planning. He's in L.A. now, so it's got to be the G8."

"What's on the agenda?" Mason asked. "Likely targets?"

Chris replied, "That's our next problem. Each is as likely as the next. Security is tight everywhere. Hitting a target this hard isn't al-Libbi's usual style."

"There was the Russia-Israel détente meetings back in '94," Chappelle reminded him.

"He missed and was nearly caught," Mason observed. "He never tried anything like that again."

"He's desperate for money," Chappelle said. "Anyway, so we bring this Marcus Lee or whatever his real name is in for interrogation."

Chris hesitated. "There's a complication. The Chinese are insisting that this Marcus Lee has nothing to do with ETIM, that he's not Nurmamet Tuman. They say we've got the wrong guy."

He saw the look on Chappelle's face change, watched what little color there was drain out of it. Henderson wanted more than anything for Chappelle to say, *Bring him in anyway.* But knew that wouldn't happen. The Regional Division Director was a political animal, and at that moment he was connecting an entirely different set of facts: the United States wants China in the G8, the United States plays host to China for the summit; U.S. Federal agents arrest a Chinese national whom the Chinese have already cleared . . .

"Let's use kid gloves," Chappelle said at last. "Send someone to check this Chinese national out. If there's something suspicious, I'll clear it higher up."

Henderson had known this was coming. He looked at Nina. "Go pay him a visit. And be nice."

The effects of the OC spray were finally wearing off. Jack was sitting inside a police wagon—a long truck, the back of which was designed with two long metal benches. He'd been sitting there, half blind and choking, for what seemed like hours, but he guessed it wasn't more than five or ten minutes. His hands were still flex-cuffed behind his back. He was the first one into the paddy wagon, and he had been shoved all the way back into the corner as the police brought in more rioters.

"Hey!" he said, pounding his head against the metal wall of the vehicle. He knew there must be a driver up front. "Hey! I'm a Federal agent!" he yelled.

A small window in the wall between the cab and the container slid open to reveal a metal screen and a police officer's face staring through it. "What?"

"I'm a Federal agent," Jack said. "I tried to identify myself to your partners, but I didn't get a chance."

"You have proof of that?" the officer said.

"You guys searched me," Jack said, remembering the hands pawing at him when he was down. "You must have found my ID."

"Hold on."

The metal shield slid closed. As the OC spray wore off, Jack's anxiety increased. His daughter, al-Libbi, the G8, Mercy Bennet . . . not a single loose end had been tied up. He had to remind himself that it had been only a few hours.

The metal door slid open again. "Sorry, pal, we bagged everything. There was no ID on you at all. Nice try, though." The shield started to close.

"Wait!" Jack said. He thought back to his struggle with the man in the blue shirt. His ID must have fallen out then.

"Look, I'm telling you the truth. Call CTU Los Angeles—"

"CTU?" the officer asked.

"Counter Terrorist Unit," Jack said impatiently. Of course, CTU was a relatively clandestine unit. There was no reason for every beat cop in Los Angeles to recognize its name instantly. He recited an emergency number. "Call that number. They'll clear me."

The cop sounded accommodating. "Okay, look, I'll do it, but I don't want you to get your hopes up. The city's pretty much gone to hell, and it may take a little while."

"I don't have a little while," Jack said.

"You may not have a choice." The metal door slid shut.

Jack Bauer fumed. He had no time to wait. For all he knew his daughter was dying, and he was sure Ayman al-Libbi was about to attack the G8. For the first time, he looked down the bench at the other rioters who'd been captured. There were four of them . . . including the man in the blue shirt, sitting on the bench opposite him and near the door. Jack looked at the person next to him, not more than a teenager. "Move," he said, sliding past him so that he was near the door and across from his target. He stared at the man without asking a question. He would ask questions eventually, but only when he knew he would get answers.

The kid who had just moved looked at Bauer. "Did you say you were a cop?"

Jack didn't answer, but the kid laughed. "You're a cop? I love it. How does it feel to get beat up by the other fascists?"

Jack sized him up: Von Dutch T-shirt, tanned skin, with that California drawl drawn out by money and time. This was the kind of person for whom everything had come easily. He hadn't even lived long enough to know what hardship was, hadn't lived long enough to know that the people he called "fascists" were usually the ones who put their lives at risk so he could have an easy life.

"I guess you're in here for no reason?" Jack asked.

The kid clearly wanted to tell his story. "Look at this bump on my forehead, man. Three cops jumped on me."

"What were you doing right before that?" Jack said.

"I threw a rock at them, but that was only—"

Jack said, "Those cops, they spend their lives putting themselves in harm's way so you can sleep at night. Most of them don't ask for any thanks or praise from you at all. Think of that next time you pick up a goddamned rock."

2:33 P.M. PST
UCLA Medical Center

"I simply won't do it," the doctor said for the third time.

Tony Almeida ran a hand through his black hair. He looked at the doctor's name tag. "Look, Dr. Gupta, this is a matter of national security. This man has information that could save lives."

"I have an ethical responsibility," Dr. Gupta said. He was young, not yet out of his twenties, with a lean, thoughtful face, dark eyes, and a stiff spine. "If I give him drugs to bring him out of the coma, it could kill him."

"As long as he wakes up first."

The doctor frowned at him, and turned to look for help from the group assembled behind him. There was quite a collection: a nurse holding a tray that contained a syringe full of some medication; the hospital's chief of internal medicine; two lawyers; and two uniformed officers who'd come in just to see the show.

None of them offered Gupta any assistance, so the doctor turned back. "Agent Almeida," the doctor said reproachfully. "I am not an executioner."

"I'm not, either," Tony said. "In fact, the only executioner around here is him." He pointed at Dyson. "I'm telling you I saw his fingers move. I don't think he's in a coma anymore, and even if—"

"You're hardly qualified to—"

"—and even if he is," Tony repeated, "the risk of killing him is nothing compared to what he knows. I believe this man has knowledge of a terrorist plot that could happen any time in the next twenty-four hours, and I need to know what it is."

The doctor hesitated. "I've taken an oath to do no harm."

Tony sighed. "I haven't."

He reached past Gupta to the nurse and snatched the syringe off her tray. Before anyone could react, he popped the protective cap off the needle and plunged it into Dyson's chest. The nurse gasped and Gupta cried out in alarm. He grabbed at Tony but the agent shrugged him off easily and removed the syringe. He watched the vitals monitor for a moment, the heart rate meter chirping steady and slow. After a moment the beeps came a bit faster, and then faster still. Dyson moaned. The lawyers sighed.

Tony leaned over the bed. "Dyson. Dyson, wake up."

The FBI agent's eyes fluttered. Tony slapped him lightly. "I said wake up."

Dyson's eyes opened. Dr. Gupta pushed past Tony and pulled out his penlight, shining it in Dyson's eyes. "Pupil reaction," he muttered. He checked the vitals. "Stable so far."

"Dyson, who are you working for!" Tony said, moving Gupta forcefully. "Who are you working for?"

Dyson blinked once or twice. His watery eyes focused on Tony for a moment, then glazed over. A slight smile turned the edges of his mouth. A thin laugh rattled past his lips. "Monkeys . . . monkey gang . . . bitten by monkeys . . ."

His lips kept moving, but the words melted into incomprehensible dribble.

"Dyson!" Tony said, shaking the agent.

The heart rate monitor picked up its pace, sounding suddenly urgent. At the same time, his blood-oxygen levels started to drop. A second later, Dyson's heart rate went from frantic to nonexistent.

2:35 P.M. PST
Mountaingate Drive, Los Angeles

Nina Myers rolled up Mountaingate Drive to an exclusive tract in the Santa Monica Mountains that overlooked the Sepulveda Pass and the 405 Freeway to the east, and the entire Los Angeles basin to the south. The owners paid for the view, so every house had one, but one property in particular occupied the sweet spot. On the south side of the ridge stood an enormous white house with a panoramic view not only of the L.A. basin, but of Santa Monica Bay as well.

Or at least it would have, if not for the Vanderbilt Complex. The Vanderbilt Complex, or just the Vanderbilt to locals, was a vast, impressive castle built into the hillside. Although constructed lower on the slope than the houses of Mountaingate Drive, the Vanderbilt was big enough to mar the view from the large white house above it. Mountaingate residents had complained, but as wealthy as they were, they were peons compared to the Vanderbilt estate, which had both money and public sentiment on its side. The Vanderbilt was a museum complex built around the private collection of a few Vanderbilt heirs. The museum was free to the public, dedicated to advancing the cause of the arts among all people, and a political juggernaut. The estate bought the property and forced the approvals through the city bureaucracy. Environmentalists had decried the development because the Sepulveda Pass was one of the few green spots left in Los Angeles . . . but everyone, from the environmentalists to the residents of Mountaingate, had to admit that the finished structure was impressive. Perched on a shoulder of the mountains, it commanded a lordly view of the Los Angeles basin. The *L.A. Weekly,* the local cutting-edge weekly magazine, had featured a cover photo of the magnificent Vanderbilt with the headline "Acropolis Now!" Thousands of tons of travertine had been imported from Italy to cover its walls and form its plazas. A private road led up to the museum, but most visitors rode an automated tram that wound up the mountainside to the wide, flat steps. The Vanderbilt housed classic paintings, an impressive photography collection, and a rare books display that included an original Gutenberg Bible and one of the original thirteen copies of the Bill of Rights.

As she gazed down on the Vanderbilt from the mountaintop, Nina decided that the museum was an excellent location from a security point of view. The single road leading up to the complex was easily controllable; the steep slopes were inaccessible by vehicle and offered little or no cover to a team on foot. The wide open skies above allowed easily for exfil of the VIPs by helicopter if the need arose. Because of its isolated location on the hilltop and the security measures that had already been put in place to protect its priceless treasures, the Vanderbilt was a desirable location for dignitaries seeking a secure but elegant meeting ground. The only variable keeping the Vanderbilt from becoming a perfectly controllable site was, in fact, the house at the end of Mountaingate Drive.

Nina parked a few blocks down from the house—a tall, white, antebellum mansion with a circular driveway. The house even had one of those little statues of a jockey in a red coat, holding out one hand, to which was attached a metal ring. Nina walked past it and knocked on the door. No sound came from inside, but an intercom next to the door came to life and a static-laden voice came through. "Yes?"

"Hello, I'm looking for Mr. Marcus Lee, please," Nina said in her nicest, most professional voice.

"Who is asking, please?" the intercom replied, and Nina knew intuitively that she was speaking to Mr. Lee.

"My name is Nina Myers, sir. I'm with the Federal government. I just have a few questions to ask."

The intercom clicked off and Nina felt her muscles tense. Was he going to rabbit? She liked action, and part of her relished the idea. But a moment later the door opened and a small Asian man of indeterminate age smiled at her warmly. "I am Marcus Lee," he said gently. "Please come in."

2:41 P.M. PST
Federal Building, West Los Angeles

Jack pulled at the flex cuffs on his wrists, more out of frustration than anything. They bit into his skin, reminding him that they were practically unbreakable unless they were severed with wire cutters. He didn't mind the pain—it helped him focus. He stared across the short space to his quarry, the young man in the blue shirt. The young man returned his stare bravely, but his look of anger and defiance soon wilted under Jack's glare.

Something bumped up against the outside of the police wagon.

"What's that?" one of the other prisoners asked.

"Someone getting beat up," said the blond kid next to Jack.

But the next sound they heard was the anxious voice of the police driver in the cab in front of them. "Get them the hell off!" he yelled, his voice pitched anxiously high. They heard several shouts from outside, then silence.

"Have you made that call yet?" Jack yelled toward the cab, but there was no answer.

2:43 P.M. PST
Mountaingate Drive, Los Angeles

Nina walked into Marcus Lee's living room and blinked in the bright sunlight. The entire back wall of the living room was made of several sets of French doors nearly two stories tall, opening out onto a wide green lawn that dropped away where the property met the slope of the hill. Beyond the grass, Nina could see the roofs of the Vanderbilt Complex, and beyond that, the glistening blue water of Santa Monica Bay. To the left, she saw white and dark smoke rise up around the Federal Building, and she heard sirens wail plaintively far away.

"What can I do for you, Agent Myers?" Marcus Lee asked.

He was polite and welcoming, which immediately put Nina on edge. Most people were at least a little nervous when they saw a Federal badge, but Lee had scanned her ID as casually as a man reading the morning headlines. He had turned and led her gracefully into the house, offering her a drink, which she declined, and then escorted her to the living room.

Nina decided to ambush him immediately. "I'd like to talk to you about your involvement with ETIM."

She watched his face closely. His eyes brightened, but otherwise he gave no reaction at all. "I'm not sure what you mean."

"Yes, you do, Mr. Tuman."

Half a beat. "Excuse me?"

"Your real name is Nurmamet Tuman," Nina said, glancing at a notepad in her hand and using the same casual tone he had used to greet her. "You told the INS that you were ethnic Chinese, but you are in fact a Uygur from the eastern province of Xinjiang." She looked up. "You're also most likely involved with ETIM."

Another half beat, but no change in his facial expression. Marcus Lee/Nurmamet Tuman was a very good poker player. "My real name is Marcus Lee," he said. "And I don't know what 'ee-tim' is."

"You knew them well enough to give them two million dollars. Did you also put them in touch with Ayman al-Libbi, or did they already have their own contact?"

Bull's-eye. Lee tensed, and Nina readied herself to go for her weapon. But instead of running or attacking, Lee put a hand to his temple and rubbed it as though she'd just given him a severe headache. "Agent Myers, I can neither confirm nor deny what you are saying. But I can tell you this. I am very well connected in the Chinese government, even to this day. I recommend that you contact a Mr. Richard Hong, who operates out of the Chinese Embassy here in Los Angeles. He may have information that will help you."

Nina felt her stomach tighten into a knot. She did not know Richard Hong, but unless she missed her guess entirely, Marcus Lee had just referred her to his case officer in Chinese intelligence, which also meant that Lee was Chinese intelligence, which meant that with a few simple words Lee had made this whole affair much, much more complicated.

"In fact, I have his card right here." Lee reached carefully into his pocket and pulled out a simple business card. He handed it to Nina with two hands in traditional Chinese fashion, and bowed slightly.

Nina read the card. "Stay here." She walked into the hallway, keeping Lee in her line of sight, and pulled out her cell phone. She called CTU and asked for Jamey Farrell.

"Jamey, Nina. Can you do a quick check and patch me through to a Richard Hong at the Chinese Embassy. If they give you the runaround, tell them I'm calling about one of his assets."

Nina waited on hold for only a minute or two, watching Marcus Lee, who had settled himself gently onto a plush white couch.

"Nina," Jamey's voice came on the line, "they tried to pass me off, but the minute I mentioned an asset, Hong was right there. Here you go."

The line clicked. "Mr. Richard Hong?"

"Speaking. Who is this?"

Nina explained who she was, and why she was there. Richard Hong paused. "I think this is a discussion best had in person." Meaning, Nina knew, no cell phones. "Can you come to me?"

"Not if Tuman is going out the back door at the same time," Nina said.

"He is no flight risk. I can promise that."

Nina considered her options. If she were concerned about protocol, she would heed the warnings and walk away. But she was more inclined to take Lee in, regardless of whatever Chappelle had said about using kid gloves. The Chinese could always come get him out of interrogation if he was that important. She was just about to tell Richard Hong that when Marcus Lee's doorbell rang. Lee stood and moved past Nina, opening his hand to the door and asking permission with his eyes. Nina nodded and followed him.

"Thank you for your advice, Mr. Hong, but I think it's important that we have a discussion with Mr. Lee. I—stand by." She stopped as Marcus Lee opened his door. Three men in dark suits and sunglasses walked in as soon as the door was open, as though they knew they'd been expected. In fact, it was Nina's presence that seemed to alert them most.

"Mr. Lee," said one of the suits. He took off his sunglasses and held out a badge, but his eyes were already on Nina. "Clay Lonis, Treasury Department. Who's this?"

Marcus Lee sidestepped and opened his arms as though trying to join Nina and the newcomer. "Mr. Lonis, this is Agent Myers."

Nina's jaw dropped. Treasury Department. Why was the Secret Service visiting Marcus Lee?

2:46 P.M. PST
Federal Building, West Los Angeles

Jack heard—and felt—another loud thump against the outside of the police wagon. This time the vehicle rocked back and forth, as though giant hands had grabbed it and shaken it back and forth. There were more cries from outside, but these were not cries of alarm. A rhythmic chanting had begun, and the wagon was rocking in sync with it. *Oh shit,* Jack thought.

2:48 P.M. PST
Mountaingate Drive, Los Angeles

Nina held out her own identification, and Clay Lonis frowned as he slipped his sunglasses back on. "A word?" he said, motioning to the door.

Nina nodded and followed him outside, first making sure that the other two Secret Service agents were staying with Lee. Nina stepped outside onto the shaded porch, stopping near the railing that overlooked Lee's circular driveway. The property was beautiful and neatly landscaped, but the tension in the air told Nina that it had just become a very complicated maze.

Clay Lonis had been cut right out of the Secret Service training manual: a little over six feet, sandy brown hair trimmed short, mandatory cleft in his chin. He kept his sunglasses on, which Nina found annoying.

"Agent Myers, may I ask your business here?"

"What does the Secret Service want?"

"You first," Lonis said with a thin smile.

Nina frowned. She wasn't sure there was any interdepartmental rivalry here. She just didn't like other people prying into her business. "I'm doing my job. Is Tuman considered some sort of security risk?"

Despite the sunglasses, Nina saw a reaction from the Secret Service agent. "You mean Lee."

Nina shrugged. "That's one name for him." She thought out loud. "But it doesn't make sense for him to be a security risk. If he really were, you guys would have rounded him up already. What's going on?"

Lonis considered her from behind his shades. "Nothing too dramatic. But it's on a need-to-know basis."

"Well, I need to know."

"Maybe you could at least tell me the broad strokes about your investigation. You guys are counterterrorist. That makes me nervous, considering my job."

Nina decided she had to give a little to get a little. "We have questions about an alias of his, and about transfer of money from Lee to a terrorist organization."

Now Lonis frowned. "That's disturbing. But it doesn't sound right. We've already done extensive background on Mr. Lee with the Chinese government. He's not considered a security risk, that much I can tell you."

Something was askew here. Nina wasn't convinced, but

one thing was clear: there was no way she could drag Marcus Lee into an interrogation room with the Chinese government and the U.S. Secret Service both screaming at her. She dropped immediately to her bottom line. "Are you guys going to be here for a while? I'm not looking for intel!" she added when Lonis started to object. "I just want to know that Lee isn't going anywhere. I have some people I need to talk to."

The Secret Service agent nodded. "Lee's not going anywhere. That I promise."

The CTU agent slid away from him and put her phone back to her ear. Richard Hong had already severed the connection, of course, so she called CTU again and had them patch her through. "I'm coming to meet you," she said tersely. "I am going to need some explanations."

"Always happy to assist," Richard Hong said politely. The line went dead again.

2:55 P.M. PST
Federal Building, West Los Angeles

The police wagon rocked so hard, the prisoners were thrown from one side of the wagon to the other. Jack Bauer braced his feet against the far side of the hold. The vehicle tipped again, so much that Jack was nearly standing upright. Then it lurched back the other direction until Jack was almost up on his shoulders.

"What are they doing to us?" the blond kid shrieked.

"Breaking us out," Jack replied. The van had been rocking sporadically for several minutes, the brief interruptions accompanied by screams and cries of alarm. Jack assumed that the police were trying to retake control of the area, but there were too many rioters covering too much territory. Either the same group of rioters retreated and returned, or new groups of rioters flooded in as soon as the last group had been driven off. Once Jack heard someone enter the cab and try to start up the vehicle, but the engine wouldn't turn over.

The rocking had been going on without interruption now for several minutes, and Jack guessed that the police had given up. Perhaps they didn't know there were detainees in the wagon; perhaps they didn't care. Either way, they'd ceded the ground to the rioters.

The wagon went up on its side again, axles groaning, and this time it hung there for a moment as if it had all the time in the world to decide. Outside, the mob hooted and cheered, but their cheers turned to disappointment when the wagon fell back to all four tires. The chanting and the rocking started again.

"They're going to kill us!" the blond kid whined.

"Brace yourself," Jack instructed. "If it goes over upside down for you, keep your chin tucked."

The chanting started again, and the van rocked and groaned. Jack planted his feet firmly on the far wall. "Get ready."

Up went the van again, the frame trembling as it teetered on the very edge of the driver side tires. Jack was ready, hoping it would tip this way and put him on his feet. But the van fell back. Immediately it tilted to the passenger side. Jack felt his world turn upside down. He was on his shoulders with his neck pressed against the metal side wall. The wagon paused, then fell flat on its side. Jack felt the impact travel through his neck like an electric shock. Outside, the crowd cheered.

1 2 3 4 5 6 7 8 **9**
10 11 12 13 14 15 16 17
18 19 20 21 22 23 24

••

THE FOLLOWING TAKES PLACE
BETWEEN THE HOURS OF
3 P.M. AND 4 P.M.
PACIFIC STANDARD TIME

••

3:00 P.M. PST
Federal Building Command Center,
West Los Angeles

Kim Bauer had been sitting on a cot in the basement of the building for almost two hours. She was in some sort of mini-hospital, with several cots set up to treat sick people, those poles on wheels with the hooks at the top for IV bags, and other machines.

They had kept the metal door to the hospital room closed, but now and then someone would come inside, sometimes to check on her, sometimes to get supplies from a cabinet. Every time she asked if she could leave, the man or woman would give her a quick "No" and rush out.

As time passed Kim's demands had become more urgent,

but the replies were even more insistent. During the short intervals when the door had been opened, she saw Federal employees, some in police uniforms and some in suits, hurrying back and forth.

But at that moment, two uniformed security guards carried in a third officer whose head was heavily bandaged. Blood still trickled out from under the bandage and onto his forehead and cheek. The other two laid him down on one of the empty cots. A doctor—the same woman who had taken Kim's blood—followed close behind to treat him.

"Excuse me, I have to go!" Kim said to one of the security officers. He looked at her, his beefy face sweaty under his round cap.

"Trust me, you don't want to go anywhere right now," he said. "There's a little trouble outside."

"Then let me call my mom," Kim said. "She's got to be freaking."

"You have a cell phone?"

"The battery died."

The cop looked harried. "Come here." He led her out into the main control room, which was bustling with activity. "Here." The man handed her a land line and then hurried off.

Kim dialed her home number quickly. Her mother picked up on the first ring.

"Mom, it's me, don't freak—"

"Kim! Thank god! Where the hell are you! You know there's a riot—"

"I'm safe, Mom. Dad got me into the building before it all started."

"He should never have let you go down there in the first place." She sounded stressed out, and Kim knew that she'd been worrying all this time. She was sure that, once her phone was charged, she'd find a dozen frantic messages.

"There was no way he knew this was going to happen, Mom. You're too hard on him."

"They all knew, Kim!" her mother snapped. "Your father always knows more than he tells, trust me. Let me talk to him."

"He's not here. He . . . went out."

Her mom said something she would have gotten in trouble for saying. "I'm coming to get you."

"I don't think you can, Mom. I think there's a lot going on outside." She looked at the wounded security officer. "I'm okay in here. You should probably wait until it calms down." She told her mother that her phone was dead and promised to call her again in thirty minutes. She hung up the phone and rubbed her arm where the doctor had drawn blood.

3:10 P.M. PST
National Health Services Laboratory, Los Angeles

Celia Alexis rubbed her eyes before looking into the microscope. It had been a long day, and news of the riots at the Federal Building had not helped her concentration. She knew Jean could take care of himself, but she also knew that if he saw people in trouble, he would ignore any danger to help them. She'd seen that back in Haiti when they were kids, and she'd seen him act recklessly as an adult. He always laughed and told her that an L.A. Sheriff's deputy was *supposed* to run toward trouble, but she knew, she *knew* that he was always looking for ways to prove he was as good as or better than everyone else. It was an immigrant's attitude he had never outgrown.

Of course, she was self-aware enough to know that she suffered from a similar disease herself. First in her undergrad class at Stanford, top of her medical school class at UCLA. She didn't have to be first, but anything less felt like failure. She had left her barefoot childhood back in Haiti, but somehow she'd managed to bring the burden of Haiti itself with her, like that hint of accent she could never seem to silence. Her friends liked it; the men in her life loved its singsong quality, but to Celia the slow roundness of her vowels evoked no images of Calypso and sun-drenched beaches, but only the dirty streets and poverty of Port-au-Prince.

Celia pressed her eyes to the microscope and studied the slide. Someone had marked this urgent—a blood sample from a teenage girl. The researcher blinked, rubbed her eyes again, and adjusted herself at the scope. But when she looked at the blood sample, the image hadn't changed.

"Ken?" she called, sitting back. There was another researcher, Ken Diebold, working at the other end of the lab counter. Like her, he was wearing a sterile suit and mask. Researchers in the laboratory wore them as a matter of habit, although Celia felt with sudden dread that in this case, the sterile environment might be necessary. "Can you come look at this?"

Diebold was decent enough, but he suffered from a deep appreciation of his own sense of humor. "What's this? The Caribbean Queen asking for help?" he said dryly.

"Just look," she insisted.

Ken walked over and, without sitting down, looked into the scope. He straightened and looked at Celia, then sat down as she moved out of the way, and looked again. "Where did this come from?" he said at last.

"CTU Los Angeles just brought it in," Celia replied.

"CTU Los Angeles?" Ken said in shock, his voice rising an octave. "This patient is inside the United States?"

Celia nodded.

"You know what this is?" he said.

Celia nodded again. "It's a filovirus. It looks like it's related to Ebola—"

"—or Marburg," the other doctor said.

"But it's not Marburg," Celia pointed out. "The shepherd's crook shape isn't the same."

"Is the patient isolated? When did exposure happen?"

"We'd better find out," Celia said, "before half of Los Angeles dies from hemorrhagic fever."

3:14 P.M. PST
Federal Building, West Los Angeles

The door of the overturned police wagon flew open. Hands reached in and pulled the prisoners out one at a time. Jack, who had positioned himself near the door, was one of the first. There was a small mob around the fallen van, cheering as each one of the prisoners was helped out. Beyond the mob, the street was empty for nearly a block, but farther down Jack saw a line of rioters pushing against a line of policemen with shields and batons. The rioters had abandoned all reason, and were ignoring the blows of batons.

"We managed to get through," one of the protestors said to Jack, like one soldier briefing another. "Those bastards did a good job holding us back, especially with those goddamned horses. But we got to you. Here." The man, who spoke with a slight Spanish accent, held up a pair of wire cutters. He stepped behind Jack and severed the flex cuffs.

"Hey!" yelled a rioter, bending down to look into the wagon. "One of these guys is hurt. His leg looks really bad." Jack glanced down. It was the man in the blue shirt. He screamed as they pulled him out of the wagon. His left leg was broken at the shin, snapped at such an acute angle that his leg appeared to have a second knee.

"Look what we found!" someone yelled from the front

end of the vehicle. Jack leaned around the corner to see three rioters pulling a half-conscious policeman from the cab. Jack recognized him as the same cop who said he'd try to call CTU. His face was covered in blood from a cut on his forehead and his eyes weren't focused. He was as limp as a rag doll and no threat to anyone. But he was wearing a police uniform, and in the rioters' maddened state, that's all it took. One of them stomped on his head.

Jack snatched the wire cutters from his rescuer's hand and shoved him out of the way. He reached the injured cop before the three rioters and, as another one raised his foot to stomp down, Jack kicked his base leg. The rioter screamed and toppled over. The other two looked at him in surprise. Jack punched one of them in the stomach with the hand holding the wire cutters. The beak of the cutters jabbed into the man's stomach and he crumpled to the floor. The third one grabbed Jack by the shirt, so Jack head-butted him in the nose and shoved him backward.

"What the hell are you doing!" shouted the man who'd brought the wire cutters.

"He's not one of us!" It was the blond kid, who'd just been pulled out of the van. "He's a cop!"

But by now Jack was a cop with a gun, having taken the policeman's sidearm. He held the 9mm Beretta level and steady at the center mass of the man who had held the wire cutters. "You're done here. All except for him." He nodded at the man in the blue shirt, who was lying on the ground. "Everyone else go. Now."

The man under Jack's gun said, "Bullshit. You don't get to—"

Jack squeezed the trigger and put a round past the man's ear. Everyone cringed away from the sound of the gunshot. Only Jack held steady. "Now."

The crowd scattered. Jack watched them until they were

too far away to pose any sort of threat. Hastily he knelt down beside the cop, who managed to focus on Jack. "You okay?" Jack said.

"H-hell, no," the cop said. "Thanks. You . . . saved . . ."

"Later," Jack said. "Looks like they forgot about you and me." He looked over toward the Federal Building, but there were no cops in sight. Everyone was either inside the building or out chasing rioters. He snatched the radio off the man's collar. "Dispatch, this is—" He looked around for the man's name, but his riot gear was blank.

"Agastonetti," the man said weakly.

"This is Officer Agastonetti," Jack said. "Officer down at Federal and Wilshire. Just outside the Federal Building. Officer down." He cut off as someone squawked back. The less detail they got, the faster they'd respond.

Jack wanted assistance, but he didn't want it just yet. He jumped back over to the blue-shirted man and crouched down beside him. The man was shuddering and sobbing from pain. There was blood on his pant leg, so Jack knew without looking underneath that the fracture was compound. His shin had snapped when the police van turned over.

Jack grabbed his face in one hand and turned his chin until their eyes met. "Your name."

The man sobbed again, but said, "Kasim Turkel."

"Kasim, you're going into shock," Jack said calmly. "Your leg is shattered and you're hemorrhaging all over the place. You're going to die, unless I get you help right now. Do you want to die?"

Kasim shook his head.

Jack sat down and sighed. "Personally, I don't care one way or the other. You can live or die, it's all the same to me." Kasim looked up at him in fear. Jack continued. "So if you want me to care, one way or the other, that is, it's going to be very important how you answer the next few questions. Do you understand?"

Kasim nodded.

Jack replied with a look of satisfaction. He tapped the barrel of the Beretta directly onto Kasim's broken leg. Kasim screamed. "Good. Let's start."

3:18 P.M. PST
National Health Services Laboratory, Los Angeles

Celia stood up as Eli Hollingsworth, the Director of NHS, walked in. He was wearing a sterile suit that had been hastily pulled over his business attire. "Show me," he said tersely.

Celia stepped out of the way and let him examine the blood sample. By the time he straightened, his face was grim and looked far older than his forty-seven years. "The data you've collected on this sample matches information we just received from Brasília. Local authorities down there in the province of Minas Gerais found a local in his hut. His body looked like it had been torn apart, but it turns out the skin ruptures weren't caused by assault. The skin had broken open due to hemorrhagic fever of a kind not previously recorded."

"Most hemorrhagic fevers originate in Africa," Celia pointed out.

"Not this one," Hollingsworth guessed. "At least, not according to current evidence. This is the only case so far. It happened in a populated area with no sterility and high probability of transference from one host to another. No one would have brought the disease down there, there's no reason to. So we have to assume that it originated there."

"But now it's here," Celia said. "Do we have more information on the patient here? Were they in Brazil?"

"CTU hasn't released it yet, for security reasons. All we

know so far is that exposure probably took place this morning around nine o'clock," Hollingsworth replied. "One more thing. There is one difference between this virus and the one in Minas Gerais. This one seems to replicate more slowly. I'd guess the local patient won't become seriously compromised until about twenty hours or more after exposure. The strain from Brazil killed its victim in less than twelve."

"So we're dealing with two strains," Celia said. "And we have no vaccine for either of them."

3:23 P.M. PST
Federal Building, West Los Angeles

Kasim Turkel screamed again, but his cries sounded thin and empty on the deserted street. The blond man was barely touching him, but he kept tapping the barrel of his weapon right on the jagged spot where his leg bent at an unreal angle.

"You are part of the Eastern Turkistan Independence Movement?"

"Yes."

"And you hired Ayman al-Libbi to come to this country and attack the G8 summit?"

No answer. Tap, tap went the muzzle.

"Yes, yes!" Kasim shrieked.

"What is he planning?"

"I don't know."

Tap, tap, tap.

"I don't know! I don't know!" he screamed in Uygur, then in English.

"He needed help once he got here," Jack said. "Where did he go? Who did he meet with?"

"I don't—"

Tap.

"Aghh!" Kasim sobbed. "I . . . I never met him before. We took him, but we waited outside. I don't know what he wanted."

"Names," Jack said threateningly.

"F-Farrigian."

Tamar Farrigian. Jack knew him. He was a fence and trafficker who usually played in the shallow end of the pool. He was a sometime informant for CTU and kept out of trouble enough to continue in that useful role. But if he was selling arms to major players like al-Libbi, his time had come.

"What did he buy?"

"Bombs. Or rockets. Something explosive. I didn't see what."

"When was he planning his attack?" Jack asked. "Where?"

There was no answer. He tapped Kasim's leg, but the man only screamed and sobbed in his native language. Jack didn't press further—it would have surprised him if al-Libbi had shared his plans with his employers.

"What about the virus?" he asked, thinking of Kim.

"Wh-what?" Kasim replied. There was genuine confusion in his voice.

"The virus!" Jack said, poking harder at the leg.

"I don't know, I don't know what that is!" Kasim insisted, once he'd stopped crying. "What virus?"

Jack believed him.

3:29 P.M. PST
Consulate General of the People's
Republic of China, Los Angeles

The Chinese Consulate was downtown, near Vermont and Wilshire and a stone's throw from Lafayette Park. A run at breakneck speed along the cliffs of Mulholland Drive to avoid the riot area, a race down the curves of Laurel Canyon, and then a hard left turn along Third Street with little regard for red lights and less for anyone else's right of way, all helped Nina Myers reach the building in under thirty minutes.

She was expected. The demure young woman in the gray dress suit took a cursory look at her credentials, then spoke softly into her tiny headset in Chinese before rising and escorting Nina to a side room with a short, wide table surrounded by thick leather chairs. Her shoes made almost no sound when she walked.

"Water?" was all she said. When Nina declined, she gave a short bow and vanished.

Richard Hong entered a moment later, as boisterous as the girl had been timid.

"Ms. Myers, how are you?" he said in a very American accent, shaking her hand vigorously and dropping down on the couch opposite her and crossing his legs. The table, made more for coffee than for meetings, came only to his raised foot, and he tapped it gently and thoughtlessly. "What can I do for you?"

Nina knew this game, and she didn't want to play it. She cut through the layers of diplomacy, if for no other reason than she knew it was not the Chinese way. "You can tell me why the Chinese government never told us that Marcus Lee was really Nurmamet Tuman, and why he is giving money to ETIM."

Nina couldn't have caught Hong more off guard if she'd jumped up on the table and slapped him in the face. The Chinese official straightened, and as he did, the diplomatic facade melted off his face. His black eyes gleamed. He looked at her, then quickly to the door, and then back, and in that moment Nina knew three things: the room was bugged; her accusations were serious enough that Hong thought men might burst into the room; and someone higher up than Hong had decided to let this all play out.

Hong tried to recover by reciting a memorized line. "There is no ETIM."

Nina started to protest, but Hong waved her off, recovering some of his former gallantry. "Oh, of course there are a few malcontents," he said. "But to call them a real organization would be like calling the Clippers a real basketball team, eh? Factual in the strictest sense, but meaningless in the practical world."

"Well, they are real enough to receive two million dollars. And Tuman is real enough to give it to them. He's also apparently clever enough to change his dossier so that no one noticed that he changed his name, or that he grew up in the heart of the East Turkistan resistance in Urumchi."

Hong glared at her in a decidedly undiplomatic way. She wasn't intimidated. Very few things intimidated her, and none of them were in this room.

There was a muted beep. Hong said, "Excuse me," and deftly plucked a mobile phone from his pocket. He opened it and listened, muttered something in Chinese, and pocketed the phone again.

"Ms. Myers, here is what I can tell you: Mr. Marcus Lee, or, as you call him, Nurmamet Tuman, is no threat to you, or to the United States in any way. Between you and me he is a former officer with the People's Army, and if you cannot guess more than that, then you are not the kind of person I think you are." By which Hong meant, *He was a spy and you are probably a spy, too, so you figure it out.* "His name was changed to protect his privacy, but I give you the solemn word of the People's Republic that he is retired." Hong placed heavy emphasis on that word *retired*.

"His name is Uygur," said Nina, silently thanking Jamey

Farrell and the other analysts at CTU for the geography lesson she'd received during the drive over. "Before he was retired, did he work in the Xianjing-Uygur Autonomous Region? Did he infiltrate ETIM?"

Richard Hong stood up and smiled warmly, as though Nina had said goodbye instead of asking a prying question. "It was great to meet you," he said in his casual American way. "I hope to see you around again." He bent down and shook her hand, stubbornly ignoring the fact that she had not yet stood up. "Have a great day." Then he was out the door, leaving Nina alone in the room.

3:40 P.M. PST
Federal Building, West Los Angeles

Jack had given up the interrogation when Kasim Turkel passed out. He knew he'd gotten everything he was going to get when Turkel gave up the name of Tamar Farrigian. He'd hoped to find out something about the virus, but he wasn't surprised that Turkel was ignorant of that. Ayman al-Libbi was notorious for playing close to the vest, and had angered his patrons more than once by withholding information from them.

A roar like falling water rolled down Wilshire Boulevard. Jack looked eastward and saw the police line break, cops stumbling backward as rioters broke through, pouring down the street like a reservoir suddenly rushing down a dry riverbed. Idiots, Jack thought. All they would do was bring out the cavalry and rubber bullets again. And for what?

Jack left Turkel on the street, intending to have the FBI or other CTU agents pick him up later. With his leg broken like that, he wasn't going anywhere. But the injured cop was another story. Jack went back to him.

"Can you walk?" he asked.

The cop shook his head. "Only if you can make the street stop wobbling."

"Come on." Jack helped him up and pulled the man's arm around his shoulder. Together they hobbled back down the road to the Federal Building, through the line of waist-high stone pillars, across the grass, and up to the glass doors. Uniformed officers on the inside opened the doors for them and pulled them inside. There was a short-haired woman with them. She held her hand out to Jack Bauer.

"Agent Bauer, Cynthia Rosen." Jack remembered her name from the telephone.

"Thanks for your help. Is there a car I can borrow? I have to get back to CTU. It's urgent."

Rosen was nonplussed. "Well, yes. But your daughter—"

Kim. Jack felt a tug at his heart, the primal urge a father feels to protect his daughter. Manufacturing the ruse that had brought her into police custody had been hard enough. Now that the immediate danger had passed, he wanted nothing more than to wrap her up in his protective arms. But he did not doubt for a second that she had indeed been exposed to a deadly virus. According to his captor, she had hours before she was in danger or even contagious. That meant the very best way to protect her was to find the people who had put her in harm's way, make them cure her, and then make them pay.

"Can you have someone escort her home, Agent Rosen?" he asked. "I've got to go. It's urgent. Now please take me to a car."

3:47 P.M. PST
Mountaingate Drive, Los Angeles

The white truck with "Sanchez Landscaping" on the side rolled to a stop at the foot of the circular driveway, where a

Secret Service agent stopped him. The Secret Service agent was dressed in jeans and a T-shirt, but his short-cropped hair, angular build, and air of authority gave him away. Of course, al-Libbi would have known he was an agent even without these clues. He had been warned that the Secret Service might occupy the house.

"Can I help you?" the young man said.

"I guess," al-Libbi said, affecting a Mexican accent nearly identical to that of the gardener he had murdered. With only a day's growth of scruffy beard, dark skin, and the accent, he could pass for Latino. He'd done it many times to cross the border into the United States, even being stopped twice and deported, once to El Salvador and once to Guatemala. "I'm the gardener here. Is there something—?"

The Secret Service man nodded as though he'd been expecting the gardener, which was indeed the case. He stepped away from the truck, turned, and muttered something into a microphone at his wrist. A moment later the front door opened and Nurmamet Tuman (whom he must call Marcus Lee) appeared, followed by another Secret Service agent in a suit.

"Is everything okay, Mr. Lee?" al-Libbi asked in his most worried voice. "I have a green card."

Tuman nodded at him. "Yes, that's him, of course it is," he said to the Secret Service agents.

The one in the suit nodded. "Okay, let him through."

Ayman al-Libbi rewarded them with his best nervous smile and eased the truck forward.

3:49 P.M. PST
Santa Monica, California

His real name was Dr. Bernard Copeland, and until a short time ago he had planned to save the world.

He stumbled into his fashionable house on Fourteenth Street north of Montana in Santa Monica, closed the door, and fell onto the floor, exhausted. He tugged a small wrapper out of his pocket, unrolled it to reveal a wad of maracuja leaves. He popped two into his mouth and sighed in relief.

Copeland had known for more than two decades that the world was spinning out of control. He'd seen the human species work overtime to destroy its own environment when he worked as a graduate biology student in the Amazon. He'd joined the EPA soon after getting his Ph.D., devoting his energies to the government's own fight to save the human habitat. But seven years at the Environmental Protection Agency had taught him the true definition of doublespeak, for he found himself under pressure not to fight off developers but to justify alliances with them. The government rationalized its permissive attitude toward industries that poisoned rivers, spewed greenhouse gases into the atmosphere, and turned acres of vibrant forestland into grazing ground for cattle. Disgusted, he had quit. To hide himself, he'd gone to work for the enemy, sold himself to a research firm studying the medicinal properties of fauna in the Amazon. It gave him an excuse to go back to the land he loved, and it gave him cover. The firm he worked for was pro-industry, and he carried its banner in public loudly and often.

In private, he began to develop relationships inside the real environmental movement. At first he met quietly with members of Greenpeace and the Sierra Club, but he knew immediately that they were too tame for his needs. He had worked inside the machinery of government, and he knew that it would grind itself slowly, inexorably, into oblivion. Stopping it would require much more radical means than they were willing to take. But, slowly, his associations in the Sierra Club brought him in contact with more radical sects, until eventually he was having coffee with Earth Firsters and taking hikes with the Earth Liberation Front. Foresighted, he had kept his name to himself, using a nickname from the eco-terrorist's favorite read, *The Monkey Wrench Gang*. "Seldom Seen Smith" received a derisive laugh more than once, but preserved his anonymity.

Copeland was no utopian. He did not expect the world to revert to some antediluvian paradise. He was neither a vegan nor an animal rescuer. He was a scientist. He had studied the data and reached the inevitable conclusion: mankind could not continue to destroy the Earth without consequences. Someone needed to stop human beings from continuing on their destructive path, and for better or worse, Bernard Copeland had elected himself.

He'd spent several years committing low-level acts of terrorism: burning down isolated work sheds owned by timber companies, spiking trees. But even back then he'd known it was only exercise. He could spike a million trees, and it wouldn't stop the world from destroying itself.

At first he used his scientific background to motivate companies to preserve his first love, the Amazon. He published papers describing the curative effects of turbocuarine, a natural muscle relaxant that had helped Parkinson's patients; he gave lectures on *Podophyllum peltatum*, commonly known as mayapple, which was the source of the etoposides used to fight testicular cancer. How, he argued, could we continue to ravage the Amazonian forest when it provided us with cures to our ills?

None of it mattered. Though revelations like those motivated some companies with promises of profit, there was just too much money being made cutting, stripping, and baring for grazing land or building housing. As the years passed, Copeland came to understand a basic principle of human nature: greed was powerful, but secondary. Fear was the prime mover of the human species. It was not enough to show human beings that the Amazon could provide them with profit. He had to fill them with fear of death and then show them that the Amazon was their salvation.

For years he had operated with this knowledge but without a coherent plan until, quite by accident, he had discovered the curative powers in the resin of a Croton lechleri tree in Brazil: The resin carried the dramatic name of *Sangre de Drago* or "Dragon's Blood." Then, through either coincidence or design influence (Copeland was not sure he believed in either), he had discovered a virus so deadly, it had never spread out of the deepest part of the Amazon. It was a unique feature of the most terrifying viruses in existence that, without artificial aid, they actually could *not* spread: they simply killed their hosts too fast. This virus was a variant of hemorrhagic fever, a distant cousin of Ebola and Marburg in Africa. Copeland was a biologist, not an anthropologist, but his own personal theory was that this virus had brought down the Mayan Empire. The common strain, which he'd discovered in a troop of Capuchin monkeys and was harmless to them, killed a human being in about twenty-four hours. In the rural Amazon, it often took more than a week to hike out of the deep jungle just to get to any kind of transportation. Explorers might have "discovered" the virus a thousand times in the last three or four centuries, but no one would ever have survived long enough to carry it into civilization.

The virus, in its native form, was terrifying. Within twenty-four hours it caused lesions in the skin that erupted so quickly that the skin seemed to come apart as though torn by giant claws. Some of the indigenous peoples, living in tiny villages at the fringes of the deep forest, told tales of *uña de gato*, or Cat's Claw.

Bernard Copeland had found his weapon.

But, with the wry observation that he could no more resist tampering with nature than the next man, Copeland had used his skills to "improve" Cat's Claw. He nurtured more and more aggressive strains, until he'd developed a strain of the virus that killed within twelve hours.

His plan was simple and admittedly vicious. He would infect people of prominence and force them to publicly acknowledge the need to preserve the rain forests, which provided the Dragon's Blood cure for the virus. If they didn't, they would die.

Of course, it wasn't that simple. Copeland had spent years gathering a team from the eco-terrorist groups, some of whom were even more radical than he. A few had even suggested simply spreading the virus around the globe, then releasing information about the cure a day later. Make the virus pervasive, they said; it was the best way to ensure that humanity needed the rain forest.

Copeland had balked. He was a scientist, and as a scientist he had calculated the odds and understood that some people might have to die. But if the virus were simply released into the human infrastructure, thousands would die, maybe millions. That was a cost that could be avoided, and therefore *should* be. Copeland had also studied the actions of classic terrorist groups like the PLO and al-Qaeda, and understood their method: it was not how many people you killed, it was how many you scared, that counted.

Time had passed, and Copeland's small army grew, though few of them knew his real name. He continued using the nom de guerre of Seldom Seen Smith and called his group the Monkey Wrench Gang, finding cover in the pure ridiculousness of the names, since no one who was not passionate about the cause would take them seriously. He found people of many persuasions in business, in universities, and even in the government, who were faithful to the environment. And when the G8 summit was announced in Los Angeles, he knew he was ready.

Or he thought he had been. The Bernard Copeland who collapsed on the floor of his Santa Monica home was no longer Seldom Seen Smith. Smith had fallen apart in the middle of the Federal Building riots, chased by the police and tracked by a Federal agent. Smith had used his one trick on Jack Bauer, the chemical marker his company had experimented with in the Amazon, to track the agent, only to find that Bauer had outsmarted him. Smith really had one of his followers infect the man's daughter, but he did not consider her to be in any danger. He had several doses of the vaccine, and it would be a simple matter to deliver it to her. In the meantime, anyone who studied the virus in her blood would be suitably terrified, which was what he wanted anyway.

From that moment on, all his plans had fallen apart. The police detective had . . .

Copeland shuddered, reliving the moment when she'd fallen into his precious and deadly stack of glass vials. Now Copeland needed the vaccine for himself. He could not be sure if he or Frankie had been exposed to one or both strains. The detective undoubtedly had.

"And she has no idea," he murmured, his words slurred ever so slightly by the maracuja. "No idea at all. She could kill thousands."

"So what?"

Copeland sat up, his heart skipping a beat.

"Relax, it's me," said Frankie Michaelmas.

She was standing in the doorway to his back rooms as calmly as though nothing had happened. He stood up and walked over to her in a maracuja haze and hugged her. He kissed her, and was too frantic and drugged to notice that her lips offered no warmth or passion.

"Don't say so what," he said at last, "don't say so what. You know what. I don't even know which strain she was exposed to. Maybe in less than a day, she could be infecting people, spreading the disease all across the city. We have to warn someone."

Frankie shrugged, dislodged herself from his arms, and sat down in a chair.

"You do have doses of the vaccine, right?" Frankie asked almost lazily.

"Of course I do. But I have to make more now. For you and me."

"Which strain do you think?" she asked.

Copeland shook his head. "No way of knowing. We have time, if we hurry. I'll call the others. They'll help."

Frankie nodded. "I'll call them. Tell me who."

Copeland paused. Secrecy had been part of his protection, both for himself and his virus. Few members of his gang knew all the other members, and as a safeguard against abuse, he had not told those willing to use the virus where the vaccine was hidden. That way, no one was eager to play fast and loose with the virus itself.

"Okay," he said uncertainly. He went over to a bookshelf to collect the contact information for his colleagues.

"Good. But don't warn anyone else. It's a disease. There's a cure. Spread the disease and tell them where to go find the cure. Best way to get our way."

So brutal, he thought, though he felt a delicious tremor in his stomach. "We have to warn them," he said again. "And we have to find a way out. We have to take the antivirus ourselves and then get out. She saw my face. She knows you're involved. And that Federal agent. I can't believe the Feds got on our tail so fast. They'll find us eventually."

Frankie nodded. "That's true. But you know that we know people that can help us with that. People with a lot of experience hiding from the government."

The impact of her words reached Copeland even through his drug-induced stupor. He put down the book containing his contacts and bristled. It suddenly occurred to him that he absolutely should not tell Frankie where to find the vaccine. "Absolutely not."

"They're your contacts," she pointed out. She reached forward to the coffee table and hefted a heavy piece of jade. Copeland had told her a dozen times the story of how he had discovered it during one of his hikes into the wilderness. She'd always liked its weight and its jagged edges. "You're the one who wanted to learn from them."

"Their philosophy! How they achieved their ends!" he spat. "We're not going through this again. They are cold-blooded killers. Their goals are petty. We are trying to—"

"—save the planet," she said like a teenager mocking her father. "Well, your reward is going to be a jail cell when they catch you. But those people can get us out of the country."

Copeland shook his head. "I haven't spoken with them in months. I have no way to contact them."

"I do."

Copeland's eyes narrowed. He forced himself to pierce the tranquilizer's veil to focus on her. "You? How did you—you have been speaking with them?"

She said yes without the slightest bit of remorse.

"They want to kill people. They'll do nothing with the vaccine," Copeland said firmly, trying to recover from his shock. "Absolutely not."

He walked over to the telephone. "We have to call someone. Warn them about the police officer. They can get her into a sterile room before she becomes contagious." He picked up the telephone.

Frankie Michaelmas stood up, hefted the heavy piece of jade, and brought it crashing down on the back of Copeland's skull. She had always wondered how many blows it would take to kill him, and now she was determined to find out.

1 2 3 4 5 6 7 8 9
10 11 12 13 14 15 16 17
18 19 20 21 22 23 24

• •

THE FOLLOWING TAKES PLACE
BETWEEN THE HOURS OF
4 P.M. AND 5 P.M.
PACIFIC STANDARD TIME

• •

4:00 P.M. PST
CTU Headquarters, Los Angeles

Ryan Chappelle burst into Christopher Henderson's office, red-faced and puffed up, looking like a small dog taking up space.

"Bauer." Chappelle said the word as though it left a bad taste in his mouth.

"Not here," Henderson said. "What's wrong?"

"This is," the Director said, holding up a mini-disc as though the very fact that he was holding it proved his point.

Henderson received the disc, opened his CD tray, and laid it down with deliberate smoothness. The video program fired up, and in minutes Henderson was watching color footage of Jack Bauer hunched down next to an overturned police van. His face wasn't clear—the video was slightly un-focused, and Jack's face was turned partly away—but Henderson recognized the slouch of Bauer's shoulders and the straw-blond hair. He was talking to a man in a blue shirt—Henderson knew it was Kasim Turkel, who seemed to be handcuffed and lying on the ground. Every once in a while Bauer jabbed at the man's leg and he twitched.

Henderson knew what was coming, but he wasn't going to make it easy. "So?" he said dumbly.

"So, we've got video of a CTU agent torturing a man in public!"

Henderson wished he could have built a wall between himself and Chappelle's invective. "You know Jack. He had a reason—"

"I'm sure Bauer had his reasons. I'm also sure I won't like them. And I'm even more sure that if this ends up on the evening news, it'll be a public relations disaster!"

"Suppress it. Where'd we get it?"

Chappelle paced back and forth, unable to contain his energy. He could be as cold as ice sometimes, but Bauer always seemed to bring out the worst in him. "That's the kicker. A protestor. Check that, a *rioter* took video footage of him. Probably one of the same people who vandalized the police wagon. And the guy wants to sell it to us for half a million dollars. Otherwise he's going to CNN."

Henderson rubbed his temples. Video was unforgiving. Context didn't matter. The public would see a Federal agent abusing a suspect, and no one would pay attention to the fact that the suspect was a terrorist putting lives at risk, and the interrogator was a man with hours left in which to save lives. "So we buy it off him, or we scare him out of the deal."

"Maybe," Chappelle said. "Because the other choice is that I cut this off at the knees by bringing Jack Bauer up on charges."

Mercy Bennet had followed Smith, on foot, from the Federal Building out of West Los Angeles and into Santa Monica. He seemed to think he'd lost her in the crowd when she had hesitated, looking at Jack Bauer, and she did nothing to dissuade him from that belief. Tailing him on foot seemed ridiculous in this day and age—he should have been followed by two or three teams on foot and in cars, switching drivers and clothing. But with no radio or telephone, Mercy could not call for backup.

So she resorted to cloak-and-dagger movements, staying as far back as possible without losing him, staying behind parked cars, street signs, and other obstacles as often as possible. Copeland seemed to be taking a zigzagging path, one block north then one block west, over and over. Twice she thought she'd lost him, only to follow the pattern and pick him up again. Losing him temporarily had probably helped her more than anything, since it reduced her chances of being seen.

His path led eventually into an upscale neighborhood of Santa Monica above Montana Boulevard. Once he was there, he seemed to relax. His pace had slowed considerably and, though she was too far back to say for sure, she had the impression that his shoulders lost some of their tension. He was on his home turf.

He ended his run at a well-landscaped brick house around Fourteenth Street, the kind of house she would never afford on a government salary. She watched him enter the house, then she made her last dash, reaching a large oak tree planted along the parkway of the house across the street, and partly shielded by a parked Chevy Tahoe. She sat there for a minute catching her breath, trying to decide what to do next, when a Toyota Prius drove into Smith's driveway. Mercy nearly cursed aloud when she saw Frankie Michaelmas get out of the car and hurry inside. A few minutes later, Frankie had reappeared carrying several small cases. She made a second trip for more cases, then got in the car and drove away. Mercy resisted an irrational urge to jump onto the hood of the car and keep it from moving by force of will. But in the end she did not think Frankie was her target. She focused on Smith.

She sat across the street for a few more minutes, recovering some of her strength and considering her next move, when a middle-aged woman with a round face, wearing a chic bandana on her bald head, came by, walking her dog. Both the woman and the dog moved with tired steps.

"Excuse me," Mercy said, "I don't want to bother you, but do you have a cell phone?"

The woman studied Mercy with a sharp eye. "Why?"

"I'm a police officer. I've lost my badge and my radio during a foot pursuit, and I need to call my department. It's an emergency."

"You don't have a badge?"

Mercy shook her head.

The woman assessed her shrewdly. Mercy could almost imagine what she was thinking: her story was unlikely . . . but who would claim to be a police officer in need of a cell phone who was not, in fact, just that?

"How can I believe you?"

"There's no harm either way," Mercy pointed out. "You can stand here while I make the call."

The woman considered again, shrugged, and handed over a small silver flip phone. Mercy dialed 911. This time she was connected—the riots, she guessed, were finally calming down, thanks to police presence and protestor exhaustion— and she identified herself. The emergency dispatcher contacted West Bureau for her. She was connected to Sandy Waldman. She rolled her eyes. Waldman, a twenty-year veteran, had been one of the many who'd mocked her ecoterrorist theory.

"Sandy, I need help," she said.

"You and half the goddamned city," Waldman replied. She could picture him sitting at his desk with his feet up, his veteran's belly rolling over the top of his belt buckle.

"I'm code five on Fourteenth Street in Santa Monica," she said, using the department's code for "on a stakeout" to affirm the dog walker's generosity. "I need units to roll here ASAP code two."

"Ooh, police talk," Waldman joked. "You're lucky. We've been code thirteen for the last couple of hours, but now we're getting back to code fourteen." Mercy hated Waldman in that moment, but she was glad to hear the department was standing down from major disaster activity caused by the riot. "I'll roll a couple of slick tops to you now."

"Thanks. Can you also run an address for me?" She recited the address of the brick house.

"Stand by."

"What do you want with that house?" asked the woman with the bandana.

Mercy understood intuitively that she'd lost her hair to chemotherapy. "It's police business, ma'am."

"But that's Bernie Copeland's house. Is he okay?"

"You know him?"

"Well, he's a neighbor," the woman said as though all neighbors should know one another. "He travels quite a bit. South America most of the time, I think, but I see him outside sometimes when I walk Honeybear." She tugged affectionately at her dog's leash.

"Ever notice anything unusual about him?"

"Not until now," the woman replied dubiously. "May I have my phone back?"

"Almost."

Sandy Waldman came back on the line with the name of Bernard Copeland and a list of interesting items, only a few of which Mercy absorbed in that moment, because just then two unmarked police cars rolled up, one of them passing the house and pulling to a stop three doors down, the other stopping short. The cops inside were uniformed.

"Tell me what you want them to do and I'll radio it to them," Waldman said. For a jerk, he was a pretty efficient cop, she decided.

"Approach when they see me move, one goes to the back and the other goes in with me. He's inside."

"Ten-four." A moment later, one of the unmarked cars rolled away to go around the block. Mercy knew he'd keep in contact with the other via radio.

"Thank you, ma'am," Mercy said, handing back the phone. She walked down two doors, forcing herself to remain calm and steady, then made a hard left turn and crossed the street at a fast pace. The cop on this street put the radio to his mouth, then hung it up and exited quickly, hurrying up beside her and nodding. Together they strode up the steps to the door, and the officer kicked it in with one stomp of his boot.

Mercy let him enter first, since he was armed, but she knew almost immediately that there would be no gunfire.

Seldom Seen Smith, a.k.a. Bernard Copeland, was lying on his living room floor in a pool of blood.

"Radio for an ambulance!" she shouted. Mercy rushed forward while the uniformed officer began to clear the house while simultaneously making the call. Mercy heard the other officer enter from the back.

She knelt beside Smith, who was facedown. The back of his skull looked like hamburger meat mixed with clumps of hair. He was breathing, but barely.

"Copeland!" she said to him. "Copeland, can you hear me?" He didn't answer. "Smith!" she yelled. "Seldom Seen Smith!"

His eyelids fluttered and then stopped at half mast. "Smith!" she repeated. "This is the police. An ambulance is on its way."

She moved into his line of sight. His eyes focused on her for a moment and his breathing quickened. His mouth worked noiselessly.

"Take it easy," she said. It seemed unsafe to move him, even though the pool of blood near his lips made his breathing wet and raspy. "We're getting you help." She knew without asking that Frankie Michaelmas had done this to him.

His mouth worked harder, and this time he succeeded in making small, moist, guttural sounds. He spoke words rather than sentences. "You," he rasped. Then, "Infected." Mercy didn't know what he meant, but a sudden weight pressed against her stomach when he managed to add, "Hours. Only."

His mouth worked desperately again. He closed his eyes and they remained closed; he coughed, spraying droplets of blood onto her knees. Copeland gathered himself and managed a few more words. No, one long word. "An . . . ti . . . dote." Then he coughed again and pushed out another fearful word. "Gone."

One uniformed cop walked back into the room. "All clear—" But Mercy held up her hand. Copeland continued slowly. "She . . . use . . . it. Terror. Vander. Bilt. Anti. Dote. She . . . use . . . it. Terror." The sounds ebbed until they were only weak rasps. Copeland opened his eyes. His right hand moved along the floor, sliding until it reached the edge of the pool of blood. Reaching clear hardwood, his dragging fingers drew dark red lines. His hand stopped, then he drew three numbers—13, 48, 57. His hand stopped moving and his eyes closed. His lips quivered and, weak and thin as the meowings of a kitten, he spoke another phrase. Mercy couldn't quite make it out. It sounded like a foreign name. "Uma," like the actress, then something about a "ghetto." Then he stopped making sounds altogether.

4:20 P.M. PST
Century Plaza Hotel, West Los Angeles

Mitch Rasher walked into the President's suite at the Century Plaza. "We're back on," he said.

Barnes looked up from the security briefing he'd been reading. "What about the riots?"

"It's going to look bad on the evening news," Rasher warned him, "but the streets are getting back to normal now. By the time you have your meeting tonight, they'll have everything cleared up."

"And security is tight up there? Nothing's been leaked?"

"No, sir. Tight as a drum. Shall I confirm with the other side?"

Barnes considered. He'd been looking forward to this meeting. He always enjoyed cutting through the red tape and slicing right to the heart of the matter. The riots, had they continued, would have made a meeting impossible and given the protestors a victory, though they'd never have known it. But, if Rasher felt the riots had burned themselves out, well . . .

"Let's do it," Barnes commanded.

4:22 P.M. PST
CTU Headquarters, Los Angeles

Jack walked into CTU headquarters just shy of four-thirty. His entire body ached; the rush dialysis had taken more out of him than he cared to admit, and he felt as if that police wagon had landed on top of him. But he had no intention of slowing down.

He walked through CTU's main floor and up to Henderson's office, his face scratched from the struggle with the police, his eyes red from OC spray, and his shirt torn. He ignored the stares from the analysts as he reached the top of the operation chief's office.

"Is there any word on Kim?" he asked without saying hello.

Henderson shook his head. "National Health Services hasn't called."

Jack gritted his teeth. The virus, he told himself. The vaccine.

Tony Almeida and Nina Myers were already in Henderson's office, along with Jessi Bandison.

"Okay, are we on top of Farrigian?" Jack asked. He had called ahead to tell them what he'd learned from Turkel.

Henderson replied. "He turned up dead. We found him in his warehouse with a bullet in his brain."

Jack didn't waste a moment's grief over a small fish eaten by a bigger one. "Inventory?"

The Chief of Field Operations shrugged. "We have people looking, but no one knows for sure."

"So we know it's explosive. But a bomb? A rocket?" Jack thought aloud. "A stationary bomb would be difficult. I can't imagine him getting it into a location, and a roadside bomb would make a lot of noise, but what would his target be? You have all these world leaders traveling separately."

"It's ETIM," Nina said. "They want China. The Chinese Premier is here to make his case to the G8."

"It's going to be hard to figure out his plan if we don't know the weapon," Jack said, his tone edged in frustration. "Turkel seemed to think it was tonight. Do we have the G8 itinerary?"

Jessi Bandison called the schedule up on Henderson's computer screen. A timetable appeared showing the where-abouts of the principals in the G8 at any given time during the summit. All eight heads of state would be attending a function at the Beverly Wilshire Hotel.

"But the Chinese Premier won't be there," Henderson pointed out. He jabbed his finger at a box on the screen that stated the Premier's location for that evening: in his suite at a separate hotel. "Al-Libbi wouldn't attack then, like we said."

Jack studied the schedule. Something was bothering him. "Why is he staying indoors?"

"What do you mean?"

Bauer ran his finger along the column for every other day and night. "His schedule is packed. He has events every day and every evening, especially evenings. The only blank spots are for sleep and some time during each day, but no rest at all the other evenings. Only this one."

Tony saw where Jack was going. "You think he has a ren-dezvous planned?" Jack was already sliding the screen over to President Barnes.

"Well, look who else doesn't have anything planned in that slot." He smiled at the others. "I'd say these two have a meeting of their own scheduled. We just need to find out where it is. Let's go over the facts we know and see how they fit."

Each member gave a quick summary of recent discover-ies. Tony reported that Dyson had died without recovering enough for serious questioning, and had mumbled only non-sense before he died. Jack cursed at that, but said nothing else. He repeated the information he'd pulled out of Kasim Turkel. Nina's information surprised them all.

"Nurmamet Tuman is former Chinese intelligence. That's about all I could get from my contact at the consulate, and even getting that was like pulling teeth," she said. "My assumption is that he was Uygur trained to spy on other Uygurs, but my guy didn't say any of that."

"Maybe he was turned," Jack mused. "Pretending to spy when his heart was still with his homeland."

Nina nodded. "I thought the same thing, but they weren't having any of it. It's hard to have a conversation when they don't even acknowledge that the separatists exist. There's one other thing." She paused. "When I was leaving Tuman's house, the Secret Service arrived. They wouldn't tell me why they were there. They seemed to know Tuman already."

"You think they're meeting at Tuman's house? That wouldn't make sense," Tony pointed out. "Too public, too small, too insecure."

Jack turned to Henderson. "We need to give them our information. Even if they won't tell us what's going on, they can at least change their plans; maybe that'll stop al-Libbi."

Henderson nodded in approval. Sometimes the best way to thwart a terrorist plan was the simplest: change a date, a time, a route. Denial of information was a primary part of counterintelligence, and counterintelligence was a foundational tool in any anti-terrorist organization. "I'll ask Chappelle. But he might be in a mood."

Jessi was standing back from the conversation, but she had continued to study the screen. "You know who else's schedule matches up," she said. "President Novartov from Russia. Remember, the contact I made was Russian, and the information on the Tuman connection was Russian."

Jessi knew what they were going to ask the minute they spoke up. Henderson put the phone in her hand, and she dialed the number. A moment later she was listening to Anastasia Odolova's melodramatic voice say, "My Jessi, what can I do for you now?"

Jessi felt extremely self-conscious with four experienced field agents all staring at her. "Anastasia, thanks again for helping before. If you have a minute, I could use a little more guidance."

There was a pause, during which the analyst was sure she could feel Odolova smiling on the other end of the line. "First things first, Jessi. Call me Anna. Now, what else can I do for you?"

Jessi looked at Bauer and the others, who were studying her closely. Bauer, especially, made her nervous. The intensity in his eyes, in his movements, always shocked her in contrast to his boyish good looks. She knew how good he was at his job, but she hoped that he never had to turn that steely focus on her. "I'm digging into this Marcus Lee situation," she said, choosing her words carefully. "Everywhere I look, Russia keeps popping up. I thought you might be able to tell me a little more about what Tuman, or Lee, or whatever he's called, might be up to."

"Well, I always have an idea or two in my head," Odolova replied. "But theories are sometimes misunderstood. It might be best if I were to tell you in person."

Not me, Jessi thought immediately. *I'm no field agent.* "I could send someone to meet you."

"No, no," Odolova said gently, but firmly. "You are Kelly's friend. I'm happy to meet with you, but no one else. And, if my idea is correct, we should meet soon. I can be at the Cat & Fiddle on Sunset in thirty minutes. I'll be wearing white." With these final words, the Russian's voice had quickened to a short, terse tone, informing Jessi that this was her only offer.

"Okay," she said weakly. Odolova hung up.

Jessi relayed the conversation to the group.

"She's not a field agent," Tony said, voicing her thoughts.

"She should go," Jack insisted. "We're missing pieces here, and if this Odolova woman can give us some, we need them. Come on."

He grabbed Jessi by the wrist and started to guide her to the stairs when the phone rang. Henderson picked it up and said it was for Bauer.

Jessi was relieved. Now she would have time to a phone call of her own before they left.

4:33 P.M. PST
CTU Headquarters, Los Angeles

"Bauer," Jack said.

"Agent Bauer, this is Ken Diebold with National Health Services. You sent us over a blood sample to examine."

Jack's attention narrowed suddenly to a laserlike focus. "Yes. What can you tell me?"

"The blood sample contains a virus . . . a sort of virus we haven't seen before. Are you familiar with Ebola or Marburg?"

Jack felt as though a hand had clenched around his heart. "Yes."

"They are hemorrhagic fevers. So is this one. We don't know much about it, yet, but we're using Marburg as a model. This subject is the second case we're studying."

"Wait," Bauer said. "My colleagues should hear this." He

switched to the speakerphone and motioned for Nina to close the door.

Diebold continued. "If our information is accurate, this subject will be contagious about twenty-four hours after exposure, and will die a few hours after that." Diebold paused. "I have some knowledge of your agency's activities, Agent Bauer. Do you have the subject in custody? Do you know when he was exposed?"

Jack felt the hand try to tear his heart from his chest. "Yes," he said quietly. He checked his watch. "About eight hours ago."

"He needs to be isolated immediately," Diebold said. "He's no danger to anyone yet, but we expect lesions to appear on the skin. Once they break open, the patient is contagious and the virus can spread."

"Isn't there anything—?"

"A virus is a difficult thing to kill," the NHS doctor replied. "There is no cure for Marburg."

"You said this was the second case . . . ?" Henderson asked.

"The other was reported to us from Brazil, from an area called Minas Gerais. We're guessing that's where the virus originates. Was your subject recently there?"

"No," Jack said. But he was distracted. Tony Almeida's eyes had widened at the doctor's words.

"Agent Bauer," Diebold said. "It's imperative that we get your subject quarantined as soon as possible. If this virus is half as contagious as Marburg, it could take out half the population of Los Angeles in a matter of days."

"I'll take care of it," Jack said. He hung up. "What?" he said to Tony.

Almeida frowned thoughtfully. "That's the second time I've heard someone mention that place. Minas Gerais, or something like that? Dyson talked about it this morning, right before he tried to kill me. He was talking about coffee. I didn't think there was any kind of connection."

Jack felt frustrated anger boil up inside him. His daughter was dying and didn't even know it, and Almeida was forgetting important information. "Did he say anything else?" he said evenly.

Tony saw the fire in Bauer's eyes and countered it with cool professionalism. "Not unless you count the babbling he did right before he died. He saw me and mumbled something about a joke I made about monkeys earlier today. He talked about gangs of monkeys."

Jack's eyes lit up. *Monkey Wrench Gang.* He turned to Henderson. "We have to find Mercy Bennet right away."

4:45 P.M. PST
Mountaingate Drive, Los Angeles

The ocean breeze blew across the southern face of the Santa Monica Mountains, cooling Nurmamet Tuman's grounds, which had turned gold-green in the late afternoon sunlight. Tuman stepped out of the house to enjoy the breeze, leaving behind the two Secret Service agents who were stationed in his living room.

Out in the backyard, his "gardener" was moving equipment and clipping the hedges. He was butchering them, of course, because that's what Ayman al-Libbi was: a butcher.

Tuman had been anxious ever since the female Federal agent had come to his door. He'd managed to hide his anxiety from her, of that he was sure. He had spent a lifetime concealing his thoughts and desires, even in the face of the most startling surprises. But although he could hide his fear from the woman, he could not hide it from himself. If one division of the government had concerns, they would eventually share it with the Secret Service, and Tuman's carefully scripted plans could all be exposed in one fell swoop.

And, adding to his nervousness, the People's Consulate had called him. Oh, they had no idea of his plans, of course. They were as blind as bats. But they had called him, concerned about the inquiries of the American government. What, they wanted to know, was "Marcus Lee" doing to attract so much attention?

Tuman approached al-Libbi and said for the benefit of any Secret Service ears that might be listening: "You're wrecking my morning glories. Please stop hacking them up!"

Al-Libbi turned toward him, a light sheen of sweat on his face, his dark eyes gleaming in the sun. He actually seemed to be enjoying this work. He nodded, tipped his cap, and went back to work.

"We have to call it off," Tuman whispered.

The terrorist stopped his attack on the hedge. "What?"

"First the Federal agent. Now my own consulate is calling me. I don't like it."

Al-Libbi jabbed the head of the clippers into the grass and rested his hands on the two extended handles. "For a man who worked as a double agent inside China for twenty years, you are very jumpy."

"I listen to my instincts," Tuman replied. "I convinced them for years that I had left my ethnic loyalties behind, that I was a party member first, a Uygur second. I could always sense when someone didn't believe me and I have that sense now. Someone out there knows that I've helped ETIM, and sooner or later that person is going to tell *them*!"

"Don't worry about them," al-Libbi said. He leaned over the handles of his clippers. "Listen, my friend, it is too late to stop this."

"It is not too late," Tuman insisted. "We'll refund your money."

"Really?" al-Libbi replied in his perfect American tones. "Did you really think I was going through all this for two million dollars?" He smiled. "I took this job because it will put me back where I belong."

"At the top of the most wanted list?"

The small smile widened across his face. "Two lists: most wanted by Western governments, most wanted by Middle Eastern employers."

"It can't happen now." Tuman stepped around so that his body blocked any view from the living room. A small semi-automatic had appeared in his hand.

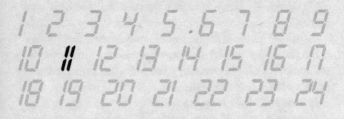

....

**THE FOLLOWING TAKES PLACE
BETWEEN THE HOURS OF
5 P.M. AND 6 P.M.
PACIFIC STANDARD TIME**

....

5:00 P.M. PST
UCLA Medical Center

Mercy drove away from UCLA Medical Center in her borrowed Crown Vic, her arm still stinging and stiff where they'd drawn the blood. As soon as the coroner and more officers had arrived at the house on Fourteenth Street, Mercy had evacuated herself to the hospital. Few of the words Copeland had spoken made sense to her, but the word *virus* rattling out of his bloody mouth nearly stopped her heart. She remembered the way he and his gang had reacted when she crashed into those vials in the other house. They hadn't run from her, they'd run from the accident. She had inadvertently released some kind of virus. She'd stopped by UCLA and asked them to run some tests. They could find nothing wrong with her immediately and released her, promising to call her as soon as they had any information.

She had to get back to her desk and regroup. Her original case had been the investigation of Gordon Gleed's death. Her intuition now told her that Copeland wasn't responsible for his murder, at least not directly. Frankie Michaelmas had done it. She seemed to have a fetish for bludgeoning people to death, and, following her practice of instant impressions, Mercy sensed that Michaelmas was far more violent in her heart than Copeland was. Frankie was her target, but Frankie had proved elusive.

Mercy stepped on the accelerator.

5:04 P.M.
Mountaingate Drive, Los Angeles

Ayman al-Libbi smiled at the gun as though it might have been a bouquet of flowers or a borrowed book. "Are you going to shoot me?" he said calmly. "That will expose you as much as any rocket attack."

"I'm a hero," said Tuman, who had thought of this option long ago. "I stopped a wanted terrorist who had somehow slipped past the Federal agents."

"You waved me through the door," al-Libbi said. "You told them I was all right. Don't you think they'll ask about that?"

Tuman continued to spin his story. "You killed the agents first. I managed to get you while you were focused on them."

The terrorist nodded appreciatively. "So you'll kill them and frame me after I'm dead. It's a good story. It will work. And here's your opportunity." Al-Libbi's eyes lifted up to look over Tuman's shoulder.

Tuman didn't go for the bluff. Not really. But his eyes

flicked to their corners for just a fraction of a second. That was all the time al-Libbi needed. His left hand grabbed the gun while his right hand struck at Tuman's face, the fingers stabbing into his eyes. Before the Uygur could even squeal, al-Libbi was holding the gun. But he couldn't use it without alerting the guards inside. As Tuman staggered back, holding his eyes, the terrorist pocketed the gun and picked up clippers. They stabbed like a snake's head. The first blow sliced the Uygur's hands, which were covering his face. Tuman recoiled from them instinctively, exposing his throat. The killer stabbed again.

Al-Libbi left Nurmamet Tuman gurgling on the grass, his throat frothing blood, and walked calmly inside to deal with the Secret Service agents.

5:09 P.M.
Cat & Fiddle Pub, Los Angeles

Jack's agency SUV rolled up to a parking space a block from the Cat & Fiddle.

"Wait," he said, pressing his hand over Jessi's forearm. His eyes flicked from the rearview mirror to the side view and back. He watched cars roll past them.

"What?" Jessi asked. She was already nervous. Bauer's silent company during their drive had raised her tension even more.

The red Camaro Jack was watching rolled past with a single driver inside. He'd seen it twice during their drive, or at least he'd seen two Camaros that looked the same. Camaros were popular with a certain type, but Jack didn't like seeing two of them. The first time he'd seen them there'd been a driver and a passenger. Classic surveillance procedures involved two or more automobiles that alternated the pursuit.

Either Jack had seen two very similar vehicles, or he was being followed by a team that had cycled through too quickly.

"Nothing," he said at last. "I'll go in first. Wait a few minutes, then come in. You'll do fine."

He waited for her to nod, then exited the car and hurried up to the Cat & Fiddle's door. Inside it was dark and cool, and would have been smoke-filled in the days when California allowed smoking. The Cat & Fiddle had a blue-collar feel that appealed to its upscale crowd. Jack hunched his shoulders a bit as he entered, being someone who'd had a hard day at the office. He didn't bother to look around, even though he caught a flash of white at the bar. There would be time for that. He knew immediately which booth he wanted—a corner table with a view of all the ins and outs, and near the emergency exit, but it was taken by a man in a blue T-shirt. There were many other empty booths, so he took one in the corner near the bar. ESPN was playing on both televisions. A waitress in her forties gave him a menu, but he ordered a beer and watched MLS soccer. Watching television gave him an excuse to keep his chin up and his eyes looking out across the room. He saw the woman in white now, and he decided it was safe to stare for a while. He couldn't see her face, but he could see the Japanese tattoo on the small of her back where it peeked over the top of her low-slung white skirt. She was blond, with narrow shoulders and long arms. It would have been a giveaway if he didn't stare at her.

Jack forced his mind into the present. This had to happen before the next thing, like firing a weapon: first load, then acquire, then fire, then assess. The virus was in Kim. They had no cure, but someone did, and he was going to find them. The way to find them was to focus on this . . .

Jessi walked in. She turned a few heads as she walked to the bar. One of those heads belonged to the man in a blue

T-shirt and a buzz cut. He went right back to sipping his beer, but his eyes had lingered on Jessi a little too long, and Jack knew that Anastasia Odolova had a babysitter.

Odolova's appearance matched her voice. Her limbs were long, lean, and toned, and she moved them in slow, dramatic flourishes when she spoke, as though she were used to holding something like a cigarette in her hand. Her face was angular and pretty, framed by straight blond hair. Oddly, she wore heavy black mascara under her blue eyes. Set against the stark white of her outfit and skin, the heavy eye makeup looked disturbing and hypnotic.

"You're Jessi, of course," Anna said. "What will you drink?"

"Nothing, thanks," Jessi said.

Anna leaned forward, catching Jessi with her mesmerizing eyes. "Of course you will, my Jessi. What else are we here for?"

Right. Appearances, Jessi thought. "Newcastle, please," she said to the passing bartender.

"You know what you like, don't you?" Odolova said, seeming genuinely pleased. "Now, what is it I can help you with?" Her voice was breezy, nothing that stood out.

Jessi did not have her skill, and did not pretend to. "Is Novartov having a classified meeting with us and the Chinese tonight? Is that Tuman's target?" she asked softly.

Odolova flicked her wrist as though tapping away the ashes of an imaginary cigarette. "See, you can tell a lot about a person from the way they order a drink. You, for instance, are very straightforward. Strong. You'd make a good Russian." She smiled lightly, and continued. "Obviously, I can't discuss

scheduling matters with you. But you may be on the right
track. Would you like to know more about Nurmamet Tuman?"

"Sure," Jessi said.

Odolova spoke in long, dramatic sentences, but the story
she told was this: Nurmamet Tuman had been a Chinese espionage agent for more than twenty years. Although he was
an ethnic Uygur, he had lost his parents and been taken to an
orphanage, where he was indoctrinated first as a Maoist and
then as a member of the newer, more "progressive" Communist Party. He had climbed the ranks of the People's Army
and proved to be adept at intelligence. But during a purge a
few years earlier, superiors who disliked and mistrusted his
Uygur heritage retired him. He was dumped in the United
States with a new name and a faked dossier, where he started
and ran a small software company. The Chinese government
kept in contact, and even used him now and then, but for all
intents and purposes he was in exile.

What Beijing did not know was that Marcus Lee had
never stopped being Nurmamet Tuman, never stopped being
a Uygur. Even while deep inside Chinese intelligence, he
continued to work secretly for the independence of Eastern
Turkistan. The Russians were sure that he had saved ETIM
members from capture at least twice in his career. Once he
was in the United States, he had a much easier time strength-
ening his contacts with ETIM until he became their largest
backer. His native Uygur loyalties were bolstered by bitter-
ness over his removal from the espionage community.

"But why attack here?" Jessi asked. "Why not do it in
China?"

"The security is too tight," Odolova answered. "Besides,
ETIM is frustrated that they do not get more attention from
the West. China controls the flow of information, especially
in the rural provinces. ETIM commits terrorist attacks in
Urumchi to draw attention, but no one ever hears about

them. If they make an attack in Los Angeles, the whole world will start paying attention."

"How do you know so much?" Jessi asked, unable to disguise her naïveté. "You're so far ahead of us. How do you know?"

"It is not so impressive," Odolova said in a way that indicated how impressive it really was. "In fact, we learned much of our information because of a minor arms dealer in Los Angeles. Some Russian-made RPG–29s were stolen, and we tracked them to this arms dealer, assuming he had bought them, when, in fact, they'd been stolen by ETIM and delivered to this arms dealer for safekeeping."

"Farrigian," Jessi said matter-of-factly.

Odolova smiled warmly. "You see, you are good at this after all. It was the missing RPGs that made us look more closely at ETIM, and that led us to Tuman."

"Do you have any proof of this?"

"None whatsoever."

Jessi's heart sank. She knew Chappelle would want evidence before moving against a Chinese national. "I thought—"

"This is not always a business of hard facts."

"Why do the Chinese trust him? They're telling us he's clean."

The Russian cast the thought aside. "No one likes to be wrong." When Jessi continued to look puzzled, she added, "They believe their own propaganda. They have no reason to think ETIM can do harm if half of them don't believe the separatists exist. They don't want to believe one of their own is a traitor."

Odolova smiled at her as though waiting. Then, after an uncomfortable pause, she drained her own drink with a flourish and said, "Now I think it's time for you to buy a drink for me."

"Oh," Jessi said. "Would you like another one of—"

The Russian agent laughed. "I mean it's your turn to share information."

Jessi felt her cheeks burn as she blushed. "Infor—? I don't know if I have any . . ."

Odolova's face hardened. The dark mascara, which before had appeared hypnotic, became ugly and severe. "The RPG–29s. Who has them? Where are they?"

"Oh," Jessi said, realizing she actually did know that information, and only too late deciding that she shouldn't have revealed it. "I . . . I don't know that I'm allowed to—"

Her counterpart brushed blond wisps away from her forehead. "I'm not running a charity service, Jessi. I gave you information because I expect something in return."

Suddenly there was weight and pressure behind Jessi. She glanced over her shoulder to find a man in a blue T-shirt standing very close, his hard stomach pressed against her elbow.

"Let's go for a drive and talk some more," Anastasia said pleasantly; but it was not a request.

The man put his heavy hand on Jessi's arm. Then things happened very quickly. As the man squeezed her arm, Jessi heard a dull thud and a loud pop. The man's eyes flew very wide, and then he crumpled straight down like a building falling in on itself. And suddenly Jack Bauer was standing there.

5:45 P.M. PST
Cat & Fiddle Pub, Los Angeles

Jack had listened to bits and pieces of the conversation, though he missed most of it. Odolova was skilled at sounding natural while keeping her voice low. When the Russian babysitter made his move, Jack made his. He slid up behind him and dropped him as soon as he laid hands on Bandison.

The Russian man was still on the ground, sobbing and holding his broken knee.

"We're done talking," Jack said to Odolova. He took Jessi by the same arm the Russian had grabbed. His grip was gentler but still firm as he guided the analyst away from the bar and past the patrons wondering what had happened to the man on the ground. Jack and Jessi walked outside into the twilight of Sunset Boulevard.

Jack carried a borrowed phone, and it rang now. He leaned back into the alcove that led into the bar, but away from the door in case the Russians followed. "Bauer."

"Jack."

It was Mercy Bennet. "Where are you? Are you safe?" he asked.

"Well, there are degrees of safe," she said with a morose tone. "CTU contacted me and gave me this number. It's been quite a day."

"The Monkey Wrench Gang," Jack said. "Smith. All those things you said. They're all true."

Mercy laughed bitterly. "I've been waiting for someone to say that to me. It's just a little too late." She told him quickly how she'd tracked Smith, whose real name was Copeland, and watched him die; she also told him that before he had died he'd told her she'd been exposed to a virus. "I got checked out at UCLA, but they haven't gotten back to me yet."

Jack felt a great weight settle on his shoulders. "Are you sure he said that?"

"Pretty damned sure."

"Mercy—" the weight that settled on him was guilt; guilt that he hadn't told her earlier what he was really doing; guilt that he had turned her into an unwitting victim in the war on terror. He still couldn't tell her the truth, not quite yet. But she did have a right to know her own fate. "Mercy, the virus is deadly. It's a hemorrhagic fever."

The line fell silent. Finally, Mercy said, "Hemorrhagic . . . you mean like Ebola?"

"Yes."

"Shit. Jack, I'm driving around. Am I . . . am I contagious?" That was Mercy Bennet. She'd just been handed her death sentence and she was worried about its effect on others.

"Probably not yet," he said hoarsely. "My daughter has it, too. She was exposed by Copeland's people. The doctors tell me she's not contagious yet, so you probably have hours left."

"I'm not going to the hospital yet." She relayed Copeland's final words to Jack. "I don't know what he meant by 'terror' but I know who 'she' is. It's Frankie Michaelmas. I get the feeling that girl makes Copeland look like a saint."

A chill ran down Jack's spine. He knew what Copeland had meant by terror. He had known all along. But still he couldn't tell Mercy. Not while he still needed her.

"You should get to a hospital. Keep yourself safe," he said. "Contact National Health—"

"Screw that," Mercy said. "If I'm not contagious yet, I'm going to get that little bitch."

"Mercy, there's more here—"

"I'm going up to the Vanderbilt Complex. That's what Copeland was talking about. I think she's going to be there."

"Mercy, wait, let me tell you—"

But Bennet had dropped the line.

"We have to go," Jack told Jessi. "This whole thing is hitting the fan in the next couple of hours. Come on."

....

**THE FOLLOWING TAKES PLACE
BETWEEN THE HOURS OF
6 P.M. AND 7 P.M.
PACIFIC STANDARD TIME**

....

6:00 P.M. PST
Cat & Fiddle Pub, Los Angeles

Jack half ran down Sunset Boulevard to reach the SUV with
Jessi Bandison in tow. He had just reached the tail end of the
big car when he saw the red Camaro parked across the street,
the driver barely visible in the shadowy twilight, his body
held steady and angled toward them.

"Down!" Jack grabbed Jessi and pulled her to the ground
as something hissed lightning-fast through the air over their
heads. He dragged her behind the SUV. *Plunk, plunk plunk!*
Rounds sank into the SUV. One passed right through the
sheet metal over his head. Jack stayed behind the rear wheel,
which offered more cover, and shoved Jessi toward the front.
"Stay by that tire. Behind the engine block!"

More dull thuds, but now from another angle, up the street instead of across. They were in a crossfire.

Jack drew his weapon, a double-stacked .45 Springfield, borrowed, like the phone. He stayed low and leaned around the tire, but the angle was bad, and all he could see was street. Cars zoomed by, oblivious. The snipers were equipped with silencers, and none of the cars realized they were driving through a gunfight. Jack slid to the tail end of the car and leaned around, switching the Springfield to his left hand and squeezing off four rounds. Unlike the snipers' weapons, his .45 wasn't silenced. The sharp report made Jessi shriek. The Camaro's side window shattered. Jack rolled back behind the SUV and switched hands again, taking a kneeling position, looking to acquire the other sniper. But there was nothing to see except Sunset Boulevard, with dozens of buildings to hide in, parked cars, and cars moving along the street. A bullet chipped the concrete beside him, and he pressed himself tighter against the SUV.

More rounds hit the SUV from the other angle. The car was turning into a bullet sponge. But the angle of impact was changing. The shooter in the Camaro had relocated, improving his position. Jack fired two rounds into the air, just to make noise. Someone would call the police. If he could hold off the shooters until backup arrived, he'd have a chance. The gunfire brought shouts of alarm and screams from somewhere on the street.

Movement. Someone dashed from a building to a vehicle half a block up from the SUV, and Jack had his second shooter. But the first shooter put rounds into the SUV over his head, shattering the rear window, so Jack rolled in his direction and fired over the top of the car parked behind his. Commuters drove by, their startled faces flashing like subliminals in Jack's eyes. He could not be worried about them now. The shooter from the Camaro stumbled and fell, but Jack wasn't sure he'd actually hit him.

How do you know you've hit your target? the words of an old tactical firearms instructor came back to him.

When he goes down?

He might have fallen, he might be faking. There's only one way to know. Front sight, trigger pull, follow through. Make sure your sights are on the target. That's where the round will go.

Jack was sure his sights hadn't been on target. The man was still operating.

Sirens in the distance. That was good. But his slide had just locked back. He dropped the magazine out and popped in his second and last. Fifteen rounds left. Jessi made herself as small as possible as Jack moved closer to her position. The shooter up the street moved and Jack fired, shattering glass and ripping through a public trash can. A man walking out of a store yelled something and dived back inside.

These weren't eco-terrorists. They were operators working in tandem—one drawing Jack's fire, the other improving his position. It was a good plan. It was going to work. And the sirens were too far away.

The shooter up the street popped up, taking aim. Jack fired to keep the enemy's head down; he had no cover or concealment from that angle; his only cover was to shoot. At the same time, car tires squealed to a stop on the street a few feet away. If there was a third shooter, Jack thought, this was going to get really difficult. But the shooter pivoted, sighting the newcomer, his rounds turning the windshield into a spider web. The driver jumped out of the car and fired at the shooter. Panicked, the shooter changed angles, and there he was in Jack's sights. Jack dropped him and his gun went into slide lock again. With grim determination he thumbed the slide release and felt it snap back. Now it was a nice blunt object.

Twilight had turned to gloom but the streetlights hadn't come on yet. Jack couldn't see the driver's face, but he saw his body swivel in the other direction. There was a hiss and a snap, and the driver cried out, his gun hand dropping. He fell away behind his car. Jack heard footsteps running onto the street. The shooter from the Camaro was closing in on the newcomer. Jack rolled around to the back of the SUV. He bolted into the street in time to see the shooter reach the new car, a silenced Beretta in his hands. The shooter saw him and tried to turn, but Jack was too fast. He grabbed the Beretta in one hand, holding it off his body, and punched the muzzle of his empty Springfield into the shooter's face. He recoiled and punched his throat. The man dropped.

Without pausing Jack dropped the Springfield, tapped and racked the Beretta, and dropped to one knee, scanning the street. There was no movement. Cars had stopped passing by. The sirens were close enough to hurt his ears.

He looked up from his kneeling position to see the driver standing over him. "Hey," said Kelly Sharpton.

6:15 P.M. PST
Bauer Residence

"I'm going to kill him."

Teri Bauer slammed the phone back into its cradle. It was her fifth call to Jack in the last half hour. Like all the others, it had gone straight to voice mail.

Kim sat at the kitchen table, one hand absentmindedly tracing the seams where the wooden leaves of the table met. She looked pale, and concern for her fueled Teri's anger.

"He did it on purpose," Teri said out loud. "He took you this morning, but he was on a case."

"Mom," Kim said in a tired teenage voice. "Something

came up. The first thing he did when that trouble started was get me out of there."

"And make you sit in a basement for three hours!"

Teri paced the length of the kitchen. The magic of the prior month had worn off. Her fear had been that it would vanish immediately; that Jack would dive right into some crisis. Instead, it had faded like a tan. She'd watched Jack's attention turn slowly but steadily away from her and toward . . . whatever it was out there that called him. Teri had worried lately that it was another woman, and the thought had not completely left her. But it didn't seem possible—Jack was driven by some desire that had nothing to do with sex.

It had nothing to do with disloyalty of any kind. She was furious Jack for leaving Kim, but she knew he loved her. Ultimately, though, Teri was beginning to sense that his deepest loyalty lay with his country. Or maybe it wasn't even his country. It was his mission.

"Are you all right?" Teri asked.

Kim was holding her head in her hands now. "Yeah. Just tired, I guess. I feel hot. I think I'll go lie down."

6:18 P.M. PST
Cat & Fiddle Pub, Los Angeles

One of the shooters was dead. The other wouldn't be eating solid food for a long time, and he was currently gagging uncontrollably thanks to his swollen throat where Jack had punched him.

Jessi Bandison hugged Kelly Sharpton, who winced visibly. His right arm was covered in blood. "Are you—?" she started.

"Not too bad," he said. He rolled up his shirtsleeve. The

round had slid along the inside of his arm, plowing a furrow from his wrist to his elbow, but never fully penetrating.

He looked a little older than Jack remembered him from his short stint at CTU. There was weight in his face and gray in his hair. Jack had worked well enough with Sharpton, though they were never friends and didn't see eye to eye politically; still, he'd drawn fire when Jack needed it, and Jack felt grateful. "She called you," he said.

Sharpton nodded. "Odolova was my contact from way back."

"I was nervous about doing fieldwork," Jessi said. "I'm sorry I didn't tell you."

Jack waved her off. The end counted far more than the means, and they were all alive.

Black and white patrol cars materialized out of the gloom. Sharpton, no longer commissioned, put his gun away. Jack held up his badge, and after a moment or two of explanation, the uniformed officers lowered their weapons and began to cordon off the block. LAPD radioed for paramedics. The surviving shooter was choking to death. "I need him alive," Jack said. "I've got questions."

"You want to fill me in?" Sharpton asked.

Jack shook his head. "You're a civilian."

"A civilian who saved your ass!" Sharpton said amusedly.

Jack nodded. "And for that you have the thanks of a grateful nation."

"That and a dollar . . ." Sharpton sighed without finishing the sentence.

"Jessi," Jack said, turning to the analyst, "make sure these uniforms keep a close watch on that one. I want him taken back to CTU for interrogation. Don't let them give you any crap about medical attention. Go tell them."

He turned away, ignoring her look of panic, and dialed headquarters on his borrowed phone. A moment later he was talking to the head of field operations, Henderson's voice echoed by the speakerphone he was using.

"They took a shot at us," Jack said, describing the attack in brief. "I guess al-Libbi's got some friends in town." He explained what Odolova had told them about the RPG–29s, and her oblique confirmation of an event happening that evening.

He summed up: "Russia, the U.S., and China are having a secret meeting tonight around seven. Al-Libbi almost definitely wants to attack it."

Henderson replied, "RPG–29s are tank killers. He's got to be going after the presidential limo. It'd take a tank round to do any real damage to that thing. But there's no way the meeting is at Marcus Lee's house. The Secret Service wouldn't have picked it even if he wasn't Chinese intelligence. So why were they there?"

Jack told him about his conversation with Mercy Bennet. "The Vanderbilt Complex."

"That makes sense," Nina Myers broke in, her voice softer and more distant from the microphone. "I was up there. Lee's house looks right down on the place. That's got to be why the Secret Service was staking it out."

"Tell them what's going on," Jack said.

"Stand by," Henderson said. The line dulled and Jack knew he was on hold.

"Never a dull moment for you," Sharpton said during the interlude.

"That's because I didn't retire."

The line came alive again. "Jack," Henderson said, "the Secret Service tells us everything is under control at the Lee house. They checked with their men up there and all's well."

It's not right, Jack thought. Ayman al-Libbi with high-powered rocket-propelled grenades, eco-terrorists with killer viruses, and the heads of three of the world's most powerful countries all meeting together. "I don't care what the Secret Service says. We need to be up there."

"Bauer." Jack recognized the angry nasal voice immediately. Chappelle. "We've already discussed options internally. I've passed along word to the President himself. This meeting is important, and the Secret Service has guaranteed security. We need to stand down."

Jack banged the phone against his forehead in frustration. "What we need to do," he said at last, "is send someone up there to have a look. I'm going. Are you sending me any backup?"

Ryan Chappelle's voice rose an octave. "Bauer, you're coming in. Right now. You've got problems you don't even know about—"

"What was that?" Jack said, shaking the phone. "You're breaking up."

"Bauer! Report back here immediate—"

"Bad connection. It's a borrowed phone, sorry!" Bauer yelled. He hung up.

Sharpton shook his head, but his eyes were smiling. "I see a lot has changed," he said sarcastically.

Bauer ignored that. He was already thinking of the fastest route to the Vanderbilt Complex. If al-Libbi was there, stopping him alone was going to be difficult. He stopped and looked at Sharpton. "How retired are you?"

6:30 P.M. PST
Mountaingate Drive, Los Angeles

It had been easy, really. Disguised as the gardener, al-Libbi had had several hours to listen to the Secret Service communications. He'd heard how they responded to communications through their ear pieces and quickly memorized their call signs. And he had always, always been good at voices.

So each time they called in, he gave the call sign in a voice that approximated the man who had possessed the ear bud. Possessed it, that is, before al-Libbi had cut his throat and dumped his body into a closet.

It was almost time. The terrorist ignored the dead bodies and hefted several large, long boxes one at a time out of the truck and carried them into the backyard. A tall screen of bamboo marked the borders of Lee's house, and hid part of the Vanderbilt Complex from view. Al-Libbi stacked his boxes there, then picked up the shears he'd used to kill Tuman and clipped a hole in the bamboo hedge. Once it was clear, he had a clear line of sight to the Vanderbilt Complex below. In fact, his sightline was clear straight to the reception hall at the heart of the building. The RPG–29s' five-hundred-meter range would be more than enough to do the job.

Al-Libbi's cell phone rang. Anyone who had his number was important enough to speak to, but he was surprised to see this particular number on his screen. "I thought we were done with our dealings," he said by way of hello.

"There's been a change in management," said Frankie Michaelmas. "I'm in charge now, and yeah, I want to make a deal."

6:36 P.M. PST
Vanderbilt Complex

If Stan Chupnik was nervous, he didn't show it. Hell, he didn't even *feel* it.

He started and finished his wardrobe slowly and fastidiously. His pants were pressed and the pleat stood up nice and straight. His shirt was wrinkle-free and as white as bone. He had shaved twice for the occasion.

After more than ten minutes of primping, Stan stood before the dressing mirror nailed to the door of the men's locker room and sized himself up. His bow tie was a little crooked, so he plucked it loose and began to retie it. No clip-ons. That was the sort of detail that differentiated the Vanderbilt from pretty much everywhere else.

Stan had worked as a waiter at the Vanderbilt—or "the Van" as the employees called it—ever since it had been constructed, and had served at every important shindig the complex had hosted. Of course, the real money was made waiting tables across the plaza at the Almandine, the five-star restaurant where dinner for four ran about four hundred dollars. That was Stan's bread and butter. But exclusive events at the Reception Hall allowed Stan to breathe the same air as celebrities and world leaders. As far as he was concerned, that was worth the loss of a few hundred dollars in tips now and then. That was certainly true of tonight.

"Did they hassle you?" Daniel Schuman was saying to one of the other waiters in the locker room. "They asked me about a thousand questions. I take that back, they asked me the same four or five questions about a thousand times."

One of the guys on the catering staff said, "What kind of questions?"

Daniel tugged at his bow tie, trying to even it out. "All about Arabs. I've been to Jerusalem a couple of times, and each time I go I try to make a side visit, you know? Damascus, Iran, places like that."

"Jesus," said the other waiter, "you're asking for trouble."

"Yeah, well, those bastards gave me some. I almost didn't get to do this gig. They'd have given it to Lopez. Can you believe that? Lopez!"

Stan chimed in. "Well, it's all your fault. What do you think they're going to do, the world like it is now?"

"Oh, and I suppose you've never traveled anywhere?" Schuman retorted.

"All over the place, baby," said Stan smugly. "But not places that raise eyebrows. I'm a big Costa Rica fan. Brazil, Peru. I love it down there."

"You surf down there?" Schuman asked.

"Some, but mostly I do hikes up in the jungle."

"I did that once," the other waiter said. "Eco-tourist stuff."

"That's right," Stan agreed with a hint of pride. "I'm an eco-tourist."

• •

THE FOLLOWING TAKES PLACE
BETWEEN THE HOURS OF
7 P.M. AND 8 P.M.
PACIFIC STANDARD TIME

• •

7:00 P.M. PST
Mountaingate Drive, Los Angeles

The sun was little more than a line of orange fire along the
rim of the world. To the east the world was dark, but over the
Santa Monica Mountains the sky looked bloody.

Jack parked several doors down from the Marcus Lee address. He and Sharpton, both rearmed, slipped out of the car
quietly and padded along the street lined with the demi-
mansions that were so in vogue. Streetlights had come on,
and Jack skirted the pools of light until he reached the correct address—a tall white house at the end of the lane, removed from the others.

The porch light was on, as were several lights inside, but
the place was quiet. The Secret Service said they had been

checking in with the agents there on a regular basis, but Jack refused to believe it. If he was wrong, Chappelle could (and would) throw the book at him.

7:07 P.M. PST
Vanderbilt Complex

President Barnes walked into the Reception Hall with a conscious and confident stride. The hall was empty except for the priceless art on the wall, a dining table with two chairs, and the Premier of China.

Xu Boxiong. The name was as inscrutable as the man, as far as Barnes was concerned. Xu stood there, at the far side of the table, his arms straight down at his sides, his round face composed into a warm but unreadable expression, neither friendly nor otherwise. Though Xu was in his sixties, his hair was jet black and thick. The Chinese leader wore a pair of Coke-bottle glasses, though Mitch Rasher had told Barnes that Xu's eyesight was perfect. He wore the glasses like curtains over the windows to his soul.

It occurred to Barnes that, in all his political career, this was the first time he'd met a Communist.

Barnes crossed the distance between them, extended his hand, and said, "Mr. Premier, it's a pleasure to meet you at last."

Xu smiled and tipped his upper body. "The pleasure is mine, Mr. President," he said in gently accented English.

And, as if the greeting had broken a spell, others flooded into the room. Four security agents, two from each country, stationed themselves at either of the two exits. Waiters entered bearing the favorite drinks of each leader. Barnes raised his glass to Xu, who did likewise. They sipped together.

"It is a shame Mr. Novartov could not join us," Xu said. "Something to do with the flu. But perhaps in some way, better. We can speak more directly."

Barnes nodded, not ready to enter the deeper discussion yet. "Would you like to sit down, or shall we admire the art?"

"I have often heard of the Vanderbilt collection," Xu replied, his small eyes scanning the room. "Perhaps a circuit around the room?"

Barnes nodded and motioned with his arm. Xu stepped forward, and together they walked the perimeter of the room, stopping at each portrait to admire it or, in Barnes's case, to pretend to admire it. He wasn't much for fine art. He passed a picture of a bearded man that evoked strength but did nothing for him, and a picture of a young man in red that he vaguely remembered as being painted by Raphael. Both he and Xu stopped, as if by some unspoken signal, before a tall portrait of Louis XIV, the Sun King.

"Now there," said Xu thoughtfully, "was a ruler."

"Not a member of the party, though," Barnes pointed out.

Xu turned to him and gave the slightest nod. "None of us, unfortunately, is perfect. But I was speaking of his leadership, not his politics. I aspire to be this sort of leader, and I am curious if you, too, have such aspirations, Mr. President."

"One can hope"—Barnes decided to take the initiative—"that your leadership will include accommodating the wishes of the nations that wish to invite you into the Group of Eight."

Xu sipped his drink. "What accommodations would those be?"

"Human rights," the American President said simply. "We need movement on human rights to stop the kind of scene we had out here today."

The Chinese leader turned to face Barnes fully, and lowered his drink so that nothing stood between the other man and him. "It is interesting to us that the U.S. is so concerned about human rights in China when it maintains detention camps around the globe."

Barnes was ready for this, of course. Politics aside, human rights was an issue close to his heart, and one that had pained him during his entire presidency. He had stuck his integrity in his back pocket countless times, but never at the expense of those who suffered under injustice.

"Sir," he said firmly, "if we are to have any sort of dialogue whatsoever, you will never again compare our detention of terrorists and murderers to the incarceration of those who simply disagree with you."

Xu did not respond immediately. He studied Barnes, the eyes behind the Coke-bottle glasses slowly traveling across the American's face. The statement, Barnes knew, had been calculated. Those closest to him knew of his famous temper, and he suspected Xu was testing him. If this was how they were going to play, Barnes thought, it was going to be a long night.

7:24 P.M. PST
Outside the Vanderbilt Complex

Mercy didn't stop her car until the bumper was touching the agent's knees. She got out as the man in the dark suit came around to the front of her car, his hand held up, palm out.

"I'm sorry, ma'am," he said, "but the museum is closed this evening for a private affair."

"I know. I called," she said, holding up the badge she'd reacquired. "Detective Bennet. I need to talk to whoever is in charge."

The agent kept his hand upheld and turned to mutter into his microphone. After listening, he nodded and turned back to Mercy. "They got your call up the hill, ma'am. I'll take you up there, but you'll have to leave the car. This way."

The agent motioned her toward the white stucco building, the station for the tram. Several more agents were there; they checked Mercy's ID again, and then allowed her onto the tram.

"Hurry, please," Mercy said. "This is urgent."

"Yes, ma'am," the agent said. The tram hummed up the hill to the Vanderbilt Complex, but it moved with interminable slowness. Mercy was sure she could have walked it faster. At last they came to the top, where the tram ended next to a set of acre-wide, shallow steps made of travertine that led up to the massive double doors of the Vanderbilt. Two more agents were trotting down the steps. One in the lead held his hand out to Mercy, who shook it quickly.

"Adam Carter, Agent in Charge," said the man. "What's this all about?"

"I told you over the phone," she said. "There's a—"

"—plot against the President, yes, you said that. What is this about a virus?"

Mercy repeated what she had relayed on the drive over. "There's an eco-terrorist group that is trying to make a statement. They have some kind of virus like Ebola and I think they are going to try to release it here, tonight."

"Do you have any idea who's delivering it, or how?" Carter asked earnestly. "Because frankly, I'm totally willing to believe you if the President's safety is even slightly compromised, but I need more information."

"I'm not sure how," Mercy admitted, "but I got the information directly from the man who plotted the whole thing."

Agent Carter frowned, and Mercy realized how odd her statement had sounded. "And where is he now, ma'am?"

She groaned inwardly. "He's dead."

"Well, if he's dead—"

"Agent Carter, please don't be an ass," she said impatiently. "The virus is real. You can check with the L.A. office of the Counter Terrorist Unit. They know about it."

Carter nodded. "I'm really not trying to be uncooperative, ma'am," he said. "You're a detective and we take local law enforcement's warnings seriously. But we've had calls already from CTU. They warned us about the house up on the hill, and our agents confirm that everything's fine." He pointed up the slope to the right of the complex, where the silhouette of a house stood out from the hilltop. She wondered what the house had to do with anything, and if Jack Bauer was there. Carter continued. "But you're not giving me anything to go on. I'm not sure that I can evacuate the President on a rumor, especially when our agents are in complete control of the environment."

"Can I at least come in?" she asked. "I don't need to see the President, but I've been around one or two of these ecoterrorists, and I might recognize someone."

Carter hesitated. She watched him oscillate between his desire to keep her out, thus eliminating a variable, and letting her in to thoroughly explore any hint of danger to his protectee. Finally, he nodded.

7:27 P.M. PST
Mountaingate Drive, Los Angeles

The street was as quiet as any street in any affluent neighborhood. Jack parked his car well away from the white house at the end of the lane and he and Sharpton got out. Jack saw no option but the straightforward approach. If the Secret Service caught them sneaking in, it would cause more trouble than it was worth. So he strode up the circular driveway with Sharpton in tow, expecting at any moment to be stopped by an agent stepping around a corner. But none came.

Jack's internal alarms would have gone off even without the security failure. There was a gardener's truck in the driveway. The trucks themselves were common enough in affluent neighborhoods, but it was rare to see a gardener at work after sunset. Jack drew his SIG-sauer, recovered from the riots, and held it low at his side. Sharpton took his cue and did the same.

7:29 P.M. PST
Vanderbilt Complex

Mercy was impressed by his demeanor. Carter was calm and professional, neither overreacting to her dire prediction nor ignoring her vague warnings. Of course, she wanted to shout at the top of her lungs that the President should be evacuated immediately, but she could not blame the Agent in Charge for his discretion. She'd given him almost nothing to go on.

She had to find something, she knew. She was desperate for some means of convincing the Secret Service that she was right. Mercy found herself doing something she never thought she would. She thought, *What would Jack do? What would Bauer do when confronted with a plot he knew to be real but without the evidence to prove it?*

He'd find another way to move the President to safety, she thought. And he'd do it without regard for himself or his reputation. And in that moment Mercy formed her plan. When she was close enough, she was going to draw her own weapon and fire. The Secret Service would take her down, she knew, but they would also evacuate the President, remove him immediately from the premises to some secure, controllable haven. He'd be safe. Copeland's plot would be foiled.

She steeled her resolve as they marched up the wide, shallow travertine steps and through the great double doors. The foyer of the Vanderbilt was more than two stories tall, with several hallways leading in different directions, with signs promising displays from ancient Greece, the Renaissance, and the Impressionist era. One especially magnificent hallway directly across from the doors led straight to the Main Gallery, a central room housing the finest of the complex's works of art. Two agents were stationed there, as well. Carter waved to them and they let Mercy pass. Art hung on the hallway walls, but Mercy noticed none of it in her eagerness to reach the gallery. The hallway ended at a T-intersection, with short hallways to either side and an archway in front, leading to another magnificent room. Four agents guarded this door, and two of them were Chinese. Beyond, she saw a table set in exquisite fashion, with two empty chairs, almost as though the dining set were an exhibit itself, the vacant chairs offering some statement about the emptiness of modern life.

"This is as far as I can take you," Carter said. "If there's anything more you can tell me, tell it now."

Mercy glanced around, but what she was looking for would not be found in art. She needed evidence, and she had none. At the far end of the gallery she saw two men strolling casually from masterpiece to masterpiece. She became hyper-conscious of her pistol's bulk against her left ribs. She would have to do it. She'd have to.

Three figures in white coats suddenly burst out of the hallway to her left, carrying silver trays topped with silver covers. Yet another Secret Service agent was with them. That agent gave a thumbs-up sign to the agents at the door. Even so, the door wardens stopped each waiter briefly, lifted the covers, and examined their contents, then waved them past.

"Detective?" Carter asked. He rested a hand gently on her forearm.

Mercy barely heard him. Something about the waiters bothered her. She studied their backs, trying to put her finger on the problem. The waiters strode almost lock-step across the floor and laid their trays on the table. With long, graceful motions, they placed precious porcelain dishes full of food onto the table.

Not all the waiters, Mercy thought. Just that one. Her eyes narrowed as she focused on a waiter with dark hair. She'd seen his back before. She'd seen it. And as he turned, his eyes fell on Mercy. In a split second his look of confidence turned to one of sheer terror, a look Mercy had seen on his face before—when she'd crashed into the vials of virus.

"Him!" Mercy yelled. "That's him!"

7:35 P.M. PST
Vanderbilt Complex

Stan felt like someone had kicked him in the liver. Seeing the LAPD detective standing there knocked the wind out of his lungs. She shouldn't be here. She couldn't be here. How could she have figured it out?

Her shout broke the spell, and Stan knew what he had to do. He bolted. But he didn't run for the exit. He ran straight to the nearest masterpiece, the portrait of Louis XIV that was taller than he was. With all his might, Stan grabbed the frame and yanked the picture off the wall. He knew the picture frame was bolted to the wall. He knew that, even bracing his feet against the wall, he would most likely fail to pull it entirely free. He also knew that it didn't matter. He didn't care about the picture, nor did he need to pull it entirely free. He just needed to trigger the security measures.

7:36 P.M. PST
Mountaingate Drive, Los Angeles

Jack moved through the foyer of the Mountaingate house. He and Sharpton had spared a few moments to clear the large front yard, and Jack had made short work kicking in the door. The house was dark except for a pale light from the kitchen shed by fluorescents built under the cabinets. Jack motioned for Sharpton to go upstairs. He cleared the kitchen and the garage quietly, not really expecting anyone to be there. If the Vanderbilt Complex was the target, then the backyard would be the best position. But Jack didn't want anyone behind him when he reached the back of the house. He moved toward the living room.

7:37 P.M. PST
Vanderbilt Complex

Alarms shrieked the moment the waiter grabbed the painting. The sirens were so loud that even the best-trained agents flinched for a moment. The Secret Service agents in the room were already moving, two of them going after the waiter and two of them covering President Barnes, dragging him toward the exit. Agent in Charge Carter moved forward, his weapon already in his hand, when he realized something unexpected was happening. A sheet of thick Plexiglas was dropping down from the top of the arched entrance to the Main Gallery.

"What the hell is this!" he shouted. The Plexiglas barrier was halfway down. He dropped underneath it and rolled into the gallery, scanning the room past his gun sights, seeing several Chinese agents eyeing him over the barrels of their own weapons.

It all happened fast after that. The two Secret Service agents reached the waiter and laid hands on him. He struggled for a moment, raising his hand. For a heart-stopping moment Carter thought he was holding a detonator. That was impossible; their security sweeps would never have missed anything explosive.

He was right. The waiter held only a palm-sized glass vial. He hurled it to the ground at the feet of the two world leaders. Security agents instinctively threw their bodies over the bodies of Barnes and Xu, but it didn't matter. The glass vial shattered, and for a fraction of a second everyone flinched. But nothing dramatic happened. Glass shards sprayed, and a tiny puff of white gas drifted up in the air and dissipated quickly. The Plexiglas shields closed down on the floor with a soft but definitive click. There was a split second of pure silence.

The next second was complete pandemonium. The two agents put the waiter facedown on the ground. The other two agents, handling Barnes, reached the Plexiglas barricade on the far side of the room and kicked at it angrily. Agent Carter leveled his pistol at the shield, then, thinking of the ricochet, lowered the muzzle. The Chinese agents were screaming in Mandarin.

Outside the gallery, Mercy, along with a crowd of other agents and staff, looked on in sheer amazement. The room must have been sealed airtight because they could hear nothing that Carter or the others were saying, but they could see them moving frantically. A moment later Carter spoke into his radio, and an agent near Mercy responded.

"Yes, sir," the agent said. "We'll get the glass lifted immediately."

"No!" Mercy yelled. The agent scowled at her. "Let me talk to him."

The agent consulted with Carter, then pulled the bud from his ear. Mercy leaned in close to him, located the speaker, and grabbed the agent's hand like it was a microphone. "Carter, it's Detective Bennet. If I'm right, that entire room is now contaminated with the virus. You can't open the doors."

"Bullshit," Carter said. He had approached the Plexiglas near her and stood there, his face red with anger. "This is the President of the United States in here and I'll blow the side of the goddamned building away to get him out, virus or no virus!"

"Then you risk spreading the thing all over the city," Mercy said.

President Barnes appeared at Carter's side. It was a surreal moment for Mercy—an LAPD cop suddenly finding herself talking to the leader of the free world through a sheet of Plexiglas. He looked exactly as he did on television, except that his face was turning pink and a vein had started to pulse in his forehead.

"What the hell is this?" he demanded. "Who are you?"

Carter listed her credentials succinctly.

"There's a virus, sir," Mercy said.

Barnes blanched. "Are you sure—?" he started to ask, but discarded the question. Of course she was sure. She wouldn't be there if she weren't sure. "How bad?"

"Fatal," she replied. "But not for a few hours at least. And I think there's an antidote. But if we open these doors it will spread—"

Barnes was nothing if not decisive. He turned to Carter. "Get rid of anyone nonessential. Seal off the whole complex. Get National Health Services on the line, tell them to prepare some kind of contained transportation for all of us to a safer location. Keep these doors sealed until we know the entire building is evacuated."

"But, sir—" Carter protested.

One of the other Secret Service agents shouted something

to Carter, who turned to see the man holding up a small device. As Carter's had earlier, Mercy's heart stopped for a moment as she thought *bomb*, but a second later it was revealed to be a portable DVD player.

"The guy who did this is a political activist, not an outright murderer," Mercy said to Carter. "I'm guessing there's a message there for you."

Carter activated the DVD player, and an image came on the screen. Mercy could just see it between Carter and President Barnes, and Carter's mike carried the message to her ears.

The image was little more than a silhouette, but Mercy recognized it as Copeland. "Hello," he said in a gentrified voice. "You can call me Seldom Seen Smith and, if you're watching this, Mr. President, you've just been infected with a deadly virus. You have approximately twelve hours to live."

Carter glanced at Mercy with a damn-you-were-right look on his face.

The DVD continued. "Our purpose here is simple. To save the rain forests of the Amazon. Your first question, of course, will be to wonder what the connection is between our cause and your infection. Let me assure you that the connection is very direct. The virus that is now replicating in your system is called Cat's Claw. It exists naturally in the Amazon. Of course, I have to confess, I've done a little tinkering with the virus. In its natural state, it kills human beings in about twenty-four hours. The strain that I have developed for you kills in half that time. I discovered it by lucky accident, but rest assured that loggers and developers will stumble upon it and carry it back to civilization soon enough. More importantly, there is an antidote . . . and the antidote also grows naturally in the Amazon. To date, I am the only person who knows from what plant the vaccine can be synthesized, and how to do it.

"My proposition to you is very simple. Go on television right now and announce that the rain forests must be secured immediately, and that all development and logging must halt. I will give you the antidote, and you will live.

"If you don't, you'll never hear from me again, and you will die. I would like you to note that I have gone to a great deal of trouble to keep the virus contained. Your location is isolated. The security system acts as a sort of quarantine zone. I have no wish to kill people unnecessarily. But you are destroying the planet, and I have to stop you. So if it comes down to it, I will spread the virus into the population, forcing them to preserve the Amazon until they can discover the vaccine for themselves. I expect my associate to be released unharmed. He knows how to contact me."

The screen went blank.

7:41 P.M. PST
Mountaingate Drive, Los Angeles

The moment the alarms sounded from the complex below, Jack shifted from his slow and steady pace to a sprint. He was through the living room in a flash. He opened the sliding glass doors to the backyard as quickly and quietly as he could, and then he was out onto the patio of the backyard.

If there were lights in the backyard, they'd been killed. A line of tall shrubs along the perimeter shielded the yard from the city lights below, so the yard was almost completely in shadow. Jack crouched down, waiting for his eyes to adjust, scanning the deep pools of darkness along the edge of the yard. Finally he saw what he was looking for—a hunched figure almost invisible against the tree line. Jack didn't bother with warnings. He leveled the SigSauer and exhaled as he squeezed off three rounds. Noise and fire shattered the silence and darkness, mixed with a startled cry of surprise and pain. Jack fired again. This muzzle flash left an after-image seared on to his eyes, an image of Ayman al-Libbi on one knee, his face contorted in pain, an RPG pointing straight at Jack.

Jack dived to the side as he heard the familiar hiss and whistle of the launching rocket. The rocket-propelled grenade smoked across the short distance and exploded into the house behind Jack. The CTU agent felt himself lifted off the ground by tongues of fire and glass fragments glittering like a starburst as the sharp, short thunder of the ordinance enveloped him. He landed in the grass, barely keeping his hands on the SigSauer. Jack forced himself up to his knees, shaking his head and ignoring the roaring echo in his ears. Something in the house was on fire, casting uneven light out onto the yard. It was enough to see by. Jack raised his weapon one-handed and found Ayman al-Libbi on the far side of his sights. Before he could squeeze the trigger, someone body-slammed him from the side and Jack went over, landing heavily in the grass. This time he lost the SigSauer completely. The person on top of him was unskilled, but an animal, throwing violent knees into his body and tearing at his face. Jack caught the assailant's arm, hooked his leg around the man's leg, and bucked his hips, rolling over and ending on top. Without looking he threw a head butt downward and felt the hard bone of his forehead smash through lips and teeth. He raised his head back and slammed his elbow down onto the same spot. Only then did he look and see Muhammad Abbas's face, now all blood and pulp.

Jack's eyes were intent on Abbas but his senses were alert, aware of his surroundings. The movement was three-quarters behind him but he saw it nearly in time, rolling away as the shovel swung at his head. The shovel head glanced off his skull, making his head ring again. There were two accomplices with al-Libbi. Where the hell was Sharpton?

Jack rolled in the semi-darkness, groping for his weapon, but then he heard someone else tap and rack the SigSauer and he knew his attackers had found it first.

"Stop," said a male voice. Abbas. Jack looked up. Abbas was on his feet, half his face illuminated by a half-dozen small fires burning in the damaged house. Beside him, holding the shovel, was a short girl with curly blond hair. She was holding Jack's pistol in her hands. She didn't hold it well, but her hands were steady and her eyes were clear and determined. She had cleared and racked the weapon. She could certainly pull the trigger.

Al-Libbi shouted in Arabic from across the yard. He sounded as if he was in pain. Abbas stepped behind the girl, out of her line of fire. "I'm going to check on him. Kill this one." He ran into the shadows.

The girl stepped forward. One shot rang out and Jack flinched, but at the same time he knew that the girl had not fired. A hole erupted in the girl's shoulder and she screamed, dropping the weapon. Sharpton, it had to be. Jack lunged forward, grabbing his SigSauer. He grabbed her by the hair and shoved her down onto the ground, making her eat grass as he turned to reacquire the terrorists. He saw them, two shadows moving in and out of the darkness. Jack fired, tracking them, but the shadows kept moving until they reached the corner of the house.

The girl. Sharpton. Al-Libbi. Jack had three elements to

prioritize. Jumping to his feet, he stepped toward the girl's feet and stomped hard on her ankle, hearing it crack. She screamed, and he knew she wouldn't be going anywhere fast. Jack ran across the yard, parallel to the house, and saw Sharpton on the ground, his body lying across the threshold. His clothing was shredded on his body and his skin had been half flayed from his bones. His arms were stretched out, the gun lying under his right hand. He ran past Sharpton and reached the corner of the house. Firelight illuminated the corner, and Jack knew he'd be visible. He leaned around the corner quickly, then pulled his head back as someone discharged rounds from a pistol. Two of them tore chunks of wood from the frame of the house. Jack kept his body on the safe side and stuck his gun around the corner, firing several rounds. Then he dropped low and sprinted down the side of the house. He zigzagged forward, but no more shots came. Jack reached the front end of the house where an open gate led to the front yard. Jack hoped for more gunfire; if al-Libbi and Abbas stood and fought, it gave him a better chance of getting them. But the front of the house was quiet. Jack ran to the sidewalk. Lights were on in the houses down the block, and a few people stumbled out with cell phones in their hands and shocked looks on their faces. Jack saw the lights of a car hurrying away, but it was too dark to catch the make or license plate.

7:49 P.M. PST
Vanderbilt Complex

The last of the food servers and administrative staff for the Vanderbilt had been evacuated. Ambulance sirens approached, and Mercy heard Secret Service agents confirm that National Health Services personnel were en route.

Inside the sealed Main Gallery, the Chinese security officers were shouting into cell phones and radios. Agent in Charge Carter was alternately talking and listening on his radio incessantly, while the other two Secret Service agents kept the waiter pinned down and peppered him with questions. But the waiter had sealed his mouth and refused to speak, smiling smugly as though the questioning was all part of the plan.

Mercy knew something had been happening for the last few minutes. A sound rolled through the Vanderbilt Complex, a muffled roar like distant thunder that resounded off the mountain canyons around them. Half the agents in the complex had suddenly rushed off, weapons drawn.

Surprisingly, the two calmest men in the entire complex were President Barnes and Xu Boxiong. Mercy, who had never been so close to real power, watched them intently. They seemed to find their focus in the midst of the crisis; their answers to questions succinct, their decisions made quickly and surely. Mercy had no idea what sort of man the Premier of Communist China was, nor did she really know much about Barnes, but this, she decided, was leadership: the ability, in fact the desire, to make decisions when decisions needed to be made.

Suddenly President Barnes was standing in front of her, his eyes studying her through the glass. He spoke to her through a radio. "Who are these people? If we capitulate to their requests, will they give up the vaccine?"

"That's—that's a problem, sir," she stammered "The man who organized this is already dead. Murdered by one of his people."

Barnes scowled. "Are you telling me there's no one to negotiate with?"

"Yes, sir."

Jack hung up the phone after a thirty-second conversation with Henderson telling him that al-Libbi was at large, that the explosions were caused by a stray RPG, that he had one suspect in custody, and that he needed an ambulance immediately. He ran through the house to the back patio. The blond girl was curled up in a ball, bleeding from her shoulder and holding her ankle.

Bauer knelt down beside Sharpton. The former agent had rolled onto his side, his chest heaving. The skin on his neck and one side of his face was seared. One of his eyes was closed. The other looked up at Jack.

"Kelly," Jack said, "hang on. You're going to be okay."

Sharpton coughed. "Lie—liar."

"Thanks," Jack said. "You got her for me."

Sharpton nodded as his good eye closed. "That's . . . two times." He never spoke again.

Jack paused, though he did not have a moment to spare. Sharpton had been a good man. Then he walked over to the girl, who looked up at him. Her eyes were moist, but she wasn't crying. "You broke my fucking ankle!" she spat at him.

He knelt down and checked her shoulder. Sharpton's round had passed through her shoulder blade and exited the hollow of her clavicle. Her shoulder was probably shattered, but she was going to live.

Jack's phone rang. He answered and heard Mercy's voice. "Jack, they told me there's something going on up the hill from here. I have a feeling you know about it."

"You could say that. You talked about a girl before," Jack said. "I think I have her."

Mercy paused. "I'd like to talk to her again," she said

ominously. "There's an emergency down here. The President and the Chinese leader have been exposed to the virus."

Jack swore under his breath.

"Jack, you there?"

"Yeah," he said. "We need to get this girl into an interrogation room. We have to find a vaccine for this virus right now. If we don't, by morning people are going to start dying."

1 2 3 4 5 6 7 8 9
10 11 12 13 **14** 15 16 17
18 19 20 21 22 23 24

....

**THE FOLLOWING TAKES PLACE
BETWEEN THE HOURS OF
8 P.M. AND 9 P.M.
PACIFIC STANDARD TIME**

....

8:00 P.M. PST
Bauer Residence

Teri sat on the edge of her daughter's bed and laid a cool wet washcloth over her forehead. "Does that help?"

"It's better," Kim said. "I hate being sick."

"I know, honey, I'm sorry. I called the Tashmans but they weren't home. As soon as they get here I'm going to go out and get you something from the pharmacy."

"You can go now, Mom," Kim said drowsily. "I'm—"

"You're not okay, honey. And if your father were here like he's supposed to be, I wouldn't have to wait."

"You sound like you hate him." Kim's words sounded both pouty and honest in the way only a teenager could speak them. Teri realized just how much of her anger she'd allowed to show. She had to fix it.

"I don't hate him, honey. I don't. But I get frustrated when he's gone so much. Sometimes I worry that he'd rather— well, sometimes I just wish he had more time to spend at home."

8:03 P.M. PST
Vanderbilt Complex

All President Barnes could think was, *If I can get through this, I can get through anything.*

He exerted every effort to sit through the crisis in complete calm. He could feel the eyes of Xu Boxiong on him at all times. Xu, who must also be exerting enormous self-discipline, seemed eager to take Barnes's measure. Through a sheer act of will, Barnes remained cool, delivering orders in measured tones, even nibbling at the hors d'oeuvres that had been trapped in the room with them.

It wasn't easy. Barnes had seen video of Ebola victims as the disease ravaged them. He did not want to die that way. And even if he didn't die in body, his political death was surely imminent. How had his security people allowed this to happen? Where were all his goddamned counterterrorist teams?

As if on cue, Carter approached him and said, "Sir, Ryan Chappelle has just arrived. He's the Regional Director for the Counter Terrorist Unit."

"I remember him," Barnes said. He stood up and walked over to the transparent shield. On the other side stood a short, balding, ferret-faced man holding a radio to his ear. Next to him stood Mitch Rasher, his closest advisor. Just having Rasher on the premises made Barnes feel better.

"Mr. President, I'm sorry," Chappelle said.

"Don't be sorry, just fix it," Barnes replied. "First, tell me what the hell is going on."

"I have some answers for you, sir," Chappelle replied, "but it's not a complete picture yet. What we know is that there were actually two terrorist plots in the works. Our agents stopped terrorists from firing rocket-propelled grenades into this building. But at the same time, an eco-terrorist group managed to—"

"I know what they managed," said Barnes irritably. "Why didn't your people know about this?"

Chappelle fidgeted and Barnes knew instantly that Chappelle was uncomfortable speaking truth to power. "Well, sir, we had people on the case. Unfortunately, we didn't learn about this meeting until the last minute."

Barnes looked at Rasher through the glass and frowned deeply. The meeting had been Rasher's idea. The secrecy had been his idea, too. Rasher, an entirely political animal, believed the stories of Xu's daunting negotiating skills and hadn't wanted to expose his man to any public scrutiny if he failed to win concessions from China. Secret negotiations were only valuable if they remained secret.

"The press?" Barnes asked.

Mitch Rasher, on his own radio, said, "Controlled. No one's come up the hill but our people, and we're putting the word out that there was an attempted robbery up here. The Vanderbilt is going along with it."

"That's something then," Barnes allowed. "Is NHS here? Do they have a vaccine?"

"ETA is five more minutes," Rasher said.

"But," the CTU man said, "but frankly, sir, we already had NHS investigating other exposures. They don't have a vaccine yet."

"So you think this idiot on the DVD was telling the truth?"

Suddenly a blond man pushed his way through the crowd of staffers and security people and began talking to Chappelle. He looked like hell—his shirt was torn, the side of his face was turning purple, and there were streaks of what must have been blood on his sleeves and pants. Barnes couldn't hear him through the radio, but it was clear from Chappelle's expression that he didn't like the newcomer.

8:09 P.M. PST
Vanderbilt Complex

". . . what the hell do you mean he got away?" Chappelle snapped. "How could you let him get away?"

Jack glared at Chappelle. "If you hadn't refused the backup I needed at Lee's house, he wouldn't have gotten away. Not to mention the fact that if I had listened to you, I wouldn't have gone up to that house in the first place, and you'd be standing in the middle of a bomb site rather than a quarantine zone!"

Chappelle opened his mouth, then shut it, realizing that everyone around them, including the President, was listening to their argument. Jack saw the wheels turning in the director's head: he had screwed up the call on Marcus Lee, but at the same time, he would never take the political heat. Lee had been cleared by the Secret Service, and they had been stationed at the residence. That snafu would be blamed on them. Thanks to Jack Bauer and Nina Myers, CTU had been the only Federal agency with any clue to what Lee was up to.

Jack glanced at Mercy to make sure she was all right. She nodded, reading his thoughts. They had a lot of talking to do; he knew that. But it would have to wait a little longer.

"Well," Chappelle said at last, "we need to find al-Libbi."

"Forget about the terrorist!" Barnes demanded. "Find me

the vaccine. According to the message, we've got less than ten hours."

Jack looked at the Secret Service man next to the President. "Bring me that waiter."

The other two quarantined agents brought him over and slammed him up against the Plexiglas. Someone held a radio to his ear.

"Your name is Stan," Jack said.

"You have to let me go," said Stan. "If you don't, you won't hear from him."

"Him? You mean Bernard Copeland?" The waiter reacted physically to the name, his facing draining of color. Jack continued. "We won't hear from him anyway, Stan," Jack said. "He was murdered this afternoon. By one of your people."

The edges of Stan's mouth sank into a deep frown. "You—you're lying."

"I think Frankie did it," Jack stated, looking at Mercy as though waiting for a second opinion. "She seems like the type."

It was the oldest trick in the interrogator's handbook, to act like one knew more than one did. Of course, in this case Jack was almost certain he was right.

The reaction on Stan's face proved it. "Oh shit," he muttered. "Oh my god. She's crazy."

"Stan," Jack said in the tone of a reproachful parent. "I want to remind you what this means. You've been exposed to the virus like everyone else in there. The guy you were counting on to vaccinate you is dead. Your life span can now be measured in single digits. Tell us what you know."

Stan talked. But in the end, what he had to say was interesting without containing anything vital. Stan's role in the eco-terrorist plot was no different from the role of true believers in any organization. He'd been recruited for his zeal and been

sold on a dangerous role, but never been told the deepest secrets of the group. But he did confirm Jack and Mercy's suspicions about Frankie Michaelmas. "She's a nutcase," Stan said.
"The rest of us wanted to find some way to get the world's attention, but she wanted to find some way to hurt people. She's
the one that got the idea of trying to contact real terrorist
groups. She said no one would really take us seriously until
we defended the Amazon the way Hamas defends Palestine."

"And look how that's worked out," Mercy murmured.

The waiter could feel the anger on both sides of the Plexiglas rise, and all of it was currently directed at him.
"Copeland didn't go for it. None of us did," Stan said defensively. "I got the feeling Frankie was contacting them on her
own, 'cause she kept coming to us with new ways to orga-
nize. We broke into small cells, and almost no one knew
everything that was going on except Bernie. Bernie liked the
part. He was really paranoid about people knowing what we
were doing, especially the Federal government."

"Let's get to the important part, Stan," Jack said. "Who
else in your group has the vaccine, or knows where to get it?"

Stan shook his head. "Man, if I knew, I'd tell you. I don't
want to die of this stuff. I know there are some others, but I
don't know them. But I'll bet Frankie knows."

Jack turned to Mercy. "I'm going to go talk to her. You
want to come along?"

8:18 P.M. PST
405 Freeway

Ayman al-Libbi sat in the passenger seat of Muhammad Abbas's rented Chrysler 300C, bleeding on the brand-new
leather seats. The bullet had blown some of the flesh off his
left side, but the round itself must have glanced off his ribs.

He was sure at least one of them was broken. But he did not think he was dying.

"Drive a little faster," he said, as cool as ever. "The other cars move faster than you do."

Abbas obeyed. "The safe house is fifteen minutes from here. You can make it?"

The terrorist nodded. "I can make it. How could I do otherwise? This whole affair has just become so much more interesting." He patted the pocket of his jacket, which contained two small glass vials.

8:20 P.M. PST
Los Angeles

"How are you feeling?" Jack asked as he headed down the freeway away from the Vanderbilt Complex and back to CTU.

"I'm fine right now," Mercy said. "I don't feel anything. Except pissed off. I feel really pissed off."

Jack took one hand off the wheel and put it over her hand. "We're going to find this vaccine. You're going to live," he said.

She put her hand over his. "Don't make promises you can't keep. Besides, there are more important people than me to worry about. Like your daughter. How is she?"

Jack gritted his teeth. "I'll call soon. I get the feeling Copeland kept his promises. If he really didn't give her the weaponized version of the virus, then she's got hours left."

"You've got to be exhausted," Mercy said. "I know I am."

"No time to be tired," he said, switching freeways and heading east. After a moment, he said, "You need to promise me something. According to the workup we got from NHS, you become contagious once you see lesions that open up. You've got to—"

"I'll do what I have to," Mercy said. "But as long as I'm not a danger to anyone, I'm staying on this case."

Jack smiled. "I always did like your attitude."

"You just like girls who can kick ass like that girl from *Alias*." There was another short silence. They both watched the blurred, impersonal lights of Los Angeles flow by on either side. Finally, Mercy said, "So what's it been? Mid-life crisis that you've chickened out of? I had block-away potential, but now that I'm up close you're not interested? What?"

Jack was glad to be driving so he could focus on the freeway. "You said you didn't want it," he said evasively. "You said—"

"I know about me and what I want," Mercy interrupted. "We're talking about you, now. I just want to know where it came from. I'm a detective, remember? I want answers. Was it just guy stuff, the need to have another woman? If it was, just tell me, 'cause I'm one of the cool chicks. I get that. I won't be part of it, but I get it."

Jack had to laugh in spite of himself. She really was one of the most centered people he'd ever met. "It wasn't just an itch I have to scratch," he said. "I promise. And I promise I'll tell you, but right now I want to focus on this."

These last words were spoken as they pulled up at CTU's Los Angeles headquarters.

CTU was a whirlwind of activity. Although the attack on the President and the firefight up at Mountaingate Drive had been hidden from the public and the media, the intelligence community was in an uproar. CTU was screaming at the CIA for its shoddy information on Marcus Lee. The CIA was screaming at the Chinese for not disclosing more. Everyone was screaming at National Health Services to provide more information on this unknown virus that had suddenly become the single most important issue in the entire world.

Jack blew through it all like a torpedo cutting through a whirlpool. Nina Myers shouted to him that his prisoner was in holding room two, and Jack was there in no time.

Frankie Michaelmas was sitting in a bare metal chair designed to do nothing for her comfort. Her shoulder had been heavily bandaged and her ankle was wrapped in a brace. Her face was pale from loss of blood, but a medic whispered to Jack that she was stable and coherent.

As Jack walked in, Frankie smiled at him. "You're the guy who broke my ankle. Did you get Ayman?"

Jack didn't bother to answer.

"You didn't get him," Frankie concluded. "You'd have a different look on your face if you did."

"You're going to tell me who else knows how to create the vaccine," Jack said. He checked his watch. "You're going to tell me that in the next three minutes."

Frankie shook her head, her blond curls matted to her forehead. "That's my leverage, man. You think I don't know the shit I'm in? I'm not giving away my only card."

"You don't have leverage," Jack said. "You're involved in a plot to kill the President of the United States. You've aided and abetted wanted terrorists. You're going to be put in a hole. The only thing you might negotiate is how far down we drop you."

Frankie looked at him, and Jack had to admit that she was cool. Whether it was desperation or pure fortitude he didn't know yet, but she played the game with force. "How's your daughter?"

Jack felt animal rage leap inside him, but he didn't let it show.

"The joke of it is that Bernie never would have let her die. He figured if he exposed her, then you'd have her checked out by someone and they'd know the virus was real. He was going to send you the vaccine no matter what. Fucking wimp."

"You don't have that weakness," Jack said.

She put aside the compliment. "He liked to pretend there were lines you didn't cross. But that's bullshit, right?" She wasn't looking for confirmation. Jack could see that whatever lines there might be, she'd crossed them long ago. "You do what you do to get what you need, and that's it. That's why the terrorists are so effective. No boundaries. That's what I kept telling him, but he wouldn't listen."

"Someone else knows how to make the vaccine. Tell me who it is."

"Amnesty. A plane ticket to anywhere I want. Five hundred thousand dollars."

"Life in prison instead of the death penalty," Jack offered, neither knowing nor caring if he could actually deliver.

"Amnesty. A plane ticket. Money," she repeated.

Jack checked his watch. "Just over a minute."

"I've read up on all this interrogation stuff," Frankie said. "I know what you guys can do, but you don't have time. Hell, you look more sleep deprived than I do. What are you going to do, make me stand up for the next ten hours? Okay, then the President will die. You don't have time for any of that psychological shit you guys do."

Jack nodded. "You're right."

He punched her hard right on her bandaged shoulder. Frankie screamed in agony. He waited for her to stop screaming. As her cries turned to sobs, she started to say, "What the—? What the—?" and he kicked her broken ankle. She screamed again.

As soon as he thought she could hear again, Jack leaned in close. "No boundaries, Frankie. No lines I haven't crossed. Wait till I start working on the healthy parts of you."

He sat back. "Before he died, Copeland scrawled three numbers on the floor. Thirteen. Forty-eight. Fifty-seven. Tell me what they mean."

Frankie sobbed and glared at him.

Jack continued calmly. "He also tried to say something. A name like Uma and the word 'ghetto.' Tell me what that means. Tell me what the numbers mean."

Frankie grinned almost maniacally through her pain. "He was always so goddamned corny."

"Tell me."

"Amnesty. A plane ticket. Mon—"

Jack leaned forward and rested his hand on her shattered shoulder. He could feel bones and meat move unstably beneath the bandages. She gasped wordlessly and shuddered uncontrollably. Jack leaned in again, but this time he noticed something at the edge of her bandages. He'd thought it was a laceration of some kind, but it wasn't. It was purple, like a bruise, but raised and spotted like a weird rash. Or a lesion.

Oh shit, Jack thought. He backed away. Frankie's shuddering did not stop. She doubled over and dry-heaved. Jack took another step backward. The lesion on Frankie's shoulder split open and bloody pus trickled out. At the same time, Frankie heaved again, and this time blood poured out of her mouth like water from a faucet.

She coughed. "The fast strain," she sputtered.

"Jack!" came over a hidden loudspeaker.

He didn't need to be told. He was already halfway out. Jack slammed the door behind him and checked his arms and hands. No blood. Was the virus airborne from inside a human body?

Jack hurried around to the observation room where he found several CTU agents, including Nina, Tony, and Christopher Henderson, along with Mercy Bennet, watching Frankie decompose. That was the word for it. Her skin seemed to simply split open as though invisible claws had torn at her shoulders and neck. She vomited blood two or three more times.

"Get NHS here immediately," Henderson ordered. "Get plastic over that door."

Jack looked at Mercy and knew what she was thinking. This was going to happen to her. And he felt a hand squeeze his heart when he knew that the same thing would happen to Kim if he failed.

8:31 P.M. PST
West Los Angeles

Ayman al-Libbi lay on the couch of the safe apartment. Despite the best efforts of the U.S. government, he had maintained a few friendships in America over the years—maintained them mostly because he did not ask favors of them. Until now. But *now* was a critical moment for him, a make-or-break moment as they said in the United States. So he had called in a very old debt from years ago in Jordan, and now he and Abbas were settled into a condominium that could not possibly appear on even the longest security watch list.

Abbas brought him a cup of tea. Ayman nodded. What would he have done all these years without Muhammad? Tonight was only one of a dozen times over the years that Ayman had survived because Muhammad was at his side. His devotion was absolute.

As he placed the tea on the coffee table, Muhammad slid his eyes over Ayman's face and body. It was not the first time Ayman had noticed this, nor was it the first time he wondered if the source of Muhammad's devotion was something more than mere friendship. Such things were abhorred in fundamentalist Islam, of course, but one heard whispers of it. Many young men who had spent their youth studying in a madrassa had experienced the subtle approach, the too-long-lingering look of another youth who could not or would not give voice to his urges. Ayman, who had long ago turned secular and cynical, now recognized such urges as the inevitable result of the separation of the sexes.

Ayman waited until Muhammad's eyes had slid off his body, then he said, "I'm going to call them."

Muhammad stopped, halfway into the seat across from the couch. "Are you sure? It's almost as risky as dealing with the Americans."

"This is a time for risks," Ayman said. He propped himself up as Muhammad handed him the phone. Ayman entered a long distance number he thought he'd never use again.

A gruff voice answered, and the terrorist said in Arabic, "This is Ayman al-Libbi. Let me speak to him."

There was a pause.

"Not too long," Muhammad warned. "The Americans will hear."

Another voice got on the line, a voice Ayman had not heard in many years. It was a powerful voice in the Iranian Ministry of Defense. "This is not Ayman al-Libbi speaking," the man said. "Ayman al-Libbi is a dead man."

"*Inshallah*," al-Libbi said, falling back on the religious expressions of his youth, "you will find it in your heart to breathe life back into me."

"You are an infidel now," the Iranian said.

"I am an infidel who holds the life of the President of the United States in his hands."

"You are a fool to say these things on the telephone."

"We are two fools then, because you will listen." Quickly, Ayman summed up his situation. "I have the Cat's Claw virus. I have the Dragon's Blood vaccine. I can save or destroy the American President. I can deliver the virus and the vaccine to you. In return, I need support here in Los Angeles.

I know you have people here, even if the Americans don't know it."

"Do others know how to create the vaccine?" asked the Iranian man.

"Three others."

There was a long pause. "You have our interest. But we must consider this. Wait for our call."

8:53 P.M. PST
CTU Headquarters, Los Angeles

Ten fewer minutes that Kim had to live. Ten fewer minutes that the leaders of two of the great powers had to live. Ten minutes closer to the violent, hemorrhagic death for Mercy Bennet.

Jack forced such thoughts from his mind as he stood in CTU's conference room with Mercy Bennet. CTU staff had covered the door to the holding room, sealing in the gruesome scene, and NHS would arrive any minute. In the meantime, CTU had been locked down in case the virus had some spread outside the room. Jack didn't think how he'd caught the virus, but he'd voluntarily locked himself into the conference room. Mercy, without explaining herself to anyone, had joined him.

"We need to figure out what those clues mean," Jack said. "Copeland may have been insane, but he wasn't stupid. He knew what he was doing when he left them."

Mercy nodded, her face settling into a calm, distant look as her detective's mind began sorting through facts. "He was trying to help. He didn't want the virus spread randomly. Whatever those clues mean, they have something to do with stopping the virus."

Jack wrote them down on the dry erase board. "Thirteen, forty-eight, fifty-seven. Is there anything in common?"

Mercy considered. "They're not prime numbers. There's no even spacing between them. They're all double digits." She wasn't forming a theory, just listing observations.

Jack rubbed his temples. He felt himself starting to wear down, but he'd been here before. His will was strong even when his body was not. "Frankie said something. Something about Copeland being 'corny.'"

"He was," Mercy said. "That whole Monkey Wrench Gang thing is corny. So is Seldom Seen Smith . . ."

They looked at each other. Jack voiced their mutual thoughts. "Is there a connection? You did all the research on this Monkey Wrench thing. Is there a connection between those numbers and that whole story?"

"Not that I know of," Mercy admitted. "But that doesn't mean it's not there. I bet it's worth searching Copeland's house again."

Jack nodded. "We need to go there right now."

"But CTU's locked down."

Jack gave her a look of disappointment. As though a little thing like a lockdown was going to stop him . . .

1 2 3 4 5 6 7 8 9
10 11 12 13 14 **15** 16 17
18 19 20 21 22 23 24

••

**THE FOLLOWING TAKES PLACE
BETWEEN THE HOURS OF
9 P.M. AND 10 P.M.
PACIFIC STANDARD TIME**

••

9:00 P.M. PST
Vanderbilt Complex

President Barnes watched his Chinese counterpart closely
as Xu, in turn, watched the doctors and technicians from
National Health Services at work. From the moment they'd
arrived, the NHS personnel had been hard at work construct-
ing an airlock made of plastic tenting over one of the two
Plexiglas barricades. Now, as the airlocks were finished, four
doctors dressed in full biohazard gear entered and the barricade slid up to allow them entry.

The four doctors trod cumbersomely over to the two
world leaders and immediately started to draw blood.

"Mr. President, my name is Dr. Diebold. I am going to
draw a blood sample to confirm whether or not you've been

exposed." The doctor spoke through a microphone built into his squarish plastic headgear.

Barnes nodded. "How much do you know about this virus already?" he asked.

Barnes could see the doctor's frown through the clear plastic face screen. "Enough to know what it can do, sir. Not enough to stop it. Not yet."

Barnes turned to Xu and flashed a smile as the other doctor drew blood from the Chinese leader. "Quite an evening, eh?" he said breezily.

"Astounding," Xu said, his eyes like thin pencil lines behind his glasses. "I am surprised the terrorists could strike so close."

Barnes, who had been briefed on all the recent events, was ready for that one. "I'm surprised, too. Of course, if a man can work for Chinese intelligence for years as a double agent without being noticed, I suppose anything can happen."

The American President smiled at the Coke-bottle eyes as the Chinese leader's face, for once, became readable. Barnes knew he would hear no more about this.

9:10 P.M. PST
Santa Monica

Getting out of CTU had not been difficult. The unit had a lockdown mode for security crises, and avoiding that would have taken some doing. But a hastily slapped-together quarantine was no problem for Jack.

Jack followed Mercy's directions to the house on Fourteenth Street. Jack expected to find squad cars in front and police tape girdling the house. Instead he found that the entire house had been tented, and the houses on either side of Copeland's had been evacuated.

"NHS is taking this seriously," he said.

They got out and walked up to the front of the house, where a uniformed officer and a harried-looking man in a burgundy sweater holding a clipboard met them.

"I'm sorry, the house is off-limits," he said. "Nothing to worry about, just some asbestos cleanup, but the city—"

Jack showed his identification. "We know what's going on. We need to get in."

The man stepped back, shaking his head. "I'm from NHS. If you know what's going on, you don't want to go in there."

Mercy started past him. "I'm the one who made the first call. I don't think there's contamination inside. He didn't keep the virus here. Even if there is, I don't care."

"Why don't you care?" the NHS man said.

"Because I've already been exposed. Now you're wasting my time."

The man's reaction was visceral. He recoiled from Mercy as she walked up to the door. She turned to Jack. "You want to stay out here just in case?"

Jack considered. Mercy knew more about Copeland than she did. If there was evidence to be found, she was better suited to find it. And he'd be no good to anyone if he infected himself. He hefted his cell phone, indicated he would wait for her call. "Go," he said.

9:13 P.M. PST
Bernard Copeland's Residence

The front of Copeland's house included an airlock similar to the one she'd seen at the Vanderbilt Complex. She entered it and then strode into the house.

It was dark. She felt around the walls until she found the light switch and turned it on. The house was very much as she'd left it, except that Copeland's body had been removed and only the bloodstains marked where he had lain.

There was a certain symmetry to Copeland's death, and to Frankie's, she thought. Copeland wanted to be a terrorist for a decent cause, and had been murdered by a more pragmatic, if cold-blooded, killer who understood that terrorism was inherently indecent. Frankie, in turn, had been destroyed by the very weapon she tried to usurp for terrorist purposes. Maybe there really was justice in the universe. But no, there would be no justice unless they uncovered Copeland's secrets and replicated the vaccine, which meant justice relied, as it did so often, on the determination and stubbornness of fallible mortals like her.

Mercy thought justice ought to choose better champions.

Thirteen. Forty-eight. Fifty-seven. The numbers had no relation to one another that she could figure out, nor could the analysts at CTU find a connection. So their relationship had to be in connection with something else. An address. Most of a phone number? Something . . .

Mercy wandered the house, soaking in her impressions of Copeland. The house was meticulously kept, befitting a scientist and researcher. Copeland had planned his viral attack on the President with the utmost care. He had even created a contingency plan for dealing with investigators like Jack and Mercy. He was a planner, he was exacting. He was also careful. His operators were fragmented, few of them knowing the whole picture. So she guessed that the numbers were a combination to a safe or a code of some kind. Copeland would keep information (meticulous) but he would hide it (careful).

And he was corny.

There was a moment in Mercy's investigations when her thinking fell into a groove, when her mind seemed to find the right element, and all of a sudden all extraneous items were redacted. Gone. Leaving only the answer before her, clear and distinct.

The book. It was that book with the stupid title. Mercy searched the bookshelf in the hallway but found nothing. She found a den with a television and two bookshelves packed with titles. Still nothing. She ran upstairs to Copeland's bedroom, and she found it. An old, nearly faded copy of *The Monkey Wrench Gang* by Edward Abbey, sitting on his nightstand. The pages were permanently curled upward by a hundred rereadings. Mercy opened it and saw notes scribbled on the first page, and the second, and the third. Some of the scribblings were illegible, others seemed to be short phrases or incomplete thoughts that Copeland had set down and forgotten.

Mercy flipped to page thirteen, and smiled.

9:30 P.M. PST
West Los Angeles

Al-Libbi's phone rang. He opened the connection without saying a word.

"You should praise Allah, my friend. Only a moment ago you went from being on our death list to being our most desired ally." It was the voice from the Iranian ministry.

"If it is the will of Allah," Ayman said, not really caring if Allah had anything to do with it, as long as he had a home. "Now, to deliver the package to you, I will need some help . . ."

9:32 P.M. PST
CTU Headquarters, Los Angeles

Jessi tapped on the glass door of Christopher Henderson's office. Henderson looked up unhappily; it had been a long day and he was looking forward to a moment's rest. He'd just sat down for a few minutes, rubbing his eyes. NHS had all but taken over CTU to evaluate the threat of the virus. He'd just gotten word from Dr. Diebold that the station had tested negative, and that all personnel were cleared.

"Do you have a minute?" Jessi asked.

"Sure," he said.

"I didn't get a chance to talk to Jack Bauer," she said. "And I haven't seen any of the updates because the NHS wouldn't let me near the computers—"

"It's all clear now," Henderson said.

"I was just wondering if Jack . . . if anyone's heard from Kelly Sharpton."

Henderson sat back. "Jack didn't—? No one told you?"

"Jack sent me back here with the prisoner earlier. That's the last thing I heard from either of them."

Henderson stood up. "Jessi, I'm sorry. There was a firefight. Sharpton went with Jack. He was . . . Jessi, he was killed."

Jessi felt all the life go out of her legs and she nearly fell. "Are you—are you sure?"

"Jack was with the body when he called in. He was— Jessi, I'm sorry. I heard you were close with him."

Jessi felt the tears start coming. She turned and walked out of Henderson's office.

9:35 P.M. PST
Venice, California

His name was Todd Romond, and he was getting the hell out of Los Angeles.

"Gone too far, it's gone too far," he muttered to himself over and over again as he stuffed clothes haphazardly into a red wheeled suitcase. There was a redeye from LAX to JFK, and he planned to be on it. In New York he could take up with some friends and disappear for a while. His New York friends were old friends, from before his Earth First! days. No one could trace him there.

Someone knocked, and Todd nearly jumped out of his skin. He ran to the door as quietly as he could and peeked through the spy hole. It was only Mrs. Neidemeyer. He opened the door and looked down on her four-foot, ten-inch frame topped with wisps of white hair. She was wearing a pale blue dressing gown.

"Todd," she said in her deceptively frail-sounding voice. Todd, a sometimes delinquent tenant, had heard how determined and persuasive that voice could be. "Your car is blocking the drive. The tenants will complain."

"It's only for a few minutes, Mrs. N," he promised. "I'm almost out of here. Please excuse me." He closed the door.

"Well, be sure it's moved!" she called a little sharply.

He'd be sure. He had more incentive than she did. All she cared about was making sure Junior Merkle didn't honk his horn and shout when he got home at three o'clock in the morning after playing drums in whatever band he was part of. Todd, on the other hand, was trying to stay alive.

Frankie had done it. She'd contacted terrorists, real terrorists, not people who spiked trees and chained themselves to bulldozers, not people like him. She'd always campaigned for their group to learn how real terrorists operated, but real terrorists blew up babies and old women. All Todd had ever wanted to do was see the rain forests survive his lifetime. He'd been willing to do a lot to make that happen, even shake the government to its own tangled roots.

Todd was an MIT graduate and had come this close to a Fulbright scholarship. He could certainly see the writing on this wall. Smith (Todd had thought of him as Smith rather than Copeland from the minute he adopted the nom de guerre) had dropped out of sight, and his house had looked like a crime scene until the big plastic tent was dropped over it. Frankie had called him less than three hours ago. All she had told him was that she was in charge now, she had backing from powerful friends, and she would get them all out of this. But Todd had listened carefully, and he guessed what she wasn't telling him. She'd thrown her lot in with murderers and terrorists, and she had given them the vaccine. Todd was sure of it—why else would they work with her?

For Todd, it was only a small leap into the mind of the terrorists: now that they had the virus and the vaccine, they would begin to wonder who else knew how to make it, and conclude that that person should probably stop breathing very shortly.

Todd was one of three people who knew how to create more vaccine. He had no intention of waiting around until the police made a connection between him and Dr. Bernard Copeland, and he certainly was not going to wait for the terrorists to blow him up. He finished packing and rolled his suitcase into the small living room. He stopped to make two phone calls, dialing and speaking quickly.

There was another knock. "Todd?" Mrs. Neidemeyer called.

Todd sighed. He swung open the door. "Mrs. N, I told you it'd be a minute. I was just—" he stopped cold. Mrs. Neidemeyer was not alone.

9:45 P.M. PST
West Los Angeles

It should have taken ten minutes on surface streets to run south from Santa Monica to Venice, but an accident on

Wilshire Boulevard slowed their progress. Jack tapped the side of the car impatiently until at last they were past the accident and rolling. Mercy shook her head. "This has got to be the only city where you can find a traffic jam at ten o'clock at night."

They turned down Lincoln Boulevard and crossed Colorado, then Pico, and soon they were in the beach community of Venice.

The first name on the list was Todd Romond, his information scribbled on page thirteen. An MIT graduate and an expert on the behavior of viruses, he had discontinued a lucrative grant with a dominant pharmaceutical company to become a tour guide organizing eco-vacations in Costa Rica. He was also one of three people who had helped Copeland mutate his virus and develop a vaccine.

This was going to work, Jack thought. They were going to find this Todd Romond and he was going to cure Kim.

Romond's apartment was a small seventies model shaped like the letter "U." The empty middle of the shape was a grass yard open to the sidewalk, with a driveway on one side that led to a carport that supported the upper-story apartment at the back. There was a car parked diagonally across the driveway.

"That Romond's car?" Jack asked, already knowing the answer.

Mercy conferred with the stats she'd written down after calling in for Romond's profile. "Yep. Looks like he's coming or going in a hurry."

"Guess which."

Jack stopped in the middle of the street and jumped out, Mercy close behind. Jack nearly stumbled at the curb, reminding himself how hard he'd pushed it all day. Jack checked the car quickly, his weapon drawn but held low at his side. Sure the car was empty, he ran to the apartment number that matched Romond's. There were lights on in the living room.

Jack pounded on the door. "Romond! Federal agents!"

No answer. Jack didn't want to wait for another warning. He stepped back and then kicked the door hard right where the bolt met the frame. The thick door held until the third try, when the wood shattered and the door swung open.

Mercy, who'd come up behind, now slipped around him as he recoiled his foot. She stepped into the room and faded left. Jack followed, his own weapon now chest-level. But it wasn't necessary.

Todd Romond lay on his back on the living room floor. There was a small hole in his forehead, from which blood slowly trickled. Beside him was an old lady, facedown, as dead as he was.

Mercy checked the kitchen, the bathroom, and the bedroom, and that was the end of that small apartment. She came back to stand over Romond's body.

"Al-Libbi," Jack said hoarsely. "We're in a race now."

1 2 3 4 5 6 7 8 9
10 11 12 13 14 15 *16* 17
18 19 20 21 22 23 24

• •

THE FOLLOWING TAKES PLACE
BETWEEN THE HOURS OF
10 P.M. AND 11 P.M.
PACIFIC STANDARD TIME

• •

10:00 P.M.
CTU Headquarters, Los Angeles

Christopher Henderson watched technicians from National
Health Services carefully wheel a hermetically sealed coffin
out of the holding room. They had sprayed the room down
with powerful chemical cleansers and collected the soiled
chemicals into special vats. They had gathered up what was
left of the girl's body, which wasn't much considering that
she'd been alive and actually participated in a firefight not
two hours earlier. That was the fate that awaited the President if they didn't do their jobs right.

A call came through from Jack Bauer. Henderson took it
at a spare computer station. "Tell me you found something."

"We did," Bauer said from the other end of the line. "We

have the names of three people who worked with Copeland.
We think they know about the vaccine."

"Good! Let's round them up."

"Agreed," Bauer replied. "We have to move fast. The first
one was just murdered. I'm standing over his body."

"Al-Libbi," Henderson surmised.

"The girl gave him the names. He's ahead of us."

"But he can't have our manpower. Give me the other
names. I'll get teams to bring them in right now."

Jack recited the two other names they'd gleaned from
Copeland's annotations: Sarah Kalmijn and Pico Santiago.
"On it," Henderson said. "I'll call you back."

10:06 P.M. PST
Bauer Residence

Teri Bauer picked up the phone before the first ring had finished.

"Honey, it's me," Jack said.

Her voice was cold and quiet. "Great, how nice of you to
call."

The tone of her voice stabbed Jack in the chest. "Teri, I'm
sorry—"

"You're not!" his wife replied, her voice rising slightly.
But she wasn't frantic or passionate. She was earnest. "Jack,
you're not, that's the thing about it. You're out there doing
your job. I know that. But it doesn't make it any easier to be
the person sitting here. There was a riot today, Jack. Our
daughter was in the middle of a riot. My husband was in the
middle of a riot. I haven't even been able to process that, and
you're probably already doing god knows what else."

Trying to stop a virus from killing half the city, he
thought. *Trying to save the President of the United States*

and our daughter. But of course he said neither of those things.

"How's Kim?"

"Sleeping," Teri said, wiping a tear from the corner of her eye. "She has a little fever and went to bed early. I'm hoping it was just all the craziness today."

The phone was silent for a minute. "Jack?"

"Sorry," he said after a second. "The connection dropped out. Just a fever, though? Anything to worry about? One of the protestors they arrested today had some kind of rash. Nothing serious, but some FBI guys caught it and said it itched like crazy."

"No, I didn't see a rash."

"Okay."

"Jack, what time are you coming home?"

Another pause. "I don't know, Teri. As soon as I can, I promise. I love you."

"I love you, too," she said, in the same voice she'd used to answer the phone.

10:12 P.M. PST
Venice, California

Jack ended the call and put his head down for just a minute. It was a moment of indulgence he could hardly afford, but he took it anyway. Teri was upset with him, but she didn't know the half of it. He would have to tell her the truth soon. By his watch he still had a few hours, even allowing for a margin of error . . . but in the end he'd have to get Kim quarantined. She would hate him then.

"You really do love her," Mercy said. She'd watched the pain on his face when he made the call, and the nearly incomprehensible anguish in his thoughts afterward.

Jack shrugged. "We've had a life, you know?"

"I guess," she said, then added, "but not really."

He had no response for that. He'd spent his savings of emotional currency on others already, including her. He had nothing to spare for a life and career that had kept her from a husband and family.

The mobile phone rang, saving him from his obligation to respond. "Bad news," Henderson said. "Santiago and Kalmijn are both gone."

"Al-Libbi?" Jack asked.

"There's no knowing for sure, but there are no signs of struggle, and certainly no bodies," the field operations chief replied. "And phone records show that each residence received a call from Todd Romond's location not long ago."

"He was already packed to go," Jack guessed. "He warned them."

"Which means they're in hiding. Let's work on friends and family and try to find them."

Henderson said, "I'll have Jamey Farrell run through video footage and electronic data. Maybe a traffic cam picked up their directions. Long shot, but we'll try everything."

"I've got an angle I can work," Jack said.

He hung up and relayed the information to Mercy. "What's your angle?" she asked.

"I'll take you there," he said. This was a moment he'd been dreading.

They drove in semi-silence, punctuated now and then by brief questions filling in bits and pieces of the day. Frankie must have been exposed to the virus at the same time Mercy was, but she'd received the weaponized version, the same one that had been used on the President. They made sure that NHS had tented that safe house as well. So far, they'd been lucky: the virus had been contained at several relatively controllable locations. Mercy herself had been lucky. It appeared she'd absorbed the slower-acting strain.

Mercy didn't realize where they were going until they pulled up in front of 16150 West Washington. Jack got out and she followed suit, a look of confusion settling on her face. "This . . . you know what this address is? This is my informant inside the eco-terrorist movement."

"I know," Jack said. He climbed the exterior steps to the second floor with Mercy in tow and went straight to the apartment of Ted Ozersky, a.k.a. Willow. He knocked, and the door opened almost immediately. Willow shook hands with Jack and let them both in.

Mercy sat down gingerly, as though she thought the floor might suddenly disappear beneath her. "What's going on?"

Jack took a deep breath. "Mercy, this is Ted Ozersky—"

"I know him, don't be an idiot," Mercy said, suddenly irritable.

"Ted Ozersky is a CTU agent."

The sentence was such a non sequitur to Mercy that it barely registered. "I'm sorry, what?"

"I'm a CTU agent, Detective," Ozersky said. The California drawl was gone. He spoke in crisp, efficient clips.

Jack had been waiting almost a month to tell Mercy the truth, and he'd known since the moment she showed up at the Federal Building that the day had arrived. But he hadn't had time to consider how to tell her, and there was very little time to spare, so it came out now in a rush.

"Mercy, all the stuff you tried to tell me this morning, about radical eco-terrorists. I knew it was all true. CTU has had its eye on them for a while, but they were tough to get inside."

Ozersky (she had stopped thinking of him as Willow the minute his voice changed) said, "I had managed to infiltrate Earth First!, but I could see that they weren't a real target for

CTU. It was their radical fringe that was the threat. Those guys are paranoid, and I couldn't get any closer. But I passed along what I did hear."

"Including, several months ago, that someone in a fringe group had contacted Ayman al-Libbi, trying to learn how he operated," Jack jumped in. "That's when Tony Almeida and I got seriously involved."

"A couple of months ago . . ." Mercy said. She was in shock.

"One piece of information that Ted passed on was the rumor that the eco-terrorists had someone inside the security services, but we didn't know who. It could have been FBI, even CTU. It could have been more than one person. At the time, I was nervous about giving our operation too high a profile.

"When Gordon Gleed was murdered, I knew the eco-terrorists were making a move. I needed someone to investigate, someone I knew was good, and that I could keep an eye on without the word getting out that CTU was involved."

"That you could keep an eye on . . ." Mercy repeated dumbly. Jack sat ramrod-straight, ready to take the brunt of her anger as soon as the meaning of that phrase seeped in. But she passed it over for the moment. She said, "Are . . . Jack, are you telling me that you arranged for me to get on the Gordon Gleed case?"

Jack nodded. "And I made sure that Ted became one of your contacts. He was able to feed you information you could use, and it never appeared that the Federal government was involved. Copeland—I didn't know his name until you found it out—Copeland was paranoid about the Federal government. One whiff of us and I was afraid he'd vanish."

"Did you know about the virus?" she asked.

"All rumors," Jack said. "But we knew that the eco-terrorists were trying to improve their game by learning from the big leaguers like al-Libbi."

The shock was wearing off. Anger crept into her voice. "This morning, at the Federal Building, you made me feel like an idiot."

"I'm sorry," he said. "But at that point we'd narrowed our suspects down. Tony believed that the mole was in the FBI, and that he was part of the surveillance team. I couldn't be sure if he was listening to our conversation. If he was, I wanted him thrown off the scent."

"But—"

"Remember, I tried to talk you out of coming to the Federal Building at all, but there's no stopping you."

Mercy's neck turned pink. "So I've just been in the fucking way . . ."

Jack smiled. "Hardly. You've done all the work. You found out about the Monkey Wrench Gang. We didn't know anything about these people except that they, or at least some of them, wanted to work with al-Libbi, who I knew was inside the country. The only snafu was when you came to see me. It made Copeland panic because he thought I was investigating him. He got Kim involved, and he kidnapped you. That threw a wrench into the works. But everything we learned about who they are we learned from you."

Mercy looked from Jack to Ted Ozersky and back to Jack. The emotions churning inside her were visible on her face. "You used me."

"I'm sorry," he said again. And he was; not sorry for doing whatever needed doing to complete the task. As far as he was concerned, that was the definition of his job. But he had an immense amount of respect for her, and he was genuinely sorry for any pain he caused her.

"The thing to do now," Ozersky said, saving them both from the tense silence that followed, "is to compare notes. Two people have gone missing. I spent a lot of time on the fringes of the group. You've spent a lot of time investigating. Maybe together we can come up with something."

The next moment was, perhaps, the moment Jack most admired Mercy Bennet. She'd just been humiliated personally and professionally by a man who, from her perspective, had nearly become her lover. But she rebounded almost immediately and plunged into a conversation with Ozersky. He talked about people he'd met on the fringes of Frankie's circle. She whittled down his list from memory, discarding people she'd investigated and found to be inactive or unenthusiastic when it came to real action. It wasn't long before they came up with a short list of contacts for both Santiago and Kalmijn that might know their whereabouts.

"Good," Jack said. "The three of us will follow up on Santiago's contacts. I'll call from the car and have Tony Almeida and Nina go after the others."

"Santiago worked at Earth Café over in Venice," Ozersky said. "We should start there. It closes any minute."

They stood up, and Ozersky ran to get his gun and badge. During the interlude, Mercy stared daggers at Jack, but said nothing. Jack already felt like he'd been through hell, and something told him it was only the beginning.

....

**THE FOLLOWING TAKES PLACE
BETWEEN THE HOURS OF
11 P.M. AND 12 A.M.
PACIFIC STANDARD TIME**

....

*11:00 P.M. PST
CTU Headquarters, Los Angeles*

Of all the times Christopher Henderson had wanted to hit
Ryan Chappelle, this was the hardest to resist.

"You authorized this whole goddamned thing without
telling me!" Henderson yelled so loud that the thick glass of
his office could not completely muffle it.

"Don't yell at me," Chappelle shot back. He was exhausted
and frustrated from dealing with a frayed and angry presidential staff for the last hour, while at the same time over-
seeing the security lockdown that kept an entire nation from
knowing its president had been exposed to a violent hemorrhagic fever. "I'll have you working postal routes searching
for stray anthrax."

"This is bullshit!" Henderson continued. "How can I do my job as Director of Field Operations when you have my people running clandestine missions behind my back."

Chappelle had just informed Henderson of Jack's operation linking the eco-terrorists to Ayman al-Libbi.

Chappelle sniffed arrogantly. "It was need-to-know. Besides, if you want to blame someone, blame Bauer. He bypassed you. Better yet, blame yourself. Aren't you one of the reasons he's here in the first place?"

"So Jack wants to run a secret operation and you give it your stamp of approval? Jack's job is to think outside the lines. I thought yours was to stick to the rule book."

Chappelle laughed; it was a thin, unpleasant sound. "You know what I notice? How everyone thinks it's great to have a loose cannon like Jack Bauer around . . . right up until the loose cannon rolls over their toes. Sharpton liked Jack, too, and now he's dead. Don't be surprised if someday you find yourself regretting that Bauer's around."

11:07 P.M. PST
CTU Headquarters, Los Angeles

Jessi sat at her desk, staring at her computer screen. She was supposed to be analyzing downloads from security and traffic cameras within a five-mile radius of two addresses, and running the facial recognition systems to see if any cameras had picked up their movement. But she knew she wasn't doing a good job. Her focus was gone. No, it wasn't gone, but it wasn't here, either. It was with Kelly Sharpton.

"Jessi, are you on it?" Jamey Farrell appeared at her side. "You look lost."

"Um, no, yeah, I'm good," she replied. "Sorry. I'm on it now."

But she didn't notice the picture sliding by her of the slim man with dark hair leaving his apartment. If she had, it might have saved more than one life.

11:10 P.M. PST
Earth Café, Venice, California

A clerk was locking the front door of the Earth Café as Jack, Ozersky, and Mercy Bennet jogged up. Jack put his hand on the glass door just before it closed. "Hang on, it's just after eleven," he said, pointing at the sign that indicated closing time was eleven-thirty.

The clerk, a dark-haired twenty-something girl with a nose ring and a very flat stomach between her T-shirt and her low-slung men's trousers, pushed on the door again, a look of panic in her eyes. "We're closing early. Sorry!" She shoved at the door and Jack relented. He watched her lock the door and then hurry behind the counter and into the back room.

"Slackers?" Ozersky wondered aloud.

"She's pretty anxious," Mercy said.

"You guys walk back to the car," Jack ordered. They all turned around and retreated to the sidewalk. Mercy and Ted continued, but as soon as they were out of sight of the doorway, Jack turned and sprinted toward the rear of the café. There was a small parking lot in back, but it wasn't well lit. Jack stuck to the shadows and reached the back of the building in no time. He touched the back door gently, feeling it locked. There was a small window above and to the right of the door. Jack hopped up onto a blue Dumpster that stank of coffee grinds and rotting vegetables, balanced himself on the edge, and looked in the window.

he window offered a view of the café's kitchen. Jack saw

the nose-ringed clerk and another employee, a young man with short hair and a goatee, standing with their backs to the kitchen counter. In front of them were two men facing away from Jack. They were small, wiry men with dark skin. They both held guns. They appeared to be asking questions. The two clerks looked terrified.

Jack pulled out his phone and sent a text message to Mercy: "**Distraction ASAP**." He jumped down, landing softly, and waited.

A moment later glass shattered at the front of the store. The girl inside screamed and one of the men shouted in Farsi. At that moment, Jack kicked in the door. His kick blew through the bolts, and the door swung open. The men inside were fast. They had turned toward the sound of breaking glass, but when they heard the door crash, they whirled around just as quickly, weapons ready. Jack dropped to one knee as bullets sped over his head. He double-tapped, and one of the men crumpled inward and fell on his face. Bullets from the other man's pistol chipped the asphalt around Jack, who calmly shifted his muzzle over and double-tapped again. The second man was falling before the two clerks thought to scream again.

Jack jumped to his feet and ran forward, kicking the weapons away from the fallen assailants. Both men were dead.

"Are you all right?" Jack asked. The two clerks were pressed as far back against the counter as possible, terror and shock and relief all visible in their eyes. "I'm a Federal agent. Are you all right?"

They nodded. The girl said, "Who . . . who are those guys?"

Mercy and Ted rushed in, weapons drawn. "Clear," Jack said. "Can you call CTU?" Ozersky nodded. Jack turned to the girl with the nose ring. "Did they ask you any questions?"

She nodded, almost unable to take her eyes off the two

corpses. "Um, yeah. They were asking us about Pico. They said they'd kill us if we didn't help them."

"Pico Santiago. We want him, too," Jack said. "Do you have any idea where he is? Do you know him well?"

The young man, who'd yet to speak, nodded. "I do. We've worked here for a couple years. Is he in trouble?"

"Not if I can help it. How well do you know him?" Jack's own body was still adrenalized from the gunfight, but he forced his voice to remain calm and firm. "We need to find him. He's not at home. We think he's afraid of these guys and he ran off somewhere. Do you know where he'd go?"

Jack saw the kid hesitate, his eyes settling on Jack's gun. He had that same look on his face Jack had seen on some of the protestors that morning, though it seemed a lifetime ago. He spoke irritably, "Yeah, I'm the government and I want him, too. But here's the difference between us and them. They want him dead, and I want to keep him alive. So tell me."

The young man straightened up. "He was working here tonight, but he just took off. Said something had come up and he had to get out of town for a while."

"Did he say where out of town?" Mercy queried. "Would he take a plane somewhere?"

The kid shook his head. "No, dude, that's not what he means. Pico's into outdoor stuff, like me. He went up into the mountains to hike."

"Give me his cell number."

"He doesn't use one," the kid said. "He says the microwaves fry your brain."

"Up in the mountains where?" Jack asked.

"Dude, it could be any—"

"Somewhere he knows," Jack said, growing impatient. "Somewhere he'd feel comfortable and safe."

The kid snapped his fingers. "Temescal Canyon. That's

his favorite spot, and you hike back there past the waterfall, you feel like you're in the middle of nowhere."

"Do any of his other friends know about that place?"

"Lots of people know about it. Yeah, Pico's got some other friends he hangs with up there. Gina's been up"—he pointed to the nose-ringed girl, who nodded—"and I've been up there with Pico and that freak girl he used to date."

"Freaky girl?" Mercy asked.

The man nodded. "Yeah, Frankie something or other."

"Thanks," Jack said. To Mercy and Ted, "Let's go."

They left the kitchen for the dining area. Behind them, the girl shouted, "Hey, what about these guys!"

Jack ignored her. If those were the last bodies he left behind tonight, he'd be lucky.

11:37 P.M. PST
Miracle Mile, Los Angeles

If the decision were Eshmail Nouri's to make, he would have strangled Ayman al-Libbi, left his body in a Dumpster, and gone back to the 213 Lounge he owned and managed just off Wilshire Boulevard. He was tempted to disobey orders and do it anyway, but that was just his independence talking. Eight years living in the United States, living and playing as an American, had given him a veneer of rebellion. But it was thin and did not seep into his heart, which had been with the Ayatollah Khomeini and was with the ayatollahs still. He would do as he was ordered, even if he thought it was stupid.

And it was stupid, in his professional opinion. The ayatollahs had seen fit to plant Nouri and his compatriots in the United States long before the Americans had increased their watchfulness. Of course, after 9/11, Nouri himself and each of his companions had been questioned, but he had already been in the country for years; he was careful to communicate infrequently with the rest of his cell, and often only through handwritten letters that could not be traced. He was indistinguishable from the thousands of Iranians who had emigrated over the years.

Which was his point. Nouri understood that he was a valuable asset. His entire cell was a precious weapon kept hidden by the ayatollahs and, if Allah willed it, they would someday come forth to strike a blow against the Americans. He knew the ayatollahs had tried to build other cells in recent years, but almost all had failed, thanks to American intelligence. To risk one of the few well-placed groups at the whim of Ayman al-Libbi, who had by all accounts become a useless infidel, seemed reckless.

Not seemed reckless, *was* reckless, based on the evidence. Mahmoud and Ali should have called in by now, whether they had obtained additional information from the target's friends or not.

Eshmail did not yet know about the virus or CTU. All he knew was that at long last his cell had been activated. They were to kill three people, one of whom was already dead, and another who would soon be eliminated.

Still, he wished he could kill Ayman al-Libbi when all was said and done.

10:54 P.M. PST
Temescal Canyon Road

Jack stopped the car in the dirt lot where the paved road ended. There was one car, a silver Volvo, already parked there.

"Could they be ahead of us again?" Mercy said as they got out.

Jack drew his gun and walked over to the car. "It's still warm and ticking." There was a moon out, but it had been a long time since Jack had hunted anyone by moonlight alone. "We should take flashlights. Have either of you been up this trail before?"

"I have," Ted said. "It's hiking, not mountain climbing, but parts of the trail are tough. The waterfall is about two miles up."

"We could call the sheriff 's mountain rescue unit," Mercy suggested.

"Do it," Jack said. Mercy got on her phone and went through 911.

"Their ETA is more than twenty minutes for the helicopter," she said after a moment. "No one's going to get here any sooner."

"Let's see what we can do until they get here," Jack said, stopping to reload the magazines for his SigSauer. He popped one magazine into the handle and racked the slide. "Let's go."

• •

**THE FOLLOWING TAKES PLACE
BETWEEN THE HOURS OF
12 A.M. AND 1 A.M.
PACIFIC STANDARD TIME**

• •

*12:00 A.M. PST
Vanderbilt Complex*

"Moving at last," President Barnes said.

Dr. Diebold, still wearing the biohazard suit, nodded. "Yes, sir. The containment tube is complete. It will take you straight down to the hazmat vehicle. You and the others will ride to National Health Services. We have a bio containment unit there."

Carter nodded. "Advance teams have already cleared the facility, sir."

Barnes turned to Xu Boxiong. "Sir, after you."

Xu bowed and smiled. There was nothing like a crisis, Barnes thought, to turn acquaintances into friends or enemies. If either country's security had botched this up, the other leader would have been at his counterpart's throat. But both countries had screwed this pooch. They were in it together in every way.

"I trust the United States will not offer too much of a complaint if the People's Republic takes stronger steps to break the separatist movement in the Xinjiang Uygur Autonomous Region?" Xu observed casually.

"Probably not," Barnes replied. "And I trust that China will offer the G8 some movement that allows us to save face on humanitarian issues."

Xu nodded. "I believe some steps can be taken."

They stepped out through the airlock and into a long, clear plastic tunnel. Mitch Rasher was there, his round body hidden behind the bulk of the environmental suit. "Everything's been handled, sir," he said. "And it's been done in coordination with the Chinese staff," he added with a bow to President Xu. "Both offices issued statements that you both came down with minor cases of food poisoning—"

"You didn't say poisoning?" Barnes interrupted.

"Of course not, sir," Rasher said. "But that was the underlying message."

"Isn't it a bit too obvious if we two made the same claim?" Barnes asked. It seemed to him a lot like asking for three cards in a game of five-card stud.

"We got lucky there, Mr. President," Rasher said, sounding pleased even through the muffled effects of his headgear and microphone. "Mr. Novartov of Russia actually did come down with food poisoning. So it all works out."

"So this containment is good," Barnes said as they reached the end of the plastic tunnel, which was attached to a huge yellow hazardous materials vehicle. "How's our other containment?"

"One hundred percent so far, Mr. President," his top aide replied. "Of course, this meeting was top secret anyway, so very few people knew you were here in the first place. The virus story itself is bound to get out—too many police and NHS personnel know about it. But your infection is known to very few."

"Until I keel over," Barnes said grimly. "Doctor, are you any closer to understanding this virus?"

Diebold shook his head inside his suit. "No, sir. I have Celia Alexis, one of my top people, working on it. But, sir, we've been studying Marburg and Ebola for years and we don't have cures for them. I understand that the terrorist who did this claims to have a vaccine. Are we trying to locate that person?"

Barnes nodded. "We have people working on it."

12:11 A.M. PST
Temescal Canyon

Jack put one foot in front of the other carefully, settling his foot into the ground gently, then putting his weight down in order to avoid making too much noise. He hadn't turned on his flashlight yet—it would do more to warn the driver of the car they'd seen at the start of the trail than it would do to illuminate his path.

This is a terrible way to stalk someone, he thought. His shoes and clothes were all inadequate for the terrain and the darkness. His SigSauer was a fine weapon, but he would have traded the pistol and all three magazines for an M40 sniper rifle with half a dozen rounds, and he might give that away for a decent pair of night vision goggles.

The Temescal Canyon trail rose steadily from its entrance off Sunset Boulevard and up into the mountains, running parallel to a thin ribbon of water that traveled a tortuous path from the mountains down to the Pacific Ocean. With the exception of a small Park Services ranger station at the entrance, the canyon was completely rustic, a gateway into the Santa Monica Mountains Preserve, a wide tract of wild land that ran along the backbone of the mountains that divided the Los Angeles basin from the inland area of the San Fernando Valley. The preserve was home to deer, rabbits, hawks, and a multitude of other wildlife. Hikers had been known to encounter mountain lions padding along the trails that wound in and out of the hills. Most Los Angelenos spent their days oblivious to the fact that this wilderness lay just outside their doorstep.

Ozersky and Mercy followed behind Jack, doing their best to be quiet. Ozersky was field trained, but he'd never been an operator as Jack had been, so his movements were a bit clumsy. What Mercy lacked in training she made up for in common sense. Even so, Jack wished he were working alone. He'd have moved faster.

The moon, nearly full, reflected enough light for Jack to see the path, except when they dipped down under thick groves of trees. Even then Jack didn't use the flashlight. Somewhere ahead were men like the men he'd encountered at the Earth Café. Those men had reacted fast to his entry. He didn't want to give their companions any more warning than he had to.

He'd been giving a lot of thought to those men at the café. Ayman al-Libbi had clearly gotten assistance from somewhere, but where? He was sure these men weren't ETIM. The two who had attacked him at the Cat & Fiddle probably were, undoubtedly muscle given to al-Libbi by Marcus Lee or the man Jack had questioned at the Federal Building. But the shooters at the Earth Café were more Middle Eastern than Chinese.

Al-Libbi might be using this whole attack as a means of getting back into the good graces of terrorist sponsors. And if he'd already found muscle to do his bidding, his plan might already have succeeded. Which also meant that Jack had no idea the size of the force he was dealing with.

There was nothing for it. He had to save Kim's life. He had to save the President. He was going to find someone who could deal with this virus, and God help whoever got in his way.

12:22 A.M. PST
CTU Headquarters, Los Angeles

A cell phone sitting on a counter kept ringing. It rang every ten minutes or so. For more than an hour everyone had ignored it—there was far too much going on for anyone to pay attention to a phone not his own. But now, after midnight, the situation with the President had stabilized and the atmosphere at CTU, although tense, was steady.

So when the phone rang again, Jamey Farrell saw that the ring was coming from a phone inside a plastic bag sitting at Jack Bauer's station. She picked it up without answering it and carried it up to the security desk. "Where'd this come from?" she asked.

The night guard had no idea personally, but he checked his log. "It was brought over from someone at the Federal Building. Bauer got himself arrested earlier and they took his cell phone."

Jamey nodded and brought the phone to Christopher Henderson. "Figures," Henderson muttered. "He loses his gun, his ID, and his cell phone, and only the phone comes back."

As if on cue, the phone rang. "Bauer's line," Henderson said.

"At last," said the smooth voice at the other end of the

line. "Am I speaking to Agent Bauer or some other agent of the Counter Terrorist Unit?"

"How can I help you?" Henderson said.

"This is Ayman al-Libbi."

12:31 A.M. PST
Temescal Canyon

Jack and the others trudged up a steep rise where the path rose up out of a gorge and onto a hilltop. Up ahead he could hear the murmur of falling water. Then, over that, he heard someone shout in alarm. He started to run.

12:34 A.M. PST
CTU Headquarters, Los Angeles

Three minutes after the phone call, Henderson had a recording of it put into a digital player. He and Ryan Chappelle played it back with Jamey Farrell listening.

"This is Ayman al-Libbi. I was given this number by a certain young woman who was also kind enough to give me a very deadly virus. As you may know already, I have both the virus and the antiviral medicine that cures it. This puts me at a distinct advantage since I also know that your President and the Premier of China have both been infected. They will both die within a few hours unless they are given this medication. I will be in touch with you soon."

Chappelle swore a long, thin stream of expletives. "According to that waiter, how much time do they have?"

Henderson checked his watch. "Less than eight hours."

12:38 A.M. PST
Temescal Canyon

Anything can happen in four minutes. The terrorists, whoever they were, could have killed Santiago a dozen times
over. Or it might not even be Santiago. The people from the
Volvo might not even be terrorists.

But Jack Bauer ran as if his daughter's life depended on it.
More shouts drifted down from above. He didn't wait for
Ozersky or Mercy. He plunged down into another dell, then
sprinted up out of it into moonlight again. The path leveled
out and the sound of rushing water grew louder.

Voices called to each other in Farsi and a moment later
several shots rang out. Jack guessed that the terrorists had
tried to dispatch their victim quietly, but had failed. Now they
were resorting to gunfire. He saw several muzzle flashes in
the distance.

Jack stopped, took a deep breath, raised his weapon, and
waited. A moment later there was another muzzle flash. Jack
leveled his sights behind the flash and pulled the trigger
twice. He heard one cry of pain and several shouts of alarm.
He'd given his position away, but now the terrorists had to
divide their attention between their victim and him.

Jack moved to the inward side of the path. Trees lined the
path from here to the waterfall he could hear ahead, but they
were scraggly trees with thin trunks. They offered more concealment than cover, but he would take what he could get.
Jack moved from tree to tree, silent now because his quarry
had gone silent.

The victim, however, was making a lot of noise. "Help!
Help!" he shouted. "Whoever's out there, they're trying to
kill me! Help!"

Keep yelling, Jack thought. *Cover the sound of my movement.*

He moved up to the next tree and stopped, listening. He could see nothing, nor hear any threat, but some sixth sense told him he'd covered enough ground. The ambush would be somewhere in this range. That's where he'd have put it.

Someone sobbed in the darkness, and Jack's muzzle swung there like a magnet to a steel plate, but he didn't fire. It was the man he'd put down. *Don't reveal your position to kill a man who's already dead.*

Footsteps behind him. Ozersky and Mercy were coming. They would draw fire. Jack prepared himself.

He heard Ozersky's heavy footsteps and Mercy's labored breathing. They'd get shot in the dark if the terrorists were any good.

Thunder and lightning erupted under the trees as the two gunmen opened fire. The minute their rounds went off, Jack found them. Jack emptied his magazine at them, and then all firing ceased. Smoothly he ejected the magazine and slid another one into place. As the snap of the slide gave his position away, he moved forward and crouched low.

"Help!" someone yelled from near the water. "Help me!"

Moans and whimpers rose up from the ground. He could hear something shuffling or rolling back and forth in the dirt. Jack moved forward quietly. Shreds of moonlight turned the area deep gray, and in the gloom he saw two figures lying on the ground, one motionless and the other twitching and sobbing. "Search them," he whispered into the darkness behind him, and moved on. He passed the third body, the one he'd shot from long range, and kicked the gun from the corpse's hand.

"Help me!" The waterfall was just ahead.

He couldn't see it well in the moonlight, but from what he could tell, the falls consisted of one short cascade from the ridge above into a wide pool, then another much higher fall into the gorge below.

"I can't hold on!"

The voice came from the darkness of the gorge. Jack pulled out his flashlight and shined it downward.

"Pico Santiago!" Jack yelled, his voice nearly blending with the rush of falling water.

"Help!"

Santiago was there, halfway down the gorge, clinging to a ledge by his hands. Jack guessed what must have happened. The terrorists had caught up with Santiago and tried to kill him quietly. He struggled and broke free. When they pursued him, he had tried to escape by climbing down the gorge. It had been a brave and stupid thing to do. There was no way to climb down that cliff at night. Santiago had fallen or slid, but had been lucky enough to catch himself on an outcropping of rocks and bushes.

"Hold on!" Jack shouted. "I'm coming down for you!"

He didn't know what else to do. Besides, he could be as brave and stupid as the next guy.

"Jack!" Mercy called out, following the beam of his flashlight. "Wait for the helicopter. They'll be here soon."

"He's not going to last," Jack said, half to himself. The flashlight had a cord, which Jack looped around his neck. Then he held the light between his teeth and started to climb down. He chose a path above and just on the waterfall side of Santiago, so that he would land on the man if he fell. Unfortunately, that put him closer to the water, so the rocks and plants he grabbed for handholds were slippery.

"I can't hold on!" the man yelled.

"You hold on, you son of a bitch!" Jack yelled.

"My hands . . ." the man moaned.

"It's not about you!" Jack yelled down at him, dropping the light from his mouth and letting it swing. He was still twenty feet above, and the going was slow. "You hold on because people are going to die if you don't!"

"Agh!" one of Santiago's hands slipped away from its hold. He was clinging by one hand.

"Hold on!" Jack inched downward, foot by foot. He willed Santiago to be stronger, to hold tighter. But in the end it was not Jack's will but Santiago's that was most important, and Santiago's broke. His other hand slipped, and Jack watched him fall away from the beam of the flashlight with a short cry.

1 2 3 4 5 6 7 8 9
10 11 12 13 14 15 16 17
18 **19** 20 21 22 23 24

••

THE FOLLOWING TAKES PLACE
BETWEEN THE HOURS OF
1 A.M. AND 2 A.M.
PACIFIC STANDARD TIME

••

1:00 A.M. PST
CTU Headquarters, Los Angeles

Christopher Henderson was convinced his headache was
permanent. He'd started the day worried about nothing
more than crowd control at the Federal Building and what
he'd thought of as Jack Bauer's overeager attempt to find a
terrorist needle in a haystack. Now he was co-managing a
crisis of global proportions with Ryan Chappelle while Jack
Bauer left a trail of bodies from one end of the city to the
other.

No sooner did they have forensics teams at one location
than Bauer was calling from another, asking for more cleanup.

Jamey Farrell was in his office giving him a summary of

the most recent information they had gathered. Her voice was hoarse from talking, but otherwise she was fresh. "The two shooters who attacked Jack on Sunset Boulevard this afternoon were definitely ETIM. We had them on a watch list, but they were never identified near any hot spots until the shooting, and they were too low a priority for surveillance. The one who survived the fight with Jack has been cooperative, but he doesn't know much more than we know."

Henderson nodded. "With Marcus Lee dead and Kasim Turkel out of commission, I'd say ETIM is back to low-priority status. What about the others?"

"Frankie Michaelmas is dead, Bernard Copeland is dead. Jack met up with two shooters at the Earth Café. Both of them are dead, but we do have information on them."

"Go," Henderson said, focusing in.

"They have nothing to do with ETIM as far as we can tell. They're both Iranians who immigrated here in '92 and '94, respectively. We have files on them, shared with the FBI, but they're scant. One was interviewed after the truck bomb at the World Trade Center in '93, and both were interviewed after 9/11, but in both cases the evidence pointed toward Saudis rather than Iranians, so they weren't pressed. Their files were kept active because they were known to attend a mosque run by a fairly vocal cleric named Ahmad Moussavi Ardebili, but they've never made a peep otherwise."

"Sleeper cell?" Henderson thought aloud.

"It looks that way. And a really patient one."

"Okay, I'll put a team together. Let's revisit our database for this cleric and round up everyone we think is a possible suspect."

1:09 A.M. PST
Silverlake Area of Los Angeles

"Last one," Tony Almeida said.

"Too bad," Nina replied. "I'm getting to like waking people up."

While Jack had gone to track down Pico Santiago, Nina and Tony had been given a list of three names—people who might know where Sarah Kalmijn was hiding. The first two had been dead ends, the individuals clearly having little or no idea what Sarah did in her spare time. This was the last address, a small house in the bohemian Silverlake area that looked down on Hollywood and central Los Angeles.

Nina walked up to the door of the little Craftsman bungalow while Tony stood farther back by one of the wooden pillars that marked a Craftsman. But before she reached for the bell, Nina drew her pistol. Tony mimicked her movement and stepped forward where he could see what Nina had noticed: the door was closed but the jamb was shattered. Someone had broken into the house.

Using hand signals, Tony indicated that he was going around the back. Nina nodded and counted to five silently, giving Tony time to get around. Then she eased the door open slowly. The house was dark. She listened, but heard no sound until a barely audible creak came from the back of the house. Tony was inside. Nina pulled a tiny Surefire flashlight from her belt and fired it up. The beam swept the living room and came to rest almost instantly on a figure lying on the floor. She swept her hand along the nearest wall and flipped up a light switch, illuminating the room.

A woman lay on the floor, a piece of electrical cord wrapped around her neck. Nina knelt beside the body without touching it. The woman's tongue was enlarged and her eyes bulged slightly. She'd been strangled to death.

Tony entered. "Damn it. I'll the call the PD. Let's get a forensics team out here."

"These guys are a step ahead of us," Nina said.

A door creaked behind them and both CTU agents whirled around, weapons ready. "Don't shoot!" someone yelled from the closet.

"Come out slowly!" Tony ordered. "Hands first, hands where I can see them!"

A pair of thin female hands appeared in the half-open doorway, followed by two graceful arms and then the complete figure of a young woman in her thirties with short black hair. She looked terrified.

"Don't shoot me!" she pleaded. "I heard you say to call someone. Are you . . . are you the police?"

"Federal agents, ma'am," Tony said. "What happened?"

"Thank god, thank god," she said, shuddering as though releasing hours of pent-up tension. She broke down in tears for a minute, falling beside the body of the other woman as tears poured down her cheeks. "I just left her there. I was so afraid, I thought they might still be here."

"Who was it?" Nina asked. "Who did this?"

"Two men," the woman said. "They broke in. I was in there." She pointed to the closet. "They attacked Susan. They hit her until she told them what they wanted, and then they—they . . ." She started to cry again.

Tony checked the closet and realized why the terrorists had missed the woman. In the back of the closet, half-hidden by a couple of coats, was the door to a tiny darkroom.

Nina put a hand on the woman's shoulder. "I'm sorry, ma'am, but it's important that we know what she told them. What were they asking?"

The woman wiped her eyes. "Th-they were asking about Sarah. Sarah Kalmijn is a friend of ours. They wanted to know where to find her. Susan told them, she did, and they killed her anyway."

"Where did they tell her to go?"

"What do you want with Sarah?"

Tony curled his lip unhappily. "Right now we just want to save her life. Where would she be if she's not home?"

The woman had started crying again, but between sobs she gave them the answer Susan had given her tormentors. Sarah blew off steam at underground parties—raves. She was a lawyer now but she hated her job and forgot her troubles by attending the raves thrown by a college friend who ran a DJ company called Goodnight's. That was all she knew.

1:27 A.M. PST
CTU Headquarters, Los Angeles

"Jamey, I need to leave," Jessi said.

Jamey Farrell looked up from her work, bleary-eyed and brain-fried. She'd been through some long days at CTU, and this one matched them all. "Can you stay a little longer? I'm just getting a call from Tony Almeida and I'm going to need some research."

"No," Jessi said. "I mean I need to leave CTU."

Jamey put down her pen. "You mean for good."

Jessi nodded. "I lost someone today—"

"I know, I heard. I'm sorry. It comes with the territory here sometimes—"

Jessi shook her head. "That's everybody's attitude. No one's even stopped to think about it. Kelly worked here. Okay, not as long as Jack Bauer or some of the others, but he had friends here. But everyone goes on like nothing happened."

Jamey set her jaw. If Jessi had been hoping for sympathy,

she was going to be disappointed. "Listen, 'cause I'm only going to tell you this once. No one here pretends like nothing happened. But if you want to work in this unit, then you have to get tougher than this. In this line of work, people die. And do you know what happens if we stop to mourn them right away? More people die. Those agents out in the field can't stop to bury every body because they're busy stopping the bad guys from killing more people. Same goes for us in here."

"I—I know . . . that's why I think I need to leave." Jessi crossed her arms like a shield. "Jamey, I missed something earlier. I was going over security footage that I'd downloaded and I saw one of those people they're looking for, Pico Santiago. I could have tracked him, I could have led Jack straight to him, but I missed it because I was upset."

"Then you screwed up. Now fix it."

"He's dead! I can't make him alive again—"

"No, but you can do your job so the agents in the field do their job and keep more people alive." She crossed her own arms. "You want to mourn the guy you had a crush on, then do it by getting the guys who killed him."

1:38 A.M. PST
Temescal Canyon

With no fear of an ambush, Jack and the others made better time down the hill. They had waited for the mountain rescue helicopter and lost a few precious minutes while Jack explained what had happened to the stricken pilots surveying the carnage, and then double-timed back down the trail.

As Jack, Mercy, and Ted Ozersky climbed back into the car, Jack's phone rang. It was Jamey Farrell. She briefed Jack on the events Almeida had reported. "Thirty more seconds and I'll have an address for you. You're taking one and Tony and Nina are taking the other. They're the two most probable locations for Sarah Kalmijn."

"Where's Henderson? Why isn't he briefing me?"

"He's out. The guys you killed may be part of an Iranian sleeper cell. Henderson is leading a raid."

"Okay," Jack said. "We keep swinging and missing. We have to hit a home run this time."

"You don't know the half of it," Jamey said. She told Jack about the call on his cell phone from al-Libbi.

"Has he made any demands?" Jack asked.

"Not yet, but Henderson and Chappelle are sure he will."

"We'll get him first."

"Here's the address." She read off a location.

1:54 A.M. PST
Rancho Park Neighborhood, Los Angeles

Christopher Henderson sat in the back of a CTU van studying a hastily generated blueprint of the house owned by Ahmad Moussavi Ardebili. The easiest way to botch a raid was failure to plan, and Henderson's five-minute pep talk with his squad hardly counted as planning. But it couldn't be helped. They were running out of time.

"It looks like there are two rear entrances," Henderson said to A. J. Patterson, his squad leader. "Send half your men around the—"

"We won't need it," someone said from the front of the van. "Look!"

Henderson pushed forward and looked out the window. They were in a well-lit neighborhood of short but well-kept lawns and fairly large houses, many of them rebuilt "Persian palaces" that were popular in the area. In front of one of these, four or five men were hurriedly running out of the houses carrying boxes, which they stowed in the back of a Dodge pickup truck.

"Moving day," Patterson said, hefting his MP–5. "Let's see if we can help."

The CTU van stopped and the agents poured out, shouting at the men to freeze. Three of them did, but two of them ran into the house, with Henderson, Patterson, and two other agents in pursuit.

Henderson was second in the door behind Patterson. There was a loud bang and Patterson fell out of sight. Henderson nearly tripped over him, but managed to keep his feet and squeeze off a burst of automatic fire in the direction of the blast. He barely had time to register that he was in a living room with a fire burning in the fireplace before someone slammed into him, pinning his MP–5 to the wall. But Patterson was suddenly on his feet again. A short burst from his submachine gun made Henderson's assailant vanish.

The entry team flowed forward, and now Henderson saw a short, squat man with a long salt-and-pepper beard kneeling at the fireplace, squealing at the sight of the CTU team as he lifted a box and dumped documents into the fire. Henderson grabbed the bearded man and hauled him away. Without regard for his own safety, Patterson stuck his hands into the fire and scooped the papers, some of them ablaze, into his arms and hauled them out. He fell on the stack, rolling back and forth with his body to stifle the flames.

"Ahmad Moussavi Ardebili, you are under arrest for conspiracy to commit terrorist acts against the United States," Henderson said, panting. He glanced at the papers. "Start going through these immediately."

1 2 3 4 5 6 7 8 9
10 11 12 13 14 15 16 17
18 19 **20** 21 22 23 24

. . . .

THE FOLLOWING TAKES PLACE
BETWEEN THE HOURS OF
2 A.M. AND 3 A.M.
PACIFIC STANDARD TIME

. . . .

2:00 A.M. PST
Fairfax District

The club was called Plush, and it was anything but. It was, essentially, a giant warehouse space with a long wooden plank that served as a bar. Only two things recommended it: the bar was fully stocked and the DJ was fantastic. Since most people went to raves to drink and dance, the setup was perfect and the club was an enormous underground success.

The ride over had been silent. Jack was completely focused on finding this last person who could stop the virus. Mercy had not had time to recover from the shock of Jack's revelation, and sat lost in her own thoughts. Ozersky guessed at the tension between them and decided to stay out of it as much as possible.

It wasn't until they reached the warehouse just off Fairfax Avenue that Jack spoke. "I'll go in alone. Mercy, you and Ted go in together. We're looking for the DJ named Goodnight. He's friends with Sarah Kalmijn."

Ozersky started forward, but Mercy grabbed Jack's arm and held him back a few steps. "I was thinking in the car. When you were telling me about your marriage, you said you and your wife had gone to Catalina for the weekend, and that it was a great weekend."

"Yeah," Jack said noncommittally.

"That's where you saw al-Libbi, isn't it? When you got back?"

"Yes," he affirmed again.

She shook her head in disbelief. "You're a piece of work, Jack. You used the vacation with your wife as a setup for staking out the docks. You're the best operator I've ever met, but you're a real son of a bitch."

2:08 A.M. PST
Melrose Avenue, Los Angeles

Tony and Nina arrived at their assignment. This club was on Melrose a mile east of Plush, designed into the shell of an old forties movie theater. The big bouncer at the door, standing six feet, five inches and built like a comic book superhero, tried to stop them, but Tony held up his badge. "Where do we find Goodnight?"

The bouncer waved them inside. "He's spinning the records, man."

Tony and Nina walked inside and were immediately assaulted by pulsing red and blue lights, strobe lights, and music with a bass line that throbbed in their chests and a melody, if that's what it was, that was repetitive and hypnotic.

"I swear," Tony said, "you could use this music to brain-wash people."

Nina looked at the crowd of twenty-somethings writhing to the music. "It's working," she said.

They pushed their way through the grinding crowd until they reached a dais at the far side. Their badges got them past that bouncer, too, and they climbed up to stand beside the sound equipment being run by a round-bodied, chubby-faced black man wearing small, squarish, black-framed glasses, who sweated profusely under his ear-phones.

"Hey!" Tony said, holding up his badge.

The DJ nodded at them, then did a double-take when he saw the badge. A look of disgust crossed his face, as he slid the headphones down around his neck.

"Man, what'd we do? I've got permits for everything."

Tony shook his head. "Are you Goodnight?"

"That's right."

"We're looking for Sarah Kalmijn."

"What?"

Tony put his face close to Goodnight's ear and said it again.

"She in trouble?" the DJ shouted back.

"Not with us. We want to protect her. She here?"

Goodnight shook his head. "Try the other club, she goes there, too. But if there's really a problem, I don't think she's gonna be there."

"Where'd she be?" Tony asked over the music.

"Her family's got a boat down in Marina del Rey. That's where she goes when things get bad."

"You know the name of the boat?"

"No, man, I don't remember. It's Marina del Rey, though."

2:20 A.M. PST
Plush

Jack accomplished his mission quickly. The DJ at Plush didn't know Sarah at all and told them to check the other club, where Goodnight was spinning that night. Frustrated, Jack turned to go, motioning for the others to follow. They pushed through the noise and the crowds toward the door.

Ted saw them first. He produced his pistol as if by magic, shouting something that Jack could not hear over the music. Ozersky shouted again and pointed. Now Jack saw the door. There were three of them, dark-haired men with guns firing at the bouncers, who fell to the ground. One of the men reached in and grabbed the doors to the warehouse and pulled them shut. Just before they closed, another man tossed something inside—a large can with a rag sticking out of it.

"Down!" Jack yelled. Ozersky grabbed the dancers nearest him and dragged them downward. Jack and Mercy dived for the floor. A moment later the can exploded, spraying flame and liquid everywhere. Burning liquid splashed on the ravers, setting their clothes on fire, and hit the walls, burning wood and posters. The alcohol-sprinkled floor caught fire. People screamed and rushed for the door. Jack barely had time to pull himself and Mercy up before the crowd surged forward.

Someone pulled at the doors, which opened inward. "It's chained!" Jack heard. "It's chained from the outside."

The liquid fire was homemade napalm, which not only ignited combustible material but also burned into the skin. The fire was already spreading. Smoke began to blur Jack's vision. He looked up and saw a window at second-story height to the left of the locked doors. "Help me!" he yelled. He shoved his way to the wall, Ted and Mercy following in his wake.

"Stand there," he ordered Ted, and the other CTU agent braced himself against the wall. Jack planted a foot on his slightly bent leg and boosted himself up, his other foot reaching the height of Ozersky's head, and soon he was standing on the other man's shoulders. Jack reached up but the window was too high. Maybe if he jumped . . .

The room was in chaos. The fire spread with unbelievable quickness. It was almost impossible to think over the heat and the terrified screams.

"Pull me." Mercy was below him, reaching up.

Jack reached his hand down to Mercy. Without hesitation, she climbed up Ozersky's back, caught Jack's hand, and mountain climbed up both CTU agents until she was on Jack's back. She reached the window. Mercy drew her gun and used its muzzle to smash the glass, then knocked out the jagged teeth of shattered glass to avoid being cut.

Mercy stuck her head out the window to assess the far side. She didn't hear the gunshot over the noise inside, but she felt it brush through her hair, nearly scalping her. She was so startled she nearly threw herself backward into the crowd.

"Gun!" she yelled, ducking her head down.

"Go!" Jack yelled. "Go!"

"Are you fucking crazy!" she yelled.

"Look!" he said. The fire raged. If Plush had a sprinkler system, it was malfunctioning. The walls were in flames. Panicked ravers pounded against the door as those behind pushed forward, crushing those in front.

This virus isn't going to kill me, Mercy thought. *Knowing Jack Bauer is going to kill me.* She gathered herself, adjusted her grip on her pistol, and launched herself upward. She vaulted over the window frame and fell almost a story to the ground below. Gunshots sounded almost in her ear. Mercy rolled on the ground and came up, weapon in hand.

It was the most lucid moment in Mercy Bennet's life. She was aware of moving quickly, but she did not feel hurried. She experienced a groove, the steady calm of a snowboarder hurtling downhill, but completely under control. She acquired the first man and put one bullet into him, then swiveled to the next. Bullets ricocheted off the ground around her. She felt one pass through the cloth of her shirt between her arm and her ribs. She laid her muzzle over the chest of the second man and squeezed. She was about to shoot the third when Jack landed on him heavily. The man crumpled under Jack's weight. Bauer smashed him in the face three times with the muzzle of his SigSauer. Jack turned toward the doors. A short, thick chain had been looped through the handles, locking the doors in place. Jack pointed his own gun at the lock and fired four times, shielding his eyes from the blast and hoping no ricochets killed him. When he was done, smoke rose up from his gun as the chain fell down.

"Help them!" Jack commanded. Mercy helped Ted shove the doors inward, against the pressing crowd.

Ozersky appeared in the crowd, yelling "Move, move, goddamn it!" The crowd inside managed to make enough space, and the next moment they were streaming out of the building.

Jack ignored it all. He knelt down beside the man he'd struck. Finally, he had one of them alive. "What's al-Libbi's plan?"

The man grinned at him with broken teeth. "Who's al-Libbi?"

Jack lifted the man's left hand, placed the muzzle of his gun against the palm, and fired. The man screamed.

"Jesus!" Mercy screamed at him. Jack ignored her.

"What's his plan?" Jack said. He didn't know if he'd gone mad or if he was thinking with perfect clarity. But he did know that time was running out, he was low on leads, and important people would die if he didn't find a solution.

"I . . . I don't know," the man said, his voice suddenly pleading and desperate.

"Tell me something," Jack threatened. "Tell me something worth knowing right now or I'll get some of that napalm you made and pour it down your throat."

The man started to speak. What he said brought Jack no closer to finding Sarah Kalmijn, but it was valuable nonetheless.

2:45 A.M. PST
Rancho Park Neighborhood, Los Angeles

Henderson and his squad divided the rescued papers into five charred piles and began to sort through them. Many of the pages were in Arabic and would need to be translated later.

"Do we know what we're looking for?" Patterson asked in a low voice. He had gone down earlier when a bullet had punched him through the vest he wore. The Kevlar had stopped the round, but the force had bruised his sternum.

"No," Henderson conceded. "But anything with American names on it. Santiago, Romond, Kalmijn . . ."

"Kalmij-n?" one of the operators said, holding up a burned scrap and mispronouncing the name.

"Kal-mane," Henderson corrected. "Give me that, please."

It was a sheet of notepaper written in English, the words hastily scribbled. Under Sarah Kalmijn's name Henderson saw the addresses of two clubs or bars, and also the phrase "Marina del Rey At Last." He guessed it was another bar.

"Call Jack Bauer," Henderson said.

2:53 A.M. PST
CTU Headquarters, Los Angeles

Bauer's recovered cell phone rang again, and this time Ryan Chappelle answered.

"To whom am I speaking now?" Ayman al-Libbi asked. Chappelle signaled for the trace to begin.

"This is Regional Division Director Ryan Chappelle."

"That sounds important," al-Libbi said patronizingly. "That's good, because my message is also important. Tell the President of the United States that he is holding five men prisoner in a secret holding facility just outside Los Angeles. You know who they are. These five men are to be allowed to go free. If this is not done within one hour, I will destroy the antiviral medicine. If it is done, I will give you the antidote. I will call again in forty-five minutes."

He hung up. Chappelle looked at Jamey Farrell, who shook her head and slapped the table in frustration. "He had some kind of router. We can beat it, but he needs to be on the phone longer."

Chappelle ran a hand over his balding head. He knew of the men al-Libbi wanted. They were Iranians the CIA and CTU were sure belonged to Iran's terrorist network; all three had history with Hezbollah. They'd been plucked out of various European countries using methods some would call illegal. They'd been bounced around from secret bases in Europe to Guantanamo Bay, but as those facilities came under scrutiny they'd been moved, so they ended up in a secret holding facility CTU maintained out in the high desert region above Los Angeles along the Pear Blossom Highway.

"I have to take this to the President," he said.

1 2 3 4 5 6 7 8 9
10 11 12 13 14 15 16 17
18 19 20 **21** 22 23 24

● ●

**THE FOLLOWING TAKES PLACE
BETWEEN THE HOURS OF
3 A.M. AND 4 A.M.
PACIFIC STANDARD TIME**

● ●

3:00 A.M. PST
West Los Angeles

Jack hurtled down the 405 Freeway chasing the last lead
they had. Tony had called him with the news about a boat in
Marina del Rey. He had no more information, so Jack had
jumped in the car, barely giving Mercy and Ted time to
climb in, before he peeled off.

"Call Jamey and have her search the harbormaster's records. Sarah's name is bound to be there somewhere." He
hung up and drove.

There was silence in the car again, but this time Mercy
broke it. "You shot that man through the hand," she said at last.

Jack nodded. "That man knows how to keep you from dying sometime in the next few hours."

"I don't have any sympathy for him," Mercy said. "But . . . but do you ever wonder if what you're doing is okay? What if sometimes they're right and you're wrong?"

Jack looked at her, his eyes steady and his face like stone. "Sometimes I'm wrong," he said. "But they are never right."

His phone rang again. "Bauer."

"Jamey," said the analyst. "Jack, Tony relayed your request. There's nothing in the harbormaster's database for any Sarah Kalmijn, or anyone else with that surname. If she really does have a boat, the slip and the boat are registered to someone else."

"Keep digging," he said, speaking shorthand. "There's got to be something." He hung up, but the phone rang yet again.

"Jack, it's me," said Christopher Henderson. "I've got something random here. It's one of those things that sticks out, but I don't know where to put it."

"Go."

"We raided the cleric's house and pulled some notes. By the way, if nothing else goes right, unearthing this sleeper cell itself was a huge security coup. Anyway, there are notes here on one of your targets, Sarah Kalmijn. I know you've already been to the clubs, but another note says 'Marina del Rey At Last.' That mean anything to you?"

Jack felt fear and dread settle side by side in his stomach. "Yes, it does," he said. "Thanks, Chris. You have no idea how much you just helped."

At the end of the day, it was that sort of teamwork that made field operations possible. One agent relaying information to another, the analysts at headquarters sifting data and digging for information. In less than two minutes Jack's headlong, purposeless race to Marina del Rey had a purpose, because one phone call to Jamey Farrell, and a few strokes of her keyboard, told him that the thirty-foot sailing yacht *At Last* was docked in slip 268, H Basin, in Marina del Rey.

It also told Jack that al-Libbi's people knew about it and would be there, too.

At three o'clock in the morning, the Los Angeles freeways worked the way they were supposed to. Jack swung onto the 90 Freeway from the 405 and arrived in Marina del Rey in less than ten minutes.

"I don't want to be surprised by these guys again," Jack said. "Ted, stay at the near end of the dock in case they come after us. Mercy, follow me down to the finger where slip 268 is, but then do some reconnaissance past that. Okay with you?"

They both nodded.   ●

The harbor at Marina del Rey was huge, a manmade project that involved digging four separate basins that were subsequently flooded with sea water. H Basin lay just off Admiralty Way. Jack parked the car in a small lot near a blue shack that advertised sailing lessons. All three got out and hurried toward the docks. The docks were lit, and they saw row after row of slips holding boats of all shapes and sizes. The main dock, running perpendicular to the slips, was accessible, but a fence ran the length of that dock and a gate at each row required a key to get down to the boats themselves.

As they set foot on the long dock, Ted took up a position in the shadows and waited. Mercy and Jack hurried down the ramp and along the dock until they came to the row containing number 268. Just then a boat engine powered up.

"No," Jack said calmly. He vaulted the fence and ran down the row of moored boats. Number 268 was near the end, and by the time he reached it, the boat—a white thirty-foot single-masted yacht—was sliding out of its space. Jack gathered steam as he ran and launched himself onto the boat. He landed with his feet on the deck but nearly bounced back from the lifelines that ran the perimeter like a wire fence. Catching his balance, he hopped over the lifelines.

"Get the hell away from me!" yelled a woman's voice, and a metal pole jabbed Jack in the face, tearing into his cheek. "Get off my boat!"

"Wait!" Jack yelled, staggered back from the blow, and nearly fell off the boat. She hit him again with the pole. Jack grabbed it to keep it from moving. "I'm a Federal agent!" he snapped. "I'm here to help you."

That did not seem to make her any happier. "Get the fuck off my boat! I didn't do anything!"

The pole jabbed him in the stomach this time. He'd had enough. Pivoting, he wrenched the pole from her hands, dropped it, and lunged forward. He jumped onto the molded bench near the wheel and caught the woman's wrists.

She was pretty and blond with short hair. Her eyes were lovely, but currently filled with panic. "Shut up and listen," he said. "I'm a Federal agent. I know all about the Monkey Wrench Gang and Bernard Copeland or Smith or whatever you want to call him. I know about the virus." At this, her panic increased, but he stifled her movements with his grip on her wrists. "I'm not here to arrest you. We need you."

She stopped struggling. "You . . . need . . . ?"

"You're Sarah Kalmijn, right?"

"Yes."

"Listen carefully because I don't have a lot of time. Part of Copeland's plan worked. The President did get the virus. In fact, several people have contracted it. But Frankie Michaelmas sold you all out. She gave the virus and the antiviral medicine to terrorists, real terrorists. We need to know how to create a new antiviral medicine or people will start dying."

Sarah looked terrified. "Do they have the weaponized version or the natural—?"

"Both. Stop asking questions," he said. "I'll tell you everything you want to know when there's time. Right now assassins have killed Pico Santiago and Todd Romond, and you're next. Do you know how to make more vaccine?"

"It's not exactly a vaccine. It's an antiviral—"

"Whatever. Can you make it?"

"No," Sarah said. Jack's heart sank until she added, "But I know where Copeland kept his notes stored."

"We searched his house—"

"Not there. It's at Santa Monica Airport. I can show you."

"Good."

The boat had drifted out into the main channel as they spoke. Sarah grabbed the wheel and straightened the boat out, the chugging engine barely giving them any momentum. She started to turn the boat around as she said, "Did you—did you say that the President has the virus? Is he okay?"

"Last update I got," Jack said. "But not for much longer."

Sarah hesitated, then said, "I have something you'll want. Hold her steady." She put his hands on the wheel and reached down into her bag. She removed a leather camera case that had been stuffed with strips of rags. Tossing the rags aside, she removed a thin vial of clear liquid and handed it to Jack.

"Is this what I—?"

"The antiviral," Sarah said. "When Bernard really started messing with the virus, I stole a dose for myself. I'm terrified of that virus."

Jack took the vial from her and put it into the pocket of his jacket. "I've seen what it does to—" He stopped. A powerful engine roared nearby, and Jack heard the hiss and splash of rapidly displaced water. A searchlight fired up, shining brightly on Sarah's boat.

"Get down!" Jack yelled, slamming Sarah Kalmijn onto the deck. Guns blazed on board the speedboat, and bullets riddled the side of the boat, splintering the fiberglass. The speedboat came closer, intending to board. Jack fired his SigSauer, and the boat veered away as someone cursed in Farsi.

Jack got off a few more rounds, but the assassins had fire superiority. There must have been four or five of them in the speedboat because they laid down a constant rate of fire, forcing Jack to stay low, covering Sarah as she murmured, "Oh god, don't let them hurt me," over and over.

The speedboat came closer. Jack stuck his gun over the edge of the cockpit and fired, but they were blind and wild shots that wouldn't slow these assassins down. Mercy was on the dock and Ozersky was undoubtedly running to some sort of position, but it would be tough for them to acquire targets from where they were. The gunfight must have awakened the entire harbor, but it would take minutes for anyone to respond effectively, and Jack was sure he had only seconds.

Jack cast about desperately for an idea. Spying the stern of the boat, he saw a silver pan attached to the railing. He knew from his trip to Catalina Island that the silver pan was a barbecue.

Gunfire slapped against the fiberglass. They'd be able to board soon. "Does this boat use a propane tank? Do you have a stove down below?"

"What? Yes!" Sarah said, holding her arms over her head and pressing her head to the deck.

"Stay here," he ordered. Jack slid along the cockpit floor, scraping knees as he did, and dropped down into the cabin. He fumbled in the dark until he found a flashlight in a cubby-hole above the stove. By its light he spun open the gas valves on each of the four burners. Gas hissed out into the cabin.

Jack crawled back onto the deck. The speedboat was ten meters away. Jack emptied his magazine at them, and they ducked low.

Now, he thought. Jack grabbed Sarah Kalmijn and dragged

her over the side of the boat away from the assassins. They both fell into the freezing water of the harbor. Jack held his breath and clamped a hand over Sarah's mouth and nose. He refused to let her drown. Kicking away from the boat, he swam under water as long and as far as he could.

3:40 A.M. PST
H Basin, Aboard At Last

Eshmail Nouri was the first aboard the sailboat, a fresh magazine in his Glock pistol. Two of his three men boarded with him while the third stayed in the speedboat.

It had been a bad night for Eshmail. As far as he was concerned, their cell had been wasted. Years of patience and tolerance had been abandoned in the blink of an eye. Eshmail had lost good friends and excellent operatives at every step. Even when his people succeeded they ended up dead! He hated the American government more than ever.

It had been a bad night, but he would make the Americans pay. Nouri stuck the muzzle of his pistol down into the cabin and opened fire. Too late did he hear the hiss and smell the gas. A ball of fire engulfed him, his colleagues, the sailboat, and the motorboat, and his bad night was over.

3:42 A.M. PST
H Basin

Jack came to the surface and gasped for breath as the fireball dissipated and the boom rolled out over the waters of the harbor.

"Jack!" Mercy called. "Jack!"

"I'm okay!" he called out. "I've got her."

Jack swam to the sound of Mercy's voice. By the time he and Sarah reached the dock, Ozersky was there, too. Sirens wailed in the distance and people, mostly live-aboards, were gathering.

"This is Sarah Kalmijn," Jack said as Mercy pulled him out of the water. "She's going to take us to Copeland's notes so we can re-create the antiviral medicine."

Mercy held up a towel she'd pulled off someone's boat. Jack took off his coat and wrapped himself in the towel. He was soaked, freezing, exhausted. But he was not going to give up now.

"Come on, we have to hurry."

3:45 A.M. PST
National Health Services, Los Angeles

The phone in Chappelle's hand rang and he answered. He'd driven over to Health Services to be with the President when the call came in. The phone had been attached to a speakerphone so Barnes could hear from inside the bio containment unit.

"I'm here," Chappelle said.

"As are others, I'm sure," al-Libbi said smugly, "so I'll be quick. What have you decided?"

Chappelle looked at Barnes for final confirmation. The President nodded. "We agree," Chappelle said. "The five will be released immediately."

"Perfect," al-Libbi replied. "Go to the corner of Olympic Boulevard and Colby. Assuming the five are actually released in the next few minutes, and assuming I get confirmation, you will find a package there." The terrorist hung up.

Chappelle picked up a different phone. "Henderson, send Almeida and Myers. Olympic and Colby. Go, now!"

Barnes, on his side of the plastic shielding, squeezed his hands together so hard the knuckles turned white. He looked at Mitch Rasher, and then at Chappelle. "Once this is over, we're going to use every means at our disposal to kill that man."

3:52 A.M. PST
CTU Headquarters, Los Angeles

CTU was as quiet as it would ever get, with most of its field agents out on assignment and half the analysts sleeping in their chairs from sheer exhaustion.

One person was still up. Jamey Farrell sat in her seat, analyzing data signals from Ayman al-Libbi's phone. His trick was simple, as the best tricks usually are. His cell phone bounced around various satellites, being rerouted so that its point of origin, if it could be tracked at all, took time to find. And of course he never stayed on the phone that long.

But each time he'd called, Jamey had narrowed her field of search. She knew he was in Los Angeles somewhere, so the signal had to bounce off a local cell station first. On his first call, she'd figured out that he was not in West Los Angeles anymore. On his second call, she knew he was calling from somewhere south of downtown.

He had just called a third time, and she had him. He was at the Los Angeles International Airport. Smiling to herself, Jamey called Jack Bauer.

••

THE FOLLOWING TAKES PLACE
BETWEEN THE HOURS OF
4 A.M. AND 5 A.M.
PACIFIC STANDARD TIME

••

4:00 A.M. PST
H Basin

Jack listened to Jamey Farrell speak, and then he knew what he had to do.

"Mercy," he said. "You and Ted take Sarah to Santa Monica Airport. Get the documents to National Health Services. I'm going to get Ayman al-Libbi. He's at LAX. Sarah, do you have a car?"

She nodded. "But the keys were on the boat."

"I'll hotwire it. Just tell me where it is."

She pointed out a Toyota Prius. Jack got in and drove away.

Mercy was feeling light-headed. "Ted, you should drive if you don't mind."

"Sure," he said. They got in the car and drove off before the police arrived. There's going to be a hell of a lot of paperwork, Mercy thought.

"You okay?" Ozersky asked.

"No," she admitted. "I don't know how much time I have left. It was, what was it? One o'clock in the afternoon."

Sarah, in the backseat, sat back and pulled her arms in and away from Mercy. "Are you saying what I think you are?"

Mercy nodded. "When your guy kidnapped me. I escaped, but I got exposed to the virus. So did your lovely Frankie Michaelmas. I spilled all kinds of the stuff, I guess. She got the faster one. I've still got . . . oh, what, nine hours left to live."

"I want to go home," Sarah said, her voice trembling. "I don't want to be any part of it. I don't want to be around you when you become contagious."

Mercy wrapped her arms around her body, feeling her joints ache. "Thank you for your sympathy." She looked at the CTU agent. "Ted, you okay with this?"

Ozersky shrugged. "I like your style, Mercy. Always did, even when I was undercover. How can I say no?"

Ozersky hadn't looked at her when he spoke. Maybe it was just because he was driving, but she didn't think so. She had the distinct impression that he hadn't wanted to reveal too much. And it suddenly occurred to her that maybe she'd fallen in love with the wrong CTU agent.

Ted Ozersky's thoughts were on Mercy. Probably too much on Mercy, he decided. And he was right. If he'd been paying more attention, he might have noticed the black Mazda that followed them out of the marina and onto the freeway.

In the early hours, the drive from Marina del Rey to Santa Monica Airport was ten minutes. Santa Monica Airport serviced small planes, mostly private planes and a few charters.

The airport made extra income by renting out some of its spare hangars and mechanics sheds to other businesses. One Hollywood screenwriter actually used a spare shed as his office, swearing that he got more work done because no one thought to come bother him down there.

Now just after four o'clock in the morning, the LAPD detective, the CTU agent, and the eco-terrorist drove down the main lane, past a pub called the Spitfire Grill, and pulled up in front of one of those sheds. Without ceremony they exited and hurried over to the shed.

"I don't have a key," Sarah warned. "Copeland actually owns a plane here somewhere, but I never got very involved in this stuff."

"I have a key," said Mercy. She drew her gun and fired rounds into the door until the bolt shattered. She kicked open the door.

The room inside was tiny, but it reminded her of Copeland: neat stacks of paper, file cabinets with labels on them, maps rolled into orderly scrolls.

"Hurry, please," Mercy said.

Sarah went to the file cabinet, pulled out a folder, and held it up. "That's it?" Mercy said. "That's it," she repeated, this time answering her question. They'd been running all night, killed people, watched people die, and now all of a sudden here it was, plain as day.

But then her knees lost all their strength and she fell to the ground. Ozersky rushed forward but Sarah stepped back, gasping, "Don't touch her! Don't! Look!"

She was pointing to the football-shaped bruise that had appeared on Mercy's neck. Ozersky did not back away, but he stopped moving forward, his hand hovering near her.

Mercy felt her skin until her fingers found the bump. "Oh," she said. "I thought . . . I thought twenty-four hours . . ."

Sarah shook her head. "It depends on the person. Maybe

you had the weaponized virus, and it just took longer to replicate." She backed away further. "I'm sorry. I'm sorry, I can't stay here. You're becoming contagious . . ."

Mercy felt like all her joints had suddenly become flaked with rust. They didn't want to move. And her head was on fire. She smiled weakly at Ted Ozersky. "Willow. What a stupid name."

"It worked," he said without much conviction.

"Go," she pushed her hand through the air. "Get that file back to your people."

The CTU agent said, "I'm not just going to leave you here."

"You're not going to get sick," she said. "Get that stuff where it can do some good. But do me one favor."

"What?"

"Send Jack Bauer. I need to see him."

If she'd been any stronger, she'd have noticed the look of pain on Ozersky's face. But he nodded and hurried out of the shed.

4:20 P.M. PST
CTU Headquarters, Los Angeles

"I know he's in there," Jamey Farrell said to Jack over the phone. "But I can't put you belly to belly."

"I can."

Jessi Bandison was standing beside her. The girl's face was drawn and sad, but otherwise she looked ready to work. "I thought you were leaving," Jamey said.

"There's work to do, right?" Jessi said. She sat down at the terminal next to Jamey and called up a window she'd already prepared. "I tapped into the LAX security cameras. Let's see if we can't find him sitting somewhere."

"I haven't heard back from your people," Ayman al-Libbi said. He was sitting in his car on the third floor of the LAX parking structure, talking on his cell phone. He had the window rolled down to keep the car from getting too stuffy. "I know two of them are dead, but I don't know about the other."

"We just had contact from one of our people," the Iranian voice said. "They've been released."

"Good. I hope now that you see my worth."

"You did not really deliver the antivirus to the Americans, did you?"

The terrorist rolled his eyes. "Of course not! The package they have is a surprise. They'll probably defuse it, but one can always hope."

"Hi there." Ayman al-Libbi looked up to see the blond man standing beside his car. He didn't have time to react as the fist smashed into his face and everything turned black.

Jack hit al-Libbi four or five more times, though he knew the bastard was unconscious and unable to feel it. Still, it made him feel better, and that's all he could ask. Opening the door, Jack dragged the terrorist's limp body from the car and searched him, removing a Springfield .45. He also found exactly what he was hoping for: two glass vials in the terrorist's breast pocket. He hoped they were what he thought they were. He used al-Libbi's shoelaces to tie his hands, then dragged the unconscious man over to his own car. It would have been easier to drive the car around the corner to that spot, but the thought of al-Libbi's face and knees getting scraped along the concrete did not displease him. As soon as he had the terrorist stuffed in the trunk, he called CTU.

4:27 A.M. PST
CTU Headquarters, Los Angeles

"Jack got him!" Jamey Farrell yelled.

CTU staffers erupted in cheers. Even Henderson, exhausted as he was, joined in.

"And he thinks he's got the antivirus for the President, for both of them."

More cheers.

Henderson said, "Call Chappelle over at National Health Services. Tell them what's going on. I want a whole team of squad cars to meet Jack wherever he is and escort that virus at high speed."

4:29 A.M. PST
National Health Services, Los Angeles

Ryan Chappelle was so happy when he heard the news, he forgot for a moment how much he hated Jack Bauer. When the information was relayed to the President, the entire NHS laboratory burst into cheers of gratitude. Even Premier Xu smiled and clapped his hands.

Chappelle was so happy, in fact, that when Jack Bauer's old telephone rang, he didn't think what it might mean as he answered.

4:31 A.M. PST
405 Freeway Northbound

When the line of police cars pulled Jack over he was expecting them. He pulled over on the side of the freeway, which was all but deserted at that ungodly hour. One of the uniformed cops said, "Sir, we've been told you have an item that we need to pick up and take to National Health Services."

Jack nodded. He carefully removed the two vials from his pocket and handed them to the officer. "Did they tell you what those are?" He knew that the administration and Chappelle had worked hard to keep the crisis a secret.

"No, sir," the officer said.

"Then let me just tell you that those two little glass bottles are probably the most important things in the world right now. Take good care of them and get them to NHS as fast as you can."

The cop took them gingerly. "Oh," Jack said, "and I have a prisoner in the trunk. I didn't have anywhere else to put him. Can you spare a cruiser to get me to CTU with my prisoner?"

Jack's phone rang. "Bauer."

"It's Chappelle," the Division Director said morosely. Leave it to him, Jack thought, to spoil a happy moment. "Listen to this."

Before Jack could reply, Chappelle activated a recording.

"This is Muhammad Abbas. I know that you have captured Ayman al-Libbi. You must know something. I have been inside the airport with vials of the virus. I have actively spread the virus among three groups traveling on three airplanes. If you release Ayman al-Libbi, then I will tell you which three airplanes and you can stop them. If you do not, you will find this disease spreading across your country. This is my leverage. I do not care if you trace my call." He even left his cell phone number.

No. No, no, no. Not after everything he'd done to catch this son of a bitch. "He could be bluffing," Jack said of the recording.

"He could be. How would we know? They did have the virus. He could have done it."

"Goddamn it!" Bauer roared. The cops looked at him anxiously, but he waved them off. "You want me to let him go? There's no guarantee that he'll tell us afterward."

"You have a better idea?" Chappelle asked.

"No," Jack thought. "Wait. Yes! I have one more idea. But I can't pull it off until al-Libbi and Abbas are together. I'll call you back."

Jack opened the trunk. Ayman al-Libbi was conscious. His face was bruised and his lip was swollen, but otherwise he seemed whole. He even seemed a little smug. "Has Muhammad Abbas called you yet?" he asked as Bauer helped his bound prisoner out of the car.

"He just did," Jack said grimly. "I think you're bluffing."

"It's always possible," the terrorist said with a twinkle in his eye. "You strike me as one to gamble. Hold me and find out."

"Unfortunately," Jack said with just a hint of threat in his voice, "it's not my decision. If we release you, where do you want us to take you?"

"Santa Monica Airport," Ayman al-Libbi said in his best American accent. "And make it snappy."

4:45 A.M. PST
National Health Services, Los Angeles

Ted Ozersky hurried through the glass doors and flashed his badge three times to Secret Service agents before finding Dr. Diebold. "This is it," he panted. "The documents from the man who caused all this."

Dr. Diebold grabbed the files and began thumbing through them. "Page Celia," he called out, and someone paged Celia Alexis. "Interesting, interesting," he said, reading the notes. "We never would have found this out in time."

Celia appeared in the hallway and Diebold handed her the file. "Look at this. There's a resin in a tree down there that contains a linking molecule. It creates adhesion between the virus and whatever antivirus we want to use. We'd never have discovered it."

Celia was both excited and concerned. "We can replicate this, but not in time. It will take hours to get samples of this resin up from Brazil. The source is Croton lecheri. The resin is *Sangre de Drago.*"

"Dragon's Blood," Diebold translated. "Well, the sooner we start, the sooner it'll be done."

4:55 A.M. PST
CTU Headquarters, Los Angeles

Henderson saw the text message come through and jumped on the phone immediately. "Tony, it's Henderson. Don't pick up that package."

"Already done," Almeida replied. "I thought this was for the President—"

"We found the antivirus. Get rid of whatever that is before it explodes. And I need you to do something for Jack right away."

1 2 3 4 5 6 7 8 9
10 11 12 13 14 15 16 17
18 19 20 21 22 **23** 24

•••

THE FOLLOWING TAKES PLACE
BETWEEN THE HOURS OF
5 A.M. AND 6 A.M.
PACIFIC STANDARD TIME

•••

5:00 A.M. PST
National Health Services, Los Angeles

President Barnes watched as Dr. Diebold hurried into the bio containment unit, followed by another doctor. Each held a syringe in his hand. "If you would please, sir, and quickly," Diebold said, indicating that Barnes should roll up his sleeve.

As soon as he did, Diebold jabbed the syringe into his arm and squeezed the liquid into his body gently and evenly. He withdrew the syringe, daubed the blood from the needle prick, and sighed with relief.

Barnes waited, but Diebold said nothing. "What, that's it?" the President said. "No fanfare? No trumpets? No choirs of angels?"

Diebold shook his head. "In this business the cure is as silent as the disease, sir. But we checked it out. You've just been injected with an antivirus specifically engineered to go after this virus, bond with it, and render it inert."

Barnes rolled down his sleeve and turned to Xu Box-iong, who had also just been injected. He held out his hand and Xu shook it. "Whatever we may say about each other and our countries in the time ahead," Barnes said, "I want you to know personally that I thought you handled this like a man."

The Chinese leader nodded. "It is these times that show us our character, isn't it true?"

5:12 A.M. PST
En Route to Santa Monica Airport

Jack's phone rang for what must have been the fifteenth time in the last few minutes. It was an extension at CTU. "Bauer."

"Bauer, it's Ted Ozersky."

"Did you deliver the package?"

"Yes, and they say they can work with it, which is good news. But that's not why I'm calling. Mercy is still at the Santa Monica Airport."

"I'm headed there now," Jack said, "but for a totally different reason."

"Jack, she's dying."

"The virus? But you just said they could create the anti-virus . . ."

"Not in time. She made me leave her. She's contagious now. I've asked NHS to send in a bio containment unit, but they're cordoning off the airport for some reason."

"I'm the reason," Jack said. "I mean, al-Libbi is the reason, but I'm taking him. Damn it!" Jack smashed his fist down on the steering wheel, breaking a section off. "I'll get to her, Ted." He hung up. And though he should have spent the last few minutes of his drive focused on the last shreds of a plan, he did not. He thought about Mercy Bennet, and what he had done to her, and what she had done for him, and he knew that the scales were not balanced there.

CTU had given him the location of the meet. It was a private hangar that had, apparently, belonged to Bernard Copeland. Jack pulled up next to the hangar, got out, and opened the trunk. Al-Libbi looked more put off by being placed in the trunk, but he'd get over it. Jack hauled him to his feet. He looked the terrorist in the eye and found nothing staring back at him. Jack didn't often wonder what made men like Ayman al-Libbi tick. They were evil and needed to be squashed.

"I'm going to kill you," he promised.

Al-Libbi laughed. "But not today, I guess."

"We'll see." Jack looked across the tarmac to a distant building. Mercy was over here somewhere. She was dying. And he was here, doing his job. That should make him feel good, that he was doing his job, but somehow al-Libbi ruined even that small reward.

Finally another car drove up, a black Mazda. Abbas got out. He waved to them, then hurried over to the hangar and pressed a button to open its huge door. As the door rolled aside, Jack saw a small Learjet. Abbas motioned them over.

Jack grabbed the terrorist by the arm and escorted him across the tarmac and stopped just outside the hangar.

"Cut him loose," Abbas ordered. Jack complied, using a small folding knife to slice through the shoelaces that had bound the terrorist.

"This is what will happen," Abbas said. "I will tell you the name of one of the compromised flights now, and you will let Ayman go. I will tell you the second flight as we taxi down the runway. I will radio the third to you as we leave American air space. These terms are not negotiable."

"You know, it's a shame you came all this way and didn't get what you wanted," Jack said to al-Libbi.

"Agree to the terms!" Abbas called.

Jack continued to address al-Libbi. "You didn't kill the President. You didn't do much for your friends in ETIM. Hell, all you did for your Iranian friends is give us a chance to wipe out a cell they had here." He smiled. "You don't even have the virus."

Al-Libbi glared at him, a little uncertain as to Jack's purpose.

"Let him go," Abbas demanded.

"Name the flight," Jack said, suddenly focusing.

Abbas named a Chicago-bound flight. Jack snapped open his cell phone and relayed the information. He shoved al-Libbi forward and followed a few steps. He continued, "I mean, you can't tell me these Iranian friends you've made, that they want you back just because you got us in an uproar. There had to be something tangible to give them. I would have thought the virus was a good start."

"Don't speak to him," the terrorist told Abbas.

"Oh," Jack said ironically, "but then you do still have a sample of the virus, don't you?"

"Let's get to the plane, Muhammad!" al-Libbi said, spinning Abbas around.

"You have it because you infected your friend there!"

Muhammad Abbas stumbled. "Wh-what?" he gasped.

"It's true," Jack said, inching forward. There was still a wide gap between him and them, but he did not want them getting too close to the airplane. "One of the Iranians told me before he died. He said Ayman was bragging about it, and that you were too blind to realize it."

Abbas stared at his companion. "Is this true?"

Al-Libbi rolled his eyes. "Look at him. He is American. They lie. To us, to themselves, to everyone! You are an idiot if you believe his lies."

"And you are an idiot if you think the Iranians would take him back if he didn't have something to offer."

Muhammad Abbas stared at Ayman, his eyes examining his entire body. Ayman al-Libbi, who for years had felt only rage and, in later years, felt nothing at all, now felt suddenly naked. Abbas, who had known his every quirk, his every habit, now sized him up.

"You did it, Ayman," Abbas said with a sense of heavy, sad recognition. "You gave them my death so that they could . . . could harvest this virus inside me." The look of pain that molded itself to Abbas's face was staggering in its depth. "You meant what you said. It really is only about the money."

Ayman al-Libbi held out his arms wide. "Muhammad," he said. Then he lunged at his colleague and pulled Abbas's gun from his belt. He fired three rounds into the man, then turned on Jack. But Jack had already rolled away. Al-Libbi ran for the Learjet.

Jack ran forward and knelt beside Abbas. The terrorist's eyes were wide open, his breath coming in gasps like a fish out of water. "Tell me the flights," Jack said. "Tell me the flights and he doesn't win." Jack patted Abbas's cheek. "Tell me the flights and you die together, the way it should be."

Abbas blinked and whispered six words. Three airlines and three cities. It was enough. CTU could figure out the rest.

The Learjet's engines whined as it taxied out of the hangar. Jack watched the jet make the turn and head toward one of the small runways. At the same time, Jack saw Tony Almeida appear out of the hangar, carrying a long tube in his arms. Jack knew what it was, and as Tony approached, he saw it more clearly: the RPG–29 that al-Libbi himself had bought in the United States. As he reached Jack, Tony took a new rocket and primed it.

"Thanks for getting it," Jack said.

"Just shoot him," Tony replied.

The Learjet was still taxiing, but hurrying away. Jack hefted the RPG up to his shoulder and took aim. "Clear behind," he said calmly. He pulled the trigger. The armor-piercing RPG hurtled through the space between them and ripped through the jet's hide. The jet exploded, fire bursting out of every window and seam in the plane.

. . . .

**THE FOLLOWING TAKES PLACE
BETWEEN THE HOURS OF
6 A.M. AND 7 A.M.
PACIFIC STANDARD TIME**

. . . .

6:00 A.M. PST
Santa Monica Airport

Jack didn't wait to see what happened next to the plane. He jumped in his borrowed car and raced to the shed number Ted had told him. He burst inside and found Mercy lying on the floor. Two lesions had appeared on her face. She looked weak, and a trickle of blood came down from her nose.

"There's a bio containment team on its way," Jack said. "They'll get you out of here."

"I think . . . ," she said, "I think it's too late."

"We've got to try."

She shrugged. "Please do. I'd like to live. I just don't think it's what's going to happen." She pushed herself to a seated position, and Jack saw more lesions on her chest. "You know, that word Copeland was trying to tell me. It wasn't Uma ghetto. I read his files. It's *uña de gato*. Cat's Claw. I was close, anyway."

"You were amazing. For the entire day," Jack said. He leaned toward her, but he did not approach too closely.

"Nah, I've been braver since then," she said. "Look over there." She was pointing at a desk across the small room, closer to him than to her, where his jacket lay. "That's my jacket."

She nodded. "I took it at the harbor. It's still wet. But look in the pocket."

Slowly, already knowing, Jack slid his hand into the pocket and pulled out the vial of antivirus. "I didn't want you to think I'd lost it. I know how important it is."

He was holding the vial that could save her. But it could also save someone else. And somehow Jack was not surprised that Mercy had lain there dying, all the time holding on to the very substance that could have saved her.

"Mercy, I'm sorry. I was saving it for—"

"For your daughter. I know."

"Mercy."

"It's okay, Jack," Mercy Bennet said. "Really. Really, it's okay. You said earlier that you're sometimes wrong, but they are never right. You are not wrong now. You are doing the right thing."

She slumped back down and coughed. When her hand came away from her mouth, it was covered in blood. "Jack, go now. I don't want you to see me looking like that."

"I can't leave you."

"If you do me one favor, do this one. Let me do this the way I want to. Take that to your daughter. It's the right thing to do."

Despite her request, Jack waited a few more minutes. The bio containment team arrived, and although there was little they could do for her, at least she wasn't going to die alone.

Jack turned and ran out of the shed. He jumped into the borrowed Prius and raced home. Traffic was getting heavier, but he managed to get there in record time. If Copeland's timetables were correct, he might have a little time to spare. But he would never know.

Jack parked the car in front of his house, dug the spare key out of its current hiding spot, and opened the door. The house was quiet. Jack hurried to the bathroom and took a first aid kit out of the closet. There was a small syringe there. He filled it with the antivirus and walked over to Kim's room. He sat down at her bedside gently and felt her forehead. She was feverish, but he could see no lesions yet.

He had exposed her to danger. He hoped never to do that again.

While she slept, he injected her with the antivirus. She would live now. He kissed her on the forehead.

He walked out of Kim's room and stumbled down the hall. At last he allowed the exhaustion to take hold of him. As he did, Teri came out of their bedroom, yawning. She looked at him, at his exhausted face. For a moment she looked on the verge of being angry at him for being out all night. At the last second she changed her mind and reached out, bringing him toward her with a hug. She would never know exactly what he did, or what might have been had he not done his job, but she could do this for him.

He softened into her hug. He thought of his bed, and sleep.

His phone rang. Teri did not release him. He eased himself gently out of her arms and did not look at her as he lifted the phone.

"Bauer."